COMRADES
IN MIAMI

JOSÉ LATOUR

First published in Great Britain in 2006 by Orion,
an imprint of the Orion Publishing Group Ltd, Orion House,
5 Upper Saint Martin's Lane, London, WC2H 9EA.

1 3 5 7 9 10 8 6 4 2

A CIP catalogue record for this book is
available from the British Library.

ISBN 0 75287 402 0 (hardback)   0 75287 401 2 (trade paperback)

Printed in Great Britain by
Clays Ltd, St Ives plc

www.orionbooks.co.uk

This novel is for Peter and Sheila, greatest of friends. And For Brian and Amy, John and Jeanne, and Ron and Carol.

PART ONE

One

O ne of Cuba's well-kept secrets is that for several years the most respected individual in the General Director ate of Intelligence was Colonel Victoria Valiente, a psychologist.

Brigadier-general Edmundo Lastra (cryptonym Gabriel) was general director, Colonel Enrique Morera (Bernardo) was his deputy, but the woman who headed the Miami desk of the USA Department had won the admiration of superiors and subordi nates alike with her long list of remarkable results. Under her guidance, the desk had submitted reports, issued warnings, and given forecasts judged extremely valuable by the country's top leadership. She had achieved this by planting new, well-trained secret agents in the Greater Miami area, activating sleepers, approving the recruitment of valuable informers, opposing the enlistment of some who turned out to be FBI informers, exhaus tively scanning public sources, and making educated and usu ally correct guesses.

Known in the island's intelligence community by the cryp tonym Micaela, Victoria was transferred to Interior's General Di rectorate of Intelligence from the Ministry of the Revolutionary Armed Forces in late 1989, in the wake of the drug smuggling scandal involving corrupt Cuban intelligence and military officers.

On July 12 of that year, the world learned that four perpetrators had been executed by firing squads.

In 1983, Victoria had joined the Ministry of the Revolutionary Armed Forces' Military Counterintelligence Directorate following graduation from the University of Havana's faculty of psychology. At the time, she had seen such tools of the trade as telephone listening devices, minicameras, and tap detectors only in movies. She was ignorant of basic cryptology, had fired a pistol twice in her life, and abhorred judo, karate, and other forms of unarmed combat. She had never traveled abroad.

Physically, Victoria was one shade below nondescript. As a child, one of her teachers in grade school had quipped that the girl's mother poured the baby and raised the afterbirth. What seemed strange to her parents and teachers alike was that Victoria obtained good marks in exams despite the fact that the asthmatic and astigmatic girl rarely read textbooks.

Even though her appearance improved notably during puberty, Victoria stood a meager five-foot-two, never weighed more than 112 pounds, had a rather homely face, and wore her mousy brown hair in bunches. The glasses needed to correct her astigmatism made her green eyes expressionless, and her figure was more angular than rounded where it counts. Neither dirty old men nor young virgin males ogled her when she sunbathed on the beach in a two-piece bathing suit.

Perhaps for that reason, from a sexual standpoint, Victoria's life had been saintly. She lost her virginity at twenty-one, and by the time she got married eleven years later she had copulated with just three men. Contrary to popular myth, this most unassuming, unattractive late-bloomer frequently experienced three orgasms in half an hour and, ten years into her marriage, enticed her husband into having intercourse two or three times a week, four if he felt like it. Lacking motivation for giving birth or a feeling of suitability for motherhood, she had popped contraceptive pills for seventeen consecutive years.

Her remarkable sexual appetite was not Ms. Valiente's most admirable quality, though. She possessed vast amounts of three others: One was brainpower.

An admirer and disciple of British psychologist Raymond B. Cattell, she had read seventeen of his forty-one books and many of his articles. Cattell was the first to postulate that the key problem in personality psychology was the prediction of behavior. He classified traits into three categories: dynamic (those that set an individual into action to accomplish a goal), ability (concerning the individual's effectiveness to reach a goal), and temperament (aspects like dispositions, moods, and emotions). After her transfer to Interior's General Directorate of Intelligence, Division of Personnel, Evaluation Department, Victoria developed her theory of how to perform a prospective spy's remote psychological profiling based on Cattell's teachings.

She studied the files of candidates submitted by field officers, rejected many, and asked for additional information about those who seemed to have latent possibilities. Then she eliminated a few more, recommended which operatives should approach each of the chosen few, and wrote scripts. With a good nose for politics, Victoria followed world events on a daily basis to choose the ones that, if reminded of a prospective or active informer, may strengthen his or her resolve to betray their government, institution, or company. She preferred the recruitment to be based on ideological affinity, but would set her scruples aside if blackmail or sex would let the cat out of the bag. In strapped Cuba, buying information was a means of last resort.

During her four years in Evaluation, Victoria profiled many possible informers: people working for MI6, the Vatican, DGSE, SISDE, FIS, the Federal Security Service, three different United Nations agencies, the European Commission, the German and Spanish Ministries of Foreign Affairs, the Mexican presidency, Amnesty International, Roche, and Aventis. All the while, she devoured books on espionage. The lieutenant in charge of Intelligence's library was absolutely flabbergasted and eventually compiled a list: In four years Victoria read 132 books, including all the classics. She was always the first to read new titles.

Eventually her judgment was highly respected and her recommendations rarely questioned. But it had not always been like that. In the early nineties, her superior officer could not believe she was serious when she argued for taking a promising candidate to Disney World to ask him to work for Cuban Intelligence there and then. On another occasion, she suggested recruiting a pious, sixty-six-year-old priest as he listened to the handler's confession. In both instances the officer, now retired, had asked her to convince him. She did it dispassionately, using her remote psychological profiling. She was so convincing that the two plans were approved. And they worked.

In 1993, a few weeks after she had astonished everyone by choreographing the recruitment of a top European scientist who agreed to pass on the results of his firm's research on an AIDS vaccine, Victoria was ordered to report to a third-floor office of the State Council at 10:00 A.M., where she was asked to take the Mega Society's IQ test.

This was quite surprising to her because, before the fall of the Berlin Wall, communist parties in power presented a rather simplistic and homogeneous official front when it came to politics, economics, sociology, and psychology. Non–Marxist-Leninist theories in the fields of social evolution and human responses were dead wrong. Dialectic materialism provided the only key that unlocked the complex behavior of individuals and societies. Having studied in the years when intelligence quotient tests were shunned as capitalist hocus-pocus, Victoria had scant knowledge about them and had never taken one.

In practice, however, having realized that this sort of prejudice rendered useless important research and knowledge, from the sixties on almost all general secretaries of communist parties had appointed a couple of their most trusted henchmen to head small, specialized units that applied techniques such as standardized tests to measure intelligence.

On her first attempt, Victoria Valiente gave forty-two right answers. According to Hoeflin's fifth norming of the Mega Test, she scored 176. In common parlance this meant that out of half a million people, only one had Victoria's high level of intelligence, emotional stability, and physical coordination.

The old man who had asked that the test be taken—simply called Chief or Commander by the members of his inner circle, Commander in Chief in public, Godfather behind his back, Comedian in Chief in Miami, and Holy Father by an abjectly submissive historian—sat back in his executive chair to ponder Victoria's results. On one hand, it was disappointing to find out that a semi-literate carpenter and a dressmaker had presented the world with a supergenius, whereas none of his children had scored above 130. On the other, looking on the bright side of things, he found comfort in the fact that among the incompetent, groveling, mealy-mouthed bastards that surrounded him, there was an individual scientifically proven to be extremely bright.

The Chief was further seduced when he began reading her secret personnel file. Born on January 1, 1959, her parents had named her Victoria because, on that day, dictator Fulgencio Batista fled Cuba. The revolutionaries proclaimed it Victory Day. Her father's surname was Valiente, so her full name, both in Spanish and in English, literally meant Valiant Victory, and figuratively, Gallant Victory. Without meeting her personally, he had Victoria promoted to lieutenant colonel and transferred to the Miami desk.

In her new position, General Lastra disregarded Victoria's objections twice. Colonel Morera overruled her on four occasions. The consequences were catastrophic. Three of those six recruits turned out to be double agents, two of whom managed to infiltrate a twelve-person network in Miami that the FBI, after a three-year stint, dismantled in 1998. On the evening he learned of the debacle from his minister of the interior, the Chief had Lastra and Morera summoned to his office.

"Did Micaela approve the recruitment of those sons of

bitches?" he had yelled, apoplectic with rage, when told who the FBI agents were.

Looking at their well-polished boots, the general and the colonel had shaken their heads.

"I knew it!" the Chief growled triumphantly.

In the adjoining anteroom an overzealous aide, upon hearing his idol rant and dreading that he may suffer a stroke or a heart attack, had the physician on duty come up. After hurried whispering, the physician knocked and entered the Olympus to take Zeus's blood pressure.

"Get out of here!" the patient had thundered, arm rigidly pointing to the door, the instant he saw the newly arrived. The doctor paled, did a quick about-face, and closed the door behind him. A pregnant, six-minute pause followed as Number One hobbled around the room. Lastra and Morera kept their gazes on the floor. Finally the Chief came to a halt in front of the officers, giving them the eye.

"Look at me!"

His face flamed; his gray beard shook with ire.

"Whatever Micaela recommends, even if it is against your better judgment, you do it. You've made great sacrifices for the Revolution; I don't want to send you into early retirement. But if you overrule Micaela again, you are finished. Is that clear?"

"Yes, Commander in Chief," the culprits had chorused.

"Okay, let's see now what we can do for our comrades."

Victoria never learned that she had been given carte blanche, but the subtle signs that she began picking up several days after taking the IQ test—whose results were kept from her—repeated themselves in late 1998: embarrassed smiles, lowered eyes, heightened consideration for her opinions and recommendations. Clearly remembering that she had opposed the recruitment of the two FBI informers, she guessed that a big shot, maybe the minister, maybe the Commander himself, had read her reports. Paradoxically, what was a disaster for the Directorate became a feather in her cap. It was not taxing at all to pretend that *she had felt sad for the jailed comrades when in fact she was exulting over her personal triumph.*

The second trait that Victoria Valiente possessed in a prodigious amount was the acting capability of a universally acclaimed theatrical performer.

Like many Cubans born, raised, and educated throughout the revolutionary era, right up into the late eighties Victoria had been a true believer. She had completed her secondary education in one of seven military schools run by the armed forces—the Camilo Cienfuegos schools—where the emphases placed on the perfection of communism and on the genius of the Chief were even greater than in civilian schools. Over the years, though, as she became privy to secret information of every nature, took English and French classes, read all sorts of magazines and newspapers, paid attention to her husband's increasingly frequent criticisms, and, from 1998 on, devoted four hours a day on average to browsing the Internet, Victoria reached the inescapable truth that communism was doomed, in Cuba and anywhere else where it had gained a foothold.

But Victoria had witnessed how the careers of many promising young people had ended abruptly because they had made the mistake of openly expressing disagreement. From the very first day that guilt gnawed at her conscience for doubting the veracity of her juvenile ideals, Victoria knew that she ought to conceal her incertitude and pretend that with each passing day she believed more and more in the Revolution and its Commander in Chief.

The third strength that Victoria Valiente had in portentous magnitude was ambition.

She had mapped out her progression. Director general and brigadier general first, minister of interior and division general three or four years later, member of the Central Committee, member of the Politburo, member of the Council of State, the sky was the limit. Victoria realized she was resigning herself to side with the losers, but all things considered, she had no choice. She was well aware that she had passed the point of no return years ago. For having a finger in every pie, she would never be allowed to travel abroad. On the positive side, sudden death notwithstanding, the Chief might be able to hold the country together for eight or ten more years. What she had to do, Victoria reasoned, was to become indispensable, steer clear of internal rivalries, never question the Chief's orders, and, after his death, avoid siding with a faction. Everyone should see in her a top-class specialist willing to serve those in charge, not the overly ambitious woman she in fact was. These guiding principles never left the innermost recesses of her brain.

Nonetheless, as time went on, Victoria's concerns increased substantially. Whenever the Chief ranted on television for hours on end, he made serious mistakes. He insulted any Latin American president who asked him to respect the human rights of dissenters, made rather barbed comments concerning European politicians who said that such a benevolent step would be most welcome, and termed traitors the Western European leftists who disagreed with his strategy and tactics.

Many of his half million viewers watched in dismay as he foamed at the mouth, wet his fingers in saliva to turn pages, then went on with the old litany.

He would proclaim over and over again that most Latin American governments were lackeys of U.S. imperialism, Cuba was the finest democracy the world had ever known, the Revolution had the best human rights record on the planet. Victoria and many other well-informed government officials, civil servants, and party bureaucrats watching him from their homes closed their eyes and slapped their foreheads in desperation. Had the man taken leave of his senses? Who was he trying to fool?

Around this same time, the Chief's closest associates began to perceive, with mounting preoccupation, his gradual slide down the road of senescence. With complete disregard for the diversity of the nation's opinions, he set forth his weirdest propositions and most extreme views with the expressions "Cuba believes," "Cuba considers," and "Cuba thinks."

Knowing how grave her country's financial difficulties were,

how weak the economy was after many years of colossal misman-
agement, Victoria couldn't believe her ears whenever the Commander criticized the policies being pursued in other Third World
countries. He would recite statistics on their high levels of unemployment, on the number of people living below the poverty line,
and on the large external debt of these nations without ever referring to similar data for his country.

For Cuba, he invariably prophesied a golden future. The island was a beacon of hope for the rest of the world. In three or
four years, watching the educational TV channel he had ordered
built in record time, his people would become the most cultured
on the planet. Cuban athletes, physicians, teachers, scientists, and
musicians were the best, its soldiers the bravest, its workers and
farmers the most patriotic. All were willing to die before returning to capitalism, the man always proclaimed at the end of his ti-
rade. Including the several million whom you know want to
emigrate, Commander in Chief? Victoria addressed the silent question to the screen of the set, turned it off, and started surfing the
Internet for senescence, senility, and Alzheimer's.

She gave it up after a few hours. This was a whole body of
knowledge that would have taken years to master, and what was
the use? The Chief had worrying symptoms: irritability, believing
in a reality that did not exist, a tendency to recount younger years
On the other hand, his memory loss was negligible, he frequently
joked and had fun, and never appeared disoriented. The most capable specialists cared for him and had unlimited access, from anywhere in the world with no expense spared, to cutting-edge
medications for retarding the aging process. The man delivered
three-hour-long speeches standing at a podium, pausing just to
take a sip of water. Being a formidable actress herself, she wondered if the Chief realized that he had failed miserably on all
counts and was just putting on an act for the many millions of
misinformed compatriots. Admitting failure was out of the question; it would imply relinquishing power, and everybody knew that
the Commander would rather die than take the backseat.

In February 1996, after the Cuban air force shot down two U.S. civilian planes, Victoria drove her neurons mercilessly before reaching four conclusions. First: The system was falling to pieces in slow mo. Second: Considering his genetic background and the medical care he got, the Chief had probably ten or more years to live and would most likely die of natural causes. Third: He would remain in power until the last day because those who could end his rule overnight would not move a finger. They feared (a) losing their privileges and (b) retaliation for having executed or sent anticommunists to prison. Fourth: Her husband was 100 percent right. Therefore, Ms. Victoria Valiente decided to have one more heart-to-heart talk with him that evening, and then suck him cross-eyed.

...

A pure Maya? was the first thing that came to Elliot Steil's mind while he shook hands with the widow and turned his I'm-a-good-guy smile on. In Miami Beach, the city of glamour, very deep tans are as common as flashy cars and dental-floss bikinis, but this lady's skin was an intense auburn, a color not easily found in people outside Central America. However, she was the racial opposite of a Maya woman in everything else: tall and willowy, emerald green eyes, Slavic cheekbones, upturned nose, thin lips. Why hadn't he noticed her skin color at the funeral? The answer came to him in a flash: She had been wearing black—hat, veil, gloves, and pantyhose included.

"Good afternoon, Mrs. Scheindlin," he said.

"Good afternoon, Elliot. Welcome. Come in, please. Make yourself at home."

"Thanks."

"Let's dispense with formalities. Call me Maria. Can you do that?"

"Sure" was his reply as he released her hand and crossed the doorframe.

"I ask because Ruben complained he never got you to call him by his first name."

Steil raised his eyebrows and gave her a wry smile. "Well, it's different. I owed him big time. My life, in fact. That made him very special to me."

"I understand. Follow me, please."

Three steps led down into a large, well-appointed living room with the kind of top-quality furniture and decor that seems standard and is not, Steil thought as he scanned the room. A huge sofa and two club chairs upholstered in striped satin, two loveseats in pearl gray leather, porcelain figurines and knickknacks atop the coffee tables and side tables made from cherry wood, beautiful floor lamps, sconces on the walls. A European-looking still life showing fruit in a bowl graced one wall. Two huge Armenian, Iranian, or Turkish rugs draped the opposite wall; a third carpet was spread underneath the striped-satin set, the only spot where the highly polished hardwood floor was not visible. Fresh-cut flowers adorned a corner. The staircase that led to the upper floor also had steps made from hardwood, banisters carved from rosewood. The smell of wax polish combined with the aromas of jasmine, rose musk, and vanilla that some expensive air freshener issued.

With long strides, the widow whisked him to a sliding glass door that looked out over a huge courtyard and a swimming pool that glistened in the sun. She slid the door open and went outside, then turned to Steil.

"I'm very much an outdoor person. I find air conditioning pleasant in bedrooms, at night. Do you mind?"

"Not at all," Steil said, trying to pin down her slight accent. European for sure, maybe German. She had a soft voice, though.

"Oh, my God," Maria muttered under her breath after shooting a glance at the pool.

Steil followed her gaze and registered a second surprise. A butt naked, suntanned younger woman lay supine on a blue air mattress that floated in the center of the amoeba-shaped pool. Her breasts were almost the same reddish brown of her nipples; her scarce pubic hair looked sun-streaked as well. Steil would have considered her scrawny had she weighed ten pounds more. Her eyes were closed and she wore a peach-colored rubber bathing cap. She looked utterly sexless to Steil.

As though slightly miffed, the widow shut the door and turned. She strolled along a gray granite path flanked by manicured lawn. It led to a cemented area with metallic furniture beneath a canvas striped in green and white. She waved her guest to a white armchair that had thick, plastic-covered cushions, then eased herself onto an identical piece separated from Steil's by a brass-and-glass cocktail table.

"Jenny, we've got a visitor," Maria singsonged. "My daughter," she added in a normal tone, "loves to sun herself. I set the bad example."

"It looks great on you."

"Thank you."

Jenny lifted her head a little, placed her hand over her eyebrows, shot a glance at Steil, then paddled the air mattress around until the headrest concealed most of her body.

"But you don't seem to get much sun, Elliot," Maria said as she reclined on the armchair.

"Well, I work in the daytime."

"I know. I guess in all the years we lived here, Ruben relaxed less than fifty hours in this courtyard. Work, work, work, always work. Can I offer you anything?"

"I'm fine, thanks" resting the back of his right knee against his left kneecap.

"Rum? Beer? Whiskey? A margarita perhaps?"

"Orange juice would be good."

"Sure. I won't be a jiffy."

Curiosity stirred inside Steil as he watched her amble over to the sliding door. In the eight years that he had worked for Ruben Scheindlin, the old man had mentioned his wife maybe three or four times, always in passing. Short sentences like "These new shoes are killing me; present from the wife," or "Have to be home by seven; wife's having friends for dinner," so Steil had never devoted a minute to try to imagine the woman until the day of the funeral. That sad morning, though, as he slipped into the jacket of his brand-new, off-the-rack black suit, he had pictured a grief-stricken little old lady crying her eyes out. To his complete surprise, Sam Plotzher, IMLATINEX's co-owner, had introduced him to a very poised woman at least four inches taller than the deceased. As he had expressed his condolences, her proud demeanor and firm handshake led him to believe that she was considerably younger than Scheindlin's seventy-eight. *Well, what do you know?* he had thought at the time, and exchanged a meaningful look with Tony Soto, who was also at the funeral. The Miami policeman and Steil belonged to that portion of humankind deeply distrustful of couples whose age difference is remarkable.

But this afternoon, six weeks later, there were no signs of mourning in her ensemble. She wore a white halter-neck top, loose ivory-colored slacks, and sandals. Her hair, cut shoulder-length, was held in place by silver strips. She had gold studs in her earlobes, an expensive watch on her left wrist, and appeared stylish in a quiet way. Maria slid the door open, went into the living room, shut the door. *Mid-fifties,* Steil guessed.

It was amazing to find out that Scheindlin had married a much younger woman. Was Maria his second wife? Had he divorced the first to marry her? Well, Steil reasoned, concerning women, some very bright, shrewd, and experienced men have been known to fuck up badly. Many of the less talented bring disgrace on themselves and their families on account of pussy. As a young dude he had twice dropped the good girl for hot, sexy babes who had dumped him after a few months. Nevertheless, it provided consolation to recall that the women who had made him act like a complete fool had great bodies. Maria had bony arms and legs, a can flat as a board, lemon-sized breasts, and narrow hips. Maybe Scheindlin had had a weakness for skinny broads. Or perhaps Maria was a decent, faithful wife whose lone extramarital love affair had been carried on with the sun. In which case he was just a narrow-minded, shallow, and backward male chauvinist who favored chicks à la Salma Hayek.

The two years during which Scheindlin had smuggled chloro-fluorocarbons into South Florida sprang to mind. Maybe he had tried to persuade his wife and daughter that excessive exposure to ultraviolet rays was risky and failed. Then the old man probably concluded that if he did not seize the opportunity, others would. Scheindlin had made a lot of money with CFCs, the visitor remembered.

Inspecting the back of the house, Steil took in the top-floor terraces that probably belonged to bedrooms, a huge bay window, the red Roman-tile roof, what appeared to be a duplex cabana to one side of the pool. The well-tended lawn had several round flower beds where beautiful plants whose names he did not know thrived. He identified, however, the purple bougainvillea that hid from view the Cyclone fence that enclosed the lot. The courtyard smelled fertile, humid, and earthy.

Coming in five minutes earlier, past the sliding gate and from the driveway, he had admired the landscaped garden, the colonnaded entry, the overhanging balcony with its wooden balustrade, the slate path leading to the impressive front door carved from oak. To the right, set back from the house, a three-car garage stood. Steil guessed that the mansion had been built in the late forties or early fifties, when real estate values in the west island of Bay Harbor Islands were affordable. In every likelihood the first proprietor paid less than two hundred thousand dollars for the one-acre tract, the architect's fees, and the construction costs. At present the widow could sell it for anything between three and four million, the guest estimated.

The day before, out of the blue, the widow had called him at the office and asked him over for drinks and a friendly chat. He told her he was honored by the invitation and would most surely attend. Then, after hanging up, he had asked Sam Plotzher whether he had any notion what Mrs. Scheindlin might want from him. Plotzher said he had met the widow at her home two weeks earlier. It appeared that she wanted to learn as much as she could concerning a company of which she and her daughter had inherited 79 percent of the shares. Sort of a test-the-waters meeting.

Steil uncrossed his legs and jumped to his feet. In the living room, supporting a tray with paper napkins and two glasses full of orange juice on the palm of her left hand, Maria was struggling with the door handle. The lady was rich but had no live-in maid; so very Jewish, he thought as he hurried to the sliding door. He opened it;

she thanked him, then came back into the courtyard. Steil slid the door shut and both returned to their seats. The guest waited for Maria to place the tray atop the cocktail table and make herself comfortable in her armchair before sitting down.

She wrapped a napkin around the bottom of a glass and presented it to Steil. "Please," she said. He reached for it, nodded, waited. She enwrapped the other glass and raised it in midair.

"Cheers."

"Cheers."

She sipped once, slowly; he took two quick sips. Freshly squeezed, pulpy, not too sweet. Good.

Maria returned the glass to the table and dabbed her lips with a napkin. "Tell me, Elliot. When did you meet Ruben?"

"In 1994."

"So, you were with him for eight years."

"Exactly."

"Now, if I ask you to rate my husband's reserve, or secrecy, or whatever you call it, on a zero to ten scale, how secretive would you say he was?"

Steil took a third sip, touched his lips with the napkin, shifted his gaze to the bougainvillea, then back to the widow. "I suppose it depended, Mrs. Scheindlin."

"Maria."

"Sorry. Most of the time he held his cards very close to his chest. With strangers I would say he was very reserved. With a lifelong friend like Samuel, or with you, I suppose he had no secrets."

Maria nodded thoughtfully, glancing at the pool. "He probably kept nothing of a business nature from Sam, nothing of a personal nature from me. But concerning the business, he told me very few things, and vaguely, as though he didn't want to bring home his problems. And I respected that."

"Of course."

"As a result, I find myself in the dark regarding a company of which me and my daughter are majority shareholders. I know practically nothing about the company or the staff. Jenny knows even less. For instance, all I know about you is that you are a Cuban to whom Ruben lent a hand when you confronted problems whose nature I don't know, that you became his personal assistant after Uri was killed, own 1 percent of company stock, and drive the old car parked on the driveway."

"That sums it up pretty well," Steil said, smiling again.

"Cutting to the chase," Maria continued, "I've asked you here today because I would like to find out more about you, Elliot. About your past and your present."

"I understand."

"Maybe you do, maybe you don't, so allow me to be more specific. Thanks to my late husband, that naked young woman over there," Maria tilted her head to the pool, "and I are rich. If I live to a hundred spending a thousand dollars a day, Jenny would still inherit a few million from me. I could sell IMLATINEX now and live without a care in the world. But I don't want to."

Maria paused and raised an eyebrow. Steil interpreted the facial expression as indication that he should ask why she was disinclined to live leisurely, but he limited his reaction to cocking his left eyebrow and crossing his ankles.

"So far my life lacks significant achievements," the widow added. "I was the wife, the mother, the cook. I wrote checks to pay house bills. I've spent a small fortune on sunblocks, and hand and face creams. I occasionally watch a movie on TV. I also read a couple of books a year. And that's all. I have no artistic vocation, no hobbies. Now that my daughter is a woman perfectly capable of fending for herself, now that I've lost Ruben, the ennui of widowhood seems to be affecting me. I intend to give a purpose to my life, do something that's interesting, worthwhile, and a little risky too, why not? Risk is the spice of life, or so adventurers claim. It's a flavor I haven't tasted. The only thing I can think of that could give me all that is perpetuating and expanding Ruben's business. Does that make sense to you?"

"Certainly," Steil said, thinking that Maria sounded well educated.

"To do that I need, first, to bone up on the company; second, hang on to two partners that my late husband considered trustworthy, knowledgeable, and efficient. I figure you guys want to see the company grow. Ruben trusted Sam implicitly, but he is sixty-eight and . . . who knows? He could be active many years more, and I most certainly hope so; or he may retire, develop an illness, or die as unexpectedly as Ruben died. Do I explain myself?"

"You do, yes."

"Ruben trusted you, Sam speaks highly of you, too. But I'm a different individual. I want to begin to know you personally."

Looking as though she was through with the introduction, Maria sipped orange juice. Steil imitated her, suspecting that the woman possessed an extremely sharp mind, perhaps some congenital business acumen as well. Housewife, mother; sure. Nonetheless, he couldn't rule out the possibility that the widow knew a lot more about the trading company than she was willing to admit. Maybe Scheindlin had updated her on all important aspects on a regular basis and now she was playing possum to see whether her partners would take advantage of her. As the Cuban saying goes: Pretend to be dead to see what kind of burial you will get.

Both glasses returned to the table simultaneously.

"I see your point, Mrs. Maria. Ahh, let me see. My father was American. He and my mother met while he was working at a sugar refinery in Cuba, fell in love, got married. I was nine years old when he abandoned us. He returned here, remarried, had another son, made money, came to be the major stockholder of a sugar refinery in New Iberia, Louisiana. An uncle of mine, pretending to be a friend of my father's, sailed to Havana in 1994 and offered to smuggle me out. Tired of communism, I said yes. Then he pushed me overboard in the middle of the ocean."

"He what?" gaping at him.

"Left me to drown in the Florida Straits. The reason was my father had bequeathed half his estate to my mother and me. Bad conscience, I guess; he didn't know Mom had died years before him. The problem was, his second wife and her son wanted me dead, too, so they could inherit everything. They offered my uncle a hundred thousand dollars to kill me. But I got two lucky breaks. A family fleeing

Cuba on a raft rescued me, and I met Mr. Scheindlin. Here in Miami, my half brother tried to snuff me twice. Your husband learned about it, wanted to know what was going on, so I confided in him and he footed the bill to find out who was after me and why. Next he introduced me to a lawyer, David Sadow."

"I know him. We are his clients, too. What happened to this uncle of yours?"

"He was murdered, by my half brother probably, whom I suspect had planted the letter bomb that killed Uri."

The wide-eyed widow, staring at Steil, shook her head in wonder. "Well, I had no idea. Ruben . . . kept this to himself."

The guest thought it reasonable to probe a little. "And how did he explain Uri's murder to you?"

"He said some guys were trying to scare him out of a line of business. Nothing else."

"Well, to cut a long story short, David Sadow took my case. My half brother was blown to pieces by a letter bomb . . ."

"What?"

"Yes, someone murdered him."

The widow stared at her guest again, so intently this time that Steil waited for her to renew the conversation. "Would it be wrong to infer that you are a very vindictive man, Elliot?"

"Yes, it would. I had nothing to do with it. I've never killed anyone."

"Oh well, forgive me. It's none of my business anyway. Go on, please."

"The whole probate process lasted two and a half years, but after deducting legal fees, taxes, the money that your husband advanced me, and other expenses, I netted one million six hundred thirteen thousand dollars."

The widow peered at Steil, perhaps a little suspiciously, before saying: "I would very much like to know why you invested one million in the firm."

Steil clicked his tongue, forced a smile, and shook his head sadly before giving her a sidelong glance. "There were three reasons for it,

Maria. The most important is that Mr. Scheindlin asked me to; my ten thousand shares came from his 80 percent of company stock. In the second place, I concluded that after all the things your husband had done for me, I would've been the most ungrateful of bastards if I had said no, taken my money, and ran. And last, because it is a good investment."

"Well . . ." was Maria's only comment. Then she released a deep sigh and rearranged herself in the armchair, her gaze floating around the courtyard. Steil drained the glass of juice, wiped his lips dry, glanced at the pool. The air mattress remained static; Jenny's right hand caressed the surface of the water. A minute went by.

"What make's your car?" Maria unexpectedly asked.

Steil frowned in confusion. "It's a '91 Chevy."

"When did you buy it?"

"In 1995. February, I think."

"Before you got your money."

"Yes."

"My manicurist owns a Lincoln, a '99 model."

"Great car."

"Where do you live?"

This is getting a little strange, Steil thought. "I rent an apartment at Virginia Street, Coconut Grove."

"Since when?"

"1995."

Maria threw her head back and laughed aloud.

Steil knitted his brow. "I must admit that you are losing me, Maria."

She turned to face him, still a trace of a smile on her lips. "Tell me, Elliot, please. How many South Florida millionaires would you say drive an eleven-year-old car? Or live where they lived when they were destitute?"

"Not many, I suppose."

"Exactly. Now, don't get me wrong, I don't mean to pry into your affairs, but like most women, I'm curious. The few Cubans I know are not so . . . how shall I put this . . . unassuming."

Steil tilted his head left and right, hesitating for a few seconds as he carefully chose his words. "Well, I guess that's one of the many important things I learned from Mr. Scheindlin. Keep a low profile. Don't flaunt your wealth. Don't draw people's attention to yourself. For me, that is sound advice, not difficult to take at all. My apartment suits me. And to be honest with you, I have my eyes on a 'pre-owned'"—he placed the quotation marks with his forefingers—" '98 Saab in excellent condition. But don't tell anyone that I buy my shoes at Payless."

"You don't!" She gawked at his feet, shod in expensive, orthopedic brown loafers.

"Just kidding. I used to, though."

There was a splash in the pool. In a reflex response, Steil's gaze went there. The air mattress bobbed gently and Jenny, doing the breaststroke, was approaching a nickel-plated ladder. He tore his eyes away from the young woman and let them rest on her mother. Maria watched as her daughter climbed up the ladder, picked up a white terry robe from the tiled poolside floor, put it on, opened the left swing door to the cabana, and disappeared inside.

"But money is to indulge in your every whim, Elliot," Maria said, still riding the same train of thought.

Unsure if the daughter was visible, he kept his eyes on the mother. "How true. But maybe because I was born poor and remained so until five years ago, I'm not . . . extravagant? Or better yet, profligate. But being rich makes me feel pretty sure of myself. I relish knowing I can do what I think best when I want to. It's a great feeling."

"I know what you mean," the widow said, crossing her spindly legs. "I was born and raised dirt poor. In Poland. People born here? Even the poorest don't realize how fortunate they are compared with their equals in many, many countries. Their peers in Latin America would consider most Miami homeless people rich if they could see what American indigents eat, what they wear. By the way, Sam mentioned you are planning a trip to Cuba soon."

"I am, yes," wondering whether she had completed the read.

"Business or pleasure?"

"Neither. I want to visit friends who are probably having a hard time. See if there's anything I can do for them."

"Are we doing much business with Cuba, Elliot?"

Steil rested an ankle on the other knee. Yeah, she had probably finished reading him, was moving to business matters now. "Well, let me give you a piece of advice first: You shouldn't mention to anyone that we are doing business with Cuba."

"That much I know. The embargo, the Trading with the Enemy Act and all that. But Ruben began selling things to Cuba in the seventies, I think."

Slip of the tongue flashed in Steil's brain. "That's my understanding, too," he said. "Last year Trans-Caribbean Trading, our Panamanian subsidiary—on paper it is not ours—brokered sales to Cuban firms for a little over a hundred million, twenty million less than in 2000. Mostly used trucks and trailers bought here, five or six locomotives, some heavy machinery, two small Japanese turbogenerators for sugar mills. The only snag is in electronics and home appliances; sales of those dropped to less than half of what we sold them in 2001."

"Why is that?"

"Cuba is buying those articles directly from Communist China. Six hundred thousand TV sets plus thousands of PCs, blenders, tape recorders, the whole nine yards. They don't need us to trade with China; it's a direct, government to government deal. Soft credit included."

"I see. And what's the perspective on our future trade with Cuba?"

Is this really what this woman wanted to question me about? Steil pondered. *No, she also wanted to pump me.* "Well, I'll be as honest with you as I was with Mr. Scheindlin."

He detected movement out of the corner of his eye. Wrapped in terry cloth, in flip-flops, her daughter was approaching them. Taller than Maria, she possessed an unusually beautiful face that compensated for her thinness. Wide forehead, big brown eyes, straight nose, perfectly delineated lips, a confident jawline, all framed in a lustrous, dark cranberry mane of hair that tumbled below her shoulders. The tan looked extremely becoming on her. Steil uncoiled himself from the seat thinking that should Jenny gain thirty pounds in the right places, she would drive men crazy.

"Meet Jenny, Elliot," the widow said, her tone of voice approaching patience.

"Pleased to make your acquaintance," Steil said as he proffered his right hand.

"Hi." The young woman gave him a weak squeeze.

"Elliot was your dad's personal assistant. Now he's managing for us."

"Oh, great," Jenny said, giving two quick nods and a flicker of a smile. Then, turning to Maria, "Mom, you using the Audi this evening?"

"I don't think so. What happened to your car?"

"Nothing. I just feel like the Audi tonight."

"Okay. Keys are in the ignition."

"Thanks, Mom. See you, Mister."

"Sure."

Jenny followed the granite path to the sliding door; Steil returned to his armchair. "Beautiful woman," he felt compelled to say.

"Yes, she is. Unfortunately she is anorexic."

"Oh."

"Doesn't she look emaciated to you?"

Steil pulled the corners of his mouth down, as if in doubt. "She's thin, yeah, but emaciated?" *A walking skeleton* was what he would have said were it not for the fact that hypocrisy had become the most encouraged form of social interaction.

"She's a fashion model. Very attached to her father; so much so that she couldn't attend his funeral. She was in denial, sedated, deeply affected. But you were about to give me your views on the company's future regarding Cuba."

"Yes, well. Mr. Scheindlin believed that as soon as the embargo ended, our business dealings with Cuba would triple. But I don't see that, the end of the embargo I mean, happening anytime soon. Not in this administration, in any case. I'm not fooled by the immediate cash payments the Cuban government is making to American firms at present. You know? After the hurricane? When the United States offered to help?"

"Yes, I remember reading something in the paper."

"That's just public relations. Trying to prove to the American business community that they are responsible trading partners. Cuba is broke, Maria. Eventually Cuban firms pay, but it takes them a long time. As long as six months. It is rumored that to pay cash to U.S. firms, they are defaulting on European firms. Anyway, I don't see Cuba turning richer anytime soon, not under communism, nor under a market economy. So even if the embargo ends, where will the money to pay for imports come from?"

Maria bit her upper lip and seemed to drift for a while. "What about foreign investment?" she asked. "Rich Cuban-Americans swear that, after Castro, they will invest heavily down there."

Steil grunted, then smirked. "Let me put it this way. Politicians in the opposition make all sorts of promises. After taking control, though, they fulfill those that further their aim to hold on to power and renege on the others. It's the golden rule of politics. Shrewd businessmen lead the Cuban American opposition in Miami, and they will invest, sure, but how much? Enough to turn the Cuban economy around? I have serious reservations about that. I don't think they will sell their holdings here and rush back to invest in Cuba."

"What about American companies?"

"Some will, for sure. Hotel chains, McDonald's, Kentucky Fried, the same companies that have invested all over Latin America. What has been the outcome in those nations? Mr. Scheindlin sent me on business trips to Panama, Mexico, El Salvador, and Guatemala. You see the golden arches everywhere, the Hiltons, the CNN bureaus. But once you leave the hub of major cities, you find considerable poverty and unemployment, barefoot people roaming the streets to see if they can eat one hot meal a day. An economy with 40 percent unemployment, owing the equivalent of two or three years of GDP to foreign banks, is far from prosperous."

"What's GDP?" Maria asked, furrowing her brow.

"Gross Domestic Product. I can't get to first base in economics, but your husband defined it as the total value of all the goods and services a country produces over a certain period of time."

"I see. What did you do in Cuba?"

"I was an English teacher."

"Really?"

"Really. I've got a BA in English Literature from the University of Havana."

A Mona Lisa–like smile flickered across Maria's face. She interlaced her fingers on her lap. "And when are you planning to go?"

"As soon as I get the visa from the Cuban Interests Section in Washington."

"You need a visa to visit your country?"

For the second time Steil grunted, then smirked. "I do. They don't call it a visa, though. It's a 'permission' or some other term they use. Communist politicians master human languages. A defeat becomes 'a setback' that shall evolve into victory in the future; the 1968 invasion of Czechoslovakia was termed 'generous assistance' offered by troops from the Warsaw Pact. Hurling eggs at someone who wants to emigrate, pushing him around, is 'an act of repudiation of the scumbags.' And Cuban citizens living abroad don't apply for a visa before visiting the island, it's a permission, a mere formality."

"Tell me something I don't know."

Steil felt mild surprise. She had mentioned Poland, yes, but he had failed to make the connection because she added something significant concerning destitute people. "You lived in Communist Poland?"

"I did. But that's a rather long and boring story, the sun is beginning to set, and I have taken up much of your time." Maria rose to her feet and, followed by Steil, sauntered over to the sliding door. "Thank you very much for coming over, Elliot."

"The pleasure was all mine, Maria."

"I'm not a businesswoman. Perhaps conducting this sort of interview at home is not what a majority stockholder ought to do," she said, a doubtful smile on her face as she opened the door.

"I wouldn't know. I'm not a businessman, either, nor an expert in human relations. But I appreciate and value your invitation. It has the human touch," Steil felt it proper to say as they crossed the living area.

"My aspiration is to forge a good relationship with Sam and you," the widow said. "I want to get involved in the business—not the minutiae, of course, I'll give you all the leeway you need to act effectively—but I want to know the market strategy we follow and why, the most recent developments, all important decisions. I will probably ask many questions at first, become a pain in the you-know-what, but I need you to help me out and provide advice on what you deem best for the company."

She had her hand on the doorknob.

Market strategy. Important decisions, Steil thought. Standard housewife vocabulary? "You are entitled to ask as many questions as you wish," he said. "It is my duty to answer them to the best of my knowledge and I look forward to collaborating with you. It's what Mr. Scheindlin would have wanted me to do."

"Thank you, Elliot. Drive carefully." She extended her hand.

"I will, Maria. Bye now."

"Bye bye."

Cruising the Broad Causeway on his way home, Steil thought that the first thing to do when he got there would be to grab and squeeze Fidelia's solid and slightly oversized behind.

At her swimming pool, floating on a white air mattress, her naked body soaking up the lambent glow of the late afternoon sun, Maria Scheindlin was reading, of all things, an article on the finer points of corporate governance in *The Economist*.

...

Born in 1950, Manuel Pardo began showing numerical precocity at the age of seven while attending the rural school two kilometers away from his father's eleven-hectare plot of land in the province of Pinar del Río. After graduation from the Faculty of Mathematics at the University of Havana in 1973, he was assigned to the Center for Digital Research. In 1976 the Ministry of the Interior bought its first mainframe, and the counterintelligence officer that monitored Pardo's workplace was asked to recommend the most capable young expert the ministry could enlist. The officer said Manuel Pardo was their man.

The security clearance revealed that he came from a nice family of sugarcane farmers, none of whom had emigrated to the United States, applied to emigrate, or was known to be a dissenter. Recruited into the Communist Youth in 1967, Pardo had married his incredibly attractive university sweetheart in 1974. Acquiescent, mild-mannered, and with a dislike for controversy, he always participated in the voluntary works and political rallies that the party convened. He followed the standing order to not talk shop with strangers, was modest, only swilled a beer or two at parties, did not smoke. To unwind he helped the wife at home, solved mathematical riddles, or practiced pistol shooting at the university's shooting range. The clumsy six-footer was not a hunk and went unnoticed almost everywhere.

Summoned to a meeting at a safe house, Pardo learned that the homeland wanted to know if he would volunteer for the silent army whose mission was to defend the Revolution without expecting recognition, fame, or glory. The mathematician could not believe his ears. Really? Would he be given the opportunity to join the State Security? Maybe, the interviewer replied mysteriously. However, in the beginning, the Ministry of the Interior required his services. Well, the somewhat disappointed Pardo said, he would gladly join Interior. Maybe if he proved himself highly competent he would be admitted to the State Security, he added. For being a university graduate with three postgraduate courses, he began his military career as a first lieutenant. A month later he was handed his identification as a militant of the Communist Party.

His life as a civilian disappeared overnight. At first his wife complained mildly; after a year she argued forcefully that their marriage was threatened. In 1985, with Pardo in Leningrad taking another full-semester postgraduate course, his spouse met a Monday-to-Friday, nine-to-five linguist, premiered for him a bedroom repertoire that her husband never got to enjoy, and once the intellectual admitted he couldn't live without her, filed for divorce. Already a major, Pardo realized that every cloud has a silver lining. Divorced, he would be able to concentrate full-time on the latest technological revolution: personal computers. And on improving his English, something imperative for those who made a living in IT. Upon his return to Cuba, the ministry placed him in a "guest house," sort of a communal dormitory for officers from the provinces coming to Havana for a few days, also utilized to temporarily house divorced officers who hadn't a place of their own.

In December 1987 he was transferred to the General Directorate of Intelligence from the ministry's Department of Automated Systems. Intelligence featured Interior's most coveted jobs. The brightest—and the not-so-bright with friends in high places—were sent abroad for long periods under diplomatic cover. Those spared the appalling scenes of capitalist misery in London, Paris, New York, or Rome had the risky mission of dealing with the foreigners stationed in or visiting Cuba. To properly defend the homeland they had to make great personal sacrifices: dining at the nicest restaurants, drinking the best liquors, smoking first-class cigars, and booking rooms at the finest hotels, all covered by an apparently inexhaustible budget. Pardo, however, never had to make such patriotic sacrifices. His orders were to establish a data processing bureau that would deal with everything, from accounting to decryption.

A year and a half later the corruption scandal erupted. After having four men executed, sentencing the minister of the interior and sixteen other officers to long prison terms, and firing the vice ministers, the Chief decided that Interior needed a cleanup. In less than a year, 61 percent of its officers were retired or transferred to army units, civilian jobs, or private firms. Nine more committed suicide. The ministry did not shrink, though;

substitutes came from Military Intelligence and Military Counter-intelligence. Victoria Valiente was one.

Although he did not have the slightest inkling that high-ranking officers from the General Directorate had negotiated the use of Varadero Beach as a transshipment point to smuggle cocaine into the United States, Pardo had seen the cleanup coming. From an ethical standpoint the ministry as a whole and Intelligence in particular had gradually changed for the worse. The minister, the vice ministers, and many generals and colonels lived in mansions, went fishing aboard state-owned yachts, had two or three private cars, and bought nice clothing and delicacies at the ministry's well-stocked discount warehouses; a few even spent their vacations abroad. A young and beautiful mistress became a status symbol, as were drinking whiskey and smoking American cigarettes. Junior officers fought to keep a straight face when their superiors harangued them about making sacrifices for the homeland and the Revolution. Now everybody knew where the money to pay for the good life had been coming from.

After the debacle, Pardo witnessed much soul-searching at party-cell meetings. Yes, the guiltless admitted, they knew of the special advantages, benefits, and perks, but what were they supposed to have done? As soldiers, weren't they subject to the principle of unquestioning obedience? Shouldn't they respect the chain of command? What would have happened had they taken their criticisms to their commanding officers? Should they have written letters to the Commander in Chief? The officers from the Political Directorate of the Ministry of the Armed Forces who conducted the debates had no reply for these questions. Their ministry faced problems of the same nature and they were keeping mum.

Throughout his years in Interior, the arrogant behavior of the big shots, the privileges they enjoyed, and the many abuses of authority committed under the excuse of defending the Revolution had reduced to nil the romantic vision of Cuban Intelligence and Counterintelligence that had been planted in Pardo, as in scores of young men and women, by the omnipotent propaganda machine.

The 1989 scandal was the straw that broke the camel's back. Pardo was left profoundly depressed and deeply cynical about institutions that surround with a veil of secrecy what they do to get away with dishonesty, immorality, and degradation. In the Soviet Union, perestroika and glasnost had progressed notably. The Soviet press available in Cuba was reporting hair-raising stories concerning the KGB. Pardo began to question the system.

In such a spirit, he met Victoria Valiente two weeks after her transfer to Intelligence. She was one of the army officers to whom he taught a ten-week introductory course in basic programming, Windows 2.0, and what then, given the country's technological backwardness, still seemed a fantastic dream: the Internet.

This breakthrough fascinated Victoria. Pardo explained how the widespread development of LANs, PCs, and workstations in the eighties allowed the nascent technology to flourish. The intrigued Victoria frequently stayed after class to ask questions. What did "single distributed algorithm for routing" mean? What was the difference between interior and exterior gateway protocols? And how did the domain name system work? She started experiencing a mild attraction for the lean, angular, soft-spoken, and beady-eyed specialist with a slight stoop. He was flattered by her curiosity. As often as not they left the directorate's headquarters together, a fifteen-floor apartment building on the corner of A Street and Línea Avenue, and once in a while Pardo escorted Victoria to her parents' in Old Havana.

He was divorced, she was single, one thing led to the other. To his utter amazement, Pardo discovered that the levelheaded psychologist transformed radically when making love. She became passionate, demanding, insatiable, and didactic. Talking uninhibitedly about sex, she informed him in detail what she liked most (simultaneous cunnilingus and G-spot stimulation), showed him how, and asked him to be equally specific concerning what he enjoyed most (fellatio), something at which she proved to be adept. She considerably amplified his rather elementary culture on things sexual, helped him to control his ejaculation, and almost always had multiple orgasms before he came, a first for the major.

There was no reason to keep their relationship surreptitious. Three months after having been introduced, almost everyone in the directorate knew that Joaquín (his cryptonym) and Micaela (hers) were going steady. In June 1990, during the final stage of the cleanup, he was one of the last veterans to be sent into early retirement.

Having acquired a reputation as an excellent database manager and network administrator, Manuel Pardo was shipped to XEMIC, the most important state-owned company in Cuba. Registered as a private consortium from its foundation in 1984, XEMIC imported, exported, had major chain stores, operated banks and finance companies, dealt in real estate, owned hotels and a fleet of modern buses for tourists, provided software systems, and dabbled in publicity. Much more independent than the socialist enterprises, with representatives in many countries and constantly dealing with foreigners, both Intelligence and Counterintelligence used it as a front. A significant number of XEMIC executives, managers, and deputy managers were active or retired officers who doubled as agents or informers. Pardo's field of expertise, however, hardly ever demanded that he meet or deal with aliens, and he was free to concentrate on the improvement or design of accounting, banking, invoicing, and inventory databases.

Manuel Pardo and Victoria Valiente got married in December 1991. She had always lived with her parents, he still roomed at the guest house, so she was assigned a one-bedroom apartment in a Ministry of the Interior building at Hidalgo Street between Lombillo and Tulipán, Nuevo Vedado. As the country's political and economic situation deteriorated following the collapse of communism, Pardo began voicing doubts about the future of their country. For months Victoria listened in silence, occasionally nodding in agreement or tilting her head sideways in doubt. 1992 went by and in 1993 the island touched bottom. Pardo became much more critical.

"It just doesn't work, Victoria," he had argued one evening. "It didn't work in the Soviet Union, it didn't work in China, it didn't

work in Eastern Europe, it doesn't work here. The Chief has to re-consider, he's an intelligent man, he's the only one with the authority to preside over a peaceful transition."

Her reaction had been a deep sigh that gave away her acquiescence and, simultaneously, her misgivings that the Commander would admit having been wrong for so many years. But she believed her husband right in that the Chief could slyly achieve a peaceful transition, if he wanted to.

Pardo greatly influenced Victoria's political evolution just by expressing his doubts. As she had gained access to information and considered taboo subjects, she had realized why doctrinaire institutions do all they can to censor what people read. Hadn't she succumbed to the nefarious influence of enemy propaganda? she had asked herself at some point. The fact that her husband had preceded her in questioning the system was very reassuring.

Unexpectedly, the Chief backpedaled—big time. He decided to repeal the law that penalized the possession of foreign currencies, thus confirming that he was willing to do the most humiliating things if they kept him in power. It was an explicit recognition of total failure: The Cubans he had personally labeled worms, traitors, and consumerists for fleeing from his dictatorship were now authorized to send hundreds of millions of dollars to feed and clothe their relatives, keep the country afloat, and forestall a popular uprising. On the day the news was announced, several of the faithful who still had a sense of shame had suffered strokes or heart attacks. A member of the Central Committee shot himself in the head, survived, and a year later died from coronary failure.

Free markets for farmers to sell their produce at prices decided by demand were created. Small private businesses, like restaurants and repair shops, also were authorized to operate. "Didn't I tell you?" an exultant Pardo had told his wife. "He will rectify. He wants to clean up the mess before he dies." Victoria had only smiled. She knew the Commander was personally and enthusiastically overseeing the beefing up of his worldwide network *of agents and informers;* quite unusual for an aspiring retiree, wasn't it? *she thought.*

In 1994, Pardo was dispatched to Toronto, Madrid, Milan, and Paris to train the staffs of the agencies of Havanatur— XEMIC's tourist division—in the latest computer programs. Although he never before had visited prosperous cities in the West, the database manager was not so much impacted by affluence as by freedom. It amazed him to watch newscasts in which Spanish parliamentarians from different political parties openly and respectfully disagreed about what was best for their country. Nobody called his opponent a traitor, a rat, or a worm just because the other was a Nationalist, a Socialist, a Christian Democrat, a Communist, or a Liberal. Legislative decisions were made by majority; unanimity was something nobody had ever heard of. Under capitalism, many nations had achieved what he had been led to believe only communist societies could: free education and health care. Countries with people living below the poverty line, yes; considerable unemployment, yes; a serious drug problem, yes; but where the majority lived better and enjoyed a hundred times more freedom than in the egalitarian, full-employment, seemingly drug-free society he belonged to.

After seven weeks of this, he returned to Cuba infected with the virus of freedom. Following a couple of days of pretty intense lovemaking, Victoria began to notice that her husband had changed somewhat. He acted more reserved, moody, pensive. "Is something on your mind?" she asked him a few times. "No, everything is okay" was his standard reply. Being in the trade, she first suspected that he had been ordered to do some secret intelligence work abroad. Her superiors, not wanting her to worry, or following the principle of compartmentalization, had kept her in the dark. Well, this was her man and she would not allow the sons of bitches to turn him into the sort of institutionalized paranoid schizophrenic that other officers and agents had become. She did not act hastily, though. She considered the pros and cons for almost a month before sitting down with Pardo to talk things over. Then, on a Saturday evening, she applied her psychological training to make a ten-minute introduction before asking her husband what was going on.

"We've been completely taken in, Victoria."

"What?"

"We've been lied to all our lives. Communism is worse than fascism. And the Chief must've known from the very beginning that it doesn't work, 'cause he's brilliant. He tricked our people into it because he realized it was the only contemporary political system that made it possible for him to wield power forever. But giving him the benefit of the doubt, thirty-five years have furnished enough evidence to persuade even the mentally handicapped that it doesn't work. But he just doesn't want to let go. He is insanely power-hungry."

Victoria had taken a deep breath. The moment of truth had arrived. She had considered four options: denouncing the man she loved, repudiating his views with every argument she could think of, divorcing him, or admitting to Pardo that she shared his ideas but there was nothing they could do, and they should keep their opinions to themselves. She had opted for the latter.

"Take it easy, will you? Let's talk this over, okay? What made you reach such a conclusion?" she had asked.

Lacking order or method, they spent the weekend discussing the abstract categories that have kept people wondering for twenty five centuries: things like truth, justice, and freedom, plus the state of the world in general, the Cuban present, and their future as individuals.

Pardo related his impressions of Canada and Europe. Victoria declared that democracy and freedom do not equal wealth. Her husband could not have failed to notice, she argued, that the countries he had visited were rich nations with centuries-old institutions. Half of humanity lived in appalling poverty, whereas communism offered security to most people: a job, health care, a home. It seemed that, after the initial frenzy, some of the people in Russia, Poland, Germany, and other East European countries were missing the benefits they had enjoyed in the recent past.

"Sure. Benefits for which you pay by becoming a slave. We are the best-educated, healthiest slaves in the whole world," Pardo countered.

"For three square meals a day, a job, a place to live, and access to a hospital, most people are willing to accept dictatorship," Victoria observed.

Pardo turned to stare at his wife.

"Three square meals a day? Don't you see how people in this same building have lost weight? I've lost nineteen pounds in three years. Give me a break. A job? Making three dollars a month is a job for you? A hospital? Lacking X-ray films and running water? Where you have to bring clean sheets and a pillow and sometimes even food to the patient? Why did I have to bring you ten inhalers from Madrid? Give me a fucking break."

The strength of his arguments kept her silent.

"Victoria, ever since we were in primary school we've been hearing that our government, the dictatorship of the proletariat, is the best. Bullshit! No dictatorship brings about sound government— or collective leadership. It's always the dictatorship of a single man. And you know why? Because at the root of dictatorship lies the basic concept of absolute control. In every leadership there's always a guy who is brighter, more cunning, more ambitious, has less moral scruples than the others, and he subjugates them and achieves absolute control."

"Okay, okay," Victoria had said, extending her arms to fend off a debate that would not take them where she wanted. "I don't have to remind you what you were and are now, nor what I am. I don't know how many people in your place of work, or in mine, think like you. Maybe hundreds, maybe a handful. I do know that, in my unit, whoever goes on record with a fraction of what you've said is immediately court-martialed, and the most benign outcome

is that he or she will be expelled from the party, sent packing, and kept under surveillance for as long as this government stays in power. And I suspect that, in XEMIC, the outcome wouldn't be much different, at least not for a guy with your background. Am I mistaken?"

Pardo had shaken his head and lowered his gaze to the floor.

"I thought so. Now, for the same reasons, I don't have a way out. They'll never send me abroad. Never. You can be sure of that. And I can't write a letter to the U.S. Interests Section here saying: 'Hey, guys, I've seen the light and want to settle in Miami.'"

Pardo had lifted his eyes to his wife's and laughed softly.

"Maybe you'll be sent abroad again soon. Then you can file for political asylum," she had said next.

"I'd never do that."

"Why?"

"'Cause it would end your career."

"Not necessarily. I can claim that you never gave me a single reason to suspect that you were considering defection."

"You'd lose your job and this apartment."

"For sure. But I can find another job. Feel free to defect if you want."

"I won't leave you behind."

"Why?"

"'Cause you are the greatest fuck on earth."

It was her turn to smile, quite naughtily. "You feel like . . . confirmation?"

So, they had taken a sixty-five minute break for an unforgettable lovemaking session in which feelings and fear were determinant. That she was willing to risk vilification and demotion for his sake aroused Pardo enormously. What blew her mind came close to the delight experienced by a woman who has just given birth to a much-wanted son. His life and well-being, from now on, were in her hands. She had had seven glorious orgasms.

Later, still in bed.

"Never express the slightest doubt to anyone," Victoria had warned.

"I don't have doubts, Victoria."

"Criticisms, dissent, opposition, whatever. At party-cell study circles, when debating the Chief's latest speech, the secretary asks you to comment on one of his . . ."

She had paused to search for the appropriate word. Exhortations? Appeals? Predictions?

"Deceptions, outright falsehoods, or stupid exaggerations?" Pardo had prompted.

"Coñó! You are a walking time bomb! Back to the study circle. You firmly state that, as always, the man is 100 percent right, and we party members must do all we can to explain his views to those few citizens who don't understand him. It's safer to be considered a moron than a dissenter."

"Victoria, I'm forty-four. I'm not retarded. I've done that a hundred times."

Undeterred, she had kept pressing ahead. "If you are mad about something you are ordered to do as a party member, and want to get it off your chest, wait until you get home. If you can't wait, give me a call and I'll meet you anywhere."

"I am beginning to suspect that you love me a little."

"I love you and I'm in love with you."

"Isn't that a redundancy?" he had asked, frowning.

"No, it's not. But let's get back to basics. If you are not going to defect and manage to conceal from everyone your dissension, you'll keep your job and I'll keep mine. By protecting yourself, you protect me. What we have to do is work as efficiently as we can, become indispensable, try to get promoted. The higher we climb, the better we'll live."

"That's opportunism."

"No. And let me tell you why not. You mentioned earlier one of those idealistic notions we've been fed since grade school. There are more. Placing the interest of others before your own, making sacrifices for the homeland, risking your life for your political ide-

*als. That is ideological crap for fools. You have to make a very con-
scious effort to leave them behind. Sane individuals think first of
themselves.*

*"A father tries to save his drowning daughter, a girl he loves
immensely, but when they both go under because she's clinging to
his neck, the father lets her go and returns to the surface. The girl
drowns, the father may have feelings of guilt for the rest of his
life, but he acted sensibly, because a sane person's most basic in-
stinct is survival.*

*"Above all other things, think of you. Of us, if you are not
defecting. Samuel Johnson said that patriotism is the last refuge
of the scoundrel."*

*Pardo had squinted as he pondered a one-liner he had never
heard before. "That may well be true, but José Martí wasn't a
scoundrel, or Ignacio Agramonte, or many others. I do know certain scoundrels who call themselves patriots, though."*

*"Same here. What I propose is not opportunism, it is adapt-
ing to a changing environment. If we can't or won't leave, we have
to fend for ourselves, keep our eyes peeled for opportunities, see
what we can do to prepare for the future."*

"What future?"

*"The new Cuba that will emerge when the Chief dies. Two keys
will unlock that future: money and power. Maybe if we could think
of something . . . I mean, what could we do so that, when the time
comes, I wield a little power and you've made a little money?"*

. . .

Fidelia disliked Tony Soto. Tony Soto reciprocated her feeling. The
Miami cop was Steil's former pupil and friend; he also carried special
assignments for IMLATINEX. Steil loved Fidelia. Therefore, he tried
to steer things so the antagonists were not compelled to spend time
together. But sometimes he simply could not.

In the beginning, things were fine. Tony and Lidia, his wife,
accepted an invitation to dinner at Steil's. A few weeks later, Elliot

and Fidelia had spent an evening at the married couple's Coral Gables home. This came to be a somewhat random practice. But over the years, as Fidelia got to know Tony better, she had reached the conclusion that—under a veneer of paternalism in her presence—the cop treated his wife as though she were his servant.

A devoted feminist ever since she became a law student at the University of Havana, Fidelia's belief in equal rights had increased notably since she emigrated to the U.S. The semiretired injury lawyer she had been working for died two months before she got a law degree from Florida International University. At present Fidelia practiced divorce, child custody, support, alimony, visitation, modifications, contempt, and paternity. She was one of the three lawyers in the marital and family law team of a firm that also practiced personal injury and criminal law from their offices on Dadeland Boulevard.

Doing the dishes after dinner, or during girl talk while the men watched a baseball game on TV, Fidelia used to counsel Lidia. "You mustn't let him treat you like that" or similar hints were dropped. Lidia had begun voicing mild criticism to her husband about his ways, but he would not listen and instead start shouting. "Fidelia says," Lidia had objected once. Tony wised up. From then on, he seemed uncomfortable and surly when the two couples spent time together. "What's eating you?" Steil had wanted to know one evening. Tony had given his version of the problem. Back at their place, Steil had asked Fidelia whether Tony had valid reasons to feel aggravated. "Aggravated? Tony? Are you kidding me?" Then she had listed the many reasons that made her believe that the real victim in that marriage was Lidia. Steil had tried to persuade her that she should refrain from giving advice to Lidia, so as not to sour her marriage.

"Okay, okay," she had said, holding up her hands, warding him off. "He's your friend. I know he helped you out when you needed it. But she is *my* friend and he abuses that poor soul on a daily basis. Worst kind of macho behavior I've seen in my life."

"Fidelia, she's a housewife, they have three children. What will happen if they get a divorce?"

"The kids would grow in a greatly improved family environment. And the sonofabitch would be paying child support until they are of age, and alimony to her for the rest of his life. I'd see to that, personally."

Seemingly, Fidelia thought things over and backed off somewhat. Their get-togethers had become less frequent, and when one took place, she tried to stay in Elliot's presence most of the time to ward off accusations of poisoning Lidia's mind behind his back. Steil appreciated her efforts to avoid confrontation and knew she was doing it for him. Left to her own, she would have counseled Lidia to file for divorce.

By Cuban standards the relationship between Fidelia and Elliot was odd. They loved each other, had cohabited for six years, and had not considered marriage. She had divorced her husband two years after his desertion. Fidelia kept a room at her mother's—a rented house in the northwest section of the city—where her son, now a high school senior, lived permanently. Danny's father had settled in New Jersey, and the teenager spent summer vacations there. Most evenings after supper she drove to Elliot's and slept there.

Besides never requesting or accepting cash from Steil, she had insisted on paying him back, little by little, the three thousand dollars he had loaned her to pay for her father's funeral in 1995. She had no clue that after collecting his inheritance money, Steil had drawn up a will and bequeathed her a substantial amount. She didn't know either that she owned one hundred thousand dollars in ten-year Treasury bonds that Steil had bought in her name and kept in his safe-deposit box.

Two days after Steil's interview with Maria Scheindlin, over breakfast, Fidelia informed Elliot that it was Lidia's birthday. She voiced her suspicion that Tony would forget the date. Either that or he would make up an excuse to be away from home. Fidelia added that she would love to ask Lidia to dinner at the Versailles, her caveman husband included, of course. Sipping strong espresso, Steil thought it over for a minute or so. Although the prospect was not enticing to him, he agreed to join them if Fidelia picked up the tab. One hour had gone by when, from her office, the lawyer phoned

Lidia, sang the Cuban version of "Happy Birthday To You" to her, then made the invitation. Tony's wife sounded ecstatic. Around noon she called the lawyer to complain frantically that she could not find a babysitter. Fidelia arranged that, too.

Lidia arrived at the restaurant at 7:25, alone. Five-feet-two, she had looked much better when she was fifteen pounds thinner, that is, before her last two pregnancies. Never forgetting that her handsome husband was five years her junior, Lidia dyed her curly hair on a weekly basis and dressed like women in their late twenties, or so she thought. That evening she was wearing a charcoal gray pantsuit with brass buttons over a white silk blouse, high heels, and ersatz gems on her fingers and ears. Her lip gloss was a fiery red and her false eyelashes an inch long.

Tony would be a little late, "You know cops," she said with a slightly embarrassed smile. They were having the main course half an hour later—sirloin steak with yucca in garlic sauce—when Tony joined them, a gift-wrapped box under his arm. Lidia beamed. Fidelia retreated into herself. He had on one of his ample short-sleeved shirts over a white T-shirt, straight-leg khakis, and moccasins. By way of apology he said he'd pinched a spook stupid enough to steal four laser disc players from a store in broad daylight, then had to do the paperwork at the station, take a shower, and change. His speech was somewhat slurred and red webbings crisscrossed the whites of his eyes. Fidelia shot a worried glance at Steil. Tony kissed his wife, then ordered a beer and a steak. After dessert, Lidia opened her gift. Fidelia could not repress a grunt when she saw the box of a blender.

The short, low noise brought to a boil the anger and frustration Tony had been trying to suppress from the minute his wife had told him of Fidelia's invitation. "You know how to expand a woman's space, Elliot?" the cop asked, a forced grin on his lips, after finishing his eighth beer of the night. Then he wiped the foam from his mustache with the back of his hand and tilted his chair backward.

"No," Steil said. He saw it coming.

"You build her a bigger kitchen."

Fidelia rested her right elbow on the table, covered her mouth with her hand, stared at the tablecloth.

"You know how many neurons a woman has?"

"Now, Tony . . ." Steil said in a placatory tone.

"Four. One for each burner on her stove."

The red-faced Lidia seemed on the verge of tears. Fidelia glared into Tony's eyes.

"Hey, don't give me the look. It's a fucking joke," the cop growled, trying to stare Fidelia down.

"Watch your language, Tony. This is a public place," Fidelia fumed.

"Don't pick on me, Fidelia," he retorted, wiggling a finger at her.

"Now, Tony," Steil said soothingly.

"Don't 'Tony' me, Elliot. Your woman has been giving me a hard time for years. Meddling with my private life. What the fuck does she . . ."

"Don't raise your voice," Steil said through clenched teeth.

"I'll damn well raise my voice as much as I want to."

"You are shitfaced!"

"I'm not!"

Steil jumped to his feet and stared at the cop. "Come with me."

"Where to?"

"The restroom."

Silence reigned in the restaurant; other patrons stared. Fidelia mouthed "Check, please" to the server and fumbled around in her purse for her credit cards.

"I ain't going to no fucking restroom," ranted Tony, practically climbing the wall with anger.

Steil was breathing hard, the veins on his temples pulsing wildly. "Tony, if you set some value on our friendship, you come to the restroom with me. Now."

Ever since he was his student in high school, Tony had seen Steil as a person in authority. Over the last few years his admiration and respect for his former teacher had increased considerably. He thought the man was a lot smarter than he would ever be. Elliot had won Scheindlin's confidence, had trounced the sons of bitches who tried to deprive him of his inheritance, had mastered trading, and it seemed he would be general manager of IMLATINEX once Sam Plotzher retired. And Tony knew Steil meant every word he said. He rose from his chair. Steil turned and headed for the washroom, followed by the cop. Hushed comments started to run through the restaurant.

Six minutes later the sullen-looking pair came back to the table. Lidia blew her nose on a Kleenex that she dropped into a glass ashtray. Fidelia was staring at and fiddling with her napkin, now atop the table.

"We think we have a solution for this clash of personalities," Steil said. "And we want to know whether you agree."

Lidia shot a surprised glance at her husband, who kept looking at his empty glass of beer. Fidelia pretended to be absorbed in the complexities of folding a napkin. Diners at nearby tables stole looks and tried to overhear.

"It's best if Fidelia and Tony avoid each other," Steil carried on. "However, you two are close friends and will remain so as long as you wish, and you may spend time together anywhere you like, except at Lidia's home, to avoid a confrontation with Tony. Tony and I are friends, too, so the same rule applies to us. Tony would be very grateful if his married life is the one subject you two refrain from discussing. You comfortable with that, Tony?"

"I am."

"Okay. Now, do you agree to this, Lidia?"

"Yes, sure."

"Fidelia?"

"No problem with that."

Thirty seconds of embarrassing silence followed.

"Tony?" Steil prodded.

The cop shifted in his seat. "I apologize. I was way out of line. I didn't mean to spoil your birthday, honey."

"Oh, Tony. I love you so much," said Lidia, tears sliding down her face like two streams that had burst their banks.

Steil rose to his feet, gave a let's-get-the-hell-outta-here nod to Fidelia, pulled his wallet out.

"I already paid," Fidelia said as she stood up.

"Let's go then."

Driving out of the parking lot, Steil took a peek at Fidelia. She had a faraway expression.

"What did you talk about when we were in the restroom?" he asked.

"What did *you* talk about in the restroom?"

Steil grinned and took the center lane. Typical Fidelia. He sighed in resignation. "I asked him if he thought his mother would find the two jokes he had told at the table funny. He just stared at the floor. Then I said he had given us a hard time 'cause he was smashed and that you don't discuss your differences with anyone when you are smashed. He said he feared your counseling might turn Lidia against him and that he loves her and doesn't want his marriage to go to the rocks. I said I don't give a damn if he likes you or hates you, but you are my woman and he has to respect you. No profanities in your presence. Then I suggested what I said at the table."

She mulled this over for a few seconds. "Your woman," she said.

"Well, you are, aren't you?"

"I suppose I am."

"You suppose?" taking the right lane, tapping the brakes for the red on Twenty-sixth, signaling a turn.

"He said I was your woman. Now you say I am your woman. It's a sexist expression."

"It isn't. Not in Spanish. 'My woman' has the same meaning that 'my wife' has. We were talking in Spanish, weren't we?"

"But there isn't a similar expression for you men, right? We are not supposed to say 'my man.' 'My husband,' 'my spouse,' 'my consort' are the proper counterparts in Spanish, legal terms without any connotation of personal possession."

"Fidelia, for Chrissake," Steil objected, looking at her. She kept staring ahead. "You wanted me to tell you what we discussed in the restroom."

"Green."

Steil rounded the corner, let it rest.

After a minute. "Well?" Fidelia asked.

"Well what?"

"What else did you say to him?"

"Nothing else. He sulked for a while. Took a leak. Washed his face. Apologized."

A second pause ensued. Steil changed to the left lane, waited for the light at the corner of Coral Way and Twenty-sixth, and turned onto Coral.

"Lidia just sobbed and apologized for him," Fidelia volunteered. "Said he's drinking too much."

"Hmm."

"I said I wasn't offended. Not to worry."

"Hmm."

"You mad at me?" she asked after a moment. A measure of uneasiness had crept into her tone.

"I'm not mad at you. Why should I be?" Then, following a brief pause, "What worries me is that I can't say you're 'my wife' because you are not; can't say you're my woman, because that makes you angry; can't say you're my lover or my mistress because it would blow the fuses in that beautiful head of yours. So what should I call you?"

She considered it. "I guess I could live with 'my love.'"

Steil smiled.

Not another word was spoken. Once in the apartment, they exchanged a few inconsequential remarks about getting ready for the next day. Already in bed, Fidelia turned to Steil.

"You know what's the most intelligent decision you've ever made?"

"Falling in love with you?"

"That's not a decision."

"Right. Then you tell me."

"To quit the booze."

Steil considered it. "You are probably right."

"Sweet dreams, my man."

"Same to you, my woman."

Two

1994 marked a new phase in the lives of Victoria Valiente and Manuel Pardo in which simulation, hypocrisy, contrivance, and a measure of concern fleshed out their textbook notion of the psychological pressures spies experience.

Pardo had full knowledge about the computer systems used in all XEMIC divisions, whose premises, managing structure, and business processes he gradually came to master. Although the Internet was in its infancy at the time, it was part of his job to browse it and learn as much as possible about data transmission and computer security. Over the years he became proficient in intrusion-detection techniques, programs that snatch passwords, digital certificates, authentication and authorization software, and in finding holes in computer security.

He paid special attention to Banco Financiero Internacional, XEMIC's bank, and to FINXEMIC, its credit card operator. He gleaned the patterns of deposits and withdrawals, the procedures followed for bank transfers, and kept an eye on the balance of several accounts abroad. Seven were with offshore banks offering tax havens, in Caribbean states with liberal bank secrecy laws that turned a blind eye on money laundering schemes.

In 1995 he learned about a Dutch company that used digital blind signatures for the transfer of electronic money, thus making the cash untraceable. Pardo realized that ordinary money was in intensive care. If somehow he was able to electronically siphon money from XEMIC, he would have to (1) disguise the trail to foil pursuit and (2) be able to retrieve it in the future. He began extensive research on money laundering.

The partly integrated, partly manual system used by Tiendas Panamericanas, XEMIC's nationwide chain of stores, to purchase goods and services and pay for them caught Pardo's eye, too. He detected duplicate invoices that had been settled, overpayments, and underpayments. Bogus invoices seemed possible, and also creating a false vendor or modifying a legitimate one in the accounting system. It looked as if there was more than one way to skin a cat.

That same year, the retired major made trips to Panama, Cancún, and the Bahamas. Barefoot Mayans tilling the soil in Mexico and the poor residents of Panamanian shantytowns showed him the ugly face of capitalism, but he felt sure that abolishing private property would make matters worse for the underprivileged. Unlike Cuba, those countries would not have a Soviet Union to pay for hospitals, schools, and electricity. And like in his homeland, efficiency and productivity would drop dismally once their economies were wholly nationalized. Pardo concluded that individuals should not expect anything from politics; every person had to fend for himself. From his meager allowance he saved on meals and hotels to buy as many software magazines (books were too expensive) as he could afford.

The General Directorate of Intelligence regained its respect and consideration of the 1960s by foiling attempts on the Chief's life during his travels abroad, expanding the global network of agents and informers, and contributing to the security, scientific research, and economic recovery of the Cuban state.

The Chief, though, was returning to the remarkable lapses of judgment he had been showing since the early 1960s. He insisted on limiting the private businesses he had authorized in 1993 to the bare minimum, remonstrated against intermediaries, and launched thinly veiled attacks against all those who sought inde-

pendence from the state in self-employment. When the United States put out feelers about ending the embargo after President Clinton's reelection, the Chief ordered to shoot down two Miami-based civilian airplanes that tried to disseminate anticommunist propaganda over Havana.

"Who could he blame for communism's failure if the embargo ends?" Pardo asked rhetorically to his wife two days after the four pilots crashed into the sea. "It's his only remaining excuse. All his claims that the embargo should end are a smoke screen. Everybody suspected that in his second term Clinton would ease or even end the embargo. So the geezer realized he had to do something out-rageous to make Clinton backtrack. It's amazing how he plays American presidents. And those hapless guys in Miami gave him the perfect excuse."

Victoria nodded thoughtfully. It had been plain murder. In a moment of early confusion, the Ministry of the Interior revealed in Granma, *the official newspaper, that a Miami-based Cuban se-cret agent had flown to Havana the day before the downing and warned that the planes were coming.*

"Do you know who Pola Negri was?" Victoria asked her husband.

"Who?"

"Pola Negri."

"I haven't got the slightest idea."

"Pola Negri was a Polish actress who died in 1987. She was a big Hollywood star in the twenties and thirties."

"So?"

"Remember that name. Have you settled on a safe way to . . . divert funds your way?"

Pardo blinked twice before nodding. Sixteen months earlier, in a long conversation, he had explained to his wife the existence of holes in computer security that created opportunities for him to steal XEMIC funds and deposit them abroad. They had agreed that she would start considering how to combine her expertise with his. They should not hurry; they had all the time in the world,

Victoria had repeated over and over. Haste unavoidably led to errors, errors to failure. She would let Pardo know when she was ready to make her contribution. Since then she had told him about the IQ test, her promotion to lieutenant colonel, and what she perceived as her increased influence in the decisions being made by the directorate's top guns. Now it seemed she was ready. Maybe what gave her the final push was the downing of the planes, Pardo thought.

"I still have to dot the i's and cross the t's. I'll let you know when I'm ready. Then I'll need money to open bank accounts abroad," Pardo answered.

"Don't you need IDs?"

"Sure. Some I can arrange by myself. You'd be surprised what can be done with a good laser printer, a late-model photocopier, scissors, and glue. But if you could get me a real passport, and one or two American electricity bills . . ."

"I'll see what I can do. How much money do you need?"

"Minimum thirty thousand United States; fifty would be best."

"Okay. Maybe Pola Negri can make us a loan."

"Her ghost?"

"Sort of. Would you like to make love, macho?"

. . .

Without making of it a fixed routine, Maria Scheindlin began visiting the headquarters of IMLATINEX, a very large warehouse on Seventeenth Avenue and 171st, North Miami Beach, two or three times a week, always in the afternoon.

The first day, escorted by Plotzher and Steil, she paced the three-hundred-foot-long building from one end to the other. Her eyes roved about with natural curiosity by the tire section, the ball- and roller-bearing section, the spools of wires and cables at the building's end. This was Plotzher's turf and he acted as guide. The forklift operators watched her with respectful inquisitiveness from the aisles, maybe wondering about the color of her skin, Steil supposed. She seemed as out of place as a butterfly floating in the private office of a Wall Street tycoon.

Steil found it difficult to believe that, in the many years she had been married to Scheindlin, she had never visited the warehouse. Once she left, he asked Plotzher.

"Hey, Sam, is this the first time she comes here?"

"First time I've seen her here."

"Don't you find that strange?"

"Strange? Why?"

"They were married for what? Twenty-five, thirty years? In all that time she never got curious about her husband's business? Never wanted to surprise him with a present or something?"

"I've been working here for twenty-seven years," Plotzher began after a deep sigh, "and my wife has never come here, either."

Steil nodded, to pretend that Plotzher's explanation had cleared up his perplexity. Then he grunted and turned to his desk. He wanted to ask: "Do you forbid her to?" "Doesn't she give a damn about your job?" "Is this some Jewish custom?" But it was not his concern and he tried hard not to pry into other people's affairs. Suddenly it came to him that, after an eight-year relationship, at no time had Fidelia shown curiosity about IMLATINEX, not once had she visited his place of work, seldom called him there. Was trading repulsive to women?

It was Steil's turn to guide Maria the second time she came to the firm. First, he introduced her to the three-man office staff in the ceilingless eight-foot-high glassed-in cubicle. Next, he provided an overview of the business: subsidiaries in Buenos Aires, São Paulo, Recife, Santiago de Chile, Bogotá, Caracas, Panama, and Mexico, D.F. He mentioned that a two-man office in San José de Costa Rica covered Honduras, Nicaragua, El Salvador, and Guatemala. He gave her a computer printout with the names of the people in charge in each country, their phone and fax numbers, and e-mail accounts, too.

Well aware that his knowledge of the company's financial condition was empirical and insufficient, Steil arranged a meeting between Maria and the firm's auditor, Leshkowitz and Bramson, at their offices in the Sabal Chase Professional Center. Out of discretion, he advised her to go unaccompanied, but she insisted on the presence of her other two partners. The Enron and Andersen scandals raged on; accountants and auditors were in disgrace, and they entered the meeting with misgivings. For a little over an hour, Ari Leshkowitz showed them the computer graphics and printouts on which he based his opinion that IMLATINEX enjoyed an enviable financial condition. Although unable to grasp the finer points, they were reassured by a few basic, indisputable facts and left the building in high spirits.

In their next meetings, Steil guided Maria through the paper trails of simple transactions. Export first, import later. He hoped to impress on her that trading companies operate on very narrow margins and that sales volume is not necessarily indicative of significant profits. His years as a teacher made Steil didactic without becoming pedantic, and one evening Maria commented on this. She, Plotzher, and Steil were in the office; the night watchman was sitting by the warehouse's main sliding door. Under the fluorescent light, her suntan made a striking contrast with Plotzher's mane of white hair. She had on a light green sleeveless dress and brown pumps, but wore no makeup. Just the same silver strips in her hair, gold studs in her earlobes, the expensive watch on her left wrist.

"You two make a great team. I bet you were a good teacher, Elliot. And Sam? You would've been a great teacher, too. You guys explain things very clearly."

"Thanks, Maria," Steil said. Plotzher signaled his appreciation with a courteous nod and a flicker of a smile. Then he added: "You are a very bright student."

Maria waved aside the compliment. She sat behind her late husband's desk, in the swivel chair in which Scheindlin had collapsed the day he died from massive cardiac arrest. For a while Steil was lost in recollections. He had lifted the old man in his arms and dashed out of the cubicle, clamoring for a car at the top of his lungs. The old Jew had died instantly, though. Even as he waited for Plotzher to steer his car into the warehouse, Steil had sensed he was holding a corpse. The body was heaved in the passenger seat, held in place with the seat belt. Steil had sat in the backseat, gripping Scheindlin's shoulders, feeling his chest every few blocks in search of heartbeats. Plotzher had kept cursing in Yiddish and hitting the wheel with the palm of his hand all the way to the hospital. That evening, as he watched Maria, Steil thought that not even she should sit where her husband had sat. Nobody should, ever.

"I'm just a housewife. My understanding is a credit to your capabilities as teachers."

"You don't take notes," Steil observed.

"I trust my memory. Besides, why should I? Every significant piece of information is stored somewhere. A computer, a floppy disk, a filing cabinet. What would be the point? I can't even dream of catching up with you guys as far as managing the company. But I trust you, both of you."

Plotzher nodded, staring at the floor. He had folded the cuffs of his shirt back a couple of turns. The dial of his old Swiss watch looked Lilliputian on his heavily muscled left wrist. Steil felt a mixture of affection and compassion for him. Although he drew a two hundred thousand yearly salary, the company's jack-of-all-trades was a millionaire only on paper; his 20 percent of company stock was the result of many years of hard work. He could sell his shares if he wanted, but Scheindlin's heirs had first option. He wouldn't, though, Steil suspected. It would kill him to be idle. Long illness notwithstanding, he guessed that Sam would die like his late boss and friend: on the job or a few hours after getting home. Men who become one dimensional as the final curtain descends on them.

Plotzher reminded Steil of his Cuban grandfather. As Maria listened to the older man's advice on the superiority of periodical external audits over trust, Steil flew in time to Santa Cruz del Norte. In his late fifties, his grandfather had lost interest in fishing, reading books, listening to music, or playing dominoes. He seemed happy only at the refinery's quality control lab: measuring pH, polarization, and sucrose in the bagasse; washing beakers, flasks, and test tubes; remonstrating that under socialism most young people have no work ethic. He died one week after complaining of pain in the abdomen that he attributed to indigestion and tried to cure with bicarbonate. The pathologist who performed the autopsy could not believe that a patient so devoured by intestinal cancer could have kept working until seven days before passing away. He harmed no one with his single-mindedness, though, Steil admitted to himself. Only those elders whose unilateralism consists in ferociously clinging to power torment others with their sick craving.

"Don't you think, Elliot?" Plotzher asked.

Steil had lost track of the conversation, but years of daily contact had taught him that whenever Plotzher posed that question after explaining something to someone, he found himself in total agreement. "Absolutely," he said.

"Yes, I've heard that before," Maria said, then heaved a deep sigh. "There's a German saying: Trust is good, control is better."

"In business, that's a truism," Steil said, thinking that he had already been silent for too long and should contribute something.

"And what about in other spheres of life?" Maria asked, rotating the swivel chair to better face the Cuban.

"What do you mean?"

"I mean, what about trusting your relatives, friends, your physician?"

Steil thought for a second. Plotzher looked interested. "It seems to me that trust, like love, evolves over time. Sometimes it grows, sometimes it wanes," Steil said.

Maria pondered implications. "Trust is a feeling, isn't it? So, its evolution depends on human interaction."

"Probably. And maybe on events external to the relationship as well."

"Like for instance?" Her challenging expression was softened by a smile.

For the first time ever, Steil noticed that she had a nice smile. Curiously, Plotzher seemed engrossed in this part of the conversation.

"Marital infidelity," Steil said, lifting his gaze to a fluorescent lamp for inspiration. "Medical malpractice." Then, leveling his eyes at her, "Legal proceedings have turned relatives into mortal enemies."

"Like when an inheritance is contested," Maria commented, unable to resist the temptation to remind the Cuban of his odyssey.

"Right."

Maria nodded and bit her lower lip. Then she drew a deep breath. "So, friendship is the feeling less . . ." she groped for words, "prone to involution, don't you think?"

"Maybe. I'm not so sure, Maria. You trust a friend, then one day he steals money from you, rapes your daughter, or in some other way betrays your confidence. Trust is in crisis all over the world. It's the scarcest of all . . ." it took him a couple of seconds to find the right qualifier, "expectations. People distrust next-door neighbors, politicians, lawyers, doctors, insurers, priests, bankers, accountants, corporations, you name it. It's a crazy world."

Plotzher stood and began unfolding his cuffs. "If you don't mind, I'll hit the road. It's been a long day."

"No, I'm through, too," Maria said, standing. "Thanks for this training session. Is it okay if I come back next Thursday? Around four?"

"No problem," Plotzher agreed. "But I didn't mean to cut short your talk. It's just that I'm a little tired."

"So am I," she said. "Philosophizing is one of the red lights that turns on when I'm feeling frazzled. Is next Thursday okay with you, Elliot?"

"Perfect."

"Okay, gentlemen, let's call it a day."

. . .

In June 1996, six hours before Manuel Pardo left Havana for Mexico's Federal District, while sitting in her kitchen, Victoria Valiente typed and printed a letter using the laptop and printer that XEMIC had loaned to Pardo. She folded, then sealed the single sheet of paper around the edges with Scotch tape. On the inside right corner of a plain white envelope she penciled a number 8, placed the letter and two demonetized ten-peso Cuban bills with

Che Guevara's signature into it, ran a wet dishtowel over the gummed side of the flap, and closed it. She stood up, sighed, and for a moment let her gaze rove over the view of Havana from her kitchen window.

Victoria knew where she would end up should it be discovered that she was using her position for personal gain. She would not be sentenced to death, no woman had ever been executed, but she would be given life behind bars. She tried to see herself in a cell of the Havana prison for women she had visited once. She would not spend the rest of her life there. After the fall of communism, she would be pardoned, for sure. But how far away was that? Five years? Ten? And her accomplice would be executed by firing squad, for sure. They were playing for enormous stakes.

Victoria turned, ambled to the bedroom, slid the envelope into the inner breast pocket of the suit jacket Pardo would be flying with, then stripped off the pair of surgical gloves she had been wearing.

"Shall we begin easing the pain of parting?" she asked her husband, who lay in bed reading a magazine.

"Right away," was his reply.

Pardo visited five Havanatur agencies in Mexico—in the Federal District, Tijuana, Monterrey, Veracruz, and Mérida. From this last city, he FedExed Victoria's letter to a small convenience store in Brooklyn owned by Rubem Rabelo, a Brazilian who had lived in New York since 1975. Two days later, around midday, Mr. Rabelo slit open the envelope, pulled out the letter and the money, searched for the number 8. He jotted the number on the inside of a new envelope, put the letter and one ten-peso bill into it, turned the pages of an old notebook that he kept in a shoebox, found address number 8, wrote it down in capital letters on the front of the new envelope, and mailed it personally that afternoon.

Victoria's letter was next delivered to the office of Agustín Izquierdo, a Mexican accountant who had legally emigrated to Houston, Texas, in 1985. Mr. Izquierdo put his ten-peso bill away *before looking up address number 8 in an address book and mailing the letter in a cream-colored envelope to forty-five-year-old Eugenio Bonis, a Cuban boatlifted to the United States in 1980 who made a living as a landscaper in Miami, Florida. Mr. Bonis carefully inspected the strips of Scotch tape before cutting them with a penknife. He read the letter several times, then fed a diskette into the disk drive of his PC and copied something from the letter before burning it.*

In November of that same year, Pardo flew to Havanatur's Chilean agency in Santiago de Chile. One evening, arguing that he had to finish an urgent report to Havana, he stayed late at the office. The somewhat pissed off Cuban office manager, before leaving for dinner at home around seven, closed the miniblinds on the windows and asked Pardo to give him a ring when he was through. What made him angry was that he had the only key to the agency's glass doors; Pardo's overtime would force him to drive back to close for the night.

Half an hour after the man left, the retired major opened the filing cabinet drawer in which the passports of Chileans hoping to fly to Cuba the coming week were kept. He chose five issued to men in their forties and fifties and made photocopies of every page. After returning the passports to the filing cabinet, he photocopied the yellow pages listing Santiago notaries. In his trips abroad, he took with him the XEMIC laptop, to check his e-mail from Cuba and to surf Internet sites that, if accessed from Havana, might suggest he was up to something. He spent the next three hours visiting sites on money laundering. After midnight, once he had called the office manager to say he was through, Pardo reclined on the swivel chair, fingers interlaced behind his head, and tried to anticipate his wife's reaction when told that he was ready to roll.

"Great" was what she said a week later as she stripped her glasses away, kissed him hungrily, struggled to pull his jacket off. They had just entered the apartment. She had begun moving her hand over the fly of his trousers the second the elevator began to

ascend. By the time he kicked the front door closed and dropped his suitcase in the living space, he had a full erection. It was only natural that she misunderstood what he said about being ready to roll. But when two hours later they were sipping cups of espresso in the kitchen, he remembered the expression he had used months before and said to his wife that he had dotted all the i's and crossed all the t's.

"Goooood," Victoria whispered. She considered the news for a minute or two, then said: "My hands are tied unless I learn the date of your next trip to Panama or Nassau a week in advance. Is that possible?"

"I can't say for sure. Maybe they'll tell me on a Monday that I'll leave on Friday."

"Okay. Let's not push it. We'll wait for the right moment. But now, honey, let's go back to bed. It's been so long."

They got lucky. Not only did Pardo learn in January that he would be flying to Panama in February 1997, but he was informed that he had to spend a week in Toronto first. Victoria declared the Toronto trip "perfect." Two days after he arrived, at 10:00 A.M., with a ten-dollar phone card and from a pay phone, Pardo called the Miami number his wife had made him memorize. As she had fore-warned him, a machine answered.

"Bonis Landscaping," a male voice said in slightly accented English. "Leave your message and I'll call you back."

Pardo waited for the beep. "Uh, I have a message for Mr. Bonis from Ms. Negri," trying to keep his voice even. "She'll be in Panama from next Sunday evening, in Hotel Las Vegas. Mr. Do-par will take her messages. That's D,o," Pardo paused, "p,a,r."

The retired major hung up and on his way to the travel agency felt sad for the half wit who had been risking his free-dom for who knew how many years in the belief that he was serv-ing a great cause.

A week earlier four dissidents had been sentenced to prison terms between three and six years. Their crime? Writing and dis-

tributing a document titled "The Homeland Belongs To All," which demanded freedom of expression, amnesty for prisoners of conscience, and participation in the island's political life. What the half wit was serving was a great tyranny, Pardo concluded.

. . .

Steil got his visa to spend a week in Cuba and booked a seat on the early morning flight on April 14, 2002, a Sunday. He arrived at the warehouse a few minutes before 9:00 A.M. on April 12, informed Sam that he would fly on Sunday, and then dialed Maria Scheindlin's unlisted number.

"Well, how nice, Elliot," she said, sounding genuinely pleased. "Is this your first trip to Cuba since you left?"

"Yes."

"First vacation, too?"

"Second, actually. In 2000, I took my . . ." Steil hesitated. Woman? Spouse? Lover? ". . . friend and her son to Spain." It came to him that "her" clarified the gender of his friend. Feminist jargon could raise suspicions.

"Oh" was Maria's immediate, discreet interjection, followed by a pause. "Well, give me a few hours to make my shopping list. Let me see. Posters? I've heard there's a great fifty-year-old rum. And this friend of mine? He kills for those Cohibas Castro smokes."

"Used to smoke."

"Really? Good. Proves he's no fool. Perhaps Jenny would like CDs, too. She loves Camerata Romeu. Why don't you drop around this afternoon, after work?"

What could he say? Nothing except that he would be delighted, but he was not. He pictured the woman serving her guests the rum few in Miami get to taste and saying "With Fidel's compliments." Her daughter would boast about the Camerata CDs to her friends. The cigars were surely for David Sadow, her lawyer, who would chew them to pieces without lighting them up. Rich people!

He had errands to run and needed time to sort his feelings out. Anticipation had been growing inside him day-by-day, minute-by-minute; it burgeoned after booking the seat. That afternoon, driving eastbound along the Broad Causeway as the receding sun glittered on the surface of the sea, Steil tried to figure out what was going on in his head. A measure of apprehension, for sure. Those who had left illegally felt the same on their first trip back. What if someone accused him of committing a crime? Being innocent offered little consolation. He could be charged with anything, might not be able to return to Miami. Unlikely, but possible.

Something more elusive crept through the recesses of his mind. Reminiscence? Nostalgia? Homesickness? He felt as though he were slipping back into the womb. It had already happened to him once, many years ago. His life in Havana was so fulfilling, he was so glad of having left behind the cultural backwaters, that he hadn't been to Santa Cruz del Norte in a long while. His grandmother was on her deathbed, and she had asked to see each of her grandchildren one last time. As the bus got near his hometown, he had observed the sky, the sea, and the clouds. His rational side had pronounced them identical to those forty miles to the west; yet they had seemed so unique, so *his.*

Walking the streets that evening, he had registered scores of changes: Scrawny girls had become attractive women, new houses had replaced old wooden shacks, ageless wooden fishing boats had been given fresh coats of bright paint, friends who had had washboard stomachs in their teens now were paunchy. He had sniffed the air, listened intently, drank the water, touched the surfaces. And the smells, sounds, tastes, and tactile experiences had brought bittersweet memories which, when he was reminded of them elsewhere, had not smelled or sounded or tasted or felt like in his hometown. The rum made in Santa Cruz had a different tang in Havana, for God's sake! He wondered if all expatriates felt the same bond with their birthplace. Probably. You were born in the North Pole, you longed for northern lights, igloos, and zero degrees Fahrenheit.

Miami could do with a cooler temperature today, he thought as he switched the air conditioner to maximum. Low eighties in mid-April. He entered the east island through Kane Concourse, took a left on East Broadview Drive, another left on 101. He suddenly noticed something he didn't register the first time he was here: There were no multiple dwellings of any kind, just the kind of fabulous estates that make you wish you were worth $50 million. Zoning restriction probably. Steil gained access to Maria's closed gate and stretched out his arm to press the buzzer in a metal box.

"Yes?" came from the speaker.

"It's Elliot Steil."

"Come on in."

The gate slid back with a buzz. He parked in the driveway while the gate closed itself. The front door swung open.

"Hey, that white cotton shirt makes you look more Cuban. Cool, as kids say nowadays," Maria said from the doorframe. Steil noticed the at-home ensemble. Green off-the-shoulder blouse, tennis shorts, leather thongs. A clip pinned her hair back.

"Pretty hot today," he said with a smile while approaching her. There was not a dash of makeup on her face.

"Yes. Some rain would be good."

They went down the steps into the living space. Maria approached the sofa in striped satin, eased herself down onto its left end, and signaled Steil to a club chair. Fine, it was a day for air conditioning, Steil thought. For two or three minutes the conversation focused on his departure for Havana. Steil told Maria what he had heard about the ill-famed five-hour wait at the Miami airport for a forty-minute flight, the tight security measures, the people wearing three of everything except shoes to circumvent the airline's baggage allowance.

"Why is this?" Maria wanted to know.

"So they can take more clothes to their relatives."

The news of the day was the forced resignation of Venezuelan president Rufo Chaviano, and they skirted the subject for half a minute. Then Maria crossed her legs, slid her fingers into a pocket of her shorts, and extracted a piece of paper that she handed to her guest. On a notepad page Steil read:

1– Camerata Romeu CDs

2– Bottles of fifty-year-old rum (don't know the brand)

3– As many boxes of Cohiba Espléndidos as you can bring.

Steil lifted his eyes to hers. "I've been told that people coming from Cuba are allowed only two boxes of cigars and two bottles of rum," Steil said.

"Well, something is better than nothing. You want money?"

"No. You'll reimburse me when I get back. If I get back."

"What do you mean if you get back?" Maria asked with a frown.

Steil dropped his gaze to the floor, clicked his tongue, and shook his head. "I suppose I'm just a little paranoid."

Maria cast a suspicious glance at her partner. "Are you wanted in Cuba for some crime?"

"Of course not. I wouldn't go if I were. I'm not crazy, you know?" he said with a grin that tried to prove his sanity. "But you never know. Suddenly a crisis erupts, flights are canceled, scapegoats are needed, you find yourself at the wrong place at the wrong time, and anything can happen."

For an instant Maria Scheindlin seemed absorbed in her thoughts, staring over Steil's head, the insinuation of a smile pulling at the corners of her lips. "I think you understand what I mean," Steil ventured.

"How so?" returning to the moment.

"Perhaps you visited Poland under communism."

"No, I didn't. Nor after communism. Can I offer you anything?"

"I'm fine, thanks," he said, crossing his ankles.

She shook off the leather thongs and tucked her legs underneath herself. "So, if you have this feeling, why are you going?"

"I have to make sure some people down there are all right," Steil volunteered, feeling his privacy invaded. "Friends, my ex-wife, relatives in my hometown." Why was he justifying his actions to this woman? He decided to probe a little. "Don't you have people you care about in Poland?"

Maria took a deep breath and shook her head. "My parents died in the eighties, under Jaruzelsky. And I don't have many sweet memories of Zielona Góra, my hometown, or Wroclaw, where I got my BA in . . ." she opened a pause for effect ". . . English literature."

"That a fact? I don't remember if I told you that I . . ."

"You did."

"What a coincidence."

"Yes. But you know what, Elliot? I don't miss the snowcapped Carpathian Mountains, or the Oder, or walking to the synagogue under the contemptuous glances of everybody. Poland was 90 percent Catholic and 9 percent communist, so we were socially ostracized."

Steil kept his eyes on hers, feeling his slight animosity abate. *There goes my theory of what expatriates feel,* he thought.

"I found happiness in this country. I met and married a great guy, had a daughter, lived a good life. I worship the sun, I love the sand and the sea; this Atlantic is so different from the Baltic. When I feel like a colder temperature, I go to Aspen or Yellowstone. Ruben asked me fifteen or sixteen years ago if I wanted to spend a couple of weeks in Poland. I said, 'No, thanks.' Why should I? To visit my parents' graves? That won't bring them back. To hear the hypocrites complimenting me on my foresight? The same bastards who reviled me when I . . . came here?"

An undercurrent of rancor could be sensed in her tone.

"But Cuba is probably different," she went on. "I'm under the impression that Castro has become a bit liberal over the past few years. Besides, he needs the money you guys spend there or send to relatives. He starts throwing Cubans living here in jail, his main source will run dry. And you are not getting mixed up in politics, are you?"

"Oh, no. Politics stinks. Here, there, everywhere."

"Way to go," Maria said, pulling her feet back to the floor in one swift motion.

"Will you stay at a relative's?" as she fumbled around for the leather thongs with her toes.

"I booked a room at the Habana Libre in Havana. In Santa Cruz del Norte—that's my hometown—I'll probably stay with relatives."

"Good. Now, listen Elliot. You are important to the company. Don't go looking for trouble in Cuba. No, that's not what I meant to say. I meant: Avoid trouble in Cuba. But should you encounter any problem, try to smooth it over, negotiate, and don't antagonize the authorities. Call me if you need a lawyer. I'm willing to charter a plane and get you back here as fast as possible if it's necessary. Okay?"

"Okay, Maria. And thank you. I really appreciate your concern, but I hope I won't have to call you."

"I hope so, too," she said, bending over to reach for the elusive left thong. Steil was only half pleased. He valued the distinction, but the notion that he could confront so serious a problem that he would have to appeal to Maria Scheindlin gave him the shivers. *Knock on wood.*

"The real reason I asked you here today was to tell you this; not give you the damn shopping list."

"Oh."

"I want to make that clear so you don't think I'm a show-off."

"It never crossed my mind." *Hypocrite.*

"Just in case. Off you go, Elliot. I'm sure you have better things to do. Take your friend to dinner, pack your bags, make love. C'mon," as she got to her feet.

That evening around half past seven, Maria Scheindlin left home at the wheel of her Audi. She drove down the Broad Causeway, took a left on U.S. 1, turned left on Sixth Street, and pulled to the curb between First Avenue and First Court. From there she walked to a post office, where she bought a ten-dollar phone card. Returning to the Audi, Maria scratched off the strip covering the card's code, drove west along Flagler, and on Thirty-seventh Avenue entered a supermarket parking lot.

A light gray van entered the parking lot next. It had PALM SPRINGS DELIVERY SERVICE and a phone number painted on its sides. The driver got out and headed for a cafeteria adjoining the supermarket. Inside the van, through a periscope concealed in a roof ventilator, a man observed as Maria got out, approached a pay phone, and tapped the card's code first, then a number. She got an answering machine.

A woman's voice said in Spanish: "Leave your message and I'll call you back."

"Next Sunday. Early morning. Habana Libre," she said after the beep, then hung up. She returned to the Audi and followed more or less the same route back home, where she cut to pieces the phone card before dropping it in the trash can. Then, heaving a deep sigh, she went to the shower.

...

Full of anticipation, Manuel Pardo awoke early on February 10, 1997, a Monday. He took a shower, shaved, brushed his teeth, and donned underwear, a white dress shirt, a charcoal gray, fine-striped, two-button business suit, a light green tie, black socks, and black lace-up shoes. It was 7:55 when, carrying a nearly full flapover tote bag, he reached the reception desk and asked the clerk on duty if the mail he was expecting had arrived. The man reached for pigeonhole 205 and handed Pardo a sealed envelope addressed to Mr. Pardo. Its back flap had been Scotch-taped. Pardo turned, swallowed hard, and walked away. He slid the envelope in a side pocket of his jacket. To conceal and control his anxiety, he had breakfast, then went to his room and carefully checked that nobody had tampered with the envelope before he ripped it open.

It contained a key and a two-line computer-printed note in Spanish:

Locker B-035. Bus terminal at the end of Avenida Balboa, near Avenida Central, Panamá City.

Pardo lifted the phone, asked the reception desk to call him a taxi, then flushed the note down the toilet.

The retired major sauntered into the terminal at 8:35, located the bank of baggage lockers, inserted the key in B-035, and extracted a paper bag folded and stapled at the top. He thrust it in his tote bag and, clutching the bulging piece of baggage as if it held Aladdin's lamp, returned to the hotel in another taxi. By now

Pardo felt sure he had not been born to be a spy. Despite Victoria's assurances that everything would run like clockwork, the palms of his hands were sweaty and he had to fight off the impulse to check whether he was being followed or not.

Back in his hotel room, dreading hidden cameras, he shut himself in the bathroom to open the paper bag. It contained fifty thousand dollars in stacks of fifty- and twenty-dollar bills, an electricity bill in the name of Jesús Ortega, a resident of 6405 SW 10th Terrace, Miami, FL 33144, and *a Costa Rican passport issued to Evaristo Consuegra, born in 1963, with the bearer's photograph expertly removed. Mr. Bonis, the Miami landscaper, had an agreement with a Guatemalan window cleaner at Miami's International Airport. He paid the man five hundred for every passport he found and thus got hold of two or three every year.*

By 10:35, Pardo had divided the greenbacks into five packets of eight thousand dollars each; the remaining ten thousand went to the inner breast pocket of his jacket. He stole a glance at his watch. From his wallet he extracted a passport-sized photo of himself, then returned to the room, fished a tiny tube of glue from the flapover of the tote bag, glued the back of the photo very lightly, and pasted it on the passport. As he let it dry for ten minutes, Pardo placed into the tote bag the five stacks of cash, committed to memory the Miami address on the electricity bill, then slipped it into his jacket. It was 11:02 when he left the hotel.

The plane returning Mr. Eugenio Bonis to Miami took off from Panama's Tocumén International Airport three minutes later.

Pardo hailed a taxi and asked the driver to head for the corner of 50 Street and Aquilino de la Guardia, to Banco Continental. There he opened a personal account under the name Evaristo Consuegra and deposited eight thousand. The bank manager that took care of the new customer photocopied his Costa Rican passport and typed on his keyboard the Miami address the man gave for his place of residence. At 12:45, Pardo finished opening a second account with Banco del Istmo. In Panama, banking hours were from 8:00 A.M. to 1:00 P.M., so he had to wait until next morning to open the other accounts he needed.

Havanatur had no agency in Panama; others represented it. Since he didn't have to clock in or out, Pardo was not subject to the scrutiny of Cubans. After a hamburger and a soda, the retired major went to work at a tour operator's office and stayed there until it closed at five.

The next morning Pardo had the Miami electricity bill scanned in an Internet café, then opened three accounts, with Banco Internacional de Panamá, Bancafé, and Banco Alemán Platina. He spent the afternoon at another tour operator. In the evening, using his laptop in his hotel room, he visited the Internet sites of five online banks in the Bahamas, Gibraltar, and in Jersey, Channel Islands. Pardo completed and printed out the personal account forms from each of the five banks under the names of the Chilean nationals whose passports he had photocopied in Santiago. Then he typed in the same names in the scanned version of the electricity bill and printed five electricity bills, to furnish proof to each online bank that the applicant resided at 6405 SW 10th Terrace, Miami, FL 33144, USA. On a separate page, he made clear that he was spending a two-week vacation in the Las Vegas Hotel Suites, at Calle 55 and Eusebio Morales Avenue, Panama, where correspondence should be addressed until February 24.

On Wednesday morning he sent the forms by courier—along with the photocopies of the Chilean passports, the electricity bills, and reference letters from Chilean lawyers and accountants—to each online bank. Pardo was proud to have forged all kinds of documents so expertly. In Havana he had scanned the letterheads of legitimate correspondence received at XEMIC, written the glowing references in English, and stored everything in diskettes. In Toronto he had them printed, then bought the tote bag to carry everything around.

On Friday afternoon the desk clerk delivered to the guest of room 205 five cardboard envelopes with the logo of three different couriers. In his room, Pardo opened them one by one. Each contained a letter welcoming the new client to So-and-So bank, saying he could make his initial deposit at his earliest convenience and naming the bank official who most gladly would field his calls and messages. A computer disk with the client's digital signature, login, and password was also provided.

Next Monday morning Pardo transferred different amounts from the Panamanian banks to the online banks. In the afternoon he visited the online banks' sites and confirmed that the transfers had already been successfully completed.

"In plain language, what does that mean?" Victoria asked three days later, on Thursday night, following intercourse.

"Having five Internet-based bank accounts means that from anywhere in the world, using a computer, I can electronically deposit and withdraw money and nobody can trace the operation to me," Pardo said.

"How so?"

"It's called Telneting. Telnet is a basic command that involves the protocol for connecting to another computer on the Internet. You lease an account from any Internet service provider to actually order the online banks to transfer the funds, thus concealing your real identity."

"But your real identity is unknown in any case," Victoria frowned. "The non-Internet bank accounts are under the name of a Costa Rican; the Internet-based accounts are under the names of five Chilean nationals."

"Right, but keep in mind that the Panamanian banks have my photograph on the Costa Rican passport."

"It's true, coño."

"There was no way to get around that, so I'll leave those accounts alone from now on; close them during my next trip to Panama. Their only purpose was to provide a legitimate source to transfer the initial funds to the online banks."

"How much is left from the fifty thou?"

"I deposited forty in Panama. The online banks required minimums between five hundred and two thousand to open an account.

68

I exceeded the minimum always and transferred seventeen thousand three hundred fifty. I spent around two hundred in taxis and couriers that I couldn't charge to XEMIC and have with me nearly ninety-eight hundred, for emergencies and future expenses."

Again Victoria frowned. She considered something before speaking. "I think you should take the cash to your parents' farm in Pinar del Río. Bury it, hide it, I don't know, but don't keep it here. Keep here only what you can say you saved from your allowance, forty or fifty bucks."

"Okay."

Victoria went to the bathroom to douche herself and Pardo finished the beer he had taken from the refrigerator after sex.

"Will we be able to pay back Pola Negri in six months?" Victoria asked after returning to bed as she slapped her pillow.

"I hope so. Maybe sooner. After I transfer XEMIC money to two of the online banks, let's say A and B, I'll shuffle amounts from A to B and from B to A before transferring most of it to banks C and D, where I'll move the money around some more prior to letting it rest in the fifth bank, E. I have to create a web of transfers so complex that the original source of funds will be untraceable. It's called layering."

"How will we pay her back?"

"With something that costs fifty-five thousand. I told you: It's impossible to spend digital money on the Internet now. She has to make a choice between real estate, a car, or a boat, something she can sell later on, or keep if she wants to."

"I don't think you ever got around to telling me why it has to be property."

"Considering your prodigious memory, if you don't remember, I didn't tell you."

Pardo paused and, supporting himself on his elbows, sat up straight to belch. Then he lay back again. "In the United States, Canada, and most First World countries, a property seller must file a currency transaction report for any cash transaction over ten thousand dollars," he began. "This report has to indicate who the buyer

69

is. But if the payment comes in digital cash, neither the bank holding it nor the seller that accepts it has the means of identifying the purchaser. So, the seller can't be accused of aiding and abetting a money launderer. They don't know who the buyer is."

Victoria sighed. "Which goes to prove that people always find a way to foil legal measures. But how do we pay back Pola?"

"With the property we'll buy. We'll have the deed transferred to her."

Victoria slid her hand down to her husband's groin and pulled at his pubes while considering something. His scrotum contracted, his penis awoke. "Are you positive that she can't be connected to us in any way?"

"I am. Grab my cock."

"All in good time. Nothing should connect Pola to Cuba. Hey, what's this getting up for?"

"Blow me."

"I said all in good time."

"Blow me now or I'll slap you."

"I dare you."

He slapped her twice, not too hard. They liked engaging in controlled S and M once in a while.

"I'll fill myself with you now," an imploring look in her eyes.

"Blow me first."

"Okay. Next time you do what I say," slithering down to take him in her mouth.

His fingers found her folds, slid inside, and began playing with her clitoris.

...

Wheeling the carry-on that Fidelia had given to him three or four years earlier, Steil ambled into Miami International Airport at 3:05 A.M. on April 14. His chartered flight was scheduled for 8:30 A.M., but passengers had been asked to arrive at 2:00 A.M. *The embargo red-eye,* Steil was thinking. *I took the embargoed from Miami,* he could say.

Having been there a few times when he or his late boss had traveled abroad, always in daytime or early evening, Steil was astounded to find the huge terminal, reportedly the third busiest in the United States, dimly lit and almost empty. Airline counters were vacant, duty-free shops and cafeterias closed. No customs or immigration officers, pilots, or flight attendants were to be seen. Cleaners wiped floors and emptied trash cans.

Looking around, he spotted a queue of fifty or sixty people about a hundred yards away, waiting to be checked in. *My fellow countrymen,* he felt certain as he approached the line. The last man confirmed in pure Cuban Spanish—filtered through a bushy and unkempt salt-and-pepper mustache—that, yes, they were all flying to Havana. The guy, and those ahead of him, appeared angst-ridden. The floor was strewn with all sorts of baggage, predominantly those known to Cubans as "worms"—cheap sacks made from hard-wearing fabric with a heavy-duty, longitudinal zipper—favored because their comparative lightness adds inestimable pounds to the airline's baggage allowance.

Getting ready for the long wait, Steil felt the sting of discrimination. For most international flights, passengers were asked to arrive at the terminal two hours before departure; those flying to Cuba from Miami were supposed to be there six and a half hours ahead of takeoff time. Thorough baggage searches were not a consequence of September 11; they began in the late seventies. No citizen or resident of the United States could travel abroad with more than $10,000 in cash, but if the place of destination was Cuba, they were allowed a mere $180 per day of stay.

Steil sighed in resignation. He knew that such unfair treatment was not aimed at Cubans as a race or nationality. He had traveled to Central American countries without experiencing limitations of any kind. It was all politics. Yet, politics become personal whether you want it or not. He was carrying a money belt with $8,000, which was $6,600 more than he legally could, and if searched . . . But what would the purpose of his trip be if he could not help his relatives and friends? Well, for a 15 percent commission, dozens of Mexicans and Central Americans living in Miami frequently traveled to Cuba and delivered thousands of dollars to designated recipients. He would save money that way. But the truth was, he wanted to see things with his own eyes. It was rumored that the situation had improved considerably since he had left in '94. Although he would not even think about giving up his job, Fidelia, or the freedom and business opportunities he enjoyed in Miami, he missed Havana and Santa Cruz del Norte.

"Hi, buddy," a familiar voice said in Spanish.

Steil turned and was pleasantly surprised to find Tony Soto. "What the hell are you doing here?" the traveler asked. His pal was wearing civilian clothes, which possibly meant he was not on duty. He had come to see him off. It was a nice gesture of affection and maybe a little concern as well.

Tony's grin seemed forced. Then Steil noticed two men standing behind his friend, their eyes fastened on him.

"I, uh, came to see you off . . . and to introduce you to these gentlemen. They want to have a word with you," the cop said, now in English and moving sideways to clear space for the strangers.

The weirdness of the situation left Steil speechless. He stared at the tallest man, who proffered his hand. Black, five-feet-eleven or so, early forties, neat looking in a beige sports jacket over a green shirt and jeans. His face glistened with a sheen of perspiration. Steil shook hands, muttering, "Pleasure" after the man said, "Glad to make your acquaintance," and in a reflex response turned to the other guy—white, mid-fifties, overweight, bald with a close-cropped fringe around his head. He wore a white T-shirt under a deep blue, short-sleeved shirt, and baggy khakis. His lips were in brackets. Second shake.

"Pleasure."

"All mine."

"Mr. Steil," the black man said in his deep voice, "we've asked Mr. Soto to introduce us because we know you are good friends and we want to ask a big favor from you. But we need privacy. Would you mind giving us some of your time in our office? Upstairs?"

Elliot was gathering his wits. Who were these guys? Had they coerced Tony into coming to the airport? "Friends of yours, Tony?" he asked, jerking his thumb toward the pair.

"Sure. They want to have a word with you, and I strongly suggest you hear them out."

"Who are they?"

"We'll show you our IDs as soon as we reach our office," the black man butted in. "We don't want to do it in front of all these people."

So, they were cops, Steil inferred. It was his first brush with the law in a long time. Somehow they had found out he was carrying too much cash. That had to be it. But why was Tony mediating? Maybe to intercede on his behalf. In any case, it was decent to spare him the embarrassment of being questioned, maybe even searched, in front of all those people. Suddenly his trip had been wet-blanketed. Ask a big favor from him? Did the sonofabitch think that was funny?

"Listen, this is a check-in line," Elliot argued. "If I lose my place . . ."

"We'll take care of that," the smiling black man interrupted. "You won't miss your flight."

Steil shook his head, clicked his tongue, grinned, took a deep breath, and nearly said something inappropriate. "Okay," he mumbled instead as he reached for the handle of his carry-on.

The white man made a sweeping arm gesture toward a bank of elevators and the two Cubans followed him. The black man brought up the rear. Steil was thinking that if this snag had to do with the cash, the strangers were probably Treasury agents. He could afford a sixty-six-hundred-dollar loss, but the trip made no sense if he went empty-handed. A Latin-looking guy loped off across the lounge, took Steil's place in the line, and said something to the mustachioed man.

Elliot was more curious than angry when he was led into a second-floor office-cum-living area. Two metal desks with PC screens, keyboards, files, papers, and phones atop them, two swivel chairs, and a filing cabinet, stood by the rear wall. Such furniture hopelessly mismatched the nice leather sofa and two armchairs, wooden coffee table, and lamps on side tables positioned near the entrance. There were modern prints on the walls, a small refrigerator, a coffee machine on an auxiliary table, and a TV set on a pedestal table in a corner. Three unseen video cameras and five microphones started functioning the instant the door was closed.

The black man motioned Elliot and Tony to the sofa. The cop chose the right side, Elliot the left. The strangers eased themselves in the armchairs.

"Thanks, Mr. Steil. We really appreciate your devoting some of your time to talk to us," the black man began as he unbuttoned his jacket. "My name is Brent Hart. I'm with the FBI." He extracted a badge holder from the inner breast pocket of his jacket, flipped it open, and flaunted the badge at Elliot, who fought to conceal slack-jawed amazement. *FBI? This wasn't about the cash?* "This gentleman," pointing to the white man, "is Paul McLellan and he's with the Treasury Department." McLellan showed his badge, too. Ah, so *it is* about the cash.

Elliot had learned that men in positions of power don't respect the fainthearted. Accept them, yes; respect them, no. "I want to see IDs, not badges, if you don't mind," he said.

Hart and McLellan exchanged a glance and Hart nodded. He was the first to pull out his wallet and hand over his identification. While Steil glanced at it, McLellan searched for his. The stony-faced Tony stared at the T-man. When Steil returned Hart's ID, McLellan reached over to surrender his. Looking at it, Steil thought, *I'm fucked. But what has the FBI got to do with it?* He gave back the plastic card.

"Well, gentlemen, I'm very curious to find out why I'm here."

Hart rearranged himself in his seat and, smiling, shrugged off Steil's concern.

"It's our impression that you've done nothing wrong, Mr. Steil. You have nothing to fear from us. For some time now, we've been on a case about which we presume you know nothing and are only marginally involved. At present, we can't disclose the nature of this case. It's classified material.

"A month ago we learned that you were planning a trip to Cuba and we want to request your cooperation concerning—"

"Just a minute," Steil said, raising his hand and looking at the floor. "No, go on."

"All we want from you is to report to us—"

"Hold it," Steil interrupted again. "I'll ask a question and I want a straight answer. Are you going to ask me to spy on someone or something?"

"No," Hart said.

"No?"

"No."

Steil cut a sideways look at Tony, who remained strangely impassive.

Steil cleared his throat. "Listen, Mr. Hart, Mr. McLellan," he said, returning his gaze to the officials. "I'm indifferent to politics. I don't give a damn about communism, the embargo, the Cuban American Foundation, or anything of the sort. I don't know anyone in Cuba remotely connected to the government or the Communist Party. And if your request has nothing to do with spying, I don't see how I might be of any use to the FBI or the U.S. Treasury."

Five or ten seconds elapsed. McLellan pursed his lips in disapproval; Hart tilted his head to the side but kept silent. Tony Soto crossed his ankles and, looking at the floor, shook his head in dismay.

"Well?" Elliot said.

"Well what?" Hart asked.

"How could I be of any use to you guys?"

"How can you find out if you don't let me finish?"

Steil pressed his lips together. The man was right. Suspecting a trap, he had lost his cool. He nodded his agreement. "Sorry. Go ahead."

"Fine. Would you like a Seven-Up?"

Looking the man in the eye, Steil accepted the offer and Hart marched to the refrigerator, opened it, and returned with the soda. Steil was not thirsty. He nodded out of a realization that they had checked him out right down to trivialities, as this was his favorite soda.

And the dickheads wanted him to know it. It gave him the creeps, but he reached for the can, pulled the tab, had a sip. Hart returned to his seat, interlaced his fingers, and started talking.

"We have reason to believe that you'll be approached by someone in Cuba. Someone you've probably never seen before, although he may try to introduce himself through a friend or relative of yours. We think he'll try to cut a deal with you. Rest assured that this guy won't harm a hair on your head. On the contrary, he'll try to win you over. And he'll ask you to do something for him here in Miami.

"We may be wrong. In that case, your trip will be uneventful and you'll let us know when you come back. But there's a strong possibility we're right and, if a stranger approaches you with a proposition, we ask you to please agree to whatever this man asks you to do in Miami and report it to us."

Hart crossed his legs, McLellan ran his hand over his scalp, Tony combed his mustache with the fingernails of his hand. Steil could not believe his ears; feeling his mouth parched, he took a second sip.

"Now, please, think about this. We could've chosen to keep you in the dark. Then, upon your return, ask you if someone in Cuba had requested you to deliver a message, make a business proposition, or in any other way act on his behalf in this country. In this scenario, suppose that, out of fear, distrust, or another reason, you refuse to cooperate, or deny having conferred with anyone when in fact you did. Even worse: No stranger approached you, neither a friend nor a relative asked you to do anything here, but we may think you are lying. In such a circumstance, you'd become a suspect in our case. We don't want that to happen. We've taken you into our confidence because we think you are to be trusted and can give us a hand."

"But there's another reason for asking you to cooperate with the U.S. government," McLellan said when Hart paused. "By helping us you will help yourself. Your future here is splendid, Mr. Steil. You arrived as an illegal immigrant, inherited an important amount of money, and are a partner in a trading company. Even though you haven't applied for U.S. citizenship, it's the American dream come true. However, the dream may turn into a nightmare if you become involved in a serious crime. I ask you to consider that."

Steil slid himself forward and deposited the can of soda on the coffee table. "I think the best thing I can do is to cancel my trip," he snapped.

"You may, of course," Hart retorted. "Then we would have to reconsider our impression that you are not involved in what's definitely going on."

Feeling cornered, furious, Steil got to his feet. "You just said I hadn't done anything."

"Take it easy, Mr. Steil. Please sit down. I said it was *our impression* that you had done nothing wrong. Maybe we are mistaken. Maybe you are thinking of canceling your trip to report this meeting to somebody," Hart said suavely.

"That's nonsense! I don't know what the fuck you're talking about."

"Elliot, sit down," Tony Soto advised.

"Shut the fuck up, Tony!" Elliot advised back, scowling in anger.

"There's no need to curse," fumed McLellan.

That stopped Steil cold. He inhaled deeply and expelled a sharp, exasperated breath. "I'm sorry," he whispered as he sat.

"Don't lose your cool, Mr. Steil," McLellan went on. "We need your help. Because of your nationality, your job, your frequent trips to Central America, and your fluency in English, you are the perfect candidate."

Steil turned his head, rested his elbow on the sofa's arm, cupped his chin in his hand, and, staring at the nearest desk without seeing it, looked askance at the proposition. His silence was respected. He knew nothing about the so-called case. He had not committed any crime, not in seven years. He refused to get involved in politics, never had. He would not do it. No government agency could force him to do something against his will.

"Gentlemen," he began, turning to face Hart and McLellan, "I won't go to Cuba. I cancel my trip. I'm sorry." Then he stood.

Hart raised his eyebrows and shook his head with compassion, regretting that things had reached this point, then moved his gaze to McLellan.

"Okay. No problem. It's a free country," McLellan said with a smile; his brackets bent outward. "You have a lawyer, Mr. Steil?" the man from Treasury asked.

"What?"

"Attorney, counselor, ambulance chaser, *abogado* in Spanish."

"Yes."

"There's a phone there. Give him a call."

"Why should I?"

"Because yesterday you drew nine thousand dollars from your savings account with Capital Bank. And I have here," McLellan extracted a folded paper from his shirt pocket, "an authorization to search you. I suspect you're carrying a sum of cash that considerably exceeds the maximum amount you can legally take to Cuba, which is exactly thirteen hundred eighty-one dollars, the result of multiplying one hundred eighty-three dollars by seven, the seven days you'll be there, then adding the hundred you can legally import in merchandise. Perhaps you are not aware that if I find on you just one dollar in excess of thirteen hundred eighty-one, you face a fine that ranges from fifty thousand to ten million and imprisonment ranging from ten to thirty years, for willfully attempting to violate a U.S. law that permanent resident aliens must comply with. So, I think you should call your lawyer and ask him to come here as quickly as possible."

...

On April 17, 1997, a few minutes past 11:00 A.M., Manuel Pardo got a phone call from the personal assistant of XEMIC's president. An unscheduled meeting was taking place in the top floor meeting room and his presence had just been requested, the woman said. The instant the retired major entered the luxurious meeting room and scanned the participants, he knew what was on the agenda. Besides XEMIC's president and his two vice presidents, in attendance were the president of Banco Financiero Internacional, a general—and vice minister—of the Ministry of the Interior, and representatives from the Central Bank of Cuba, the Ministry of Electronics and Communications, and the Ministry of Science and Technology.

The day before, the corporation's president began as soon as Pardo complied with the request to sit down, persons unknown had siphoned off $1,600,065 U.S. from a Banco Financiero Internacional bank account in the Cayman Islands.

The man paused to let it sink in. Pardo had been anxiously waiting to hear it from the horse's mouth. He knew that, for Interior, everyone was a possible suspect, including the presidents of the bank and the corporation, but if the corporation's network administrator were not informed of what had happened, it would have meant he was in boiling-hot water. He had rehearsed his part painstakingly, with Victoria as acting coach, and now, his fear assuaged, he was ready to play it.

"How much?" he asked, his eyes wide with disbelief.

The president repeated the amount.

"But how . . . ? I mean, banks have security systems, all sorts of . . ."

Pardo feigned hesitation. The inept bureaucrat who had reached the top after many years of seven-day, eighty-hour weeks and considerable boot-licking was shaking his head.

"They did it online," the man explained. "Two withdrawals, one for . . ." he glanced at his notepad, "$785,414. The other for $814,651."

"Oh," Pardo exclaimed, then let a few seconds slip by before jumping from his seat. "But online they leave a trail!" he said enthusiastically. Another reflective pause. "Unless they used Telnet," sounding discouraged by the prospect.

"That's exactly what they did. The trail evaporates at a Canadian Internet service provider. The lessee of an account fed them a false name and listed as place of business a vacant lot in Montreal."

The other participants watched as Pardo reflected on this. "But to find out our bank's codes and passwords . . ." The script said he had to leave it there, and he did.

"Yes, we also suspect it's an inside job," the bureaucrat said, "but we need proof. The Ministry of the Interior and the Central Bank preside over the commission formed to investigate this. I want you to collaborate with them. You'll be joining forces with . . ."

While nodding gravely to each commission member he was introduced to, Pardo felt slightly sad. He and Victoria had achieved a masterstroke and they could not claim credit for it. It was not fair.

That evening, telling the story to his wife, ". . . but I nearly peed in my pants with laughter when the general, Silvestre, you know him?"

"No."

"Well, he drew me aside after the meeting was over and said, 'Major, you are our man here. If someone can find out who did this, it's you. This is my direct line,' he gave me a note with his number. 'You need something, find out anything, I want to be the first to know.' Can you imagine? He wants to be the first to know!" Pardo laughed heartily.

Victoria was a little worried over her husband's gradual transformation. From a sexually unimaginative, lackadaisical mathematician with utopian social notions, Pardo had become a go-for-it realist with superb sexual skills. But he had also turned fearless and overconfident. She believed that a little fear was beneficial; confidence was great, overconfidence dangerous.

"Be careful, macho," she warned. "Now everybody will be on the lookout. Before this, you could check all the programs and records, enter all the Web sites, nobody was on the alert because nothing remotely similar had happened. Now it'll be different. There may be someone in Interior, or in Science and Technology, or in Communications, expert enough to track you down."

"Victoria, trust me on this. Nobody, nowhere, can track me down."

"Just be careful."

At the first meeting, the experts from Science and Technology and Communications wholeheartedly agreed with Pardo's intelligent suggestions. He in turn okayed, without any reservation, their suggestions. The laymen nodded their approval without understanding a single word of cyberspeak. Work began.

Three weeks later General Silvestre called a meeting at 10:00 A.M. in his office. The three experts admitted their failure; they had not been able to detect how the intruders got into the system. Banco Financiero, they explained to the bureaucrats, had top-of-the-line software, no holes in its security, cutting-edge intrusion-detection techniques. Somebody had got in, but they could not say who or how.

The general banged on the table with the palm of his hand, startling the others. "This is unacceptable, cojones*," he yelled. "We got robbed and you tell us that everything is perfect? The security, the software, the hardware? Well, the guy's got fuckware and right now he may be fucking us blind.* Me cago en su madre*."*

Pardo had to call forth all of his self-control to not laugh himself silly. "Excuse me, comrade general," he said instead. "We've changed all the authentication and authorization software. It's impossible for . . . whoever entered the system to repeat his feat."

I shouldn't have said feat, *Pardo immediately realized.*

"Feat? You call a robbery a feat, comrade?"

"Sorry, comrade . . . It's just that . . ."

"What Comrade Pardo means," barged in Ariel Camacho, the expert from the Ministry of Science and Technology who had taken a liking to Pardo, "is that from a purely technical standpoint, what was done is a tour de force."

"I take a crap on the tour de force," bawled the general. "It must've been that traitor," he added.

Five weeks before Pardo's swindle, a midlevel, thirty-five-year-old executive of Banco Financiero Internacional stationed in London had applied for refugee status. The man had been admitted to the party at twenty-three, served in Angola, enthusiastically

waved little Cuban flags at political rallies, and told anyone willing to listen that the Commander in Chief was the greatest person in world history. Two months after being posted to London
with his wife and five-year-old girl, he had defected.

The experts had looked into the possibility that the fleeing executive had pulled off the job or had provided the required information for others to pull it. The unanimous conclusion, reported
to commission members during the fourth meeting, was that the
man lacked the background knowledge, essential information, and
computer expertise to do it. Despite this, the paranoid general, who
could not tell a computer from a typewriter and needed to close
the case, kept insisting that the "traitor" was the thief.

"Perhaps he's in cahoots with other undetected traitors hoping to be sent abroad soon, then they apply for political asylum
and get their share. ¡Hijos de puta!"

Nobody said a word. The general gulped half a glass of
water, returned the glass to the table with a thud, wiped his
mouth with the back of his hand.

"Now, comrades," he said, "we have to solve this case. I
want you to begin anew, clean the slate, start from zero, double-
check everything. Above all, you must take appropriate measures
to secure the systems, software, or whatever you call security in
your gobbledygook and vouch that this will never happen again.
If it does, many people will be sent packing. Not you; guys from
S&T, Communications, and the Central Bank. You have nothing
to do with what happened, you are just lending a hand; Interior
appreciates that. But people from Banco Financiero? From XEMIC?
I wouldn't give a penny for their jobs if this ever happens again."

Although the culprit was never found, the fact that for the
next two years and five months no unauthorized transfer of funds
took place made the swindle sink into obscurity. Pardo traveled extensively during this period. On a trip to Canada he electronically
paid fifty-eight thousand U.S. dollars from the "E" bank account for
a vacant lot in Guelph, Ontario. Through the go-betweens in Brook-

lyn and Houston, he mailed the bill of sale to Mr. Bonis, the Miami gardener. Nine days later, at 10:00 A.M. precisely, from a Montreal pay phone he punched the Miami number he had memorized and got the machine. "Bonis Landscaping. Leave your message and I'll call you back. If this is Mr. Dopar, Ms. Negri says thanks." Pardo waited for the beep, then said: "Tell her I appreciate her help."

In 1998 and 1999 the former major traveled to London, Barcelona, Milan, Frankfurt, and Paris. In each of those cities he opened Internet accounts with local providers. Following his wife's instructions, in Paris he rented a safe-deposit box at a Credit Lyonnais branch and stored in it one floppy disk that Victoria had asked him to spirit away. She had made him promise that (1) upon his return to Cuba he would hand over the key to her for safekeeping, (2) he would not make a copy of it, and (3) under no circumstance would he try to learn what the disk contained. Feeling sure that it was something very secret and of great importance, he kept his word, believing that in certain matters the less you know the better. Victoria had taken some substantial life insurance policy, he concluded.

When in August 1999 the head of procurement at Tiendas Panamericanas, XEMIC's nationwide chain of stores, defected in Madrid, Pardo was ready to strike again. On September 14, $1,235,760 vanished from a Tiendas Panamericanas bank account in the Bahamas. The network administrator was ordered back from Paris the day after the fraud took place and he returned immediately, thus convincing the detectives that he had nothing to do with the swindle. Concealed in his shoes and underwear he brought with him $10,000 in hundred-dollar notes.

After the inquiry commission finished its work in December of that same year, Pardo was sacked. Everyone believed that the General Directorate of Counterintelligence had made him a scapegoat after they had failed to detect that a senior executive of Tiendas Panamericanas was getting ready to betray the Revolution *and embezzle the people's money. It was clear as day, General Silvestre said. For over ten years the Judas had traveled hundreds of times abroad, making contacts in many countries. A Barcelona ISP operated the Internet account utilized to make the withdrawal, and the bastard now lived in Spain. Lacking concrete proof, though, no extradition request was presented to the Spanish government.*

The sonofabitch had been very clever, Silvestre concluded. He had never shown curiosity about computer hardware or software, accounting, or banking transactions, as the depositions given by his subordinates confirmed. Until his final day in Cuba, the bastard had pledged his support for the Revolution, participated in the rallies and voluntary works, expressed profound admiration for the Chief. How could Counterintelligence have detected his real feelings and evil machinations? Impossible. Nonetheless, it was decided that Pardo and the chain's database manager had to go. The chain's specialist, a mother of two recovering from a mastectomy after contracting breast cancer, had suffered a severe nervous breakdown during the investigation and was still hospitalized. They were made an example, anyway. An example of what? Nobody knew.

Victoria and Pardo knew they had to show deep sadness and embarrassment for what had happened. Behind doors, however, they screwed like oversexed rabbits: $2.6 million salted away in a Jersey, Channel Islands, bank and twenty thousand buried at Pardo's father's farm proved to be a strong aphrodisiac. Ariel Camacho, the Science and Technology computer expert who had learned to admire Pardo's professionalism while working with him in the commission, arranged for the disgraced major to make a living as a computer specialist in the Institute of Meteorology.

"And I've been thinking, Victoria," said Pardo to his wife after a month on the job, the Sunday afternoon he returned from the island's westernmost lighthouse, the Faro de Roncali, *overlooking the Yucatán Strait, "that we should start considering how to get out of here fast, in case we have to."*

Although she had never discussed it with her husband, the lieutenant colonel had been mulling over the same thing for a while. Life had taught her that the wisest always take precautions and have alternatives. "Would you care to elaborate?" she asked.

"Sure. The institute has stations all over the country. Some of them are in pretty inaccessible, almost deserted posts by the coastline. The most important ones have radar to track hurricanes, computers, two-way radios, and other instruments. I told you my job includes thorough maintenance checks of the computers in Pinar del Río and Havana Provinces every two or three months, and reconfiguring those that crash. When I go there, in my spare time I can fish and pretend to bird-watch, befriend rangers and coastguardsmen, check what kind of security they keep on boats, clock the patrol boat's rounds, that sort of thing."

"It's not a bad idea. But be careful."

Aware that the change in her husband's life was too profound not to affect him, Victoria boosted his ego constantly and followed circuitous paths to provide indirect psychological counseling. Pardo adapted well and by January 2002 had everything ready: He and his wife could escape whenever they wished, or needed to.

Victoria's career had peaked thirteen months earlier, at 3:30 A.M. on December 5, 2001, when the Commander, true to his lifelong habit of working nights, had her summoned to his office. First she was promoted to full colonel, then conferred the Heroine of the Republic of Cuba medal. Her job was so secret that just three others attended the ceremony: the minister of the interior, General Lastra, and Colonel Morera.

Catching a glimpse of the dictator's inner circle astonished Victoria. Men who usually wore somber expressions chuckled at every cheery comment the Chief made. Knowing that he hated interruptions, they kept a respectful silence even when a pause lasted for a minute or two. They took down every significant word he said in their notebooks. None gave an opinion unless directly asked. General Lastra, a ten- to twelve-cigar-a-day smoker, knew better than to light a Lancero in his presence. The brand-new colonel left the Palace of the Revolution thinking that what was alternately referred to as respect or admiration came across as undiluted fear to her.

Next week Victoria was presented with a well-appointed two-story penthouse on Paseo Avenue, a four-door Tico, a Dell Pentium-3 desktop computer, and an Acer laptop. What elevated her to the very privileged status that precious few Cubans enjoy, however, was to be granted unfettered Internet access from her home. Ms. Victoria Valiente had truly arrived.

Forced to return the laptop after getting sacked from XEMIC and restricted to browse only weather sites from the Institute of Meteorology, Pardo lagged considerably behind in his field, which had progressed by leaps and bounds in two years. For this reason, the perks he valued above all others were access to the Internet and the laptop. His overconfidence grew disproportionately as well. In his opinion, Victoria was beyond the reach of surveillance, criticism, or impeachment. Nobody would dare to mess with her. And this led him to commit a grave mistake.

"YOU WHAT?" yelled Victoria when he told her he had accessed his offshore bank site from home.

"Hey, what're you getting excited about? Calm down. Now you are one of the untouchables. Nobody on that server will check the sites you visit."

"Oh, Pardo, don't you know there are only two untouchables in this country? That everybody else can be screened once in a while? Don't you realize you've seriously compromised everything we've achieved so far?"

"Take it easy. Nothing will happen."

"Pardo, honey, you had performed admirably. Today you screwed up atrociously. Let's try to figure out how to cover your tracks and, if we can't come up with an ironclad excuse, how best to face the consequences."

Three

F lying over the Florida Straits, a disgruntled and crestfallen
Elliot Steil scanned the sea below from his window seat.
Maybe in that exact spot he had floated in desperation in
the early hours of June 5, 1994, the victim of a conspiracy of which
he had known nothing. His first encounter with death. And today,
seven hours earlier, he had been unwillingly dragged into . . . what?
He had not a clue. And he had not had an option. The sons of bitches!
Every month thousands of people exceeded the amount of cash they
could take to Cuba; some were doing it for a living and nothing happened to them.

"Are you blackmailing me?" he had asked in astonishment, feeling his anger about to erupt, after McLellan suggested that he should
call his lawyer. Then, seething with indignation, he had blurted:
"Arrest me, goddammit, take me to court. I'll tell the whole world
what happened here tonight."

Tony had saved the day by calming him down. The cop had
walked him to a corner, gripped his arm, whispered in his ear, gesticu-
lated, urged him not to be a shit-eater, reasoned with him for almost
fifteen minutes. Elliot would be a fool if he refused to go along, Tony
had contended. In the post–September 11 national hysteria, refusing
to collaborate with the FBI on a case that involved a country accused
of being part of the Axis of Evil was tantamount to high treason.
Was Elliot willing to go to prison? Had he considered that he might

have to spend all his money in fines and legal fees? That he could lose his job and Fidelia as well? "For Chrissake, Elliot, chill out, think," his friend had said over and over.

"Tony, I don't even know what I'm supposed to do," he had objected feebly.

"You don't have to do anything, dickhead, that's the beauty of it. Didn't you hear what the man said? You go to the places you want to go, visit the people you want to visit, fuck the beautiful *putas* if you feel like it, and if—you hear me?—if someone approaches you with some suspicious-sounding proposal, like delivering a letter, a package, or a message to somebody here, you say yes, fly back, and make a report. C'mon. Let's talk to these guys. Don't strike an attitude. Say you're sorry. You flipped your lid. C'mon, c'mon."

Following his acquiescence, they had taken it from the top. Hart gave him a crash course in what informers do. He had to commit to memory as much as possible; taking notes was out of the question. The FBI agent wanted detailed descriptions of people who asked Steil to do something for them in Miami, from mailing a letter to giving a message to someone. Where he had been approached had to be reported as well. And, most important of all, he must remember who he had to contact in Miami and what message he had been told to pass on. Hart insisted that Elliot must not agree to the proposition immediately, especially if it stank of being unlawful. Were that the case, he should make himself difficult to persuade and pretend to dread a brush with the law to see if he was offered money, threatened (here Steil had chuckled), or asked to act out of patriotism. If neither of these overtures was tried, then he should say he would do it as a big, one-time favor.

At 4:35 A.M., his money belt intact, his pride in tatters, he had returned to his place in the queue. The Latin-looking agent who he had been told was keeping his place was standing behind the guy with the salt-and-pepper mustache, with a dozen or so newly arrived travelers behind him. The cop, detective, snitch, or whatever the man was immediately turned on his heels and hurried to the exit.

What would Fidelia say should she learn what had just happened to him? She would rant and rave about governments and their agencies, curse politics and politicians, remind him that the first time he had mentioned his desire to visit Cuba, she had objected in the strongest possible terms. Women and their sixth sense.

Having sex on Friday night, he had felt wetness on her face, and found her silently crying. "What's the matter?" he had asked. Stupid question. He knew what the matter was and there had been nothing to discuss. Fidelia had started sobbing disconsolately. He had pulled himself out and lain at her side. Then she had rested her head on his chest and cried herself to sleep, her fingers twitching every few minutes.

They had debated his trip on five or six different occasions since Christmas. She had been firmly against it. "You can send money, clothes, and medicines with a mule. You can afford it," she had argued a couple of times, as if he had not known. Once she had asked: "Are you still in love with Natasha?" Natasha was his first wife, a hopeless mental patient for many years now. "Elliot, tell me the truth, do you have a son or daughter in Cuba I don't know about?" He had tried all possible means to reassure her, calmly explaining that he considered it his duty to lend a hand to relatives and friends; that he longed to pace the streets of his hometown and the city in which he had lived for so long. All to no avail. Then he had tried to laugh off her fears and reservations. Nothing had persuaded her, she had never agreed.

"Is this your first time back?" the overweight, very light-skinned black woman next to Steil was asking. She appeared to be well into her sixties.

"Yes, *señora*."

During takeoff she had been slipping the beads of a rosary through her fingers, but as soon as the plane leveled off she dropped the rosary into her purse. She carried several thousand dollars in gold and precious stones on her. Chains, medals, bracelets, rings, earrings, and anklets. It had to do with status. Some impoverished Miami Cubans even rented jewelry when visiting their relatives in Cuba, had themselves photographed alongside a Lamborghini or a Ferrari Testarossa—while the rightful owner had lunch or dinner at some fancy Miami Beach club—to prove how well they were doing in *La yuma* to their friends and relatives. Cuban criminals had killed a few to rob them.

"And when did you leave?" she asked after a moment, too obviously trying to strike up a conversation.

"In 1994."

"Almost yesterday. I left in '61. Can you imagine? I've visited eleven times, not counting this. The first was in '78. I used to work at Woolworth's before the revolution. The ten-cent store at the corner of Galiano and San Rafael. You ever been there?"

"No, sorry," he lied, then turned to the window.

"Well, the ten-cent was the most beautiful department store in Havana," the woman went on, undiscouraged by the snub. "Now it's in ruins. Last time I was there, I nearly cried. Why do they let things deteriorate so much?"

Her traveling companion, in a foul mood, abstained from answering and kept looking at the clouds and the sea. The woman sighed and clammed up. He saw a merchant ship sailing dead south. Elliot estimated that the shortest route to the Panama Canal would be considerably westward; to South America much more to the east. Was this one of the U.S. ships transporting American agricultural produce to Cuba? Probably. Having baited the hook with a billion dollars of potential annual purchases, the old fox had American farmers drooling, and administration officials seething. In the future he would demand trade reciprocity. No country can only buy from another, he could correctly argue. But not now. Now he was just buying and immediately paying with cash. Establishing a good reputation with the farmers, businesspeople, and traders who hadn't been born or were kids when he had assured worried folks the world over that he was not a communist. Guys who had not yet reached middle age when he was exhorting Third World countries to default on their external debts. The man knew that, given the chance to make money, businessmen overrode other considerations, Steil concluded with a sigh. Well, they would learn their lesson in good time.

Elliot turned his gaze from the sea below to the horizon straight ahead and yes, there it was, still a hazy promise in the Gulf's palette. Emotions failed to stir inside him. His admiration for Cuba's geographical beauty and for the kindness of its people had been tempered by the unpleasant realities he had experienced there, by the years of frustration and discrimination, by the tiny percentage of bastards he had had to deal with. Even though Christopher Columbus had allegedly termed the island "the most beautiful land human eyes have ever seen," Elliot speculated whether the emotion of discovery had carried the admiral away. Were it possible only to consider their nature and nice people, most countries in the Caribbean may be justly proclaimed Gardens of Eden.

Nonetheless, when after a minute or two he watched the sea turn from indigo blue to cerulean to the sapphire of shallow waters, as he squinted at the sun's blinding reflection on the sand of a beach resort, then delighted in the lush green of planted fields, in the reddish tones of the soil, in the olive-colored hills, he felt an indefinable, enervating nostalgia. Elliot was scanning the coastline for Santa Cruz del Norte when the captain announced over the PA that within a few minutes they would land in Havana, where the temperature was 28 degrees Celsius and humidity 85 percent.

The bejeweled lady pulled the rosary out, closed her eyes, and began to mouth prayers. Elliot stared at her. That woman had to love or miss someone or something in Cuba very much. Obviously terrified of flying, she had visited on eleven different occasions over twenty-four years. For whom or what did she submit to something she dreaded so much? A religion? Her parents? A son or daughter? A lover? Friends? Her neighborhood? He would never know.

The Havana skyline diverted Elliot's attention from the praying passenger. For the first time he was seeing the Cuban capital from a plane. He searched for the highest structures: the National Capitol, next the José Martí monument in the Plaza de la Revolución, the FOCSA, the Habana Libre Hotel, in which he had booked a room. The sprawling metropolis looked peaceful, dreamy, its pockets of poverty invisible. Elliot figured that had capitalism gone unimpeded, now the horizon would be dotted with hundreds of shining glass-and-steel skyscrapers. Was it better to have kept its architecture frozen in time, the old contaminating American cars blending in with it? Highly debatable, he thought.

Approaching the runway, he was pleased by the asymmetry of ploughed and planted fields. Buildings gained in size, the roads got wider, the trees and palms bigger; several men hoed what seemed like a recently planted sweet potato field. Bump. Aaand bump. The praying woman heaved a sigh of relief and, grinning, started what turned into a round of applause. Her rosary swung wildly in all directions and the silver crucifix scraped Steil's left cheek.

"Ouch."

"Oh, *señor,* I'm so sorry."

Steil inspected the palm of his hand. No blood. "No problem, *señora.* It's nothing."

"Let me see. There's a small scratch, but no bleeding. A crucifix will never harm anyone, *señor.* The Lord has touched you. Maybe I was his instrument. If not, please forgive me."

"You are forgiven, *señora,*" Steil said, thinking that some heavenly intercession would be most welcome.

"I'm so excited! And you?"

"Yes, I'm excited, too."

The plane taxied to the oldest of three terminals, reserved for national flights and for those from or to Miami. The young immigration lieutenant who took Elliot's Cuban passport and the form he had filled out on the plane looked self-important and wet behind the ears. Apparently surprised at finding an Anglo name on a Cuban passport, he asked where Mr. Steil would be staying and seemed relieved when the visitor said "Habana Libre." Next the officer wanted to know when he would go back to the United States. "In a week."

"Where did you live before leaving Cuba?" Elliot dictated the address.

"Visiting relatives?"

"And friends," he added. The man stamped his passport and waved him to the baggage claim area.

A uniformed young woman approached him and volunteered to find his carry-on. He nodded and surrendered his receipt. Forewarned that trained dogs sniff every piece of baggage for drugs and explosives, Steil braced himself for a long wait. Twenty-five minutes went by before the conveyor belt began spewing out "worms," suitcases, carry-ons, and cartons sealed with all sorts of sticky tapes. Three-quarters of an hour elapsed by the time the young woman found his carry-on. He tipped her a dollar and moved along to where four customs inspectors were asking passengers whether they had something to declare and, in seemingly random manner, inspecting one out of every ten or so pieces of baggage. Steil's won the lottery and it was superficially examined. From Transtur he rented a Mitsubishi Lancer at $125 a day. He had been told that visitors were milked dry mercilessly, but this rate made him click his tongue, smile, and shake his head sadly.

An hour and a half after landing, Elliot Steil took a left onto Rancho Boyeros Avenue. Well aware that many Cuban drivers disregard speed limits and traffic regulations, he chose the center lane and concentrated on being careful. Waiting at stoplights, he gazed around with curiosity. Yes, some buildings had been repaired and painted, lawns were well tended, no potholes in the road. However, this was the red carpet for tourists; he had to wait and see. Pedestrians were not in rags, yet crowded bus stops and tractors hauling big trailers crammed full of people—the Cuban contribution to mass transit, known to passengers as "camels"—suggested that transportation was still a mess. The avenue widened from six to twelve lanes and became spotless after the Calzada del Cerro intersection, yet the view was spoiled by antediluvian vehicles spewing dense black smoke from their tailpipes, a slew of mangy dogs, and the slogans on government billboards promising to never surrender to aggressors.

Alone at last in Room 2124 of the Habana Libre, Elliot scanned the cityscape. The blinding sun made it seem bleached. Charcoal gray asphalt formed intersecting quadrants. Parks and tree-lined streets added green spaces. From an architectural and zoning standpoint, a city akin to many others. What made it different were intangibles:

its unique problems, culture, economy, politics; in two words, its people. Most were gullible, kind, more inclined to heroic deeds, music, and loafing around than to the boring routine of work. Many waited for the solutions to their problems to fall into their laps. He had been one of those. It was the inevitable result of smothering individual initiative.

The danger of generalizations dawned on him. He was being unfair to some and forgiving to others. Then he felt judgmental, which is to feel stupid. He wanted a drink, so he called Fidelia instead, let her know his room number, unpacked, and took a shower.

...

While doing the wash, Victoria had been pondering how to fix Pardo's grave error. All the explanations and subterfuges she could think of sounded difficult to believe and she was sure the server's administrator would report that an online bank had been accessed from her computer. Her husband refused to see any danger, accused her of being overly negative, and had not helped her with her list of possible justifications. Upon hearing her front door close, she dropped the last piece of freshly laundered clothing into a white plastic basket and hurried into the huge living area.

"What does he look like?" she asked eagerly.

Pardo took off his green Pinar del Río baseball cap, pocketed his keys, left Victoria's laptop and a newspaper on the coffee table. "Standard. White, my height, weighs around 180 pounds, my age or so. You dress him in Cuban threads, take away the rental, he's just a regular habanero *walking the streets."*

Victoria gave a slight approving nod. Like all professionals in her trade, she empathized with people who escape notice. "He rented a car?"

"Yep."

She disliked that. What if he had an accident? "Room number?" she wanted to learn next.

"2124."

She turned and approached a nicely upholstered, wraparound sofa in a corner and slid onto it. She invited her husband to join her with a glance, a tilt of her head, and three slaps on the seat. Pardo reached the sofa, sat, rested his right arm atop the back of the piece of furniture. He noticed that Victoria was wearing shorts and a short-sleeved blouse over nothing else. Doing without underwear was part of their mating ritual. They had had sex on Wednesday and Friday evenings, but it seemed that the risks they were running had made their sex life more intense.

"Give it to me," she said.

"Now? Here?"

"I mean the story."

"Oh. Well, it wasn't difficult at all. He left customs disoriented, craning his neck around, like all first-timers. That was sign number one. Number two was that he approached a rental agency, signed the papers, and left the terminal speaking Cuban Spanish with the guy from the agency. Nobody was there to greet him; clue number three. When the agency guy was going back inside the building I asked him: 'Hey, I'm here to pick up a man I've never seen before. Was that Señor Martínez?' And he said no, that was Señor Steil. So, I started the car and beat him to the Habana Libre. I was sitting in the lobby by the time he approached the reception desk. I waited an hour, went to the hotel's business center, hacked into their database, and learned his room number. Piece of cake."

"What baggage did he bring?"

"A medium-sized roll-on."

"What color?"

"Black."

"Twenty-two inches? Twenty-six? Four wheels? Two wheels?"

"Hey! I don't know! I think it has two wheels, but I'm not sure. Why do you want to know that for?"

"Just testing your powers of observation, Mayor."

"Why don't you test my powers of fucking you right now?"

Victoria mulled this over. "Okay," she said at last. "Let's first hang the laundry out."

Pardo picked up the white plastic basket and a small cotton sack with clothespins, then they both climbed the spiral marble staircase to the upper floor. She led the way along the hall connecting three bedrooms and two bathrooms, opened a door at its end, and entered the building's tiled rooftop. The former tenant, a Ministry of the Interior mayor who defected in Mexico and presently lived in Miami, had affixed two T-shaped metal frames to the four-foot-high wall bordering the covering. Plastic clotheslines connected the frames.

On tiptoes, Victoria began hanging the bed and table linen first. Holding the basket and the clothespins, Pardo took a deep breath of seabreeze and scanned his surroundings. Only the Cohiba Hotel was higher than their building, and the striking view never failed to amaze the former country boy. The vast Florida Straits to the north; the long seawall known as Malecón and the most populous part of the city to the west; the rocky coastline and the classy Miramar to the east; middle-class El Vedado to the south. On lower rooftops, sheets, towels, and clothes billowed gracefully. A flock of pigeons flew over their heads. From the street came the sound of traffic and a trace of exhaust fumes.

He fastened his eyes on Victoria for nearly a minute. He enjoyed watching her small, firm breasts as they moved up every time she raised her arms, then fell to place when she turned to get hold of another piece of clothing. His first marriage had made him conclude that women with great bodies and lovely faces are neither necessarily bright nor fantastic in bed. He doubted very much that any other woman could give him the sexual pleasure that the physically nondescript Victoria so enthusiastically rendered to him year in, year out, so he had never cheated on her. He considered it unlikely that he would ever find a person, male or female, as brilliant as his wife. To watch such an extraordinary human being doing menial house chores inflamed him with desire.

"I think we should get there a little earlier, around eight," she said while pinning the final piece, a shirt.

"Why?"

"Just in case he decides to go out, or arrives late. We've got to make contact tonight. I don't like his driving around. He may decide to go to Santa Cruz del Norte. Then you'd have to go alone, 'cause I have an important meeting tomorrow morning. And what if he has an accident and is taken to a police precinct or to a hospital?"

"Victoria, please, think positive."

"Best way to think positive is to take precautions."

"Okay, we'll be there at eight. Now, what do you say to . . . ?"

"Let's shower first," putting her arm around his waist.

...

Elliot's former mother-in-law, Josefina Montes, had been crying on his shoulder and clinging to his neck for almost two minutes. Her husband, Gustavo Cano, was patting her back and mumbling words of comfort.

"Josefina, please, it's a cause to rejoice, not to cry," he kept repeating as he eyed Elliot with an apologetic look. "Elliot will think he makes you sad. C'mon mother, please, stop crying."

After a lousy sandwich (four dollars) and a Coke (two-fifty) at the hotel's cafeteria, he had driven to his ex-wife's, in Santos Suárez. Off the beaten track he found potholes, decaying buildings, and neglected lawns. His rental was stared at suspiciously. He should have anticipated this would happen. Out of touch with Cuban reality, he had acquired the behavioral patterns of American businessmen abroad: the nice hotel, the rental, the myriad superfluities, from the shaving cream to the shoehorn. With just a glance, people knew he did not belong. Maybe he should not have rented the car; taxis abounded. Not wanting to alert Natasha's neighbors of his arrival, he had eased the vehicle by the curb two blocks from her home.

Now he felt like running away. When Gustavo had opened the front door for him, he had seen a ghost in the hallway. The apparition first squinted, then gaped at him for a couple of seconds before bolting into her bedroom. The levelheaded, cheerful, beautiful human

being that he had loved madly, the woman who had taken his sexual
desires to new heights and had given him the best orgasms of his life,
his junior by six years, had turned shockingly gray-haired, toothless,
and wrinkled. Unaware that Elliot had seen his daughter, Gustavo
embraced him and gave him the instant he needed to recover. The
old man had stepped back to examine him from head to toe. He had
been muttering something about how well his sometime son-in-law
seemed when Josefina had appeared in the doorframe to the kitchen,
drying her hands on a dishtowel, asking who it was. Then her placid
expression evolved into a combination of bewilderment, happiness,
sadness, gratitude, and love that shook Elliot. She had run into his
arms and he felt the wetness of her tears on his shirt. Having recovered, he now had enough sense to start pretending. He seized her by
the arms and stepped back.

"You look wonderful, Josefina. Well, perhaps a trifle overweight,
but it suits you."

"Oh, Elliot, my son. If it hadn't been for you . . ." wiping her
cheeks with the edges of her hands.

"Gustavo looks fine, too. You better watch out, Josefina. I've
been told young Havana chicks prefer older men," interrupting her
to change the subject. He feared she was getting ready to thank him
for the few thousands he had sent over the past seven years.

Gustavo said, "You still tickle the hell out of old people."

"And . . . Natasha, how is she doing?" He was asking because
he was supposed to.

"I'll go fetch her," Josefina said, and turned on her heels with a
teenager's alacrity. Gustavo's gaze followed his wife, a touch of compassion in his eyes.

"Natasha has worsened, Elliot," the man said sadly when Josefina
closed the door to Natasha's bedroom behind her. "All possible treat-
ments have been tried to no avail. We keep her heavily sedated and
under constant observation. You can't find something with a cutting
edge in this house. We've had to get rid of all the knives, scissors,
needles, sewing needles, and safety pins. I keep my disposable razor
here," Gustavo pulled the object from a side pocket of his trousers,

showed it, and slipped it back into the pocket. "Before starting to cook, Josefina goes to the neighbor's to cut and slice what she'll use. But sit down, please," he said pointing to the well-worn couch. Steil complied and glanced around.

The living area had been freshly painted and looked classy. Beautiful paintings, drapes, vases, antiques, and knickknacks left behind by Natasha's wealthy grandparents when they emigrated in the sixties still hung upon walls or adorned side tables and the coffee table. From a framed enlargement taken on their wedding day, his adorable young bride smiled gleefully. Josefina was a wonderful cook and the smell coming from the kitchen was mouthwatering.

"She's lost all interest in herself," Gustavo went on after easing himself into his favorite armchair. "Josefina bathes her daily, feeds her, combs her hair, cuts her nails. She refuses to go out, dye her hair, go to the dentist. It's hopeless, I tell you, it's hopeless," this said as though he was relieved that, finally, he could unload his innermost worries to someone.

There was much sadness in his voice. Steil wished to allay Gustavo's desolation with a few well-chosen words, but could not. After having glimpsed his ex-wife, anything he said would sound insincere. A thought that had never crossed his mind flashed ominously. Who would care for Natasha when both her parents had died?

"When she goes critical, we have her committed to the psychiatric hospital for two or three weeks. She gets better there, not because they give her special medication she takes the same pills we give her here—but because she's afraid of the place, so she quiets down and they send her back. Then a new cycle begins."

Steil rubbed his hands and lifted his gaze from the floor when something occurred to him. "Maybe if I get a copy of her medical file, I could have it translated, then send it to some psychiatric hospital or research laboratory in the States. There may be new drugs unavailable here that I could send you."

Gustavo pondered the suggestion, tilting his head to one side, then to the other. "It's a long shot, Elliot. Her doctor says she's taking forefront medication, very expensive, imported from Switzerland."

"You have to pay for it?"

"No, it's supplied free of cost."

"Well, in any case . . ."

Although smothered by the walls and the door, the men overheard Natasha bawl "I SAID NO!" at the top of her lungs. "I don't want to see him! Throw him out of here! Get out and tell him. NOW!"

Gustavo and Steil exchanged embarrassed looks.

Josefina bolted out of her daughter's bedroom and pulled the door shut. She hurried to Steil and Gustavo. They got to their feet. "Please forgive her, Elliot. She's . . ." she groped for words, trying to say something that wouldn't be "out of her mind" or "not herself anymore."

"Don't worry, Josefina. I know how it is. I'll leave now."

"Oh, no, Elliot, please! I beg you. Stay for dinner. You must tell us how you are doing, where do you live. You still a teacher?"

"No. I'm working for a trading company. But I can't stay, Josefina. I have other things to do, people to see," he lied. "Thanks anyway. Let me give you something." He fished into the inner breast pocket of his jacket. "There's three thousand here. It's for you."

"No, Elliot," Gustavo said. "It's too much. We don't need that much."

"Throw out the sonofabitch, goddammit! I told you to throw him out!"

"Keep it. I don't know when I'll be able to come again, or to send more."

"But—"

"I'm leaving now. Take care. I love you. The three of you. She loved me immensely and you cared for me like a son. I'll never forget that. Bye."

Josefina began to sob inconsolably. A single tear slid down Gustavo's cheek.

Elliot marched to the front door and turned the lock he had operated thousands of times when he had dwelled there. He waved good-bye. Gustavo and Josefina seemed petrified.

"THROW HIM OUT!"

He exited, closed the door, trotted down three steps, strode past the garden, opened the gate, and gained the sidewalk. Then he heaved a deep sigh.

...

Victoria named it "the prehistoric fuck." She had discovered the position in a movie she could not remember. One of those made in the wake of Kubrick's 2001: A Space Odyssey *in which the actors, dressed in furs and with advanced prosthetics and special effects makeup, play the hunters and gatherers that thirty or forty thousand years earlier roamed the plains and forests of Western Europe.*

She still remembered the scene vividly. Inside a cave, by the poor illumination coming from smoldering embers and a torch, ten or twelve hominids were spending the night. Some slept, others sat on their haunches gnawing on pieces of meat. Farther into the cave, the camera discovered a copulating couple. The beardless female, on all fours, was being penetrated from behind. The male bumped into her bottom spasmodically, wanting to reach his orgasm immediately. Yes, Victoria had sadly admitted to herself, in the Pleistocene probably no male thought about the female's pleasure. Anal or vaginal sex? Victoria had wondered next. Vaginal, she decided. Primitive people clearly grasped the raison d'etre of every organ.

Having never made love in that position, she had wanted to take a shot at it for years, but her previous sexual partners had always tried to talk her into sodomy, and she feared that if she told them what she wanted, they would try to force their way into her rectum. Eventually, with Pardo she had satisfied her curiosity. It was great! She loved it! The hominids had not been so ignorant after all.

Gradually they refined the position. Doubled over in bed, leaning on her forearms, she raised her pelvis as high as possible.

Behind her, also on his knees, he would guide his penis to the entrance of her vagina, penetrate her in his entire dimension, stay there for an instant, grab her hips firmly, pull his penis back to the point in which merely his glans remained inside her, and then push it in again. Pardo fondled a nipple while doing this. After she revealed her desire to be beaten with moderation, he alternated caressing her breasts with spanking her. When her buttocks were smarting, she had magnificent orgasms.

That Sunday afternoon in April 2002, though, he did something for the first time ever. While inside her, he sucked his forefinger to lubricate it with saliva, placed its pad on her anus, then slid the tip inside her rectum.

"Ouch," Victoria complained feebly. From her tone, Pardo knew he could disregard such lame protestation. She had already come twice, once riding him; the other while her husband licked her. He started flexing his finger slowly, buried his penis deep inside her, spanked her once.

Supported on a forearm, the left side of her face on the pillow, Victoria brought up her free hand to her clitoris and began stroking it gently. Her rectum contracted spasmodically, its numerous nerve endings reacting to the wiggling intruder that acted undecided about leaving or going all the way in. She wanted to prolong the newfound pleasure when Pardo spanked her hard. It was too much. Victoria realized she would soon have an intense orgasm.

"Ay, macho, come with me. You are the best! I'm almost there . . . Ay, coñóooo!"

Watching Victoria thrust herself against his groin, hearing her singing his praises, and ranting at the height of her sexual ecstasy proved too much for Pardo as well. He ejaculated profusely. After a few moments he began to lose his erection and pulled his finger out. She left her clit alone. Feeling exhausted, both collapsed in bed trying to get their breath back. A minute went by.

"How was it?" he asked.

"Oh, great, macho, just great."

"Next time I'll put cold cream on my finger."

"Yeah, that would be best. And also . . ." Victoria paused, then laughed herself silly.

"What's the matter?" Pardo asked, smiling uncertainly.

It took her nearly a minute to regain control and wipe away the tears sliding down her temples. "I was thinking that if you grew your fingernails as long as the Chief does, I wouldn't let you."

Pardo chuckled. Millions of Cubans, aghast at the length of the man's perfectly manicured fingernails, joked that he was competing with Snow White's stepmother. "Don't worry. You know I always do my nails on Sunday mornings. From now on I'll pay special attention, have them short and filed for you whenever you want them."

"Way to go, my man, waaay to go," feeling proud of the lover she had created.

For a while nothing was said. Then Victoria turned her head to her husband. "Shouldn't we scale down the loan somewhat?" she asked.

"I don't think so," Pardo responded. "The equation has too many variables."

"You sound so mathematical."

"But it's true. We don't know how long we may be forced to stay there, if we have to take a roundabout route to Paris, how many plane tickets we may need, if we have to bribe someone."

Victoria took a moment to reflect on the evening's operation. "You think Steil will buy your cockamamie story?" she asked.

"Probably not. But it doesn't matter. You said he just has to tell her the date, right? Everything else is irrelevant."

"It's so annoying to play dumb," she moaned.

Pardo turned his head to stare at his wife. "Well, darling, you brought him into the picture. I suppose you have a valid reason for it."

Victoria kept her gaze on the ceiling. "The reason is that a backup man is always essential. I have the guy to learn what needs to be learned and do what needs to be done. But what happens if he dies on us? Or crashes his car and becomes paraplegic? Or is arrested?"

Pardo thought she was being overly negative one more time, but refrained from telling her. "I see. Well, I'm sorry if you don't like my yarn. It's not so bad."

"It's lousy. Let's rehearse it one last time."

"Now?"

"Now."

"I feel like a nap."

"Now, Major," after giving him a peck on the cheek.

...

Sitting behind the Mitsubishi's wheel for several minutes, Steil stared through the windshield and reflected on what he had just witnessed. He had done all he could. Even though money would not improve Natasha's condition in the least, it would ease her parents' suffering and keep all three well fed and clothed for a couple of years. Their combined income as retirees was less than twenty dollars a month and a pound of ground beef cost three dollars, a bottle of cooking oil two. He forced himself to push the drama out of his mind and turned the ignition.

Rolling around the corner, he drove to the Polytechnic Institute in which he had taught English for seventeen years. Nobody would be there on a Sunday, which was perfect. He had decided against paying a visit. On one hand, party members on the staff would not welcome him; sure as shooting they had been told that he had illegally emigrated "to the Empire." On the other hand, if some colleagues greeted him in a friendly manner, they might be reprimanded for welcoming a "traitor."

Steil was pleasantly surprised when, from a block away, he noticed that the huge building had been recently painted. Getting nearer, he observed that the windows that had been broken and boarded-up when he left were repaired now. Or were they new? He eased the vehicle on the other side of the street and turned off the ignition. As far as he could tell, the former Catholic school had never before been refurbished. Inside and out? He could not tell. Maybe the urinals and toilets stolen in the seventies had been refitted; maybe there were new blackboards and erasers, too. On its roof a billboard proclaimed, THANK YOU, COMMANDER IN CHIEF. Steil clicked his tongue, shook his head, and smiled sadly. After forty years of neglect, such praise for renovating the excellent school built by the Brothers of the Virgin Mary in the fifties seemed excessive.

"Hey, mister, Chiclets?" someone said in English.

An extremely handsome light-skinned black boy, twelve or thirteen years old, had approached the driver's door and was leaning on the window frame. Big brown eyes, wavy black hair, a Roman nose, full lips blessed with a luminous smile. A textbook example of how racial mixture bears the most beautiful humans.

"Knock it off, Champ. We're birds of a feather," Steil said in somewhat dated Cuban slang.

"You Cuban?"

"What do you think?"

The boy made a U with the thumb and forefinger of his right hand, took it to sucked-in lips, and whistled shrilly. "The dude's Cuban," he shouted, waving in quick come-on gestures.

Such news brought two other boys of approximately the same age to the driver's door. One was a textbook example that racial mixing doesn't always bear beautiful people: mulatto, short, overweight, slightly cross-eyed, a chipped front tooth. The other was white, green-eyed, scrawny, with a lock of blonde hair over his forehead. All three had on ragged clothes and scuffed trainers.

"You Cuban?" the white boy asked suspiciously, eyeing Steil's foreign attire.

"Aha."

"How come you drive rented wheels?"

"'Cause he flew the coop, you dickhead," the handsome boy said to his pal. "You live in Miami, right?" addressing Steil.

"Yeah, I do."

For Steil this offered fresh confirmation that Cubans living in their homeland still could not rent cars from state-owned rental companies. The catch was that no u-drive private companies were in existence. He also corroborated that one thing had remained the same from the time he left: All kids believed that if a Cuban resided abroad, it had to be in Miami. He shook his head and smiled.

"You've got Chiclets or don't you?" Chipped Tooth demanded a straight answer. The Chiclets brand from Adams, the American company, had dominated the market in precommunist Cuba to the extent that it became synonymous for chewing gum. Like Frigidaire for refrigerator, Canada Dry for ginger ale, Delco for the device that sends electricity to the spark plugs. The rather long list of Anglo brand names substituting for the correct term in Spanish made purists of the national language angry.

"No, I don't have Chiclets, but I can buy some for you guys."

"Cool," Chipped Tooth said. "A fiver will do," reaching his hand out for the money. Handsome gave a wink and a sly smile to Blondie, who shook his head reprovingly.

"Now, wait a minute," Steil said, theorizing that perhaps Chipped Tooth had the sharpest mind. "You think I'm a shit-eater? Five foolas for Chiclets? Stop buggering me."

Disappointment shone in six eyes.

"Take me to the nearest 'shopping,'" Steil suggested, meaning the dollars-only store. "I'll buy you some Chiclets and a soda."

Chipped Tooth dashed around the hood, pulled open the passenger door, and sat alongside the driver. It took Handsome and Blondie an instant more to slide into the backseat. Steil started the car.

"Straight ahead for three blocks," Chipped Tooth said, "then take a right."

Steil pressed the gas pedal. "What grade are you guys in?" he asked.

"Sixth," they said in unison.

"Same class?"

"Yeah," Handsome said.

"You like your humanities teacher?"

The kids howled, rolled their eyes, and lolled their tongues.

"What's that supposed to mean?" Steil asked.

"You know," Blondie said. "She's a dish. Big caboose, melon-sized tits, great face."

"Man's ape shit about her," Chipped Tooth said.

"Oh, really? Am I? And who was jerking off in class the other day?"

"I don't jerk off in class!"

"You were, I saw you. The day she came with the blue miniskirt."

"I wasn't jerking off!"

"Shut up," Steil commanded. "How old is your teacher?"

The three boys exchanged questioning glances.

"She's pretty old," Handsome said, "like twenty-five or so."

Steil suppressed a smile. To this crowd he was Methuselah. In his mind's eye, he could see the beautiful teacher's predicament. Pubescent pupils, their hormones starting to stir. Girls wanting to copy her in every respect; boys drooling all day long; males on the staff making passes. You have to love the profession. It was not wise to wear a miniskirt to class, though.

"Take a right on this coming corner," Chipped Tooth instructed.

The store was small yet well stocked. Steil bought a fair-to-middling pair of sneakers, two polyester pullovers, and baggy shorts for each kid. They slurped six Cokes, split among them two dollars' worth of chewing gum, were refused packs of Salem. Steil drove them back to their block feeling, for the first time ever, like Santa Claus.

"Hey, mister, what do you have to do to move to Miami?" Handsome asked from the passenger door after Chipped Tooth shut it.

Steil realized his mistake. The feeling of self-satisfaction left him. What could he say that would not smack of propaganda?

"First you have to grow up, then seek your parents' permission."

"Is that what you did?" Blondie wanted to know, sounding suspicious.

"That's what I did. Got to go now. Take care, guys."

"Thank you, mister," all three said simultaneously, clutching their plastic bags with one hand, perkily waving from the sidewalk.

...

Even before leaving Miami, Steil had been disinclined to visit the Havana apartment building in which he had dwelled for over twenty years. It was Sunday, everybody's day off, and his homecoming would create a stir. New tenants aside, he expected that most of his former neighbors would be glad to see him, but Steil felt certain that party members would not welcome him. He had decided to go on Monday. He smiled as he imagined the reaction of Sobeida, the black retiree who had bought his groceries for several years. She would probably shout, jump, cry, laugh, embrace him, kiss him, and make the sign of the cross on his forehead.

Then he thought about visiting Susana Vila, the economist with whom he had had a four-year open relationship. Had she remarried? Moved? Did she still have her job as cashier in the supermarket? He could find out; not on a Sunday afternoon, though. Besides, fire sleeps beneath the ashes, and he was against resurrecting old love affairs. Well, maybe she would shut the door in his face. After all, they had had sex two days before he vanished into thin air and had never told her about his project. He had not communicated with her in eight years, either.

A huge yawn reminded Steil that he had not caught a wink in thirty-six hours. The adrenaline rush elicited by Hart and McLellan's blackmail had worn off. The depressing experience at Natasha's had acted as a real downer, too. So he steered the car to his hotel and handed over the keys to the parking valet at 7:25 P.M.

In his room he considered getting supper. He was not in the mood to go out, not tonight. Room service maybe? Not hungry, either. He brushed his teeth and, yawning several times, undressed and crawled in bed at five minutes to eight. One minute later someone knocked at the door. Frowning, Steil threw back the cover, got up, and strode barefoot to the threshold.

"Who is it?"

"Mr. Steil, we haven't met," a man's voice, in Spanish. "I beg you to please give me a few minutes of your time. I need to talk to you concerning past business dealings between the firm you work for, IMLATINEX, and my firm, XEMIC Corporation."

Steil was too surprised to react. A few seconds slipped by. In the hall, Victoria gave a nod and a wink to her husband.

"Mr. Steil?"

"Yes."

"Did you hear what I just said?"

"I . . . ah . . . yes. But . . . I'm here on a private visit, not a business trip. Besides, as far as I know, your firm, what did you say its name was?"

"XEMIC Corporation."

"Is that a Cuban firm?"

"Mr. Steil, pleeease. Your discretion is prudent but unnecessary. The late Mr. Scheindlin was our business partner for many, many years. He talked very highly of you. Please let us in. I can't tell you what the matter is from the hallway. I assure you it's of the gravest concern to my firm."

Elliot's mind, churning at top speed, flew back to the Miami airport office fifteen hours earlier. Again he saw Hart, McLellan, and Tony Soto, their voices overlapping in his memory. The guy out there knew that his boss had passed away. Elliot knew that IMLATINEX's Panamanian subsidiary did business with XEMIC. He had not considered the possibility that the FBI's demand could be related to his firm's dealings with Cuban business concerns. Everything seemed to be interconnected; fate was threading a pattern too complex for him. Had the man said, "Let us in"? How many were with him?

"Mr. Steil?"

"Are you alone?"

"A subordinate is with me."

In Spanish, in which the final vowel generally defines gender, *subordinada* is feminine. A woman mixed up in this conundrum? "Let me put something on. I was already in bed."

Elliot took his time donning the slacks and polo shirt he had worn after the midday shower. How the fuck had these people found him? Who told them he was here? Cuban State Security? Was he becoming a reluctant go-between for the FBI and the State Security? What the hell was going on? Should he admit to these people that IMLATINEX had been doing business with Cuba for over twenty years? Definitely not. He could say he had never been informed about such deals. Yeah, he would do that. And from then on, improvise.

He put on his loafers, ran his hands over his hair, approached the door, and turned the handle.

Steil eyed the smiling pair warily before motioning them in. The ungainly guy appeared to be in his late forties, was of his same height, twenty or twenty-five pounds leaner. He had lines on his forehead, sunken brown eyes, long teeth, and a protruding Adam's apple. The man extended his right hand and Steil felt forced to shake it. The short woman, several years younger than her escort, gave him a bashful smile, as though embarrassed for invading his privacy, and proffered her hand, too. Brown straight hair cut to her shoulders, green eyes behind plastic-framed glasses, thin lips, firm chin. She wore a cream-colored blouse, brown knee-length skirt, high-heeled shoes, and held a purse and an attaché case. Both smelled nice. The Cuban obsession with perfume.

After closing the door behind him, Steil noticed that the man, who was gazing around the room, walked with both feet turned out at a hundred-degree angle. She was narrow-hipped, had a scraggy behind; not much of a knock off, he thought. Both appeared to be neat, pleasant, forthcoming, and unremarkable. No Hart and McLellan these two. Steil waved them to the two wood-and-vinyl armchairs by the picture window.

"Can I offer you something?" he said, pointing at the small re-frigerator. It behooved him to be polite, he thought.

"I'm fine, thank you," Pardo said.

"No, thank you," Victoria declined as she placed her purse atop the coffee table separating both armchairs and put the attaché case on the floor. She tugged on the hem of her skirt.

There were no other seats, so Steil sat on the edge of his bed and crossed his legs, resting his forearms just above his knee. "My name is Elliot Steil, I'm Cuban, I've been living in Miami since 1994, and I work for IMLATINEX. Now, may I inquire who you are?"

"Of course," Pardo said. He extracted a business card from his wallet and presented it to Steil. It read Carlos Capdevila, Vice President, XEMIC Corporation.

"Very well," Elliot said pocketing the card. "But could I see IDs, please?"

"Sure."

The billfold reappeared and the tourist was handed a XEMIC plastic identification card with the visitor's photograph. It specified that Mr. Capdevila was vice president in charge of procurement. "Thank you," Steil said, giving back the ID. "May I see yours, Miss?"

"Absolutely."

Elliot learned that Berta Arosamena was XEMIC's general director of procurement for the American continent.

"What can I do for you?" he said as he gave back her ID. Victoria cast a questioning glance at her husband: the pliant deputy asking her boss's permission to proceed. Pardo nodded his approval.

"As you know, Mr. Steil," she began in a soft tone, "IMLATINEX has been doing business with XEMIC Corporation for almost twenty years. During that time . . ."

"Excuse me for interrupting, Ms. Arosamena. What you just said forces me to—" Steil said and immediately regretted it. Would he ever learn? But it was too late to backtrack. "It's news to me that my employer has been doing business with your firm. I've never seen a document that supports your allegation. In point of fact, U.S. federal law forbids . . ."

Victoria nodded and smiled condescendingly before barging in. "We are well aware of all the laws, rules, and regulations that the United States has enacted to implement the criminal blockade against the first free territory of the Americas, Mr. Steil."

Oh, my God, she's going to read me the Gospel, Elliot thought. Victoria stole a glance at Pardo, who, according to the script, slightly shook his head to say, "Skip the politics."

"But we didn't come to discuss that," she added, picking up the attaché case and clicking it open. "The firm you work for is the parent company of Trans-Caribbean Trading, right?" she asserted.

"Well . . . we do business with a Panamanian company thus named, but it's not a subsidiary of IMLATINEX, as far as I can tell," Steil said.

"Well, it is, Mr. Steil. Take my word for it," Pardo said, a bit smarmily. "I understand your cautiousness; we are not here to make you admit that or any other thing. All we want is that you hear what we have to say, okay?"

"Okay."

"Go on, Berta."

Victoria cleared her throat. "These are some 1995 and 1996 Trans-Caribbean documents," she said, handing over to Elliot a batch of papers. "They prove we've been doing business with your trading company for many years. We have a filing cabinet containing four drawers of correspondence, invoices, banking documents, bills of lading, packing lists, faxes, and e-mails to and from Trans-Caribbean dating back to the late seventies."

For a little over a minute Steil flipped pages, pretending to inspect the printed material. They were genuine, all right. Thinking it prudent to keep his mouth shut, he handed her the batch back.

Pardo rubbed his hands and slid his backside to the edge of the armchair. "Now, Mr. Steil, there are certain business practices in the world that we, as a matter of principle, strongly condemn. One of them is the concession of bribes or payoffs to government officials. They are standard practice all over the world. Everywhere— well, not everywhere, but almost everywhere in Latin America— sellers pay under-the-table money to government buyers. When we began dealing with Mr. Scheindlin, he offered us a kickback. We refused the money yet signed our first deal with him. Perhaps that made an impression. To make a long story short, Mr. Scheindlin developed sort of a . . . certain respect for us, began seeing things our way, and eventually volunteered to do us a favor. A very special favor, I should say. He offered to purchase American pharmaceuticals for us.

"In the beginning we were distrustful; the first order was for only five thousand dollars," Pardo continued. "But he supplied what we needed at good prices. In the past fourteen years, serving as intermediary, he purchased almost 3.7 million dollars' worth of medicine for us, mostly hemostatic drugs to treat cancer patients. We advanced him the cash and a list of what was needed. Then he tapped his sources, did whatever he did, we don't know what, and after a couple of months, shipped from a third country, we would get the cargo. It'll never be known how many Cuban lives Mr. Scheindlin saved by fronting for us. Blockading the sale of pharmaceuticals is repugnant."

Steil became increasingly suspicious that he was being spun a line. Advanced the cash? Nobody did that, least of all Cuban officials. Had Scheindlin been buying medicine for Cuba, he would have known; his late boss had confided much more sensitive issues to him. He battened down the hatches.

"I agree," he said.

"We anticipated you would, sir," Victoria said with a solemn expression. "You were born and raised here; you emigrated merely eight years ago. Your presence here means that you still love your relatives and friends, your people."

"I must admit I do." Steil let it hang there.

"We will always remember Ruben Scheindlin," Pardo continued. "Maybe someday it will be possible to tell the world what Mr. Scheindlin did for Cuba. Not anytime soon, though. Not as long as the embargo remains in place."

"Of course."

"The extremely serious problem that we confront now is that when Mr. Scheindlin passed away, he had in his possession one hundred thousand dollars we had given him to buy medicine."

"What?"

"You heard right. A hundred thousand in cash. And we need to find a way to recover that money."

Elliot rubbed his face to suppress a smile, felt that he needed a shave. These two were elevating implausibility to new heights. Next, they would coax him into helping them out. Hart had been right. The FBI man would be delighted to learn about this blatant attempt to pull off a swindle. However, pretending to be a half-wit may be grist for his mill.

"I can see that. Your wanting to recover the money, I mean. What I fail to see is how you can do it."

"We need help for that," Victoria admitted. "Would you be willing to lend us a hand, Mr. Steil?"

Hart's instructions blinked in Elliot's mind. He should not give his straightaway consent to anything, nor to anyone. He had to make them persuade him. "I . . . I don't know," he said, trying to look fraught with uncertainty. "I might be willing to, provided you don't ask me to do something that's against American laws . . . or that . . . compromises my future . . . or that . . . costs me money."

"We wouldn't dream of—" Pardo began.

"Excuse me, sir," Steil, cutting the man short, as if all of a sudden he had visualized the many risks ahead. "Let me make myself clear. Mr. Scheindlin was a multimillionaire, he had adopted American citizenship many years ago, he had dozens of acquaintances among judges, politicians, and government officials. If he had a brush with the law, he could retain the best lawyers, make a few calls to pretty influential people, wriggle free of any tight spot he found himself in. I'm nothing. I'm just a resident. I haven't applied for U.S. citizenship—"

"Something that speaks volumes," Victoria, inspired.

"I don't have influential friends or money, so I won't do anything illegal and, unfortunately, regarding Cuba, practically anything you do in the United States is considered so. I've been saving money for several years to make this trip. I have a job to protect. So, Mr. Capdevila, Ms. . . . excuse me, I forgot your name."

"It's Arosamena. But, please, call me Berta."

"Thank you. So, Mr. Capdevila, Ms. Berta, if you don't jeopardize my future, I'm willing to help you out, even though I can't see how."

The visitors smiled. Pardo jumped to his feet and proffered his hand. A confused Steil shook it. Victoria remained seated, pretending to be pleased.

"Thank you, Mr. Steil. We assure you that we won't ask you to do anything that would jeopardize your freedom or your job," Pardo said, then snuggled down in his seat. "We just want you to answer a few questions we have, then explain our problem to someone."

"Seems feasible. Ask away," Steil said.

. . .

Victoria snapped shut the attaché case, lay it on the floor, crossed her legs, and reclined against her seat. Pardo fixed his gaze on the carpet to formulate the list of questions that he and his wife had prepared, then rehearsed for a week, in the agreed-upon order.

"Is it correct to presume that heirs to Mr. Scheindlin have assumed control of IMLATINEX?" minding his choice of words lest he make a mistake.

"Yes. Mrs. Maria Scheindlin, his widow, and Jenny Scheindlin, his daughter, own most of the company's stock."

"Are they involved in the day-to-day operation of the firm?"

"No. Sam Plotzher, the minority shareholder, and I take care of that."

"Are you the manager?" Victoria asked.

For a second Steil wondered how much these people knew. Ruben Scheindlin had been a very private man; he would not have revealed the inner workings of his company to strangers. Just in case, he decided to be truthful.

"I guess I am. Not officially, though. I was Mr. Scheindlin's secretary, or personal assistant, take your pick. Since his death, Sam and I have shared managerial duties, sort of: I take care of the office, he takes care of everything else."

"So, you tell the office staff what to do, make deposits, place orders, negotiate contracts, sign checks, supply the raw data to your accountant, that kind of thing?"

"Both Sam and I sign checks and contracts. But yes, I do the other things you say."

Victoria concentrated on gauging the subject's reactions. They were dancing around him, asking meaningless questions. However, those feints were laying the groundwork for what would come later. Steil's body language showed that he harbored suspicions, was leery; that was natural. Had he been relaxed and comfortable, all her alarms would have gone off.

"Do you have any idea what Mr. Scheindlin may have done with our money?" Pardo asked.

"None whatsoever."

"Do you think he may have deposited it in one of your firm's bank accounts?"

Steil shook his head emphatically.

"Perhaps stashed it in a safe-deposit box?"

"It's a possibility."

"Or in a safe at home?"

"Maybe."

"Mr. Steil, we can't fly to Miami to search for the money, nor can we file a petition in court to be reimbursed by Mr. Scheindlin's heirs."

"I know that."

"So, if someone close to the Scheindlins could find out where our money is and help us recover it, our gratitude—and in this case I've been authorized to say that 'our' applies to the corporation's president, too—would find proper expression. Such an individual would be granted authorization to travel to Cuba whenever they wish, invest here, buy real estate, anything that is not in violation of Cuban law."

Steil locked eyes with Pardo, moved his gaze to Victoria, returned it to Pardo. "That's very generous, but how can I help you? I'm sure that your money wasn't deposited in one of IMLATINEX's checking accounts; all deposits are related to legal business transactions. Mr. Scheindlin never told me that he was doing philanthropic work for Cuba. If he rented safe-deposit boxes for his private use, I wasn't informed. I don't know whether or not he had a safe at home, and even if he had, I can't go there and open it."

"Maybe his wife could," Victoria said, thus ending the long yet indispensable preamble.

Steil considered the suggestion. "I guess she could," he admitted. Then the entailment made him frown. "Are you implying I should tell her what you've told me here tonight, then ask her whether she knows where the money is?"

"It's so rewarding to deal with intelligent people," Pardo asserted.

Victoria registered that Steil had been flattered by her husband's accolade and smiled a Cheshire Cat grin. Humans were so easy to manipulate; especially men. She uncrossed her legs.

"Well . . ." Steil said, busy examining the possibilities. "What if she doesn't know anything?"

"End of story, Mr. Steil," Pardo said. "I mean, what else could we ask you to do? If you don't know where the money is, if she opens her home safe—supposing Scheindlin had a safe at home—and it's not there, if she has no knowledge that her husband kept a safe-deposit box somewhere, or if she finds the cash and refuses to give it back, Cuba lost one hundred thousand dollars. Simple as that."

Once again Steil wasted a few seconds considering things. Pardo and Victoria held their breath, feeling they were getting close to clinching it.

"And if she finds it and is willing to give it back to you?"

Victoria and Pardo exhaled. They were home.

"Then," Pardo said, "we would go wherever you want us to. Not Stateside, though. You know how difficult it is to get a visa."

"Yeah, I've heard," Steil said. "But . . . nobody can leave the United States carrying a hundred thousand in a briefcase. It's a serious crime and now, after September 11, airport security is . . ."

Pardo smiled. "Let's not put the cart before the horse, Elliot. Can I call you Elliot?"

"Sure."

"First things first. If the money is found and the widow is willing to give it back, we'll find a way. Mr. Scheindlin had no problem moving cash around. Unfortunately, he never told us how he did it. We would have to see first how things play out. Maybe a sympathizer of the Revolution . . ."

"Tell us about Mrs. Scheindlin," Victoria interrupted her husband.

Steil shifted his gaze from Pardo to Victoria to Pardo to Victoria again. Office etiquette prohibits underlings from cutting off their bosses in the presence of strangers. Maybe these two were lovers; sex tears down hierarchical barriers, he thought. Pardo realized that his wife's intrusion was his fault; they had agreed to discuss how to recover the cash and bring it back to Cuba at the second meeting. Victoria perceived that Steil knew something was amiss.

"Well, I can't say much," Steil began, "because I never met her until Mr. Scheindlin's funeral. She seems a very nice lady, intelligent, well educated, polite."

"Do you know if she has an opinion regarding Cuba?" Victoria asked.

"No, I don't. We've only discussed business matters."

"Well, you must be pretty tired, Mr. Steil," said Pardo, retaking the initiative with a wide smile. "Everybody in Havana knows how many hours visitors to Cuba put in at Miami's airport, and I'm sure you feel like going to bed. However, we need to meet again before you fly back to agree on how to stay in touch. Are you flying back next Sunday?"

"Yes, I am."

"What do you say if we meet next Friday?"

"That's okay with me," Steil said. "My schedule is pretty open. In your office?"

Pardo tilted his head and squinted, pretending to ponder how to broach what he and Victoria, after extensive debate, had agreed was the greatest weakness of their plan. "It would be best to meet here or at some other public place, and there are two reasons for it," he began, trying to conceal that his answer had been carefully prepared. "State Security has instructed that Cubans living in the United States are not to be allowed into ministries, party offices, and military units. XEMIC is included in the list. We think that unfair and discriminatory, but what can we do? Maybe they know things we don't know, and if something happens, if there's an electrical fire and a Cuban residing in the United States visited the building three or four days earlier, they'll term it sabotage and say we are to blame for disregarding their instructions."

Steil thought this was probably true. The understandable psychosis of the early years, driven by terrorist attacks, an invasion, guerrillas, and the October 1962 missile crisis had evolved over time into an irrational and groundless paranoia stoked up by the State Security through all available means. It is a tenet of communism that people must always have an enemy to blame for the system's shortcomings.

"So, the president of the corporation instructed us to hold this conversation here," Pardo continued, "explain this . . . prohibition to you, should I deem it necessary, and request your understanding. That's reason number one."

Pardo took a deep breath and pretended to be worried. Victoria was discovering that, although he occasionally missed a cue, she had married a fairly good actor. He was upstaging her!

"Reason number two is more . . . how can I put this . . . personal. I've been authorized to explain it to you, though. The top echelon of our government hasn't been informed about the . . . unorthodox way we've been buying U.S. pharmaceuticals. They never asked and we never said. I can understand that. Sometimes statesmen don't want to know how a certain thing is done. I think it's called deniability. Therefore, we haven't told them about the missing money. Eventually we'll have to if we don't recover it, but we dread that the comrade president, Berta, and I will most probably be fired. And, as you may realize, we want to do everything possible to keep this under wraps until we've done all we can to recover the money. Including meeting you in private and off the record."

As he nodded in feigned understanding, Steil thought he had to hand it to them. These two had planned the con very carefully, for weeks, maybe months. Just to make them sweat a little more he asked, "And how did you learn that I work for IMLATINEX and that I was coming to Cuba?"

"That's my turf," said Victoria, keeping to the script. "We had your name from correspondence between your firm and Trans-Caribbean. Then, in 1998 I had a meeting with Mr. Scheindlin in Panama. I hadn't seen him in two years and found that he had aged considerably. This worried me and I mentioned it to comrade . . . I mean, Mr. Capdevila."

Pardo nodded in approval. "I remember," he said glancing at her. Then his eyes went to Steil: "Berta brought to my attention the fact that Mr. Scheindlin was an old man. She said: 'If he passes away anytime soon, we would lose an important business partner and col-laborator.' She also suggested we do something about it."

This time Victoria respectfully waited an instant, making sure her boss had finished speaking.

"In that same meeting, for some reason I can't remember, Mr. Scheindlin mentioned your name, said you were Cuban," she continued. "I was curious. 'Cuban you say? With such a name?' He smiled, nodded, and said you had emigrated in the early nineties. Your name stuck, got me wondering. I thought that maybe you would come to visit relatives and it might be interesting to meet you, see if you would agree to speak on our behalf to the new owners after Mr. Scheindlin passed away, maybe even ask them to keep doing for us what Mr. Scheindlin did. So, I gave your name to Foreign Affairs and asked them to let me know if you ever applied for a visa. Nothing happened for four years. Then, about two months ago . . ."

Victoria paused because nothing else needed to be said. Steil nodded again and concentrated on keeping a straight face. They were good. State Security officers probably. "I see," he said. "Well, then how about Friday evening, right here?"

"Sounds perfect to me," Pardo said.

"Excellent," Victoria added.

"At eight," Steil specified.

Victoria and Pardo got to their feet and Steil stood up as well. They shook hands.

"I don't think you can appreciate how much we value your col-laboration, Mr. Steil," Pardo said by the door.

"Oh, yes. I can," Steil said, permitting himself a wide smile. "I lived here until 1994. I know how the system works. And I'm afraid you might spend time in jail if that money doesn't turn up."

"We know," Pardo concurred, "we just didn't want to be dramatic."

"I'll do what I can."

"Good night, Mr. Steil," Pardo said.

"Good night, Mr. Capdevila."

"Pleasant dreams, Mr. Steil."

"Same to you, Ms. Berta," turning the handle.

Back in bed, lights off, Steil found himself unable to loosen up and sleep. Once again he was experiencing the mental state he had gone through twenty-eight hours earlier in Miami. He reviewed over and over what the rival duos had said, tried to make connections and guess what lay behind the layers of verbosity. Hart and McLellan had strong-armed him into collaboration, and he hated that, but they knew this was going to happen and were straightforward about their goal—go there, someone will approach you, hear what they want from you, agree to do it, then report to us. The two Cubans had done the opposite: sweet-talk him into cooperation and conceal the reason for it behind a load of baloney. However, it seemed they were not aware that the FBI wanted to know what the State Security was up to.

Five or six months earlier, Steil recalled, a senior analyst in the Defense Intelligence Agency had been arrested and charged with spying for Cuba. In 1998, twelve Cubans who had settled in Miami in the early nineties were arrested and accused of operating a spy ring. In 2001, five of them were given long prison sentences. Both cases had been extensively covered in the U.S. media, and Steil had conscientiously read numerous articles about them and watched many pieces in the evening news.

While living on the island, he had dismissed the much-touted capacity of Cuban Intelligence to penetrate foreign governments and anticommunist organizations as party-approved pablum spoon-fed to unsuspecting citizens. It seemed he had been wrong. Obviously, the intelligence and counterintelligence organizations of both countries were waging a cloak-and-dagger war and he had been caught in the crossfire. In the afternoon he had felt like Santa Claus; now he felt like a sitting duck.

He tossed and turned until two, when he lost consciousness.

Four

Having overslept, Elliot left his hotel room a little after 10:00 A.M. on Monday morning. He wore the faded jeans,white short-sleeved shirt, and old black lace-up shoes he had brought with the express purpose of blending into the crowd. Elliot placed the previous evening's bizarre interview on the back burner and, skipping breakfast, asked the parking valet for his rental. He admired April in all its glory: low seventies, cloudless sky, cool breeze blowing from the east, brilliant sunshine. He drove to his old neighborhood listening to Radio Reloj. The news of the day was that president Chaviano had been reinstated in Venezuela. He parked the car three blocks away from Sobeida's apartment building and ambled over, searching for changes.

Everything seemed to be in the same sorry state or more dilapidated. The exception was a recently refurbished private home, with a two-toned, highly polished '56 Chevrolet Bel Air in mint condition and a '98 gray Citroen in the driveway. He had no recollection of the gleaming white grilles that now secured its doors and windows. Maybe the head of the household made a living in the tourism industry, or relatives abroad paid for everything. Perhaps the residence had been purchased by an artist who performed or sold works of art abroad, or by someone operating a profitable private business. A foreign sugar daddy or mommy who had fallen under the spell of a

Cuban woman or man might be footing the bills. Whatever the source, Elliot felt sure that (1) its dwellers were secretly envied, (2) the block's informers kept them under surveillance, and (3) many would say the proprietor flaunted his or her wealth.

Fifteen or twenty years earlier, Elliot had concluded that socialist equality, theoretically conceived as an upward spiral toward communal riches, in practice became a collective nosedive into poverty. Such dismal failure, he had observed, generated envy—and its twin brother, severe criticism—toward those who prospered. It was considered irrelevant if an individual's well-being took place within the existing political framework or independently of it. The high-ranking officials who were given the comfortable homes abandoned by the fleeing upper and middle classes in the sixties, rode in new cars, and got supplementary rations of food were rebuked as sternly as those who enjoyed the same standard of living with money coming from relatives abroad or other legal sources. The overwhelming majority of Havana's dispossessed felt they had been cheated into swallowing the equality pill. The consolation prize for stupidity seems to be criticism of the smartest, he had resolved.

"Teacher?"

Elliot slowed down, half turned, looked back, then stopped. He frowned at the swaggering young man who had passed him an instant before and was now eyeing him with a doubtful expression on his face. The muscular, swarthy, beardless, baby-faced hulk struck him as being eighteen or nineteen years old. He had never taught English to students under fifteen and, having departed in 1994, the youngest in that year's class now were in their mid-twenties.

"Are you talking to me?" De Niro–like.

"Didn't you use to live in that apartment building," the young man, pointing with his arm, "many years ago?"

"Eight years ago, yes."

"I live there. And I remember you."

"Oh, you do? Well . . . thanks. And you are?"

"I'm Lemar," proffering a hand the size of a catcher's mitt.

Elliot took it feeling senile. The four-foot-tall, ten-year-old kid had turned into a Samson capable of knocking him out cold with a slap in the face.

"*Coño,* Lemar, how many ration cards you got?" It had been a popular late-twentieth-century Cuban joke played on tall, beefy guys and gals. Lemar answered with a sheepish grin. He seemed good-natured, as were most men capable of crushing almost any opponent in the first thirty seconds of a fight.

"How's your grandfather?"

"He died."

"Oh, sorry to hear that."

"You know, three-pack-a-day guy."

"Yeah, I remember. And your grandmother?"

"She's okay. Are you on your way to say hello?"

"Well," scratching his head, "yes, in fact I am."

Lemar nodded and hesitated, not sure whether asking what he wanted to ask was an indiscretion. "Word is you sailed to Miami on a raft. Is it true?"

"Yeah. I wouldn't recommend it to anyone, though. You in college?"

"Nah. I dropped out of high school. Then the army drafted me. I'm on a forty-eight-hour leave."

"It's still two years, right?"

"Yep."

"Used to be three in my time."

"Fuck."

"And you'll be discharged in . . . ?"

"Twenty-one months and five days."

Steil raised his eyebrows and shook his head compassionately. "Well, I guess there's nothing you can do about it."

"I could do something about it, if somebody told me how to make a raft and sail to Key West."

"Don't think about it, Lemar. It's madness. Well, I guess I shouldn't keep you any longer. Take care."

"You too, teacher. Bye."

Lemar was the first of five former neighbors that Elliot bumped into before entering his old building. People seemed genuinely glad to see him, wanted to know how he was doing. Where had he settled? Had he married? Was he still a teacher? What did he do for a living there? He was deliberately shy and unassuming in his answers. He worked at a Miami trading company, made a decent living, was still divorced, had come to visit relatives in Santa Cruz del Norte and friends in Havana. When he knocked on Sobeida's door, it was a quarter to twelve.

Contrary to expectations, she neither shouted loudly nor laughed merrily. She did gasp, embrace him, kiss him, and then cry and cry and cry. Holding her, he felt her ribcage. Sobeida had lost fifteen or twenty pounds, which seemed strange: He had sent her enough money to feed herself decently, maybe even lavishly. She appeared older than he expected her to look as well. How old was she? he wondered. Sixty-something. She had dissolved her childless, common-law marriage in the early eighties, both her parents had died in the town in which they had been born—Limonar, in the province of Matanzas—in the same decade. Sobeida was an undereducated, lonely woman who tried to brighten up her days by memorizing and repeating the city's latest political jokes.

When she regained composure, they sat on the couch, and Steil learned from his friend that she had been diagnosed with cervical cancer. Unable to remember the precise medical terms, much less how to pronounce them, she wailed that six weeks earlier she had tested positive to a gynecological examination routinely performed every two or three years to all females between ages twenty-five and sixty-five. She had been taken to a hospital and the doctors had looked into her with a periscope.

"Periscope, Sobeida?" struggling to keep a straight face.

"Or some name ending in scope . . . Then they took a sample for a biozia and said I had carcinonga."

Sobeida admitted to living in terror since then. She was scheduled to undergo surgery to remove her cervix and uterus in two weeks. She had no appetite, slept merely two or three hours at nights, could no longer go shopping for her clients. Steil comforted her. Most patients that were diagnosed early on lived many more years, he said, then invented the story that sufferers whose affected organs had been surgically removed registered a higher rate of survival than patients treated with chemotherapy. Cuban doctors were good. She would get well. Then he told her about himself.

She had not had lunch yet and he was hungry. Sensing that a change of air would do her well, he asked her to put a dress on then drove to El Aljibe. The Seventh Avenue restaurant is famous in Miami for its excellent roasted chicken and outrageous prices. Both things were true, Steil confirmed. During the meal, the host increased his guest's inventory of jokes with a few doing the rounds in Miami. After dessert, over a nice cup of espresso, feeling elated for the first time since her malignancy had been diagnosed, Sobeida became her real self.

"The Chief stages a rally at Revolution Plaza. A million people gather. After the national anthem, he addresses the crowd: 'I have some good news and some bad news. The good news is that Cuban scientists, the best scientists in the entire world, have achieved a gigantic breakthrough that will astound the world and deliver one more punch to the criminal blockade imposed on our heroic people by the United States. Starting tomorrow, we will be able to feed ourselves with stones.' The crowd grumbles in disgust. 'That's the good news? What's the bad news?' a guy hollers. 'The bad news is,' the Chief explains, 'we haven't got enough treated stones, so we will begin by giving each and every citizen one ounce of stone per week.'"

Back in her apartment, Steil gave Sobeida five hundred dollars, repeated his assurance that she would make a speedy and full recovery after the operation, then began saying his farewells. The old woman started sobbing silently; Steil felt dismayed. He gave her a peck on the cheek, turned, went outside, and closed the door behind him.

On Tuesday morning, Elliot paid a visit to the Colón Cemetery before driving to Santa Cruz del Norte. There were flowers for sale and he bought a dozen roses. His mother's remains had already been moved to a charnel house and now lay in an ossuary. Standing in front of the crypt, he surprised himself by turning over in his mind the same pseudophilosophical misconceptions everybody thinks in graveyards and felt ashamed for it. What was he doing here? Carmen was not a pile of bones. She was what he remembered of her, what her three living siblings and numerous nephews remembered of her, the few faded black-and-white photographs kept in Santa Cruz del Norte. So, what was he honoring here? Bones? Steil turned, left the charnel house, and dropped the roses in a trash can. Cremation would have been the right thing to do.

After driving through the tunnel under Havana Bay, the memories of his mother gradually receded. Following Avenida Monumental and the Vía Blanca, Elliot moved into rural Cuba. By the time he left the town of Guanabo, he was so seduced by the greenness of the countryside to the right that he veered off the freeway, followed a dirt road for a hundred yards or so, pulled over, and got out. With both hands in his pockets, he strolled along the shoulder of the road, taking in his surroundings. A wooden house painted orange with a roof of red tiles could be seen half a mile away, birds chirped atop overhanging branches swaying in the breeze, cows grazed behind a barbed-wire fence, butterflies fluttered about. To the north, east, and west the sky was perfect blue; to the south, a snow-white cloudbank broke the monotony. Being April, he knew that around three or four o'clock dark clouds would be massing over the center and south of Havana Province; rain would come down in torrents to the south of San José de las Lajas and Aguacate; to the north of that imaginary line it was just a possibility. Everyone is a meteorologist where they were born and raised, he chuckled.

His spirit rose and he took a deep breath. The countryside smelled of earth, dew, pollen, cattle dung, grass, seabreeze, and aromatic plants. The distant crow of a rooster reached him. Was he a country boy at heart? He found such ambivalence rather surprising. When he had completed his military stint he thought he hated Santa Cruz del Norte, wanted desperately to settle in Havana, and was overjoyed when they moved there. Now, having resided for many years in the Cuban capital, plus eight more in Miami, he longed for his birthplace. A trip to his roots, maybe to the seed itself. Old age knocking.

A jeep was closing in on him fast, leaving behind a cloud of red dust. The Gaz scraped to a halt by the surprised tourist and an army lieutenant in battle dress deftly jumped to the ground. A corporal remained at the wheel. Both wore webbed belts and sidearms. In a flash Elliot realized what was about to happen. A rental meant a foreigner. The army counterintelligence officer from a nearby military outfit had been notified that a probable CIA spy was scouting the battlefield.

"Good morning," the officer said as he saluted.

"Good morning."

"Oh, you speak Spanish."

"I'm Cuban."

The lieutenant squinted. Reading him like an open book, Elliot waited for the inescapable question.

"You live in Cuba?"

"No, I live in Miami."

"Can I see your passport?"

The man first inspected Steil's passport, then the copy of the rental car lease.

"Well, sir," returning the documents, "this is a military road, civilians are not authorized to drive through. I ask you to please return to the freeway."

"No problem. I just wonder why you don't put up a sign. You wouldn't have to drive over every time someone feels like stretching their legs," Elliot said tongue-in-cheek.

The lieutenant appeared to consider it, but said nothing. Steil was pulling the driver's door open when he heard the officer's last question.

"Is your name Cuban?"

"No, it's American."

Twenty or thirty seconds later, in the rearview mirror, Elliot saw the man duly logging something, maybe the rental's plates and his name. Clicking his tongue, forcing a smile, and shaking his head sadly, he gained the freeway and sped to Santa Cruz del Norte.

...

Compartmentalization is enforced in intelligence and counterintelligence agencies to ensure ironclad secrecy. Exceptions are kept to a bare minimum. For instance, no psychologist worth his salt will perform the remote profiling of a possible top-level agent based on distorted data. The recruit's real age, sex, race, nationality, education, profession, place of residence, and personal history must be evaluated if a well-founded opinion is to be given. The candidate may be assigned a cryptonym, but the information has to be genuine.

This textbook case of centralism became known in Cuba as The First Sacred Rule. Consequently, as soon as compartmentalization was transgressed, like when a large meeting was convened, everyone assumed the agenda had nothing to do with their bread and butter and dismissed it as so much crap they were forced to put up with and paid little heed to.

Which was the attitude that Tuesday morning inside the General Directorate of Intelligence's small and dimly lit theater, where thirty-seven poker-faced officers in mufti were attending the postmortem of the failed coup in Venezuela.

An hour-by-hour report covering the four days had been hastily assembled from the coded bulletins filed by colleagues under diplomatic cover in the Cuban embassy in Caracas, by three illegals in the cities of Barquisimeto, Maracaibo, and Barinas, and by numerous news wires. Edited portions of CNN, CBS, NBC, and Fox footage, taped at the Institute for Radio and Television, were being shown on two big-screen TV sets. The captain operating the VCR had a copy of the report. He inserted and ejected cassettes in coordination with the day, hour, and specific event that the narrator, Lieutenant Colonel Mario, was referring to.

Victoria watched as Chaviano was taken away from the Presidential Palace in the middle of the night. Days earlier, facing cameras and microphones, the man had boasted he would never surrender. However, he had meekly relinquished power the instant a general placed him under arrest. "For the good of the country." "To avoid bloodshed." Cambronne, a division general under Napoleon, came to mind. He had allegedly responded "Shit!" when, during a pregnant pause at the Battle of Waterloo, an English general bade him to sur-render. A sanitized version has him crying, "The Guard die but not ever surrender." Many of his soldiers died all right, but not him. Years later he married an English aristocrat and served one of Napoleon's worst enemies: King Louis XVIII. Men are so conceited and words are so cheap, Victoria mused, that women should be wary of both. She respected Salvador Allende, the late Chilean president, because he had been that most uncharacteristic of animals: a down-to-earth, unpretentious, levelheaded, well-balanced politician who secured his place in history by choosing honorable death before undignified surrender.

Victoria judged the silence of the audience deceptive. She felt sure that most of those men and women, if not all, considered Chaviano a fucking coward. But well aware that he was a favorite of the Chief, not one would dare say it aloud, thus evidencing that they were not models of bravery either. Cuban adults from all walks of life, especially the older and better educated, knew the Commander believed that anyone who thought different was mentally deficient, morally corrupt, or a traitor.

Latin American history abounds in utopians who seized power to straighten things up and became dictators in their own right, she reflected next. The rich people who exert power and authority fail to see the limit of social victimization. Revolutionaries make out the limit, promise to rectify what is wrong, and by peaceful or violent means seize power. Then the new ruling class gradually turns myopic and the cycle repeats itself.

Now the screen showed a smiling and waving Chaviano as he returned to the Presidential Palace for his third crack at power. The narrator, keeping his voice neutral, directed the attention of viewers to the security detail surrounding the man and commented on obvi-ous flaws. Victoria couldn't judge the technicalities of protecting a president, but the haunted faces of two white men in their thirties looked familiar to her. Cubans from the Chief's security detail, prob-ably. She wasn't surprised, though. The man was obviously and openly doing all he could to help Chaviano.

Fully aware that, after the Cuban fiasco, a communist revolution was unthinkable in Venezuela or any other South American nation, the Chief nevertheless realized that his ardent disciple had ended his isolation in the Latin American corridors of power. He had secured the daily supply of fifty-three thousand barrels of vital oil on favorable prices and credit terms. And the Commander's hands were clean. His admirer had been elected in fair and free elections. For these reasons, several thousand Cuban doctors, nurses, teachers, and sports instructors had been shipped off to the most miserable and remotest regions of Venezuela to care for, teach, and train the destitute. Chessboard pawns, she sadly reflected. She, her boss, the ministers, and the generals were all chessboard pawns manipulated by the all-powerful at the pyramid's vertex.

"What do you think?" whispered Col. Enrique Morera, cryptonym Bernardo, in Victoria's right ear. She returned to reality. General Lastra and his six closest collaborators were sitting in the first row of seats. To Victoria's left, Col. José Manuel Campa, cryptonym Paco, twiddled a cigarette between his fingers, desperate for a smoke. Victoria hated Campa because, since getting married, he was the only man she would have loved to mess around with. It made her mad to feel so attracted to a sonofabitch who only eyed broads who had hooters and hefty behinds.

"A victory of the people," Victoria, after turning her head, whispered back. "United, the people shall never be defeated," she added. The slogan—a rhyme in Spanish—was coined by Chilean socialists during Allende's tenure. The only epigram she could think of to call Chaviano fainthearted. Morera, nobody's fool, permitted himself a smile. Allusions such as Victoria's were much appreciated in Cuban officialdom. The party line had been toed, nothing improper had been said, and yet the sarcasm was perfectly clear.

"Rumor has it that, on Saturday morning, Felipe called Josep to see if José María would grant Rufo political asylum," Morera commented.

"Really?" a surprised Victoria said.

"It's a rumor."

"I see."

Victoria's mental wheels turned fast. Labeling the news a rumor meant that it was in the public domain everywhere except in Cuba. Felipe was the Cuban minister of foreign affairs, a hysterical zealot; Josep was Josep Piqué, his opposite number in Spain; José María was José María Aznar, the Spanish president; Rufo was Chaviano's first name. So, the Chief had crossed off Chaviano on Friday night, after he was arrested. Amazing. Well, Victoria mused, the Chief had to be inured to the hardships of power. Probably no other living head of state, aside from perhaps Saddam Hussein, had seen a greater number of his favorite presidents, prime ministers, and other highly placed officials fall from power or die on him; more of his ministers, generals, and party bureaucrats fail him somehow. She recalled the day when the chief of the Cuban air force landed his private plane in Miami and filed for political asylum. At the time, *she* had felt humiliated.

Yet, the Commander liked Chaviano enough to arrange for his exile in Spain, thus owing big to Aznar, a political right-winger he would love to see ousted from power. Once again she had to admire the Chief's cunning. A less experienced helmsman would have provided safe haven to Chaviano in Cuba. However, the Commander had figured out that such a move would compromise his disciple's future. Should the man spend two, three, or more years exiled in Havana, he would be reviled, labeled his puppet. On the other hand, no European country under a right-wing administration could be accused of aiding and abetting Chaviano.

"Have you heard any rumor about José María's response?" Victoria whispered.

The subalterns in the second row of seats strained unsuccessfully to overhear the big shots.

"Word is he said he would consider it if Rufo himself asked for it."

"Well, luckily the people prevailed. Now we don't owe a thing to José María, provided the rumor is true."

"Oh, yes, we do owe him. Just by agreeing to consider it, we owe him. One of these days, before the end of his term, he'll ask us to discourage a Basque Nationalist from flying to France to plan terrorist attacks, or he'll seek a pardon for a counterrevolutionary serving a prison sentence."

Victoria held Morera in high esteem. Chief of the USA Department and her superior officer, he had always treated her as a friend. Rigid implementation of The First Sacred Rule prevented her from really knowing how good the man was, but the respect with which his superiors treated him made her suspect he had performed outstandingly well during the lifetime he had devoted to Intelligence. His lugubrious manner reflected something that she had not been able to pinpoint. Dashed hopes? Disillusionment? Sexual frustration? He had the deepest lines she had seen in a forehead, the result of many years of worrying and repressing his feelings.

Rumor had it that he was not promoted to brigadier general in 1995 because his only son led a notoriously debauched lifestyle. It was also said that Morera was being nudged into retirement after the jewel of the crown, the DIA agent he had personally handled, was arrested seven months earlier. Only five people had known about her: the Chief, his brother, the minister of the interior, General Lastra, and Morera.

After her arrest was made public, though, Morera had taken Victoria into his confidence and given his version of why she was nabbed. Carelessness had been his diagnosis. He had instructed her to go to the WIPE program and destroy the file every time she got a radio message or a disk and warned her not to leave prepared information that was not ciphered in the house. But from the shreds of information he'd been able to compile, it seemed she'd had a lapse, or two, or three, nobody knew how many. And this was in Washington, where the FBI was best equipped, Morera had reminded Victoria. Not forgetting that humans tend to disclaim responsibility when things go wrong, Victoria thought nonetheless that Morera was probably right. Most spies get overconfident.

Considering a two-minute pause sufficient, and as though bored stiff by the Chaviano report, she leaned to her right and changed the subject.

"Any sign that the Gypsy has let up?" she whispered. The Gypsy was Cuban Intelligence's name for David Szady, chief of the FBI's counterintelligence division. After his people broke the Wasp cell and three years later rooted out the most highly placed Cuban agent in the United States, his Cuban adversaries schizophrenically admired the man in secret and hated him in public. They suspected Szady felt the same for Cuban case officers. It was the ultimate mark of professionalism.

Morera tilted his head right, left, and pulled down the corners of his mouth. "Not to my knowledge. I assume he's doing his job; I'm certainly trying to do mine," he said.

"How soon can I wake up a few sleepers?" Victoria asked.

"Not yet. Maybe in a few months."

"How about broadcasts?"

"Only those authorized."

"One day the Commander is going to ask if this is as good as it gets."

Morera just smiled wrily. Victoria knew he would not say one more word. She decoded the smile as: "He knows we are in very deep shit."

The postmortem was almost finished. The captain operating the VCR froze a close-up of a joyful Chaviano on the screen. Lights were turned on. Lieutenant Colonel Mario stole a look at General Lastra and was pleased to get an approving nod. A captain who after several years still had not shed the suspicious expression of rookies ranted: "Viva Chaviano."

"Viva," mumbled the other participants before they started to file out.

...

Returning to Santa Cruz del Norte after so many years turned out to be quite an experience. Before anything else, Elliot visited three homes: In the first two lived his aunts, in the third roomed his uncle. Exactly the same happened at each dwelling. Someone young opened the front door of a poverty-stricken yet shipshape household, eyed him curiously while he asked for his relative, then bawled, "Grandma [or Grandpa], a comrade is asking for you!" Almost a minute after he had been shown in, one of his aunts or his uncle, in well-worn clothes and scuffed shoes, came into the living room adjusting their glasses. Brows were knit, an instant of hesitation ensued. "No! Is it you?" was gleefully screamed next. He was hugged to the point of suffocation. He hugged them tightly, too. Then came the shouts: "Run, Elisa! Run, Jaime! Run, Ernesto! Hurry! Elito, the son of Carmita, is here!"

The older women wept and unusual mist could be seen in the eyes of those hombres who had retired or worked the afternoon or graveyard shifts. Elliot's eyes clouded somewhat. He was then steered to each home's best rocking chair and forced to sit in it. Somebody turned off the blaring ancient radio, another turned on an old fan, a third hauled chairs from the dining room and bedrooms. The youngest among the women (someone who had been six or seven the last time he'd seen her, years before leaving Cuba) was ordered to brew coffee as the rest of the family sat around him and gabbled away a hundred questions that he tried to answer no less precipitately. Within ten minutes or so, the delectable girl who had been exiled to the kitchen presented him with a timid yet dazzling smile and a demitasse of very strong aromatic coffee that tasted delicious. For the first time in many, many years, Elliot Steil felt at home.

That same day he had to muster all his willpower to refuse the numerous glasses of fragrant rum waved under his nose. Boasting that he had been on the wagon for eight years was out of the question; in Santa Cruz that's considered weakness of character, AA a club for sissies. You have to be man enough to indulge in drinking bouts when you feel like it and to turn down invitations when for some reason you cannot touch the stuff. Teetotaling there is almost as insane as celibacy. Hence, he concocted the story that he had been diagnosed with a fatty liver five weeks earlier and the doctor had ordered him to not touch a drop for the next six months. This brought nods of understanding and looks of commiseration from all.

Meals were disappointing. Although he was served the best available, fresh herbs did not counterbalance the lack of spices and cooking oil. Lacking pork sausage and bacon, a red bean potage was tasteless. A red porgy short on onions, red pepper, garlic, and basted in sunflower oil rather than olive oil lost half its allure. Was good Cuban home cooking to be found only abroad? Perhaps the kitchens that cooked for certain comrades were well stocked, he mused.

Next morning he started asking for old friends and acquaintances in an updating process that proved full of surprises. Apparently, none of those who emigrated had settled in Miami, or even Florida, which was amazing. Roberto Molina, a classmate, the son of a fisherman, became a mechanic on a Cuban fishing trawler, jumped ship in the Canary Islands, and now owned five camels that he rented to tourists in the sands of Fuerteventura. His father showed Elliot snapshots of his buddy proudly parading his beasts of burden. Manolo, still living in town, was assistant manager at the Havana Club rum distillery. Somewhat embarrassed, he declined the invitation to chat with Elliot, maybe because as a member of the Communist Party's Municipal Committee he was not supposed to. Rosa, a pediatrician mother of three who had sat next to him in fourth, fifth, and sixth grades, drowned in Guatemala while crossing a swollen river to attend to an infant dehydrating from diarrhea. Etelvina entered a convent at the age of thirty-eight. Evelio resided in Brooklyn, had married an Algerian woman, fathered two boys and two girls, and earned his bread and butter giving thorough maintenance checks to the escalators of the city's subway. Due to a serious back condition, Pedro had taken early retirement from the sugar refinery, where he operated a centrifuge for thirty years. When last heard of, Ricardo was playing maracas for a Japanese orchestra in Kobe. The once incredibly beautiful Carmina, now an overweight and gray-haired woman in her midforties, sold homemade ice cream from the front door of her wooden house. Miguel, Fernando, and Roberto sailed the small boats their fathers had inherited from their grandfathers and made a living by daily casting lines a mile off the coast.

The topic of illegal emigration, although painful, surfaced repeatedly because everybody had been led to believe that Elliot had fled to the United States on a raft. As in every other town on the island's northern coast, young people were acquainted with the rudiments of sailing and knew how to swim. Low salaries averaging ten dollars a month and unemployment made many sick and tired of suffering serious privations. To compound the problem further, scores believed that after a couple of years in the Florida Keys or Miami, they would be driving brand-new Jags and living in three-bedroom houses with pools.

According to Fernando, Samuel Timoneda, the town's historian, began keeping a tally in 1980. Since then, 137 residents of Santa Cruz, Hershey, and the immediate surrounds had illegally sailed northbound. Of these, 115 had either landed safely in one of Florida's counties or been intercepted by the U.S. Coast Guard and returned to Cuba. The missing twenty-two had left fourteen families in the most macabre corner of limbo, unable to make up their minds on the absentees' birthdays whether they should rejoice or weep.

By Thursday morning, townsfolk had grown accustomed to seeing Elliot walking around. He sniffed the air to enjoy the fragrance of molasses blowing from the south, the smell of the sea from the north or the east, or exhaled hard to get rid of the stench from nearby oil wells blowing in from the west. Downtown Santa Cruz, although clean and tidy, had remained pretty much the same. In the outskirts, new influences were to be found by the score. Ugly, four-floor concrete boxes had been built to house the families of the managers, engineers, technicians, and plain workers who operated a huge power generating plant erected a few miles to the west, on the shoreline, in the late eighties. The staff of the new paper factory, and those in charge of the oil wells drilled and laid pipelines all over the municipality, also lodged in those apartment buildings. The expanded rum distillery, allegedly the biggest in Latin America, was preeminent. The sleepy, neighborly Santa Cruz del Norte that he yearned for no longer existed.

Upon hearing that the wandering outsider who had been born there was now living in Miami, a few newcomers eyed him distrustfully. He returned their stares. What were they doing in his hometown? Their shoptalk dwelt on turbines, generators, boilers, steam, megawatts, tons of oil, cubic meters of gas, and qualities of paper, whereas native Santacruzians talked sugarcane, sugar, molasses, rum, and fish. A little cigar-rolling and tourism had been added to the local economy of late. Elliot sensed that although the recently arrived and the old-timers were trying to adjust to circumstances, underlying mistrust survived. They would intermix, like everywhere else in the history of mankind, for sexual reasons. Electric-oil-paper boys and girls would be marrying sugar-and-rum girls and boys, begetting sugelectoilrum boys and girls.

After delighting in the forgotten pleasure of napping in a hammock, Elliot spent Thursday afternoon at the dollar store at Fourth and Thirteenth buying presents in which sizes were not a requirement. Three oscillating fans, a dozen queen-size sheets, a dozen pillowcases, a dozen mosquito nets, six air-pressure kerosene lamps, a dozen flashlights, two dozen batteries, three blenders, six pressure cookers, assorted cutlery, nine bottles of perfume, fifteen bottles of nail polish, ten brushes, ten combs, almost a pound of hairpins, five dozen disposable razors, six cartons of cigarettes, two boxes of cigars, a dozen bottles of rum, six pair of sunglasses, and two dozen handkerchiefs for a total of $1,257.85. After helping him load everything in the trunk and backseat of the rental, the store manager said the luscious brunette at the perfumes counter had asked him to please tell the client she'd be delighted to have dinner with him. Steil just clicked his tongue, shook his head sadly, and turned the key in the ignition.

That evening, as he watched his wide-eyed aunts, his uncle, and other family members opening boxes and gasping in surprise, shaking their heads in dismay, and deploring that Elito had spent so much money, Elliot reflected that the innocence, candor, generosity, and honesty displayed by people born and raised in rural Cuba had to be perplexing for those who live where scheming, distrust, and suspicion are essential to survival and success. If in his childhood part of their kindness had rubbed off on him, only traces remained.

Twenty-five people dined on fried chunks of pork, the combination of rice and black beans known to Cubans as Moors and Christians, fried green plantains, and lettuce-and-tomato salad. Dessert consisted of boiled and sweetened halves of guava. After coffee, rum began to flow.

Politics briefly became the topic for the first and only time when a blackout wet-blanketed what over the course of time had turned into a boisterous party. A collective moan was heard before everyone, kids included, ranted about the government, the system, and the Chief. Elliot just smiled in the dark. Two of his cousins explained to him that when one of the Chief's interminable speeches was being broadcast, at no time was the power cut. Plants postponed scheduled maintenance, the oil reserve was tapped, breakdowns were fixed in a jiffy. As others slid the new batteries into the new flashlights, Elliot told his cousins that it had always been the same, dating from the time when he was a teenager: speech, power; no speech, it was anybody's guess. The air-pressure kerosene lamps could not be lighted because there was no kerosene at Aunt Carmina's, so the rest of the dinner party took place by romantic candlelight, with many sitting on the floor. When in the dead of night, laden with presents, Aunt Tatica and Uncle Eusebio doddered out for their homes accompanied by nine of Elliot's slightly pickled cousins, seven sleepy children of the cousins, and three dogs wagging their tails, flashlights were made unnecessary by the trillion stars and the full moon that softly illuminated the packed-earth trail, the surrounding fruit trees, and the tall royal palms. Seldom had Elliot slept sounder.

On Friday morning, the power was restored around 8:00 A.M. As their nephew packed his things, Aunt Tatica and Uncle Eusebio returned to Carmina's to say their final good-byes. Elliot gave five hundred dollars to each and got into the car without looking back, because to see them cry unashamedly was more than he could endure. Havana-bound, a mile or so after leaving town, he took a moment to ease the rental along the shoulder of the freeway, turn off the engine, and get off. His gaze scanned the surrounds. Straight ahead, the new apartment blocks hid from view most of Santa Cruz. To the left, tame bluish waves lapped soundlessly against the rocky coastline, swirled around its crevices, and retreated. Gulls circled overhead. On the horizon, a merchant ship sailed east. To the right, beyond the low green hills, the refinery's two chimneys spewed a whitish smoke that looked virginal compared to what the power plant was vomiting. Nodding a good-bye, two tears rolled down Elliot's cheeks. Then he dried his eyes, blew his nose, took a deep breath of seabreeze, slipped back into his sonofabitch personality, and drove along.

. . .

That evening, as he watched Victoria and Pardo ease themselves into the two wood-and-vinyl armchairs by the picture window, Elliot was considering that not in the least did the bad guys seem bad. If something besides unremarkable, they looked the parts they were playing: bureaucrats trying to save their asses. He mulled that, on a ten-point scale, the nine-point bad guys seem deserving of trust, esteem, and respect; the ten-point bad guys come across as the nicest individuals on earth. It occurred to him that, for almost a century, Hollywood had succeeded in making people believe the opposite and had reaped a rich harvest from such disinformation.

Hands were shaken, smiles flashed, pleasantries exchanged. Victoria was better dressed in a plain, nut-colored pantsuit, a white blouse, brown medium-heeled shoes, and a red purse. Her husband wore a chocolate-colored sports jacket over a white shirt, khaki trousers, and brown loafers. Two tired business executives after a grueling day at the office. Sure, they would have a beer, if it wasn't too much trouble.

"You won't have one?" Pardo asked when Elliot, having served them, poured half a can of Seven-Up in his glass.

"I don't drink alcohol," he said while easing himself onto the edge of his mattress.

"Oh."

Elliot thought he saw a glint of respect in the woman's eyes, as if she had just reevaluated her opponent. Pardo emptied his glass by swallowing eagerly, just a man quenching his thirst with something cold, indifferent to what it was. Victoria only took two sips and ran the tip of her tongue over her lips. Both left their glasses atop the coffee table separating the armchairs at the same time.

"First of all, Mr. Steil," Pardo began, pocketing the handkerchief with which he had dabbed at his lips, "the president of the corporation has asked me to convey his gratitude. We know you are doing it for Cuba, but as you rightly pointed out, you will be helping him, too, and both of us. It's one of those situations in which the personal side can't be separated from the business side and, whatever the final outcome, we shall always remember and value your collaboration. He sends you this as a token of his appreciation."

Pardo extracted from the side pocket of his jacket a small, gift-wrapped package that he passed on to the surprised Elliot. After unwrapping it, he opened a box that he suspected contained a wristwatch. A pure silver Meisterstück Solitaire Mont Blanc fountain pen lay in the box's velvet-lined interior. Examining it, he thought it a well-considered gift. Top quality, expensive, very appropriate for impressing customers when signing contracts. A motivational gift, not payment for services rendered.

Elliot could not know he was overestimating his opponents. In 1994, a Madrid tour operator had presented the pen to Pardo, to express his gratitude for having had his computer upgraded and his programs updated for free. Considering it too princely for his work environment, Pardo had never used it and remembered it when thinking of a gift that would please Steil.

"Well, tell Mr.—what's his name?"

"Everardo Bencomo."

"Okay, tell Mr. Bencomo thanks. But maybe he has acted hastily, maybe Mrs. Scheindlin won't find the money, or will refuse to give it back."

"I said, 'Whatever the outcome,' we would be grateful to you, Mr. Steil."

"Elliot," said Steil, pretending that the gift had wheedled him into increased friendliness.

Victoria drew out an inhaler from her purse, uncapped it, shook it, put it in her mouth. Steil forced himself to turn his gaze away from her and locked it on Pardo. She pumped the inhaler twice, recapped it, and dropped it into the purse.

"Okay. Elliot then. Let's agree on how to stay in touch," Pardo proposed.

"I don't see any problem with that," Elliot said. "Give me your phone number. I'll call you."

Pardo raised his eyebrows and, gazing at the carpet, scratched his cheek. His expression implied there *was* a problem with that. "First time we talked," Pardo began, "you made very clear that you'd cooperate provided we didn't ask you to do something that would jeopardize your freedom or your job. We promised we wouldn't and we want to keep our word."

"So?"

"Go on, Berta."

Victoria took what tried to be a deep breath and crossed her legs. "Have you heard about the patriots sentenced to long prison terms by a federal court in Miami?"

"Are you kidding?" Elliot, with a smile. "Who hasn't?"

"Well, the problem is that, a few weeks after the patriots were arrested, our government warned ministries and state-run firms, and foreign companies in Cuba, too, to be careful when making or receiving calls to or from the United States. New gizmos that ETECSA, the Cuban phone company, had installed showed that many phone calls between Cuba and the United States, in particular between Havana and Miami, were being tape recorded. It's what we were told, but you don't have to be an expert in espionage to figure that an American agency, the FBI or the CIA, is tapping lines, bugging phones, or doing whatever has to be done to falsely accuse other patriots or friends of our Revolution of spying for Cuba."

"I see," Elliot said, really seeing what would come next. But something was nagging at him. The woman's talk, sprinkled with slogans, platitudes, and catchphrases, did not fit in with her. She seemed too intelligent and cultured to express herself like the flesh-and-bones robots preferred and recruited by tyrants.

"Therefore," Pardo, retaking the lead, "for your protection we should agree on a simple code so you can tell us what you found out without endangering your future in any way."

"Excellent."

"So, here's what we suggest. First, don't call from your home or office. Buy a phone card and call us from a pay phone that's far from your home or place of work. Call us after sundown. Darkness makes it more unlikely that a friend or relative sees you and wonders who you are calling. Okay?"

"Okay."

"Don't mention names. Neither Berta's, nor mine, nor Ms. Scheindlin, nor yours. You'll be talking to me or to Berta, so you just address us as 'chico' or 'chica' or 'buddy' or 'cousin.' If you need to refer to Mrs. Scheindlin, call her *Señora*. It's the only name in code you have to remember: Mrs. Scheindlin is the *Señora*."

"The *Señora*, okay," Elliot, in acquiescence, easing into it. "Now, I've been mulling over your problem these last few days, trying to sort out how to go about it. As far as I can see, there are two possibilities: Either Mrs. Scheindlin knows or can find out where the cash is, or she doesn't and can't. If she doesn't know and can't find out, it's over; as you say, end of story. If she does know or manages to find out where the dough is, three things are bound to happen, of which two could be against you. She may deny knowing where it is because she doesn't want to give it back; in that case, it's end of story, too. The same thing happens if she tells me she knows where the money is but refuses to give it back because she thinks it's not yours, or for any other reason. Therefore, I would be reporting something positive only if she has the money and is willing to return it to you. Am I right?"

"You are right, Elliot," Victoria and Pardo said in unison.

"So, how should I go about it?"

"We think," Victoria, taking the floor and pushing up her slipping glasses, "the call gets complicated only if she has the money and is willing to give it back. To give us bad news you just have to say that Uncle Gustavo passed away—or any other name, we don't have to agree on a name in particular. Then we exchange condolences, say he was such a nice man, and hang up. Next day Mr. Bencomo, Mr. Capdevila, and myself inform the government that we've lost one hundred thousand dollars and then go home, pack suitcases for the things we'll need in jail, and kiss our children good-bye."

Uncomfortable looks and forced smiles were exchanged.

"But in case she finds the money and is willing to give it back," Victoria proceeded, "we ought to agree when, how, and where."

"It's what I figured," Elliot said, watching his step, fully alert.

"In that case you would say that Uncle Gustavo has fully recovered and now wants to spend a week in Key West, from day A to day B in so-and-so month. Mr. Capdevila, or I, whoever is on our end, will say it's great news—and we'll mean it, too; probably never before or after in our lives will we be more relieved. Then we'll predict that the son of a gun will live to a hundred, bla, bla, bla, and you'll tell us the name of the Key West hotel where, on the last day you mentioned, someone will pick up the money for us, at 11:00 A.M., in the lobby."

As they had anticipated, Elliot frowned before making the right question. "And who will take the money to Key West and give it to this representative of yours? Mrs. Scheindlin?"

Victoria shot a sideways glance to Pardo, who cleared his throat, as if realizing he should not take a stab at it but had been ordered to.

"I assumed you would be willing to . . ." probingly.

"Your assumption is 100 percent wrong, Mr. Capdevila," the muscles at the base of his jaw bulging.

Elliot had made his retort without thinking, peeved to discover that they wanted to make him their messenger boy, but his reluctance was what Victoria and Pardo expected, thus furnishing further confirmation that Elliot Steil was on the level. Had he agreed to take the money to Key West, they would have grown suspicious. Maybe he would suggest the obvious next. A little more prodding was necessary and the script said those lines were to be delivered by the spurious XEMIC vice president.

"Carlos, please," Pardo said, to mollify Elliot. "Of course, I understand. How stupid of me. But perhaps you have a friend who, for a small fee, would agree to do it?"

Tony Soto came to Elliot's mind. Tony was a cop; he had been approached by the FBI to make the introduction. The way things were going, perhaps Hart would want to involve him in the follow-through. But not knowing if his friend would approve, Elliot decided against mentioning him.

"Listen, I know many honest people, but transporting a hundred thousand in cash is dangerous. What happens if the guy is robbed? Or if he steals the money and says he was robbed? Whoever is willing to pick up the cash for you could pick it up at Mrs. Scheindlin's home in Miami Beach, then take it to Key West. Isn't that possible?"

A huge wave of self-complacency surged in Pardo and Victoria. They had planned it that way and painstakingly rehearsed it, word by word, to prompt Steil to suggest the obvious. The outcome had been as expected. Were they good or were they good? But her husband appeared to be flummoxed, Victoria noticed, as though that notion had not crossed his mind before. Her *macho* had a remarkable thespian talent.

"Well, yes, I suppose so," Pardo said. "Okay, then you tell us exactly the same thing, that Uncle Gustavo got well, that he will be in Key West between day A and day B in so-and-so month, and our man will go to Ms. Scheindlin's the last day at 11:00 A.M. How does that sound?"

"Sounds better to me. I don't know if she would agree to seeing your man at her place."

"If she agrees to give it back," Victoria observed, "why wouldn't she do it at her home? That way she doesn't have to move around with a briefcase full of cash."

Elliot nodded in agreement. "I guess you're right."

"What's her address?" Pardo asked as he extracted a notebook and ballpoint from his shirt pocket.

Steil dictated Maria Scheindlin's address and immediately added: "Now Carlos, Berta, I want it to be clearly understood that your emissary or representative or whatever you call it, will approach this woman only if she has the money and is willing to give it back. Under no circumstance will you, or anyone from XEMIC, the Cuban government, or the Miami Cubans that sympathize with this government, contact her if I report that Uncle Gustavo has died, okay?"

"Okay," husband and wife said simultaneously, repressing their desire to whoop and clap.

"Good. Now tell me your phone number," wanting to wrap it up.

"Certainly. You know you have to punch 537 first, then 832-4969."

Steil pulled his wallet out, extracting the phony business cards they had given to him last Sunday. "Loan me your ballpoint," he said.

"I'm going to ask you," Pardo said as he presented the pen to Elliot, "to rip up those cards now."

"Why?" Steil asked while reaching for the ballpoint, almost in the same instant that the reason for the strange request came to him.

"You are returning to Miami on Sunday. I know it's very unlikely, but suppose you are searched at the airport. Those cards say we are with XEMIC, a Cuban corporation . . ."

"Enough," Elliot said. "I understand."

He read the name on a card and gave it to Victoria, then surrendered the other to Pardo. On one of his business cards he jotted their phone number.

"Anything else?" he asked.

Pardo uncoiled himself from the seat. Victoria and Elliot imitated him.

"I can't find the words that would properly express . . ." Pardo began.

"Hold it, Carlos," Steil said, raising his hand. "You've very properly expressed your gratitude already. We'll have to see how things pan out. But the possibility that you recover that money seems very small to me."

"I know, but you are our only hope. Remember that you have three new friends in Cuba. Mr. Bencomo, Ms. Berta, and myself."

"Who won't be of any use to you in jail," Berta said in jest. This time the smiles were real.

"Thanks again for the pen."

Hands were shaken and Elliot escorted them to the door, opened it, closed it after they left. He folded down his hypocritical smile and hissed, *"Hijos de puta."*

...

On Saturday, after verifying that Old Havana's skid row remained in the same sorry state, Elliot bought presents in tourist shops. Next he visited two places he regretted not ever having been to: the old Presidential Palace, built in the twenties and decorated by Tiffany, and the Cuban gallery at the Museum of Fine Arts. Despite his orthopedic shoes, the many hours of walking around and standing made his feet hurt. He returned to the hotel after sunset. The lobby was teeming with a slew of young, good-looking women in tight-fitting clothes. A few let him know they were available by making eyes and smiling at him. A scalper tried to sell him a ticket for the evening's baseball game. He had supper in his room, packed, and went to bed early.

Victoria and Pardo made love twice on Saturday: after sunrise, before she left for the General Directorate, and before falling asleep close to 1:00 A.M. Victoria closed her eyes wishing she could find out how many men made love to their wives two times the same day after eleven years of marriage. Or was it that danger is the greatest aphrodisiac? She signed off before finding the answers.

On Sunday, Elliot's plane departed at 10:52 A.M. and landed in Miami forty-three minutes later.

And a few minutes before midday on Sunday, in full regalia, Victoria Valiente swaggered into the smoke-filled office of Gen. Edmundo Lastra and, standing at attention in front of his desk, saluted and said, "Permission to speak, Comrade Gabriel."

Lastra lifted his eyes from a file that contained an update of the orbits of American spy satellites over Cuba. It had been obtained from public sources at the request of Army Intelligence. The general felt sure that important hardware was going to be moved when no satellite was passing overhead. Which hardware he had not a clue. Compartmentalization.

Too surprised to return the salute, Lastra realized that something was wrong, and with the circumspection and self-control with which he always faced crises, he rested the Lancero, which he had lit minutes earlier, in a glass ashtray. The courtesy shown to head honchos in the General Directorate of Intelligence was quite relaxed and excluded military manners. Desk and case officers wore mufti most of the time. Full-dress uniforms and ribbons were for the reviewing stand in anniversaries, promotions, and funerals. It was a Sunday. Had someone died? Lastra stared at the most intelligent of his "intelligents." The only other time he had seen Micaela wearing her five-pointed gold star had been five months ago, that early morning when the Chief had pinned it on the jacket of the full-dress uniform she now had on.

"Hey, what's the matter?" Lastra asked, half smiling in puzzlement, showing cigar-stained teeth.

"Comrade Gabriel. I suspect that my husband, retired major Manuel Pardo, is a thief and has betrayed the Revolution."

PART TWO

Five

Elliot Steil was dashing along a concourse, dragging his roll-on behind him, when from a side door Brent Hart waved for him to come in. Frowning, Steil approached him and crossed the threshold into a maintenance corridor with pipes painted in different colors exposed along the ceiling. Cleaning materials and aluminum portable stairs had been left by a wall.

"Hart, for God's sake, I just landed. I want to go home, unpack, see the woman. We'll meet after lunch. Is three o'clock okay with you?"

"You were approached?"

"I was."

"We need to talk now. Don't get cagey on me, Steil. This is a serious matter. Give me an hour."

"An hour?"

"Plus maybe two or three more tomorrow."

"Hey, I gotta work tomorrow, you know?"

"Steil, don't make things more difficult than they are, please. Is the term debriefing familiar to you?"

"I've read a few spy novels."

"Then you know I have to see you before anyone else does. C'mon. Just an hour. I promise."

Hart guided Steil through the maintenance corridor, up one flight of stairs, then out to a public hallway that led to the office in which they had met a week earlier. The instant Hart closed the door, Steil asked him if he could use the phone to call Fidelia.

"Sure. Tell her you'll be late 'cause your baggage is missing."

He tapped her cell phone number.

"Hello?"

"Hi, honey."

"Elliot, where are you?"

"At the airport. Where are you?"

"At the airport, waiting for you."

Elliot mouthed "She's here" to Hart. The agent shrugged his shoulders.

"Listen. I figured you'd come. It's why I called. I may be delayed. My baggage is missing. Why don't you go home and wait for me?"

"No, I'll wait here."

"Okay, I hope this doesn't take too long. Then I have to get through customs. You know how it is, coming from a country that belongs to the Axis of Evil," he said, slyly smiling and winking at Hart, whose involuntary frown of annoyance showed that he found the sarcasm not in the least amusing, and that he was fluent in Spanish.

"No problem, I'll wait. I've missed you."

"I've missed you too. Take care."

"Where are you calling from?"

"Pay phone."

"In the baggage claim area?"

For several years now, Steil had been considering whether falling in love and having to deal with smart women is a blessing or a curse. He had not been able to make up his mind. "Yes, there's one, for staff. A Cuban who works here let me use it, as a favor."

"Okay. Love you."

"Love you, too. Bye-bye."

Steil gave Hart a forty-six-minute overview of the two meetings held in Room 2124 of the Habana Libre. In an adjoining room, wearing headphones and watching five of a twenty-screen bank of monitors, Paul McLellan, who in fact worked for the Office of the National Counterintelligence Executive, not the Treasury, and Nathan Smith, the bureau's chief of counterintelligence at the South Florida field office, hung on Steil's every word. The Cuban provided physical descriptions of Capdevila and Berta, dictated the Havana phone number he had been given, and said he suspected a swindle. The FBI man did not interrupt once. The copious notes he took prevented Steil from realizing that they were being videotaped, but as the story progressed, Hart's countenance changed from moderate curiosity to visible interest to well-guarded excitement. He seemed mildly surprised when Elliot mentioned Berta's comment regarding phone calls between Miami and Havana.

". . . then Capdevila said it had been a pleasure, Berta gave me a nod, and they left" was how Elliot finished his report.

Hart retracted his ballpoint with a click, put it in his shirt pocket, breathed deeply, arranged himself in his seat, and grinned fleetingly. "You've done a great job, Steil. Thanks. The bureau really appreciates your collaboration."

Elliot wondered if the man was getting even for his Axis-of-Evil leg-pulling. "Collaboration, Hart?"

"Involvement is better. I stand corrected. Berta's last name doesn't come to mind yet?"

"No. It'll come."

"I wasn't aware that IMLATINEX is the parent company of this Panamanian trading company . . ." Hart flipped the pages of his notebook as Steil shook his head, "Trans-Caribbean Trading, that's been selling things to . . ." again the FBI man took a peek at his notes, "XEMIC."

"To my knowledge, IMLATINEX is not the parent of Trans-Caribbean. They just buy from us. I don't know who their clients are."

"We'll look into it. Okay. Now we have to agree on what you'll tell Mrs. Scheindlin and consider how she may react to the news. Maybe Scheindlin bought medicines for Cuba, maybe he . . ."

"No, Hart. Take my word for it. Had he done that, I would've known it. These people made that up to give credibility to their cock-and-bull, and a humanitarian touch, too."

"But Scheindlin frequently traveled alone. He could have met them abroad, done things for them you wouldn't have known about."

"He did travel alone, but can you see him transporting a hundred Gs in cash? A businessman who knows the law? Give me a break."

"He could've rented safe-deposit boxes abroad. Or deposited the cash in a bank. Who knows? But let's not speculate, we'll see. Will you call the widow tomorrow?"

"Of course. She's my boss. Besides, she asked me to buy her rum, cigars, and CDs."

"And you did?"

"Sure."

"Fine. Then try to give it to her on Tuesday. Preferably in the evening. We need to meet tomorrow to agree on what you'll say to her."

"What's to agree? I just have to deliver a message."

"That's right. But we've got to have a good handle on any of the questions she may pose to you, consider alternatives, like what to do if she asks you to call these two and tell them that the uncle died, or that he's alive and kicking. This real or imaginary cash is McLellan's concern; he may want to hear everything straight from you. So, would it be possible for you to meet us tomorrow, say at 8:00 P.M.?"

"Do I have an alternative?"

Hart lay back against the seat and seriously eyed Elliot. "No, Steil, you don't. But let me tell you something. I admit that your . . . involvement in this was . . . how should I put it . . ."

Elliot wondered why the man was choosing his words so carefully. Hart was thinking that, if the videotape became an exhibit in court, he didn't want the jury to learn that his informer had been coerced into cooperating.

". . . at our insistence" was the best Hart could come up with.

"Your insistence?"

"Call it as you wish. Nevertheless, your cooperation is vital to a federal investigation, and we'll have to meet frequently to discuss things. We can do it in a friendly way or in a hostile way. Good rapport is preferable. So, don't cop an attitude on me, okay? You don't like doing this; I can understand that. I don't like—well, never mind. I would be very grateful if tomorrow at twenty hundred hours you would go to this house . . ."

Hart paused for a few moments to pull the ballpoint out, scribble an address on his spiral notepad, rip the page off, and give it to Elliot. After glancing at it, the Cuban folded it, then slipped it into a patch pocket of his sports jacket. Hart returned the ballpoint to his shirt pocket.

"Now, Steil, let's talk confidentiality."

"How exciting."

Taxed by the sarcasm, Hart lifted his gaze to the ceiling and took a deep breath.

"You have a reputation for being discreet and reserved; it's a trait we appreciate," he began as he locked eyes with Elliot. "But we are not asking you to be reserved or discreet. We are asking you to seal your lips, period. You are now in possession of information not to be shared with anyone, not your lady friend, not Tony Soto, anyone. What you just did, folding that note and putting it in your pocket, is a mistake. Suppose your lady friend finds it and gets curious. Who lives there? she may ask herself. Suppose she suspects there's another woman in your life and tries to . . ."

"You've made your point, Hart. Leave her out of this."

"That's exactly what I want, to leave her out of this," the agent snorted. "And leave Jenny Scheindlin, Sam Plotzher, and all the other people you know out of this, too. If you hadn't forgotten Berta's last name, I would've asked you to commit that address to memory and destroy the note. But seeing that your memory is bound to fail you, I'm asking you to put that paper someplace where no one can read it, until tomorrow evening, and later, once you leave the house, to destroy it."

"Okay," Elliot said begrudgingly, putting the paper in his wallet.

"Concerning this case, you make reports to me, to agent McLellan, or to any other federal agent that McLellan or myself bring to a meeting. You share your suspicions, doubts, and worries with me, with agent McLellan, or with any other federal agent present. We think you can keep a secret. So, why am I telling you this? I'm telling you this because, as far as we can ascertain, you've never before been involved in undercover work, you are not prepared for it, so we have to teach you a few basic rules and you have to pay attention and follow instructions. You must clearly understand that an indiscretion or a mistake on your part could jeopardize a very important case on which the bureau has been working for some time. Have I made myself clear?"

"Very much so, Agent Hart," Steil said testily.

"We've told police officer Soto he's not to ask you questions regarding what you're doing for us. He promised he wouldn't. Neither are you authorized to reveal your personal views on this to Mrs. Scheindlin. Only if she asks what you think, you tell her. She asks if you think it's a swindle, you say yes. She doesn't ask, keep your opinion to yourself. She's free to act however she judges best. She asks you to refer what you were told in Cuba to her daughter, Sam Plotzher, and her lawyer, we have no objection. She pays for a full-page ad in the *Miami Herald* announcing that XEMIC is trying to extort money from her, we won't interfere. She asks you to keep your mouth shut, don't tell a word to anyone, you are only too happy to oblige. Understood?"

"Understood."

"Okay, we'll talk further about this tomorrow evening. Maybe you think I'm bullshitting you, but I honestly appreciate your help."

"Yeah. May I leave now?"

"You may. Agriculture inspectors will ask you whether you're bringing in agricultural produce. Did you?"

"No."

"You bring cigars?"

"A box of Cohibas."

"Tell the inspector. He'll let you through. Then you take the nothing-to-declare line. C'mon, I'll show you how to get there."

...

The Cuban minister of the interior in 2002, the first individual to be awarded the Hero of the Republic of Cuba medal and the second promoted to lieutenant general in the Cuban army, was unquestionably a courageous man who had lived a hectic life. He was eighteen by the time he joined the rebels in the mountains of eastern Cuba in 1957. In the sixties he fought anticommunist guerrillas ("bandits" in partyspeak) in the highlands of the central part of the island. In the seventies and eighties, following to a tee the Chief's strategy, he had led Cuban soldiers to victory in battles waged on African soil. The number of men he had seen die grisly deaths was anybody's guess; his nice dreams would have been considered odd by many people, let alone his nightmares in which rivers of blood flowed, a slew of the men he had executed chased him, and poisonous African serpents bit his arms and legs.

This sad man inured to the cesspool of war had been appointed minister of the interior in June 1989 for five reasons. First, his predecessor was to be taken into custody under corruption charges. Second, the Chief had realized that new and irreversible geopolitical realities would make interfering in the internal affairs of other countries extremely risky; stationing troops abroad would be suicidal. Third, at no time had the comrade questioned or disobeyed a decision made by the Chief or by his brother. Fourth, he publicly prided himself on revering both men. Last, he was a member of the Politburo and vice president of the State Council.

Having awoken at noon on Sunday, April 21, 2002, once the assistant on duty reported that nothing compelling demanded his presence at the ministry, following a hearty brunch, and knowing that the Commander was sleeping, the minister of the interior sat down to relax and have a few. He knew the routine: The Chief would be getting up around five or six, eat a light supper, and head for the Palace, where he'd spend the night working. Therefore, the minister intended to take a shower around sixteen hundred hours, sip a cup of strong coffee, and be ready to report to the Chief's office with a clear head should his presence be required. He just had a mild buzz on when, at 2:12 P.M., General Lastra called and asked for an urgent meeting. Having been told that Victoria Valiente, one of the darlings of the Commander, had something to report, the minister agreed to be in his office at 3:00 P.M. He ordered a servant to brew him a strong demitasse of coffee. If there was bad news, he wanted to be the first to know.

He didn't pursue his duties with such zeal because he was overly committed to the cause of the poor and hungry of the world. After so many years of exerting authority and power, enjoying privileges, and rubbing shoulders with the high and mighty, to him the cause of the dispossessed had come to be sloganeering intoned to the ignorant masses. The reason for his wanting to be the first to learn bad news was that the comrade minister had appointed himself second protector of the Chief's health. The Chief's brother was immovable in his position of first protector.

In April 1996 the minister of the interior had sent for the man in charge of Patient One's medical team and asked him what he could do to keep the Commander in perfect health. The doctor explained that, at seventy, that was impossible. Sooner or later cancer develops, or a stroke or heart attack takes place, or Alzheimer's sets in. Most old people, however, are retired or semiretired, thus being partially insulated from the stress and unpleasant realities of daily life, the MD added rather didactically. But a seventy-year-old man at the helm of a nation endures a hundred times more stress than most people. When such an individual, to make matters worse, insists on being informed about all things that happen, important or unimportant, good or bad, of a political, economic, social, or military nature, his chances of suffering a myocardial or cerebral infarction increase exponentially.

Thereby, the doctor recommended limiting as much as possible the amount of bad news reaching Patient Number One. He further advised that, when giving awful news was inevitable, it would be prudent to make sure this was done after he had taken one of the three hypotensive pills he took daily, and to have the mobile medical unit on duty ready (two intensive care specialists, four nurses, two ambulances, four drivers, and six paramedics) in case something happened. The patient had to follow a strict diet as well. And it would be formidable if the Chief could be persuaded to speak less. The doctor feared that one of these days, something malignant would develop in the Chief's larynx or vocal cords. Human organs were not meant to be overworked so savagely for so many years. The minister did not argue with the head of the team. It was easy to write prescriptions and make recommendations; convincing the patient that he had to behave was not.

Almost six years had gone by and things were inescapably worse. The Chief misplaced documents, accused aides of tampering with his things, lost track of what he was saying. His lifelong custom of blaming others for his mistakes had taken on massive proportions. His famous memory was slipping. In June 2001 he had had a ten-minute blackout while making a speech in a town close to Havana. Cuban TV was broadcasting the rally, CNN got the tape, and the whole world saw him collapse. His hypertension was serious; a stroke much dreaded by his confederates. So, the minister had decided that concerning Interior's fields of activity: intelligence, counterintelligence, police, the penal system, and emigration, he would decide, in consultation with the Commander's brother, which bad news inevitably had to reach the Chief and which they would keep under wraps.

This serves to explain why, as Col. Victoria Valiente finished relating her suspicions, the minister of the interior felt relieved. He uncoiled himself from the seat and began pacing his office, hands behind his back, eyes on the floor. Victoria and her boss kept a respectful silence. General Lastra had persuaded her to change into her olive green uniform: short-sleeved jacket lacking name tag, trousers, and black pump shoes. At each point of the jacket's open collar, three white stars. Lastra opined that the full dress uniform, the gold star, and the ribbons were overkill.

Maybe he had been good-looking in his twenties, Victoria judged as she watched the minister go back and forth. Not a spunk, though. He was five-feet-six or seven at most, with regular features, but lacked the sort of fascinating personality that makes women excuse physical mediocrity. Now he was just a flabby, balding old man thick around the middle and with age spots on his forearms and hands. Didn't look like a hard-on at all, certainly didn't act like one. She tried to picture him in his undies: skinny white legs, the waistline of his boxer shorts below his potbelly.

Yet he wielded enormous power. In a country where the media deifies only the occupants of slots One and Two, and Two is the head of the armed forces, many believed that whoever calls the shots in the arcane areas of national security, police, and prisons is indisputably Number Three, who is slated to be the next Number Two. Such a promising future turned him into a George Clooney for many young and beautiful female officers who Victoria had seen making eyes at him during anniversaries, festivities, and political rallies.

As Victoria considered all this, the minister was pondering if what he had just learned was bad news. Victoria had seen what she thought was a bank statement blink on the screen of her laptop; she had found a few thousand dollars hidden in a closet that she felt certain her husband could not account for; the guy (what was his name? Calvo? No, Pardo) criticized the Chief with increasing and worrying frequency, or so she said.

The minister acknowledged that the man had most certainly been in the right place—XEMIC—at the right time—from 1991 to 1999—in the perfect position—network administrator. But he needed evidence in order to act. Had Victoria put two and two together and made five? Maybe her husband had asked her for a divorce, and she wanted to frame him and send him to jail. After all, the brilliant psychologist didn't exactly make men turn their heads; he would not blame Pardo had he fallen for a better-looking woman. The minister had seen people do worse things out of jealousy. He remembered that many years ago, in the province of Camagüey, a man was sentenced to death for engaging in counterrevolutionary activities. His wife and her lover had framed him, planting C-3 and detonators in his closet. Fortunately, the woman lost her nerve six hours before the scheduled execution time and confessed everything. Her lover had been executed; she was sentenced to twenty years. Perhaps other innocent men had not been so lucky.

But even if Victoria's suspicions turned out to be right, had Pardo been the lone culprit or just an accomplice in the theft the Chief knew nothing about, he saw no reason to inform him now. If Victoria was right on the button, once the case had been solved the Chief would be informed that her loyalty had reached the point of turning in her husband. That would make the Commander happy! Glowering, he would ask what crime Victoria's husband had committed and then he would learn that Pardo had stolen, or helped others steal, $2.7 million. Yes, that was the way to do it, after the case had been solved. The minister turned to face Victoria.

"Well, Comrade Colonel, what do you propose we do?"

It was precisely what Victoria had hoped for; everything hinged on the minister asking that question. She had seen him articulate the same request several times in the past and had heard many stories in which the man, after learning about a problem, asked subordinates if they had any suggestions. The opposite of the Chief, who always knew the best course of action. She turned her gaze to the floor as though considering her answer, then looked the minister in the eye.

"Comrade Lieutenant General: I have carefully reflected on this. I place the interests of the homeland, the party, and the Commander in Chief above everything else. My personal feelings are secondary, but I would like to clarify one thing. I loved my husband very much; I thought my feelings for him would never decrease. But when I found that cash and remembered that Pardo had been discharged from XEMIC because over two million dollars were *electronically* stolen, that at the time he was the corporation's network administrator, and that he had traveled abroad on many occasions and could have retrieved the money, or deposited it in a bank, or invested it, I felt sure he had stolen that money or helped others steal it. And in an instant something crumbled inside me: my love for him. I can't love a thief, but above all I can't love a man who betrayed the confidence that the Revolution placed in him."

Moments of respectful silence followed as Victoria bowed her head, removed her glasses, took a tiny handkerchief to her eyes, then dried her nostrils, put on the glasses, pocketed the handkerchief.

"I respectfully suggest investigating if my husband acted alone or has accomplices," she went on, "whether or not it's possible to recover the money before arresting him, or them. I feel sure he hasn't spent his share, or the whole amount, depending on whether he acted alone or not. Well, maybe he has squandered ten, twenty, or thirty thousand, but I believe the remainder is stored somewhere, in a foreign bank possibly. He traveled extensively. I told you I saw a statement. My husband acted very nervous over my seeing what was on the screen and clicked on Exit immediately. I wasn't trying to sneak up on him. I was bringing him a cup of coffee . . ."

"Yes, comrade, you already explained that. Tell me what you advise to try to recover the money," the minister, throwing a sidelong glance at General Lastra.

"I'm sorry. I'm so nervous and ashamed. Forgive me, Comrade Lieutenant General."

"You are forgiven. Go on, please."

"My advice is this. I confront my husband with the cash he has at home, tell him that I saw the bank statement on the laptop's screen, and demand that he come clean with me. I tell him that I am sick and tired of the Revolution and the Commander in Chief, that I kept this from him thinking there was no way out. Then I say I suspect he stole the XEMIC money. I ask him if he acted alone or if he got a cut, ask him where he has his share. If he admits he stole the money, I compliment him, term it the cleverest thing he could have done. If he has it abroad, then I tell him we should flee to Mexico, the Dominican Republic, Jamaica, or any other country from which he can access his bank account, or we can travel to where the loot is stashed. Once we get our hands on it, we will move to some faraway country, Australia or India or some other place, and begin a new life."

Victoria fell silent. The minister took his eyes away from her and again paced the room. General Lastra bit the end of a Lancero and lit it. After a little over a minute, the minister came to a halt in front of Victoria.

"Then what?"

"Then, Comrade Lieutenant General, it depends on what he admits and denies. He can't say the cash is not his. No relatives, friends, or colleagues of ours have set foot in the new apartment. How will he react? What will he say? I have no clue. Without wishing to sound conceited, I believe he hasn't defected because he is very much in love with me, albeit not enough to live an honest life. I will try to corner him. I don't think he'll lie to me. But I can't predict what he will say. However . . ."

She opened a dubious pause.

"What?"

"I realize that, in this case, there's no reason to trust me just because I've been for some years in Intelligence. Should I be taken at my word? You may be wondering. Has my husband been playing the field and I want to take revenge? Well, so you can have irrefutable evidence of this face-to-face that I'm suggesting, I ask you to consider installing mikes at my home, maybe even one of those tiny TV cameras Counterintelligence has, and tape my husband's reaction to what I'll say to him."

It looked as though Victoria had nothing more to recommend, and the minister returned to his executive swivel chair, snuggled down in it, reclined, and stared at the ceiling. Despite so many disappointments along so many years, humankind never ceased to amaze him. Victoria's willingness to film the whole thing so others could watch what went on dissipated his suspicion that she was framing Pardo. It also made plain as day that this Heroine of the Republic was a bitch. And she felt sure the man loved her very much! He could not imagine what she would do were she to think that Pardo hated her. However, he had learned many years ago that personal feelings should not be allowed to interfere with the job at hand. It might be another interesting video to watch.

The minister also considered that this was one of the handful of women in Cuba who could lift a handset, punch a number, and ask to be granted a private audience with the Commander, feeling sure that it would be conceded. He doubted that she would dare go over his head, but with premenopausal women, he never felt sure. Those flashes and mood swings! If he overruled her proposal, might she complain to the Chief that the minister of the interior had forfeited the opportunity to recover all or part of $2.7 million? Not probable, but neither impossible. Take nothing for granted was his motto. He rotated the chair somewhat to his left to face Victoria.

"Suppose he admits that he has all or part of that money abroad, Colonel. Suppose he likes your idea of betraying and fleeing to another country. Then what?" he probed.

"Then, Comrade Lieutenant General, the decision is yours to make. I'll abide by your orders. If you decide that we ought to do all we can to recover the loot or part of it, especially now that the Revolution needs every penny, I'd probably have to make him believe that I'm willing to leave with him, agree to what he proposes concerning arrangements to leave Cuba. If you decide that the money is best considered lost, as far as I'm concerned you can arrest him and charge him with embezzlement. The tapes would be incontrovertible evidence."

The minister turned to his chief of intelligence. "What do you think, Lastra?"

The general cleared his throat. "Well, comrade, I think that Comrade Colonel Victoria has proven that her loyalty to the Revolution is extraor—"

"I know, Lastra, I know. What do you think of Victoria confronting Pardo with the cash, asking him where it comes from, saying she wants to defect, and taping the whole thing?"

"It depends, Comrade Lieutenant General, on what you decide concerning the total stolen. If you consider it lost, there's no need for that. We just search the apartment, find the cash, demand to know to whom does it belong. If Pardo loves Victoria as much as she thinks he does, he'll admit it's his. We'll ask him where all that cash comes from, remind him that when he was XEMIC's network administrator a bundle of money disappeared. He'll confess eventually and that will be all. We won't be able to recover the rest of the money if he and his possible accomplices transferred it abroad, but we will try him and sentence him to life without parole.

"But if you want to try to recover the rest of the money, I think that what Comrade Victoria suggests is a good starting point. We should tape their exchange, see how he reacts. Again, if he loves Victoria so much, he'll be overjoyed when she says she's willing to defect. Maybe he reveals where the money, or his share of it, is. Then we'd have to meet again, study the situation, and redefine our objectives. I don't think we can see the whole picture or make all the right presuppositions here and now."

The minister considered things for a while. His secret reserve fund had reached an all-time low of forty-four thousand dollars. As the saying goes, Cuba was in debt "to the eleven thousand virgins and additionally owed one peso to each saint." That year's sugar output was expected to be the second lowest in the history of the Revolution; the world price of the sweetener was depressed, too. Tourism had collapsed after September 11. By closing their intelligence base in Lourdes, the Russians had shaved off $200 million from the revenue planned for 2002. The oil bill would exceed $1 billion. As a student of war history, the situation reminded him of Dunkirk, an economic and financial Dunkirk. Therefore, he would not get any cash for his secret reserve fund. But if he could recover part or all of the stolen money, maybe the Chief would let him keep some.

"Okay, I approve Victoria's plan. Lastra, clear this with the guys in Surveillance. Victoria, Lastra will let you know when your apartment is operational, then you tell us when you'll proceed. We'll meet a day or two after you have this exchange with your husband, examine results, and decide our next moves. And thanks, Colonel. You are a true revolutionary."

Victoria jumped to her feet and stood at attention. "I serve the Socialist Revolution," she hollered.

...

That evening, in their bedroom, the deathly pallor of his skin frightening, Pardo collapsed in bed.

"You what?" he mumbled.

"Take it easy and hear what I have to say. I got it all figured out," a smiling Victoria said.

. . .

Elliot crossed his legs and watched as Maria Scheindlin, bubbly as a girl finding an unexpected gift, opened the plastic bag he had just handed her. She pulled out two blue velvet pouches that contained bottles of rum and placed them on the coffee table. She extracted one and read aloud from the label.

"'Isla del Tesoro.' So, this is the famous rum aged fifty years."

"Or so they say."

Next, Maria took out five CDs by Camerata Romeu and a box of Cohiba Espléndidos, which she also deposited on the coffee table.

"Good. David Sadow will be thrilled. So will Jenny. Thank you very much, Elliot. So kind of you. How much do I owe you?"

Elliot drew his wallet out and produced three receipts. "The cigars were three hundred eighty-five, the rum . . ."

"Elliot?"

"Yes?"

"Just tell me the total, please."

"Six hundred twenty."

"Okay, I'll write you a check. And throw away the receipts, please."

The widow stood from the sofa in one swift motion, ambled to a closed door, opened it, and disappeared into the library. Lost in reflection, Steil returned the receipts to his wallet, pocketed it, then with unseeing eyes contemplated the still life on the opposing wall. The previous evening, at an FBI's safe house in the NW section of the city, Hart and McLellan had made him repeat his Sunday report word by word, probably fishing for contradictions. Remembering Berta's surname—Arosamena—was the only addition he had made. Then the agents had proceeded to give him instructions for this evening's meeting. Basically, Hart reiterated what he had said at the airport, McLellan emphasized the need for secrecy, but the gravity with which both men treated the whole case had made Elliot realize that something serious was at stake. He wanted out badly.

But even if he were sent to the sidelines after making the phone call to Havana, the firm's future worried him. At the airport, Hart had mentioned that they would look into IMLATINEX's connection with Trans-Caribbean. Maybe he should have omitted that. Before the agent had said they would look into it, the inescapable implication eluded him. So stupid of him. What would happen if the FBI found that the guys in Panama were nothing more than Schindlin's figureheads? Would the federal government fine IMLATINEX for violating the Trading with the Enemy Act? Would he, as a Cuban, be considered an accomplice? Worse, an agent? He had to start searching for documents proving that the Panamanian company had been established almost twenty-five years before he settled in Miami; that it began trading with Cuba in the seventies. And talk to a lawyer. Who? He could not ask Fidelia to recommend someone. She would demand to know why he needed a lawyer, and that would start a fight. Was he going back to his old habits? Concealing serious problems from her? Steil heaved a sigh of quiet resignation.

Maria came back, a check dangling from her right hand. She was wearing a sleeveless yellow cotton blouse, a green knee-length skirt from a lightweight fabric, and leather thongs. She looked better with her hair hanging loose about her shoulders. Same gold studs in her earlobes, watch on her left wrist. Steil scrambled to his feet.

"Oh, for God's sake, sit down Elliot. Save those manners for strangers. You make me nervous. Here you are."

"Thanks." He smiled, put the check in a side pocket of his guayabera and eased himself down onto his club chair. The beaming Maria got back to the sofa, crossed her legs, tugged at the hem of her skirt. Steil got ready to do what he was so reluctant to do, what he never would have done under different circumstances. He had patiently told

Hart and McLellan that, had he been acting of his own free will, he would have sent Capdevila and Berta to hell, absolutely refusing to tell such a ludicrous tale to Maria Scheindlin. It was the logical thing to do, he had argued further. Maria would judge him stupid, or an accomplice in the swindle. Hart had smiled enigmatically and advised him to say he had done it to protect Mr. Scheindlin's reputation.

"Well, tell me. How's Cuba? How are your friends and relatives?"

Elliot's grin appeared forced as he broached the subject. "Now, let me see. Cuba is much better than when I left. However, were it not for the dollars sent by Cubans living abroad, the country would be in ruins. I found my relatives in fairly good health, a friend is not so well, she's been diagnosed with cervical cancer."

"Oh, I'm sorry."

"Thanks. But I must tell you that something quite . . . strange happened to me, and it concerns you, so I think—"

"Concerns me?" knitting her brow, losing the smile.

"Absolutely. Listen, the Sunday before last, same day I arrived, as I was getting ready to go to bed around 8:00 P.M.—hadn't slept a wink the night before—a guy who identified himself as Carlos Capdevila and a woman who said her name was Berta Arosamena knocked on the door of my hotel room . . ."

Having told it twice before, he finished the story in less than thirty minutes. After Elliot revealed that, according to his two visitors, Scheindlin had been trading in pharmaceuticals with Cuba, Maria looked mystified. When he said they claimed that, at the time of his death, Scheindlin had in his possession one hundred thousand advanced by XEMIC, Maria covered her open mouth with the palm of her hand and kept it there for close to a minute. She still had not articulated a single word a minute after he finished. Hart had instructed: "Don't say anything after you are done, don't move, don't breathe. Wait for her reaction." He was doing exactly that.

"Well, Elliot," she said at last, "this is . . . news to me. I didn't know Ruben was . . . doing that. It's so hard to believe. I mean, I knew he was trading with Cuba, but not medicine, he never traded in medicine. Did you ever hear Ruben talk about medicine?"

"Never, ma'am."

Shaking her head in wonder, Maria was gazing at the carpet spread underneath the coffee table. "Is it possible these people lied to you?"

"It's perfectly possible."

"But then, is it possible Ruben was doing this for them?"

"Nothing is impossible, Maria. The first time you invited me here you asked how reserved I thought Mr. Scheindlin was. I said with strangers he was very reserved. You said he didn't bring business matters home. Maybe he was much more secretive than we were aware of. In the last six months, IMLATINEX's bank accounts haven't registered any inexplicable hundred thousand deposit, or a few mysterious deposits that added together approach a hundred thousand. I'm certain of that. I checked it yesterday. All our revenues come from legitimate sources well known to me. But what these two said is not impossible. Now Cuba is buying from American companies on a cash basis. It's possible that Mr. Scheindlin asked for the money up front. He may have had personal bank accounts abroad, or safe-deposit boxes, or a safe here at home, to deposit or store cash he didn't want to flow through American banking channels. I don't know. These people think you know or can find out. And that's what they're asking you to do. That you tell them whether or not you know where their money is, and if you find it, whether or not you are willing to give it back."

Maria's expression reflected bafflement and disbelief. Elliot suspected she had no clue what to do, where to begin, and felt sorry for her. She moved her eyes to the sliding door that opened into the backyard and took a moment or two to think things over.

"Well," she said at last, "I have to check a few things to get to the bottom of this. I mean, we're not talking about nickels and dimes here. But help me figure this out, Elliot, please. I'm very confused. Play devil's advocate. Let's consider the first thing that comes to mind: that this is a complete fabrication, Ruben never traded pharmaceuticals, no such cash exists. If so, are these two out of their minds? How can they think I'll give them a hundred thousand in cash just because they concocted an incredible story? When you're trying to con someone, you have to offer something in exchange for the money. They haven't offered a thing, except for this 'gratitude' that would allow me to invest and buy real estate in Cuba; but that's bull. Besides, I'm not interested. The Cuban government can't take me to court, they didn't furnish any proof, either. So, are they crazy? Did they look crazy to you?"

"No, ma'am, they didn't."

"They made no threat."

"No, ma'am."

"They didn't say 'If she doesn't gives us back our money we'll set her home on fire.'"

"No, ma'am."

"You are not hiding something so as not to scare the life out of me."

"No, ma'am."

"Elliot, you make me feel like I'm a hundred years old. Stop ma'aming me."

"Yes, m . . . Maria."

"So, if they are not crazy, if they didn't make any threat, if what they're so politely asking is for me to check my husband's safe-deposit boxes and personal bank accounts and, should I find one hundred thousand unaccounted for, to please consider if I would be willing to give back what's theirs, then: What the fuck is this, Elliot? Pardon the swearing. I guess I'm freaking out."

Elliot fought off a smile, crossed his legs, and moved his gaze to the front door. He couldn't say what he suspected: that this was a State Security operation in which the money and all this crap about Scheindlin buying medicine for Cuba was just a cover for something much more sinister. That the FBI was on the alert. That she and he were just fifth-billing actors in the play.

"Maria, I don't know."

"You are so helpful."

"Listen, you've spent a few minutes thinking about this. I've been considering the whole thing for nine days and I'm still unable to find a rational explanation."

Maria bit her right thumbnail for an instant, then rearranged herself in her seat.

"Okay, let's then consider what seems impossible. It's true, Ruben was doing this for them, when he died he had the money. What should I do?"

"That's for you to decide, ma'am. Sorry. Maria."

"I know it's for me to decide, Elliot. I'm asking your opinion."

"As long as you don't shoot the messenger."

Maria chuckled and the tension abated somewhat.

"I think the first thing you should do," Elliot began, "is to check if among Mr. Scheindlin's personal papers there is some deal with medical supplies: tenders, invoices, packing lists, something like that. Regarding the money, he may have had personal bank accounts abroad, by now you probably know which. You could check the statements, see if a deposit for a hundred thousand took place two or three months ago. Another possibility is that he kept the cash in a safe-deposit box here in Miami or in some other country in which he had rented one. Do you have a safe here?"

"Here at home?"

"Yes."

"Sure."

"Have you checked it lately?"

"It's not there. I've opened that safe many times since Ruben died. I have twenty-odd thousand dollars in it, important papers, stocks and bonds, and my jewelry."

"I see. Well, I can't think about any other step you could take."

"Suppose that, against all odds, I find that the Cubans' claim is true."

"Then you decide if you are going to give it back or not, and let me know your decision. I call these people, tell them either that their uncle died or that he recovered completely, and gracefully bow out."

For a moment Maria looked taken aback. "How chivalrous of you," she said reproachfully.

Steil shook his head, clicked his tongue, and smiled mirthlessly. "Try to see it from where I stand, Maria, please. I am a Cuban citizen;

Cuba has been designated part of the Axis of Evil by the present administration; some Cubans living here have been condemned to long prison sentences for spying for Cuba; I just got back from Cuba. Should this . . . thing be made public, I could be accused of being an enemy agent, be deported . . ."

"Okay, I understand," Maria said lifting a hand, staring at the floor, not wanting to hear more. "Let me ask you something: Who knows about this?"

"Nobody."

"You haven't told anyone?"

"Not a soul."

"Could you please do me the favor of keeping it like that? I don't want to see Ruben's name at the center of a political scandal for trading with Cuba. And you know he traded, not medicine maybe, but many other things."

"I won't tell anyone, Maria."

"Okay, thanks. Now, Elliot, I need to be alone. I'm so confused . . ."

"I understand, Maria," getting to his feet. "I shouldn't have agreed to deliver this message to you. Only now I realize it was a mistake. I apologize."

"It's okay, Elliot. There's no turning back the clock now," she said, with an expression that Steil interpreted as, *"You are either a fool or their partner."*

"I had two things in mind: Mr. Scheindlin's reputation and the future of IMLATINEX," as he ambled to the front door.

"I understand," reaching for the knob. Her tone said she did not.

"Well, if there's anything else I can do . . ."

"No, thanks, Elliot. You are Cuban, you may be accused of being a spy, you may be deported. Hopefully in a few days I'll call you, ask you over, and ask you to make that phone call to Havana and say whatever I decide you have to say. I would make it myself if I were fluent in Spanish, to minimize your involvement. But I'm not. After hanging up, you gracefully bow out."

Stung by how cowardly his words sounded, befuddled by the disappointment in her voice, Steil inclined his head. "Sorry, Maria."

"Thanks for bringing the presents," she said, opening the door.

Steil stretched out his hand. "Don't mention it. Good night."

"Good night, Elliot." Maria pretended she had not seen the proffered hand.

...

"Three sets of cameras and mikes: two in your living area and one in your bedroom in case he goes in there. In the living room, camera one sweeps from the wall facing the street to the dining room and from the center of the living room to the wall facing the front door, where the wraparound sofa is. Camera two sweeps exactly the same area from the opposite end, that is, the front door, the two loveseats in front of the sofa, and the coffee table. The whole area is covered. He can sit by your side or facing you, he can change seats, stand, move around, we'll be watching him. The set in your bedroom faces the bed, the side tables, and the window. Surveillance says that when couples have arguments in their bedrooms, they almost always sit or lie down in beds. But it would be best if you confront him in the living room."

"I suppose all this paraphernalia is conveniently concealed."

"Micaela, please, these people are pros."

"Of course."

They were in Lastra's office, the chief of intelligence behind a beautiful desk of African cedar presented to him by the president of Angola, Victoria in one of the two cedar club chairs upholstered in genuine antelope hide facing the desk. The general had on a checkered shirt, khakis, and gleaming brown loafers. Victoria had a light brown sweater over her white blouse, blue jeans, and moccasins. Lastra always had his air conditioner at full blast and whenever she was asked to present herself at his office, she put on the sweater. It was Wednesday, April 24.

"The monitors, VCRs, and the operator on duty are stationed a few floors below," Lastra continued. "Let me know when you are ready to go ahead. I want to have a couple of men watching, too, in case Pardo gets violent . . ."

Victoria's wistful smile and the way she shook her head from side to side several times prompted Lastra to ask: "You don't think he will?"

"I told you, Brigadier General. Pardo loves me."

"Good. But the men will be there in any case, to be on the safe side. Since this isn't a regular stakeout, Surveillance would appreciate it if we could wrap it up ASAP so they can dismantle the whole shebang and install it somewhere else. They are as hard pressed for men, money, and equipment as we are."

"I see. What about tonight?"

"That would be perfect. Where does he keep the money?"

"Didn't I tell you?"

"You said in a closet, but where? A drawer? In a molding?"

"I thought I had. When we moved to this apartment we stored many books and magazines in a closet of an empty bedroom. I was looking for an old issue of *Psychological Bulletin* and noticed that, in the middle of his pile of computer magazines, one bulged. I pulled it out and found an envelope with a wad of hundred-dollar bills, sixty-four to be exact, stored between the pages."

Lastra mulled this over. "Have you considered the possibility that he hid it there because he wanted you to find it?"

"Yes, I have. And this provocation I'll carry out allows for that possibility. I'll say I saw the bank statement on the screen, a few days later I chanced on the money, then I made all the right guesses. I react accordingly. Which reminds me, have you had our server's network administrator check my account?"

"Yes, and you were right. An offshore bank website was accessed." Lastra lifted an eyebrow, interlaced his fingers behind his head, reclined back on the swivel chair, gazed into her eyes. "You are the psychologist. Tell me. What makes an honest man become a thief overnight?"

Victoria considered it. "In this particular case, and in many other cases, as you well know, maybe traveling to capitalist countries made Pardo renege on his principles. Remember our coordinator for Western Europe in the eighties?"

"I remember him. You weren't with us then."

"I wasn't, but I read his file. Born and raised in a farm, fought the bandits in the mountains of Escambray, joined Intelligence when he was nineteen. Clever, followed orders, majored in law, had a beer every month or so, didn't smoke, model guy. So, he gets appointed resident director for all our illegals and informers in Western Europe, stationed in Prague. Then, less than a year later, Mr. Perfect steals the fund for expenses, drives to Paris, walks into the American embassy, and betrays his country. Why? I have a theory about it."

"Out with it."

"Cubans born after 1959 grew up in a very austere environment, lacking articles that are taken for granted in rich countries, from sanitary napkins to laptops. When they travel to those countries, some suffer a shock. Every Tom, Dick, and Harry has what no Cuban has. Capitalism begets consumerism. And what's the first thing a consumer needs? Money. And what's the easiest way to get your hands on the money you need to live as those people live?

"Then look at the other side of the coin. We have thousands of men and women in this country who grew up in well-to-do Cuban families. They were middle class, a few were upper class. They should have left Cuba. And what did they do? They betrayed their class and sided with the working class. Some of these people are members of the Central Committee, officers in the armed forces, ministers, vice ministers; they enjoy privileges. But the majority are intellectuals, doctors, lawyers, retirees. They eat what they get on the ration card, ride 'camels,' stand in line for hours. Yet, almost all those who travel to the United States to visit relatives return to Cuba. They don't defect, they don't steal, most have a sympathetic attitude toward the Revolution. They had the opportunity to make a choice and live with the good and the bad consequences of that choice."

Lastra just smiled and seemed lost in reverie for a while. Victoria had heard that he came from a rich family that owned hundreds of hectares of grazing land and thousands of heads of cattle in the eastern part of the island. Rumor had it that he had attended college in Kentucky, or Alabama, or another American state before joining Intelligence. Old photos proved that when young he did not have his present glum manner. Another victim of the profession, she thought. She liked him because he was a stickler for efficiency, cared for his subordinates, and never acted superior toward others.

"Then how do you explain Cubans born after 1959 who travel to First World countries and remain faithful to the Revolution?" asked the general.

"They are living proof that the majority don't succumb to the siren calls of capitalism, that we've been able to teach the new generation the importance of upholding our principles. Unfortunately, my husband belongs to the minority."

"Right."

Lastra opened a drawer, extracted a Lancero, bit its tip, and lighted it with a throwaway. "So, are you certain you'll do it tonight? I have to tell Surveillance."

"I'll do it tonight, Comrade Brigadier General."

"Fine. Anything else?"

"Just one more thing, Comrade. He'll probably want to make love tonight. I can't refuse, so I'd appreciate it if you tell Surveillance not to watch or tape that."

"Don't fret. I will. Take care, Colonel."

"You too, comrade."

...

Tony Soto seemed deeply embarrassed. Perched on a bar stool, talking in a low voice, his tone apologetic, he watched the circles he was drawing with the bottom of his glass on the mahogany bartop at Charlie's Lounge. Frequent tongue-clicking and shoulder-shrugging went with the soft tone and downcast eyes, the unconscious body language Cubans learn from the cradle when providing justification for an action they regret. It can also be seen when one is self-deprecatory, usually following the admission that you put your foot in it. Although hearing Tony attentively, the teacher in Elliot could not fail to notice how many expressions in English and in Spanish have the same signification. He had just discovered another: *Put your foot in it* is *meter la pata* in Cuba.

Tony said he had requested Elliot's presence at the bar to excuse himself for introducing Hart and McLellan. As a police officer, he could not refuse to collaborate with law-enforcing agencies, Tony argued. Besides, they had asked politely, made it seem like it was a favor. Tony also thought he could mediate in case Elliot lost his cool, as indeed he had. But he felt lousy about the whole thing, and he wanted Elliot to know it.

"Don't worry, Tony. It's okay. They were right. I was appr—"

"NO! I don't wanna know. You can't tell anyone."

"For God's sake, Tony. You were there, you know they said someone would approach me."

"Didn't they say you can't discuss this with anyone?"

"They did."

"So, don't."

"Hey, don't panic. I won't tell you anything. Jesus, I've never seen you so scared. What's the fucking matter?"

"Nothing is the matter. It's none of my business and I just don't wanna know, okay?"

They remained silent for almost a minute. Tony finished his beer and ordered a refill. Steil sipped his Seven-Up. The barman poured Tony's third beer and the cop swilled down half without even tasting it, wiping a knuckle across his lips and mustache. Once again Steil registered how much his former pupil had aged in eight years. He had developed a gut that hung over his pants and lines on his forehead and wrinkles in the corners of his eyes that hadn't been there. A few white hairs shone on his temples, too. Lidia was five years his senior, and in 1994, Steil had predicted that eventually she would come across as his mother, not his wife. Another prediction that turns out to be wrong, Elliot thought. Now Lidia was thirty-nine and looked forty-something. She never touched the stuff, followed strict diets, dyed her hair, and spent a fortune on face and hand creams as well. Tony just pumped iron. He came across as forty at thirty-four. If he kept up his lifestyle for another ten years, she would end up looking younger than him.

"Elliot . . . I wonder . . . if it would be possible, you know . . . to keep from these people that I occasionally do things for the company. They may think, you know, that a police officer shouldn't get involved in . . . well, you know, debt collecting, helping out with difficult clients, contacting customs, and stuff, you know . . ."

"I know," Elliot said, thinking about American buzzwords. Some people just had to interpolate "you know," or "fuck," or more recently "basically" into each sentence. And this was not restricted to the undereducated. The media was in love with "basically" and "having said that." Today he was very language-oriented, he admitted to himself.

"They may tell Internal Affairs and, you know, make things tough for me."

"Tony, I won't tell them a word. But be sure that in the next weeks, maybe months, these people will place the company under a magnifying glass."

"Really?"

"Positive."

"Why?"

"You don't want me to tell you."

"Right. So, you think I should get lost for some time?"

"No, you should keep visiting the warehouse as frequently as always. If you stop going, everybody, and I mean everybody, from Sam to the night watchman, will wonder what the hell's the matter with you, why you aren't visiting."

"Right."

Tony took a gulp, wiped his mustache. "This McLellan guy," he said, "nobody knows him. Hart's on the level; folks say he's been around for a while. McLellan is new in town."

"He showed me his ID. He's from Treasury."

Tony Soto slapped his forehead and rolled his eyes in desperation. "Teacher, for God's sake, stop being so naive, will you? FBI,
NSA, and CIA officers have a desk drawer full of authentic IDs with
their photos on them. They can be Treasury, State, ATF, whatever
they need to be. They have a closet full of uniforms: army, navy, air
force, police, you name it."

"You watch *The X Files*?"

Tony Soto inhaled deeply, then blew the air out with puffed
cheeks. "Okay, I'm paranoid; you're sane. You know best."

"Don't get all worked up, Tony. I appreciate your advice. So,
McLellan is not from Treasury. Where's he from?"

"Be damned if I know. But these guys with the bureau, the company, the way they look at you gives them away. It's like, you know,
like they suspect every human being over five years old is a criminal,
or a spy. That morning? At the airport? McLellan was looking at you
like that."

Steil took another sip. "Well, I'm not. I've got nothing to worry
about."

"Just watch out."

"Okay, I will. How're Lidia and the kids?"

"She's okay. Esther has a cold, Jenny and Tony Jr. are fine," said
Tony before guzzling the rest of the beer.

"Fidelia is all right, too."

"Ooops, sorry." The cop belched.

"It's okay."

"Listen, I'm worried, okay?"

"I said it's okay," wondering how many times they had babbled
the most popular exclamation in history.

"Okay. Now I got to go, okay?" Soto said, lumbering off his
stool.

"Okay."

"You coming?"

"I'll finish this first."

"Okay. See you, Teacher."

"Take care, Tony."

"You, too."

...

General Lastra pressed the eject button, recovered the black plastic container, turned on his heel, with a few steps reached the minister's desk, and placed the videocassette on top of the confidential news bulletin for April 27. Then he approached his armchair, facing the lieutenant general, and eased himself in alongside Victoria.

The minister was impressed, with reason. First, he had just watched a textbook example of what the counterintelligence community terms "provocative approach." Second, the video proved that, generally speaking, opposite-sex manipulators obtain better results; that female psychologists possess the basic understanding of the mind to excel at it; and that a brilliant female psychologist trained in the black arts of deception, acting, and blackmail was simply invincible. Third, for the umpteenth time he had irrefutable proof that besotted men act like fools, something he knew by his own experience. The results were very revealing and, even so, disappointing. Despite the fact that Victoria's interrogation of her husband had been masterful, although Pardo admitted he single-handedly had committed the biggest heist in Cuban history, even though they could try the sonofabitch and sentence him to the death penalty, the money was out of reach. The bastard had it in an offshore bank, under a false identity. The documents proving that Pardo was the bank's client, the only one who could make a withdrawal, were also abroad. Recovery seemed impossible. Should Cuba request devolution, the bank would demand proof, beginning a lengthy legal process. The media would turn the whole thing into an international circus. And if in the end the improbable happened and a court of law ruled in favor of the Cuban State, scores of creditors to whom the country owed billions would be suing, asking to be paid from such an asset.

Not wanting his two subordinates to realize he was at a loss concerning the next step, knowing that they were waiting for his reaction and that he had been silent for too long, the minister got to his feet and started pacing his office, hands behind his back, pretending to be deep in thought. He was frustrated that most of the time he was doing one of two things: taking orders from the Chief or prompting his subordinates for suggestions. He yearned for the simplicity of the battlefield: attack, defend, or retreat; fire or hold your fire; live or die; victory or defeat.

"Well, comrades, what do you think we should do next?"

Lastra raised his eyebrows and pulled down the corners of his mouth to indicate that what he would be saying had a preliminary and exploratory nature. "Well, Comrade Lieutenant General, the money is irrecoverable, so, in my opinion, we ought to arrest Pardo, try him, and ask that he be given life."

The minister energetically nodded in agreement before addressing Victoria. "You share the General's view, Comrade Colonel?"

"With all due respect, Comrade Lieutenant General, Comrade Brigadier General, I beg to differ."

"Oh?" the minister uttered, bushy eyebrows raised in admiration. He could not remember the last time a subordinate had dared to differ with something he had given a nod to. But this was his resident genius. "Would you please tell us what do you propose?"

"I respectfully suggest we offer my husband a deal, comrades."

"A deal?" both said in unison, balking at the prospect.

"Permission to elaborate."

"Granted," the minister, burning with curiosity.

"I couldn't sleep last night. I spent the whole night thinking. At the start I was seething with rage, but at a certain point I remembered Felix Dzherzinsky's definition of a Cheka operative: a burning heart and a cool head. So, I tried to think with a cool head. And I came to the conclusion that we should offer Pardo a deal.

"Had my husband passed State secrets to the enemy, had he conspired with others to assassinate the Commander in Chief, the minister of the revolutionary armed forces, or any other Politburo member, I would propose executing him by firing squad. Had he spent the money he stole, I would be in agreement with you, Comrade

Brigadier General: Give him a life sentence. Were it possible to recover the money without his participation, I would be of the same mind: life sentence. But as you saw in that video, without his active and willing participation, I'm afraid the money will be lost forever."

Victoria took a moment, as if to collect her thoughts. What she wanted was to let it sink in.

"Now, what is more important and beneficial for the Revolution in these historical days we live? To punish a thief or to recover the money? In my humble opinion, to recover the money. Can you imagine how many tons of medicine 2.6 million dollars buys? We've learned some very important things. Pardo acted alone, there were no accomplices, no split, he has it all. Well, not all. As you heard him explain, he spent around a hundred thousand buying forged documents, traveling, and opening standard bank accounts so he could later open off-shore bank accounts and deposit the stolen money without raising suspicions of money laundering. But 2.6 million dollars, exactly 96.3 percent of what he stole, could be recovered if he cooperates.

"Next let's try to imagine how Pardo will react if someone presses our buzzer, I fling the main door open, three or four comrades from Operations barge in and, without giving any explanation, arrest the two of us. We ask what the matter is, why we are being taken into custody, they don't say a word.

"After ten or twenty hours incommunicado in a cell, you take Pardo to a room and show him that video," Victoria went on, pointing to the cassette on the minister's desk. "He'll panic. He'll realize he'll soon face a firing squad or, with the best will in the world, shall spend the rest of his life in prison. Pardo is a retired officer, he knows our prisons are no tourist resorts. He'll think of me, too, I'm sure. In that video I admit that I hate you, communism, and the Chief; so, he'll assume I'll be tried and sentenced as well. After the tape ends, the comrades take him back to his cell without asking him a single question. You let him think it over for a day or two. Then you offer him a deal."

"What deal, Comrade Colonel?" asked the mesmerized minister, marveling at Victoria's cunning plot.

"You say to him: 'You will be tried and sentenced; to death by firing squad probably. Your wife has been stripped of all her decorations; she'll be tried and sentenced, too. However, due to the financial situation that the country faces, the High Command has decided to offer you a deal. Give us back the money you stole and we'll let you stay in the country where you have it, once you've given it back. Then your wife will join you.'

"I know this man: He'll jump at it. He has no choice. Maybe he'll try to obtain some concession for me, possibly demand that I am to be released from jail. You agree to it. Maybe he starts figuring how he could get away once he's abroad. Maybe not, if he wants me to join him after he gives it back. He may consider it a stroke of luck that the two of us remain alive and free abroad. He'll figure that as a computer expert he can make a living anywhere. Then, what we have to do is make sure he keeps his word on his end of the deal."

Victoria finished her presentation. General Lastra and the minister exchanged swift glances. Both men were taken aback by her presence of mind, the strength of her reasoning powers, and the boldness of her plan. Not since the eighties had something so daring and convoluted been attempted. Lastra tried to remember the Yiddish term for imaginative and risky behaviors. It did not come to mind.

"Now, just a minute, Comrade Colonel," the minister said as he returned to his chair. "I have several questions."

"So do I," Lastra made known.

"Go ahead, Lastra."

"After you, Lieutenant General."

"No, you go ahead."

"Okay. Victoria, let me see if I've got this straight. You are assuming that after Pardo agrees to this . . . offer we make him, we put him on a plane to wherever he says he has the documents and the money, and he will go to the bank, fill a suitcase with cash, and meekly hand it over to our people?"

"That's not necessary. He can transfer the balance to a Banco Financiero account."

"Why won't he run away?"

"Because two of our men will be with him and because he loves me. We tell Pardo that as part of the deal, two comrades will pretend to be his bodyguards abroad. He'll realize it's an elementary precaution we have to take; he's not stupid and he knows we aren't either. He needs a passport and a plane ticket, so we'll know where he is going beforehand. One or two days before he leaves Cuba, we send a comrade there. The other will fly with Pardo. From then on, they'll eat with him, sleep with him, go with him everywhere."

"Fine," admitted Lastra rubbing his hands and staring at the floor. "But tell me, what will keep Pardo from hollering: 'Help! Police! These two are Cuban agents! They are kidnapping me!' in the middle of the street."

"You warn him that, should he do that, I will be convicted of treason and spend the rest of my life in prison."

Lastra and the minister exchanged looks. Watching the video had persuaded them that Pardo adored his wife, kissed the ground on which she walked. He had admitted he could not live without her, asserted he had stolen the money to provide for both of them after the Commander died and Cuban communism collapsed. He had conceded that she was the only reason he had not defected the last time he was abroad. It baffled her superiors. In a free country, with enough money to buy all a man could dream of, from a nice home to the most beautiful women, why had Pardo returned to Cuba? Both generals wondered whether Victoria exerted some mysterious control over her husband's mind that made him fully dependent on her to continue existing, or if she was the only one he could get it up with. Neither officer could think of any other reason for an intelligent, mature man to act so nonsensically after eleven years married to such a physically plain woman. Now she had betrayed him. Witch!

"I don't know, Victoria. This idea of yours is too . . . complicated and risky," the minister, to deemphasize his interest.

"Complication is a relative concept, Comrade Lieutenant General. To judge it, we must contrast it with the goal we hope to achieve. I wouldn't propose this for fifty or one hundred thousand dollars. But for a 2.6-million-dollar payoff, I don't think my plan is overly complicated. As to risky . . . I don't know. I've always been a desk-bound officer. I've never been to war, never run risks; you are much better judges on that than I'll ever be. But I'm sure you two have run risks a thousand times bigger.

"On the other hand, what have we got to lose? In our first meeting, Comrade General Lastra said we couldn't see the whole picture then. I respectfully opine that neither can we see it now. Let's take the next step, the false arrest, see how Pardo reacts—I assume the comrades will videotape what he does and says. Afterward we meet again, watch the video, reevaluate the whole thing, then you make your decision. The homeland needs that money."

"What do you think, Lastra?"

The chief of intelligence scratched his head. "I don't like it, either, Comrade Lieutenant General. But on the other hand, we lose nothing if we go ahead with the first part of Colonel Victoria's plan: storming the apartment, arresting them, offering Pardo the deal. Then we meet again and you decide what we should do."

"What will happen after Pardo gives the money back and you don't reunite with him?" asked the minister. "He may go to the press, denounce that we've kidnapped you. Blow the whole deal sky-high."

Victoria shook her head and rearranged herself in the armchair. "I doubt very much that he'll go to the press. I mean, journalists will ask questions: Who are you? When did you arrive? What are you doing here? Why did the Cuban government allow you to travel here if you and your wife were in jail? Eventually he would have to admit that he's a thief. On top of that, I propose an active measure. The minute he gives the money back, the comrades play for him a videotape in which I tell the truth, that I discovered the money and denounced him, that I put forward the ideas of videotaping his confession at our home and my false arrest, that I hate thieves and traitors, that I don't love him anymore and will divorce him. That should keep him quiet."

Again, the generals exchanged sharp looks. *The sleazy bitch!* the minister thought. *He'll blow his brains out,* thought Lastra. Both looked unfazed but were not.

"You've thought of everything," the minister said suavely.

"I tried to, Comrade Lieutenant General. But plans are one thing, reality another. We'll have to see how things turn out."

"So true. Well, let's proceed with the false arrest then."

"Give me a week, Comrade Lieutenant General. My approval of what he did, my willingness to flee Cuba with him, has made the traitor so happy and overconfident that I want to reinforce such appropriate psychological well-being one more week, make plans for our future abroad, fill him with anticipation, which is such an enjoyable feeling. Then the shock of the arrest will be even more intense."

You lowly cunt, thought the minister as he nodded approvingly.

Whore, thought Lastra, who failed to infuse his cheerless smile with kindness.

"Do you agree with delaying this for a week, Lastra?"

"If Victoria thinks it will make things easier for us . . ."

"Then we'll operate on . . ." the minister glanced at his desk calendar, "May 3 around 11:00 P.M. That okay with you, Victoria?"

"Perfect, Comrade Lieutenant General."

"What about you, Lastra?"

"No objection, comrade."

"Then you'll have to excuse me. I have a rather long report to read before a meeting at the Council of State this afternoon."

Chutzpah flashed in Lastra's mind. Yes, that was the Jewish term for this kind of thing. Well, Mossad was not doing so badly.

...

At 4:48 P.M. on Friday, April 26, Elliot was on the phone with Buenos Aires, checking technical details in a contract for copper-chromium and copper-chromium-magnesium rotor bars, when Maria Scheindlin entered the warehouse's glassed-in cubicle. She greeted the data enterer first, then approached Elliot's desk. He mouthed "Long distance. Give me a minute," then returned his gaze to the fax in which he was checking off quantities and specifications.

She moved behind her late husband's desk, sat on his swivel chair, crossed her legs. In addition to the ever-present watch, gold studs, and silver strips, she wore white slacks, a crimson silk blouse, and sandals. As Elliot wrapped up the conversation, she cast glances around the office, noticing things for the first time or looking for changes. Sam Plotzher was nowhere to be seen. The data enterer slipped into his jacket, getting ready to leave.

"Good evening, Mrs. Scheindlin," the man said before departing.

"Good evening, Chris. Say hello to the wife for me."

"I sure will. Thanks. Bye," he said, waving to Elliot, who returned the good-bye.

It was 5:03 when Elliot rested the handset in its cradle. "Hi, Maria. Glad to see you."

"Glad to see you, too. Be advised that now you are Jenny's 'favorite Cuban,' her exact words. David Sadow was less enthusiastic: He said you were okay. Coming from him, that's quite a compliment."

Steil smiled and placed his ballpoint in the pocket of his blue polo shirt. "The deliveryman gets the credit? Didn't you tell them you paid for it?"

"I thought it best to heighten your standing with the heiress and the family lawyer."

"So self-effacing of you, Maria."

"Well, maybe some of your self-effacement has rubbed off on me. I dropped by to see if you'd have time now to give me some background on our business in Brazil. I'm thinking of spending a week in São Paulo and I would like to go to the office, meet the guys face-to-face, you know."

"Absolutely. Let's move to the PC. I want to show you some graphs first."

For a little over an hour, Elliot filled Maria in on both Brazilian offices: São Paulo and Recife. Not having personally met the staff, his summary lacked substance on the human side. It was just products, sales, clients, margins, the rate of exchange of the real, and even some wild speculation on how Lala's candidacy to the presidency could affect the country's future. At a quarter past six he was through.

"Well, I'm amazed," Maria said. "Do you follow our other subsidiaries with the same thoroughness?"

"No. Brazil and Argentina demand more attention. Brazil due to the volume of business there; Argentina because of the economic crisis."

"I see. Nice presentation, Elliot. Thanks. Now I wonder whether it would be possible for you to do me another favor."

"Sure. What is it?"

"To call Havana tonight and say uncle is recovering and he'll stay at the Wyndham Casa Marina between May 3 and May 8."

Not believing his ears, Elliot anyhow realized that Brazil had been just an excuse in case other people were around when she got there. Maria had realized that were she to arrive, talk to him for a couple of minutes, and leave, others might have wondered what was going on. He stared at her for so long that she raised her eyebrows and widened her eyes in admiration, an unspoken *What's the matter?*

"Let me make sure I've got this straight," the bewildered Elliot said. "You found the cash and are giving it back?"

Maria turned her head away and let her gaze rove around the warehouse, a gesture meant to express mild irritation.

"Elliot, you very clearly explained to me the reasons why you want to 'bow out' at this stage. They are valid reasons. I understand. Maybe it's just that I wouldn't like to have on my conscience that three people went to jail because they lost a hundred Gs. So, please, don't ask any questions. Just make the call, all right?"

Again, Elliot stared at her. What would Hart and McLellan think? They thought it was a mistake that he had told Maria Scheindlin that he wanted out. Steil had given her the perfect excuse to cut him off, they had argued. He did not tell the agents that that was exactly what he wanted. But suddenly he regretted being excluded. Would he make up his mind? Did he want in or out? Out? Okay, he was out. So, why was he disgruntled? No backtracking was possible, though.

"Fine. Let me jot down the name of the hotel in Key West," pulling out the ballpoint.

"Wyndham Casa Marina."

Elliot tore a page from his desk calendar and wrote on it. "And the dates?"

"Between May 3 and May 8."

Elliot finished taking the note and lifted his head. "Anything else, Maria?"

"No, Elliot, and thanks for your help. I really appreciate it," getting to her feet.

"My pleasure, Maria," standing up, too.

"Where's Sam?"

"He said he'd spend the afternoon at customs and then go straight home."

"Okay. Give him my regards."

"I will."

"Take care, Elliot."

"You too, Maria."

That evening, from the safe house and after enduring a few "We told you so's" delivered by the exasperated Hart and McLellan, Elliot dialed 5378324969. He assumed that the strange-looking machine attached to the line, with numerous dials and blinking lights, was a tape recorder. No tapes or cassettes were visible, though. There were three rings before someone lifted the handset in Cuba.

"Hello."

"Hi there, buddy, how're you doing?"

"Hey, *mi hermano,* great to hear from you. I'm fine, thanks. What's the latest about Uncle Gustavo? We're worried."

"He's fine, was released from the hospital yesterday and, you know what? He's feeling so well he plans to spend from May 3 to 8 at a Key West hotel: the Wyndham Casa Marina. Sunning himself by the pool and watching the half-naked babes, he says."

"*Coñó*, that's great!" Lights blinked madly in the machine. "I'm overjoyed."

I bet you are, Elliot thought. He said instead: "We are very happy, too. Please call the rest of the family and let them know."

"I will, sure. Tell uncle the whole family is dying to see him. When he comes we'll roast a pig for him. And tell me, how are you doing?"

"I'm fine, thanks."

"Okay. Let's hang up then. I don't want this call to cost you too much. Thanks for the good news."

"The family is the family. Bye, now."

"Bye, and thanks again."

Six

At quarter past 1:00 P.M. on Saturday, April 27, Manuel Pardo left the Institute of Meteorology, an old building located on top of a hill in the town of Casablanca, on the eastern shore of Havana Bay, and performed his daily routine of covering the 1.5 kilometers to Avenida Monumental on foot. Once he got to the eight-lane freeway, however, rather than crossing it to board a westbound bus to Vedado, which he always did, Pardo remained on the side of eastbound traffic. He ambled nonchalantly to a bus stop and sat on a granite bench.

At half past 1:00 P.M., Victoria Valiente keyed in the number to set the alarm and closed the door to her cubicle on the eighth floor of the General Directorate of Intelligence. On her way to the elevator, she produced an inhaler from her shoulder bag. Once inside the metal cage, Victoria punched the basement button, shook and pumped the inhaler twice, recapped it, and dropped it into the bag. When the door slid open twenty seconds later, she marched to her parking space.

Moments later her Tico ascended the ramp to A Street, rolled around the corner at Línea, and at the next corner turned right onto Paseo Avenue. After Calzada, Victoria shot a glance at her apartment building across the median divider and tried to breathe deeply. At the foot of Paseo, she took a right onto Malecón. The day was clear and a little humid; the sea a bit choppy, as always after midday when the eastern breeze gained in strength. Victoria shot a glance at the U.S. Interests Section as she drove by, then concentrated on her driving.

Intelligence and Counterintelligence officers were on 24/7 call, but since the mid-seventies—when the number of divorced people soared dramatically in Interior—a conscious effort had been made to allow them to spend Saturday afternoons and Sundays with their families. Complete on-duty schedules were drawn up six months in advance in order to make family plans for the weekends possible. Deskbound guys seldom saw their quality time disrupted.

In contrast, most public holidays were exhausting for members of the Ministry of the Interior. Beginning at midnight two or three days earlier, all officers, enlisted men, policemen, and cadets, including maintenance staff and excluding prison guards and firefighters, were given special chores. They had to stake out the homes of dissenters and ex–prisoners of conscience, or stand watch on the rooftops of tall buildings, direct traffic, shut off streets, intensify the surveillance of diplomats and tourists, inspect manholes and mailboxes, and so forth. This was the weekend before Labor Day, May 1, in Cuba. The high-ranking officers that had not been invited to the reviewing stand from which the Chief would wave to those taking part in the march would gather at the ministry to watch the parade from the rooftop. Victoria already had her invitation for the reviewing stand.

At 1:46, she drove through the tunnel under Havana Bay and within two minutes pulled over a few meters before reaching the bus stop where her husband waited. Upon seeing the Tico, Pardo got to his feet and hurried to the car. He yanked open the passenger door, plopped in the seat, closed the door. Victoria stared at him for a few moments and smiled. He returned her smile. She poked him in the ribs; he stuck his tongue out at her. Nothing was said. When she pulled away, Pardo turned the radio on and tuned in to a four-hour-long pop music program.

For the next sixty-five minutes the car sped east to Matanzas, capital of the Cuban province of the same name. Every minute or so

Victoria shot a glance at her rearview mirror. Once the traffic got lighter past Guanabo, Pardo fished into his wife's shoulder bag, extracted a powder compact, and used its mirror to scan the road behind every five or six minutes. A traffic sign announcing Santa Cruz del Norte made Victoria remember Elliot Steil. She glanced briefly at her husband, who nodded and smiled. Seven minutes before reaching their destination, Pardo returned the powder compact to the shoulder bag and for a while delighted in the spectacular view of the Yumurí Valley.

Victoria parked in front of Teatro Sauto, the hub of Matanzas's cultural life. The couple got out and Pardo removed a bulging duffel bag from the trunk before Victoria locked the car. They covered four blocks on foot to a dollars-only taxi stand, boarded a Peugeot, and asked the cabbie to take them to the Meliá Habana Hotel, in Miramar, La Habana. This made the driver a happy man. He could get a two- or three-dollar tip and return to his hometown later in the day with tourists or upper-class Cubans on their way to Varadero. A perfect day. Half an hour after entering Matanzas, Pardo and Victoria began retracing their course to Havana.

At 4:25 P.M. they ambled into the Meliá Habana, used the restrooms, reunited in the lobby, had a hot dog and a soda at the cafeteria, then returned to the hotel entrance and asked the doorman for a taxi. This time a more spacious Hyundai slowly ascended onto the driveway.

"Take us to Güira de Melena," Pardo ordered the cabbie once the hotel employee was out of earshot.

The road to Güira de Melena was dotted with royal palms, fruit trees, vegetable gardens, potato fields, sugarcane and banana plantations, and fields of numerous cash crops. A few cows and horses grazed. Fifty- and sixty-year-old American farm tractors—contaminating monuments to the Cubans' mechanical ingenuity—plowed a rich, dark red soil. All sorts of houses, ranging from magnificent residences built by rich people decades before the Revolution to modest wooden huts roofed with palm fronds, flanked the blacktop. Pardo knew that many plots were privately owned, and as such, were productive and cost-effective. Wherever private businesses had been authorized to operate, they had proven across-the-board superiority over state-owned competitors for many years now. But as the saying goes, nobody is blindest than he who refuses to see, he thought, and clicked his tongue. Victoria looked at him inquisitively. He smiled and dismissed her concern by shaking his head.

In Güira de Melena the couple shopped around for some time before approaching a man behind the wheel of a '53 Buick Roadmaster parked in a street that flanked the town's central park. Would he be willing to take them to Mariel, a port on the northern coast of the province? The guy said he would, for fifteen dollars; Pardo haggled him down to twelve just to act according to custom. The jalopy's windshield lacked the sticker authorizing it to operate as a private taxi, so the hacker would vehemently deny ever having driven anyone anywhere, should he be asked. The piece of junk was his, he was trying to make an honest buck, but to the government he had a hustle going.

It was 6:15 P.M. when they departed Güira de Melena. In reply to Pardo's gentle inquiring, the cabbie explained that the diesel engine of a Romanian tractor had replaced the car's original 325-horsepower, V-8 engine. What he didn't say was that the diesel engine had been stolen from a state farm. Victoria considered this a sample of the real Cuba that she and people like her had no clue existed. They retraced to San Antonio first, then turned left to Guanajay. At long last, they got out of the car on the outskirts of Mariel around 7:30. The cabbie U-turned and waved a good-bye. They waved back.

Having never been there before, Victoria looked around. Two chimneys were spewing whitish smoke against the setting sun. "Cement factory" clarified Pardo, who was eyeing her. She assented. As in most Cuban towns, tall buildings were almost nonexistent. Two or three kilometers away, along the shoreline, new-looking construction caught her eye. "Free trade zone," Pardo explained. She nodded again. The white flashes of a lighthouse marked the west side of the harbor entrance.

From here, Victoria remembered, 120,000 Cubans had emigrated to the United States in 1980. The Chief had seized the opportunity to empty his penitentiaries and pack off a few thousand criminals and a handful of spies to Mr. Carter. The violence unleashed by the "Marielitos," as the criminals came to be known in the United States, was one of the situations that helped Reagan defeat the incumbent president in that year's election. Close to twenty-two years had gone by when the thirty-ninth U.S. president had announced he would visit Cuba in May, hoping to improve relations between both countries. Did he really think he could? Victoria believed that candid, principled souls ought to abstain from seriously engaging in politics. Carter seemed principled to her, he may just pretend to be candid, she speculated.

"Let's go," Pardo said.

They started walking, holding hands. Most close-by homes were of bricks and blocks with concrete roofs. Simple in design, they had the botched-up look that many modest private houses constructed by self-help groups share. As it was perfectly natural to expect, the cement utilized to build them had been stolen from the nearby factory. It was dark already and Pardo guided his wife through a maze of streets lacking sidewalks in which potholes abounded. Public illumination was nonexistent, and night had fallen by the time Pardo knocked on a wooden front door.

"Who is it?" a gruff voice asked.

"It's me, Pardo."

A potbellied, suntanned man with dark brown hair and an impressive mustache on an otherwise clean-shaven face opened the door. Victoria judged him to be between thirty-five and forty, five-feet-ten, around 180 pounds. He wore a Cuban navy uniform, the rank of ensign on its epaulets.

"Welcome," he said, a smile playing on his lips. "Come on in."

They crossed the threshold and the navy officer closed the door. "Meet my wife," Pardo said to the host.

"Diego, pleased to meet you," the man said, extending his hand.

"On an occasion such as this, I'm not just being formal when I say the pleasure is all mine," Victoria, taking it.

She thought his smile virile and attractive. Victoria quickly scanned the place. According to Pardo, Ensign Diego Amieba had divorced two years earlier, and she assumed that the framed photograph of a two- or three-year-old boy atop the old Russian TV set was the only remains of the failed marriage. The living area looked as unkempt and dusty as any other Cuban bachelor's home. Most of the furniture was old: a precious-wood sofa with wickerwork back and seats, two matching armchairs, two rocking chairs, a coffee table, a modern nest of tables with a radio and knickknacks, an oscillating fan. Upon a wall, a cheap decorative rug showed an adult lion lying down on the floor of a living room, a smiling boy reclining on the beast. On the opposite wall hung two framed color prints of the Chief and his brother in full dress uniforms.

"You know how it is," Amieba said, having watched Victoria inspect the place.

"Yeah, I know. I have the same prints at home," she lied.

"You do?" with a big smile. "But sit down, please, sit down. Give me a minute."

Pardo nodded and the ensign disappeared inside a short hall. Victoria chose an armchair, her husband a corner of the sofa. They exchanged an affectionate glance and kept their agreement to remain silent indoors. She checked in her mind what Pardo had told her about the navy officer.

Always on the lookout for safe escape routes, her husband had met Amieba three years earlier while providing regular maintenance to meteorological equipment in Mariel. He had carefully nurtured the relationship because the ensign was the skipper of a cigarette speedboat impounded by the Cuban government from drug smugglers and converted into a patrol boat. If nothing else, Pardo hoped to learn the procedures, habits, and mentality of coastguardsmen. A fourteen-year veteran of the Cuban navy and a party member since 1993, the ensign had been based in Mariel for ten years now, having previously served aboard a Soviet Pauk II fast patrol craft which was decommissioned in 1997 for lack of spare parts.

The navy had always been the Cinderella of the Revolutionary Armed Forces, lacking a fairy godmother and prince. From the very beginning, the Commander had realized what only a half-wit would have failed to perceive: Should an American administration invade Cuba, he couldn't confront the U.S. Navy or Air Force. The October 1962 missile crisis and the Soviet Union's hasty pullout confirmed this. Therefore, both Cuban services were designed essentially as reconnaissance forces. Should there be a war, it would be waged on land.

Intervention in Africa somewhat modified such a strategic concept for the air force. The navy's expansion, however, had been limited to manning three outdated, diesel-powered Soviet subs that escorted Cuban transport ships across the South Atlantic. After 1994, the decay of the Cuban navy precipitated. Lacking spare parts, frigates were stripped down, patrol boats moored, their SS-N-2 Styx missile batteries mounted on rolling platforms and placed near beaches to repel improbable amphibious assaults. The Cuban submarine base was converted into a tourist facility in 1998. Demoralization infected officers and enlisted men alike. In 1999, ensign Amieba was appointed skipper of the thirty-five-foot cigarette with twin two-hundred-horsepower outboard engines.

Every time he spent a couple of days in Mariel, Pardo tried to devote at least one evening to playing dominoes with Amieba and a couple of his subordinates, or have a beer or two with the ensign, or simply chat amiably about any conceivable subject, from baseball (both were rabid Pinar del Río fans) to what they did for a living—Pardo pretending to be as aroused by fishing and sailing as Amieba was genuinely interested in computers. In the jokes he told, or in those that made him roar with laughter, and in other seemingly light comments, Amieba reflected dissatisfaction with his present condition and bleak prospects.

Still, one night in December 2001—when their friendship was over two and a half years old, two shots of rum had exacerbated the ensign's frustration, and nobody was around—Amieba admitted to having failed as a naval officer, a husband, and a father. His job consisted of intercepting compatriots fleeing from misery and in picking up "bombarded" bales of cocaine, he had sadly acknowledged. The woman he loved had pulled up stakes and moved in with a farmer seventeen years her senior who made more money in a week than he did in three months, Amieba had further revealed. The guy bought his kid the clothes and toys he could not afford. Persuaded that the ensign craved a fresh start, Pardo decided to test the waters.

"So, why don't you set course north seven degrees west one of these nights and start living the good life?" he had asked jokingly.

"You think we haven't discussed it?" had been Amieba's serious reply.

Pardo admitted to Victoria that the "we" had been no less surprising to him than the admission of the ensign having considered it. Amazing! Had the rest of the crew been reluctant to defect, the use of force would have been unavoidable, but if all were in agreement... From then on things had been as easy as pie. The other three sailors were young, single, and the word "Miami" made their eyes sparkle madly. Pardo had promised to pay Amieba ten thousand dollars for two tickets, one for himself, the other for his wife, a secretary in the Ministry of Basic Industry. Additionally, Pardo would give each sailor a thousand bucks. The ensign figured the money would tide him over until he found a nice job, skipper of a pleasure yacht, for instance. He knew his crew would cheer, embrace him, jump in with both feet on D-night, but Pardo had insisted on not telling them in advance. On April 27, 2002, Amieba already had spent nine weeks anxiously waiting for Defection Night.

"Okay, this is it," he said coming back into his living room and unfolding a map that he placed on the coffee table. "You take a bus to the town of Cabañas, go to 92 Maceo Street, and stay the night at Perla's. Don't mention my name, say someone recommended her. Then, tomorrow evening, you get to the coastline west of the town. Following a dirt road that begins here, one kilometer past the last house, you'll see an empty wooden house on the beach, its windows boarded shut . . ."

...

On the three-foot-tall, cedar credenza behind General Lastra's desk, seven telephones were aligned. The red set communicated with the Commander in Chief, the blue one with his brother, and the green with the minister of the interior. The white set linked Lastra with the chief of counterintelligence, the yellow one with the chief of military intelligence, and the gray phone connected the general with the chief of military counterintelligence. The black set was used to call or answer calls made by lesser mortals. Each had a tiny light that flashed intermittently when ringing. General Lastra was reading a message sent by an illegal based on Isla Morada ever since 1979, when the white set rang and blinked on and off at 11:23 A.M. on Sunday, April 28.

"Lastra," he said into the mouthpiece.

"How are things going, Mr. Cloak-and-Dagger?"

Lastra smiled. "I'm not complaining, you contemptible repressor of independent journalists and human-rights activists."

The man on the other end of the line, Gen. Edmundo Fernández (cryptonym Timoteo), head of counterintelligence, chuckled. "They haven't seen anything yet," he sneered. "I'm told the Chief's patience is wearing thin. He may unleash us anytime. I'm considering bringing back a couple of the Batista geezers and have them teach us how to conduct interrogations."

In 1958, Fernández's father had been tortured to death at a police station. His poorly concealed desire to avenge his dad had made him a star in counterintelligence in the sixties. His thirst for revenge hadn't been quenched yet. Lastra thought it prudent to change the subject.

"Don't talk trash. So, what have you got for me?"

"It seems this genius of yours didn't sleep at her place last night, neither did her husband. The car is not in the building's garage, either."

Lastra frowned. "You sure?"

"It's what the super reports."

"Reliable guy?"

"Quite."

Lastra had to think a moment. "Okay. I'll look into it. Thanks a lot, Edmundo."

"Take care, Lastra."

"Bye."

After hanging up, the head of Intelligence lighted his midmorning cigar for the third time and mulled things over for almost ten minutes. Two weeks earlier, dreading that Pardo could hurt Victoria, he had asked Counterintelligence to keep an eye on the dude. He had not made that decision lightly. High-ranking Intelligence officers or their spouses are not kept under surveillance for any but the most compelling of reasons. Although Pardo did not strike him as being prone to violence, he nonetheless wanted to play it safe. So, Lastra had dropped by General Edmundo's office, explained things to him, and asked him to tap his informers at the Institute of Meteorology and the apartment building. No round-the-clock, full-fledged surveillance was deemed necessary. He just wanted snitches to report whether Pardo was absent from work, or if loud-voiced arguments or strange sounds came from their penthouse. Watching the video with Pardo's confession had lessened his concern; he had not called off the monitoring, though.

Today was Sunday, he remembered. Maybe Victoria, playing the part of the loving wife reveling in the prospect of fleeing Cuba, had taken Pardo somewhere for a second honeymoon. No, she would have let him know in advance. Maybe their car broke down, or they had an accident. No, he would have been notified by now. Lastra got to his feet and strode purposefully to a filing cabinet, opened the top drawer, and extracted Victoria's file. He flipped its pages on the way back to his desk, then used the black phone to dial her home number.

"Leave your message," said the psychologist's machine after the fourth ring.

Lastra hung up, scanned the personnel file some more, then lifted the white phone and punched zero.

"Edmundo."

"Ah, listen, Edmundo. Could you ask the police to be on the lookout for a light blue Tico, plate number HM-83212."

"Sure. Your genius's?"

"Yeah."

"Nationwide?"

Lastra considered it. "Might as well, yeah."

"You want the driver followed, intercepted, questioned, arrested?"

"No, no, I just want to know where it is and the driver's description."

"Okay. Will let you know."

When asking their checkpoints, cruisers, and traffic cops to locate vehicles, Cuban police had established priorities: State Security requests had top priority. State Security was how the General Directorate of Counterintelligence was popularly known; the IDs of its officers had the letters DSE in green diagonally superimposed—initials for Departamento de Seguridad del Estado in Spanish, the name first used by the services in post-Batista Cuba. *El boniato,* the sweet potato, was how lower-rank SS officers called the most frightening identification that could be flashed to Cuban citizens, including police officers. All of which explains why less than three hours after talking to Edmundo, at 2:17 P.M., as he was having lunch at home, General Lastra's cell phone vibrated.

"Gabriel."

"Timoteo. Give me a call."

Having been warned that the U.S. Interests Section in Havana had installed technology to monitor cell phone calls, high-ranking government officials were under orders not to talk about sensitive matters "over the air." Lastra pocketed his cell phone. His wife gave a deep sigh of resignation: Once again, her husband's meal would get cold. The general fished a small phone book from his shirt pocket and, while approaching his secure line, looked up General Edmundo's office number. He lifted the receiver and punched it.

"Edmundo."

"Why still in the office?"

"I've got my hands full. Fucking Jeffrey is wining and dining a few counters this evening."

Jeffrey was Jeffrey De Laurentis, political counselor at the U.S. Interests Section. "What do you got for me?" Lastra asked.

"Your Tico is parked in front of Teatro Sauto, in Matanzas. It's locked up."

Lastra remained silent for a minute, mental wheels churning at top speed.

"You there?" asked a somewhat impatient Edmundo.

"I'm here."

"So, what do you want?"

"Thank the police and get them out of this. And if you can spare a couple of men in Matanzas, ask them to keep the car under observation and to let me know the minute someone gets into it."

"Consider it done."

"And Edmundo . . ."

"Yes."

"I don't like this. I may have to call you back in a while."

At 5:41 P.M., General Lastra finished his report to the minister of the interior.

"And what do you suggest, Lastra?" prompted the minister. He was quite pissed off. There seemed to be a concerted effort to spoil his Sunday afternoon drinking habit.

"An immediate, top-to-bottom search of the apartment and, if we don't find clues as to where she might be, a nationwide all-points bulletin. I recommend faxing photos of her and Pardo to the police, Coast Guard, and Immigration. Suspects wanted for questioning on a murder case, to scare everyone into immediate action. We'll give Victoria a false name."

The minister frowned. "Coast Guard and Immigration, Lastra?"

The general nodded.

"Why?"

Sure that this question would be asked, on his way to the ministry Lastra had come up with a plausible reason to mask his worst fear. "Because I suspect Pardo somehow discovered Victoria had taken him for a ride and has kidnapped her, Lieutenant General. He may try to steal a boat or a plane, holding her hostage."

"Okay. Go ahead. I'll call Operations and order the apartment searched. Meanwhile get the all-points bulletin and the photos ready."

"Yes, Comrade Lieutenant General."

A few minutes past 7:00 P.M., the man in charge of searching the apartment reported the place empty. At first sight, no bloodstains or signs of struggle were visible. The team would begin combing the place immediately. Lastra returned the handset of his black phone to its cradle and locked gazes with his secretary and jack-of-all-trades, summoned to the office two hours earlier. Amado Pernas, a not-too-bright, fifty-five-year-old captain and dyed-in-the-wool Maoist, had been with Lastra for eleven years now. Maintenance and cleaning staff were denied access to his boss's office for security reasons, and Pernas was also in charge of cleaning up, polishing the furniture, changing light bulbs, whatever.

"Fax the all-points and the photos to the officer on duty at the ministry. They'll take it from there."

...

Victoria and Pardo stealthily approached the tumbledown, empty vacation home described by ensign Amieba the previous night. They wore black jeans and boots, long-sleeved shirts—hers olive green, his dark blue—and black gloves. Their faces were mud-caked. She carried the now lighter duffel bag. As a boy at his parents' farm, Pardo had grown accustomed to hearing owls calling, bats screeching, and crickets chirping at night, whereas Victoria found every animal sound slightly unnerving. The seabreeze had died after sunset; half an hour later an inland wind started blowing.

They had been furtively watching the sequestered house from a distance for nearly two hours, making sure no hobo had taken refuge in it and that none was lurking in the immediate vicinity. They had sat on the ground by a huge mango tree on the other side of a four-thread barbed-wire fence. Feeling his wife tense, once again Pardo explained why Amieba was so sure he could sneak into Key West undetected. Simple reason: He had done so twice, on official trips to bring back state-owned fishing boats stolen by other escapees. Considering those trips excellent opportunities to put to the test U.S. naval detection techniques, Cuban Military Intelligence ordered Pardo to furtively approach Key West in the middle of the night. The U.S. Coast Guard had been informed beforehand of the day of arrival, not the time. And they failed to pick up his craft on the first two trips.

On his third, the U.S. Interests Section in Havana had peremptorily demanded his estimated day *and* time of arrival.

The beach house had fallen in disrepair over the years, but if refurbished inside and out it would be habitable again. The biggest problem its owner faced, Pardo supposed, was how to get his hands on the necessary planks of wood, as lumber ranked first on the list of hard-to-find building materials. They went around the house and, exactly as Amieba had predicted, weak moonlight revealed a rustic, five-yard-long by two-feet-wide wooden platform sticking out from the land into the sea, a ten-foot boat moored to it.

The sea was calm, the tide ebbing, and tame waves licked the shore with a lover's gentleness. Fleeing crabs and scurrying rodents sought refuge in the scarce wild coastal vegetation. Pardo relieved his wife of the duffel bag before testing the platform's firmness with a step-by-step careful approach. Waiting on the shoreline, Victoria looked back a couple of times and found it comforting to touch the inside-the-pant holster that nestled her Tula-Tokarev, 7.62mm semi-automatic pistol. Her husband boarded the boat and found, to port and starboard, resting lengthwise on the boards for oarsmen and passengers to sit, two eight-foot-long oars. He sat with his back to the bow, hauled the duffel bag in, and waved Victoria to come over. Moving swiftly, in less than fifteen seconds she was sitting astern, facing Pardo, who then released the mooring line, pushed the boat away from the platform, affixed the oars to the outriggers, and began rowing into the open sea. It was 10:19 P.M.

As her husband sculled, Victoria cast worried glances at the shore. To the east, the faraway lights of Cabañas could be seen. To the west and north, all was dark. The clear sky was simply spectacular. She gripped the duffel bag firmly and tried not to think what would be happening to her and Pardo if Amieba turned out to be a military counterintelligence agent. Following instructions, Pardo stared fixedly at the darkened house to keep the boat on a straight course, perpendicular to the coastline.

"Time?" he asked, breathing hard.

Victoria took off her gloves before pressing the light button of her Casio. "10:27."

Pardo nodded and kept rowing.

Nearly two minutes later they began hearing the *chug-chug* of low-revved marine engines growing louder.

"Get ready," Pardo warned.

Victoria pulled out a penlight from a pocket of her shirt. Again, she pressed the light button of her watch and fastened her gaze on the dial. The boat was rocking slightly now and her stomach churned. At 10:30:00, she pointed the penlight west and turned it on for two seconds.

On board the cigarette boat, Amieba lowered his infrared binoculars and made a tiny course correction.

Victoria dropped the penlight into the duffel bag, tightening its drawstring. Encouraged by the rising crescendo of the approaching cigarette, Pardo stopped rowing. The swaying increased notably. Victoria began washing her face with seawater. Pardo imitated her. Suddenly she vomited all over the bottom. Out of the blackness, the dark silhouette of the patrol boat loomed. A mooring line fell behind Pardo, who turned, grabbed it, and pulled. A second line fell on Victoria's lap. She breathed deeply, swallowed hard, and hauled. Both vessels joined sides.

"Welcome aboard, comrade," a young sailor said as he extended his arm to Victoria Valiente. Smiling at the "comrade," Victoria hauled the duffel bag and passed it on to him. When he stretched his arm out for a second time, she closed her fingers over his wrist and, in one swift motion, was hoisted over the gunwale.

...

The cockpit had bolster seats, two behind the windshield for the pilot and the copilot, a backseat for three passengers. To starboard, sitting at the helm and facing numerous dials and switches, Amieba half turned to stare at his passengers. A Chinese Tokarev pistol in a hip holster hung from his webbed belt. To port, an AK-47 lay at the feet of the crewman acting as copilot. The two coastguardsmen who helped the couple aboard sat on the back, where a second AK-47 lay. The blue lights of the light bar were off. The Cuban flag flew astern. The radio babbled in Spanish.

"You seasick?" Amieba asked Victoria.

"A little, yeah. I'll be okay," she said with a rueful smile.

"Fine, go to the cabin. Both of you. We've got work to do here. Sit down and brace yourselves. In a few minutes this baby will take off."

In the dimly lit cabin, Pardo and Victoria found a custom leather wraparound sofa, a small dinette area, a V-berth, a stainless steel sink, a cooler, and freshwater outlets. Pardo served Victoria a glass of water. As she was drinking it, the engines revved up notably and they sensed a change of course. Pardo sat by her side and they held hands. The din of the twin outboards was bearable until, at 10:54, they were thrown against their seats as "the baby took off." Lights were then turned out. The ensuing uproar, vibration, and occasional jumps as the patrol boat bounced over waves were too much for Victoria. She threw up the water she had drank and added some of her bodily fluids. Pardo careened her to the V-berth and she lay down feeling physically exhausted. Every half an hour or so, she took out an inhaler and pumped it twice.

The ordeal lasted one and a half hours. At 12:20 the outboards were gradually taken down from full tilt to the barely audible chug heard earlier.

"Have we arrived?" Victoria probed.

"I don't think so. We should be close, though."

A minute later, soaked to the skin, Amieba entered the cabin. Having their eyes adjusted to darkness, his smile reassured them. "We're almost there, guys, almost there. How are you feeling, ma'am?" Sniffing the vomit made his smile vanish. "Not well, right?"

"To tell you the truth, not well at all. But getting better. Why are you drenched?"

"Every time the hull hits the water at fifty miles an hour and there's a little headwind, the cockpit gets sprayed out."

"Of course. How stupid of me."

"It's okay. Now, let me explain what I'm going to do. We are sixteen nautical miles or so from Key West. I'm monitoring the U.S. Coast Guard frequency; their radar hasn't picked us up. So, I'll try to sneak in. Lights off, slow approach, it'll take an hour, maybe more. If we suddenly pick up speed again, it means they are coming after us and I'm trying to run aground on Higgs Beach, South Beach, wherever, so we classify as "dry feet" arrivals. If you are going to wash and change, do it once I get back to the cockpit. Not easy in the dark, especially for you, ma'am. But we can't turn on the lights."

"No problem," Pardo said.

"Think you could give me my money now?" asked Amieba.

Without saying a word, Pardo turned, rummaged through the duffel bag, and extracted something wrapped in a page of *Granma,* the official newspaper of the Communist Party, and the penlight. "Here you are. A hundred one-hundred-dollar bills. Count it."

The newspaper page made the ensign chuckle; he let it glide to the floor. Pardo turned the penlight on, pointing its beam down. Amieba flipped over the wad peering at the corners of the bills, not counting, just checking that all had the right number. Then he drew a plastic bag out from a flap pocket of his trousers, dropped the cash into it, slipped a rubber band off his wrist, put it around the bag, and dropped it into the flap pocket.

"Thanks," he said.

"No, thank you. Could you send your men in now, Amieba?" asked Pardo. "I want to pay them. We'll wash and change after that."

"Great. One by one. Okay?"

"Okay," Pardo agreed.

Uncertain whether Amieba had explained clearly to his men how they would go about it, before giving them their money Pardo briefed the soaked sailors. He and his wife did not exist. They were seeing things. No civilians were on board. The crew had sailed to Key West on the spur of the moment, sick and tired of Cuban misery. INS officials would interrogate them separately, make promises, offer deals, give their word. But none of this would be fulfilled if so much as one of them admitted that they had transported civilians. Instead, all would be tried and sentenced as human traffickers and sent back to Cuba. They would most probably be searched, Pardo warned. If their cash was found, what could they say? That it had fallen into their laps, like manna from heaven? It would be obvious they had not fled Cuba on the spur of the moment, so he advised them to hide it somewhere before turning themselves in.

Not before reaching Tampa would he and his wife go to the INS. Once there, they would say they had arrived in a raft. Should they be nabbed in Key West, they would say the same thing. In the event one of them, or the whole crew, bumped into him or his wife at a cafeteria, in the street, or in jail, greetings, winks, and every other sign of recognition were strictly forbidden. Under no circumstance would he and his wife admit having sailed in the cigarette boat.

"Understood?"

"Understood, comrade."

No offense was meant or sarcasm intended when using such a term. Over the years "comrade" had become a household word to such a point that sometimes a son or daughter answered a parent's question with "Yes, comrade." Victoria, however, was addressed with the more respectful *señora*. All three had an identical reaction when given their cash: wide-eyed admiration at pocketing twenty fifty-dollar bills. Each young man politely thanked Pardo before returning to the cockpit.

"Feeling better?" Pardo asked his wife.

"By the minute since we slowed down."

"Want to wash and change now?"

"Let's do it."

Once they rinsed their faces, Pardo emptied the duffel bag on the wraparound sofa. Victoria took off her gun, keys, jeans, shirt, boots, and underwear, then slipped into pantyhose and a strapless, black lacy bra. Next, she donned for the first time an elegant, albeit somewhat dated, black halter-neck evening gown bought by Pardo in Madrid in 1998. She put on black moccasins and reached for a plastic bag containing new, high-heeled black shoes. Finally, she seized a black purse that had inside a brand-new wallet with two hundred and fifty dollars, cosmetics, and the key to a safe-deposit box in Paris, France.

Meanwhile, Pardo undressed and donned cream-colored slacks, a white dress shirt, a dark blue sports jacket, and brown loafers. He put a money clip with four thousand dollars in one-hundred dollar bills into the left side pocket of the slacks, slipped his wallet with nine twenty-dollar bills into the back pocket, inserted his wife's gun over his lower back. The Costa Rican passport with his photo, and a CD with banking information went into the inner breast pocket of the sports jacket.

Following this, he thrust the discarded boots and clothing into the duffel bag. He pulled the drawstrings tight, seized it, reached the entranceway to the cabin, stooped, and went out. Amieba concentrated on steering and peering into the darkness. His copilot was holding the infrared binoculars to his eyes. The other two coast-guardsmen sat in the backseat, AK-47s on their laps, in wartime silence. Pardo could see city lights not too far away. The sea was calm. The outboards hummed quietly.

"Chief," the youngest sailor warned Amieba in a hushed tone after seeing Pardo emerge from the cabin. The ensign turned in his seat, spotted Pardo, looked him up and down, raised his eyebrows, and gave him an approving nod, saying "You all dressed up" with his expression.

"This bag . . ."

Amieba shushed him, then beckoned him over.

With two steps, Pardo was at his side. "Voices travel far over water," the ensign whispered. "What do you want?"

"This bag holds the old rags we wore and two pairs of boots," Pardo explained, his voice lowered to a whisper, too. "They shouldn't be found here. I want them to sink to the bottom. Any problem with that?"

Amieba considered it for an instant. "We'll see to it. Give it to Jesús, the guy to my left" was his reply.

Once the youngest sailor had the duffel bag, he cast a questioning glance at the skipper for instructions. By jerking his thumb out twice, the ensign signaled to get rid of the bag. Then his forefinger pointed at the bottom of the boat. Jesús assented, loosened the drawstring, bent overboard to port, held the bag by the strap until it filled with seawater to the top, pulled the drawstring tight again, then let the bag go. It dropped sixty-five feet to the bottom.

"Thanks," Pardo said, then went back inside the cabin. He addressed Victoria. "We are nearer to Key West, I suppose."

"How do you know?"

"City lights look pretty close."

"Oh."

For the next fifty minutes, like a nearly invisible virus invading an organism several trillion times its size, the purring outboards slipped the cigarette in. To fight off what she judged an acute attack of anxiety, Victoria closed her eyes and breathed deeply. She couldn't stop turning over in her mind the events that had taken place in the last few hours. Pardo kept checking the immediate parts of their project. They had considered two possibilities—arriving undetected or getting caught—and had plans for both. They sat on the wraparound, Victoria comfortably against the back of the seat, Pardo hunched forward as the gun prevented him from reclining, both staring at the entrance. Following what seemed like an eternity, they felt the boat scrape something. Were they motionless now? It seemed so. The outboards barely whispered. Victoria pressed the light of her Casio. 1:35. Amieba came into the cabin less than a minute later.

"Would you please go ashore, comrades?" displaying his best smile.

"You've got to be kidding," Victoria mumbled in a quivering voice.

Unbelieving, they went up. The cigarette was moored to a ten-slip, five-foot-wide dock, alongside a Chrysler 26 Cruiser sailboat, across from a Thomas Point forty-three-foot power cruiser. Side-moored at the end, too huge to fit anywhere else, a two-deck, over one-hundred-foot power cruiser dwarfed the other vessels. To their left, a slick-looking, two-story white building with a pagoda-like blue roof and a verandah sparkled against a fuzzy background. Somewhat behind it, to its right, a five-story building identically painted seemed the overgrown mama's boy of the nearer construction.

"Hurry, Pardo," Amieba, urging him. "I can't waste a second."

"But what's this place?"

"How the fuck should I know?"

Pardo leaped out first and helped Victoria. Jesús stood on the dock holding a mooring line, looking uptight. Pardo waved to Amieba and his crew, gave Jesús a pat on the back. Victoria blew kisses to those on board, kissed Jesús on his cheek. Holding hands, the couple ambled away along the dock. They heard the outboards coming to life and turned. Jesús had hopped in, the boat was going out again.

"C'mon, let's move on," Pardo whispered.

They reached the end of the dock, crossed between mama and her big boy. After fifty yards or so they found a sign that read HYATT MARINA RESORT. Victoria paused, extracted the high-heeled shoes from the plastic bag, shook off the moccasins, put on the new shoes, dropped the moccasins into the bag, and abandoned them behind a shrub. Two minutes later they were in Mallory Square.

...

The first thing Pardo and Victoria did when they found a diner was to use the restrooms. Afterward, although only one customer was sitting at the counter having a cup of coffee, they chose a table at the back. The server, accustomed to tourists, was not in the least surprised by their accents. Victoria asked for a cup of chamomile tea, which she sipped slowly. Her husband devoured a huge Cuban *medianoche:* thin slices of Southern-style ham, lacey Swiss cheese, roasted pork, and pickled cucumbers in a special bread onto which mustard and butter had been generously spread. What made *medianoches* unique were the bread and the pork, in particular a pinch of sugar and something else in the bread dough, malt maybe? He downed it with a beer.

"This is excellent," he commented halfway into the sandwich.

Victoria wondered how it was possible that her husband could be so flip as to sit there eating a damn sandwich with so much relish. Men!

Later, waiting for his change, Pardo registered what he hadn't noticed in the darkened cabin or under the streetlights: Despite having put on a little makeup in the restroom, Victoria looked gaunt and pale, with dark crescents under her eyes.

"How are you feeling, Vicky?" he asked solicitously.

"Better. These shoes are killing me, though."

Pardo wondered how it was possible that his wife, after such a grueling experience, still recovering from an asthma attack, on the cusp of an amazing life change, could complain, of all things, about a fucking pair of shoes. Women!

The server put a plastic plate with the change on the table.

"Could you call us a cab, please?"

"Sure," the woman said and marched away. Pardo left two one-dollar bills on the plate.

"You tipping two dollars for a sandwich, a beer, and a cup of tea?" Victoria murmured.

"And a phone call."

"Yeah, and a phone call."

"Vicky, this is Key West. You don't want to attract attention, you tip generously. You want this woman to remember us forever, you leave her a quarter."

Victoria breathed a sigh. "Okay, sorry. I forgot."

In the cab's backseat, Pardo reclined after sliding the gun to his left side. The cabman drove them to the bus station at Twenty-seventh Street, but warned them that it would be closed at this hour. Pardo asked him to wait while they got out and questioned a security guard. The man said the next bus to Miami was a Key Line Express that departed at 5:00 A.M. Pardo's watch read 2:32. He thanked the man and went back to the taxi.

"Hey, my friend, where can we spend the next two hours?" he asked the cabbie.

The man half turned in his seat and raised his eyebrows. "There're a zillion places. Sloppy Joe's, Hard Rock Café, there's this nice Irish pub on Grinell Street, Finnegan's Wake . . ."

"No bars, please," Victoria pleaded.

"Ma'am, this hour, churches ain't open."

"C'mon, honey," Pardo said to his wife in English, squeezing her hand, "let's check out this Irish place. You don't have to drink alcohol. Just a soda or something."

Victoria agreed, realizing they had no choice. Tonight, for Latin-looking foreigners, staying outdoors was not such a good idea. The plan was that, once they hid their money, Amieba and his guys would walk into town, find a police officer, and give themselves up. Then ringing phones would awaken every official in Key West; more phones would get journalists on their feet. Definitely not a good time to be on the street.

This was why they let themselves be taken to 320 Grinell Street. Steil gave the driver a ten, told him to keep the change, and asked to be picked up at 4:30.

"Place closes at four, Mister."

"Okay, at four then."

It was a two-story wooden structure painted white. Through a double door flanked by shop windows and potted plants, they entered a quaint pub where polished dark wood reigned. At the curved bar, talking in low tones, nursing their drinks, sat two white-haired overweight men. The bartender looked bored. Patrons stared at the latest arrivals on account of their clothes. Everybody else was wearing T-shirts, shorts, and sandals or flip-flops.

They chose a table for two at the back and took the place in. Flags and pictures on the walls, a small bandstand, lamps hanging from the ceiling. Three nearby tables were occupied by people who, judging by their slurs and the boisterous fun they were having, would wake up tomorrow afternoon with a lousy hangover. The place was evidently winding down, its staff looking tired. A longhaired, good-looking brunette server strode past tables and approached them with a giant smile, as if waiting on people made her the happiest person in Florida. When Victoria said she was not having anything, the brunette refined her act, began wheedling the customer. How come? With so many wonderful drinks to be had? A margarita? A frozen Kahlua? A pina colada? This elicited a smile from Victoria. Why couldn't Anglos pronounce the letter *ñ*?

"No drinks, thanks."

"How about a sandwich, a dessert maybe?" moving to food.

Victoria cocked her head and stared at her.

"A Cutie pie? An Irish bread pudding? How about hot apple pie with vanilla ice cream?" the waitress probed.

"Hot apple pie?" Victoria asked, and the young waitress knew she had this Latino woman in the bag.

"Yes, ma'am. Homemade."

"Okay, I'll have a portion."

"And to drink?"

"Iced tea, maybe?

"Excellent choice. And you, sir?"

"Just a beer."

"Draft, domestic, imported?"

"Ah . . . whichever."

"Whichever sir?"

"Heineken."

"Be right over."

Her first encounter with the consumer society impressed Victoria.

"Did you see that?" she asked Pardo.

"What?"

"The quality of the service? Mommy wouldn't let me go to bed on an empty stomach."

"It's how the system works. She probably earns a basic hourly wage, plus a commission on sales. She wants us to leave her a nice tip, too."

The young woman came with their order less than a minute later. Having found the pie and the ice cream delicious, Victoria perked up a little.

For the nth time they distractedly made the comparisons and reached the conclusions 99 percent of Cubans make and reach when traveling abroad. Individuals think about helping others only after their basic needs are satisfied. Communism goes against human nature, ergo its failure. For Cuban servers, the client is the enemy because they earn the same miserable wage if they serve fifty or five hundred on their shift. Where the dollar is the valid currency, they must donate part of their tips to the government. Since there is little motivation, clients are not welcome. They interrupt conversations, thwart watching a favorite TV program or listening to music on the radio, interfere with eyeing the chicks with the hefty behinds going by. Barmen and kitchen staff put less rum in the *mojito* and serve meager portions to sell surpluses on the black market. But it was not a revelation; they had discussed this many times in the past few years.

"The furniture here seems pretty old," Pardo, changing the subject. He was beginning to tire of discussing the same topic over and over.

Victoria gazed around thoughtfully. "Yeah, trying to preserve an ambience, I guess. You saw the photos on the walls? The thirties, Hemingway, that sort of thing."

"The tourists probably eat it up."

"Probably. But you know what? I'm sick and tired of old things. Havana is frozen in time. I want to see modernity, *macho*.

They kept shooting the breeze, Pardo ordering a second beer. There were periods of silence as well, five, six minutes long. They had discussed every step of the way so many times and at such great length, there was no need to do it again. What they yearned for was a place to sleep.

"Victoria. You are incredible."

"Why is that?"

"When you told me you had denounced me to the minister, I almost peed in my pants."

"It's why I told you after doing it. You would've been against creating a diversion."

"I would've been against *that* diversion. My life was at stake."

"No. It wasn't. Had it been, I wouldn't have done it."

"It worked."

"Of course, it had to. Now, if you hadn't accessed your account . . ."

"I know," raising his hands to ward her off. "I know. It was so stupid of me."

"We all make mistakes."

"You don't."

"Everybody makes mistakes, *macho*. Everybody."

The white-haired men at the bar lumbered off their stools and took their leave. The young waitress eyed the remaining clients warily. At 3:53, smiling to pretend she hated to spoil the fun, she left the tabs on the tables.

"How much?" Victoria wanted to know.

"Fourteen bucks," Pardo said, taking his wallet out.

"I can't believe it," seizing the check, reading the total, putting it back on the plate. "Fourteen dollars for a pie, a scoop of ice cream, a glass of iced tea, and two beers?"

"And an hour and a half killing time here, Vicky. This is a tourist town. But I don't expect prices to be much cheaper anywhere else. This is the U.S. of A. You better get used to it."

"We are being fleeced. And on top of that, you'll tip her two?"

"Three, 'cause she doted on you."

"That's . . . over 20 percent."

"Such a cheapskate."

The cabbie was waiting for them. Pardo thought it prudent to not get to the bus station before it opened for the day, so he asked the driver to take them to Hemingway's house. Yeah, he knew it would be closed, it was okay. The hacker, happy as long as his meter was ticking, drove them there and then suggested they take a peek at Jackson Square, the Audubon House and Gardens, and Land's End Village. At this last place Victoria checked her watch. 4:28. She nudged Pardo with her elbow and tapped the Casio dial.

"Okay, friend, take us to the bus station now," he requested.

A police cruiser, flashers gone mad, rounded a corner and sped away. The cabbie grunted. Amieba and his men could be the cause for the cop's hurry, both passengers thought.

"That cheap watch of yours doesn't go with such an elegant dress. Take it off," Pardo whispered in her ear. She mulled on that, nodded, and complied.

At the station, Pardo was asked for a photo ID to buy the tickets to Miami. He had not foreseen this, and it surprised him. An ID to buy two bus tickets? Victoria was in the restroom at the moment. Thinking that security was tighter here than he expected, he showed his Costa Rican passport to the man, then forked over $106. Eventually, at a quarter past five, northbound from the airport on U.S. 1, the most hectic hours of their lives now past, they relaxed. The air conditioner made Victoria shiver, and she rubbed her arms up and down. Pardo took his jacket off, concealed the butt of the gun under his shirt, and covered his wife. They reclined their seats, and by the time the bus crossed through Boca Chica Key both were sound asleep.

. . .

A little after half past five in the morning on Monday, April 29, General Lastra's full bladder made him get up. Mulling over Victoria's disappearance, he shaved, brushed his teeth, brewed espresso, and lit his first Lancero of the day. A few minutes past six, Lastra abandoned the five-bedroom, two-story residence in Nuevo Vedado—built to order in 1957 by a very rich Cuban lawyer who three years later emigrated to Spain—in which his wife, two daughters, two sons-in-law, and five grandchildren still slept soundly.

Driving his Lada to Línea and A Street, he experienced a foreboding that he would soon learn something bad concerning the psychologist. She had either committed suicide, been abducted, murdered, or had flown the coop. She would be given a quiet burial if she had killed herself. If abducted, they would find her. Had she been murdered, she would get a hero's funeral and her assassin would be executed by firing squad.

He feared the worst possible outcome: desertion. Why would she? he wondered. It was unlikely she had been recruited by an enemy service. Some things work both ways, though. You pull a fast one on them, they pull a fast one on you. It happens everywhere. Ask Jacoby, Wilson, or Hughes at the DIA. Tenet or McLaughlin at the CIA. Sessions, Freeh, or Mueller at the FBI. If she hadn't been recruited, what had made her chicken out, feel frustrated, unhappy, or whatever pissed psychologists off? He could understand that the many millions living in misery wanted to flee, but not her. She had recently been presented with a wonderful apartment and a brand-new car. She could buy whatever she wanted at the ministry's special shop, was a member of the most exclusive Cuban clan, the Chief's clan. At no time had she shown reluctance to fulfill her duties, nor express the slightest doubt about anything. A crisis of conscience perhaps? There was no reason for it. She had nothing to do with the repression of peaceful dissidents, prisons, the sort of thing that may weigh heavily on an officer's scruples over the course of time. He could not make sense of it.

If she had defected, Cuban Intelligence would lose Miami. Five cells, fifteen top-level agents, an excellent cobbler, three cutouts, and dozens of informers—he made a mental note to check the exact number later in the day. Even if she didn't turn them in, assuming that she had was a basic rule. In a week, two at most, they had to consider that the rival services were feeding them crap through the exposed networks. Such a loss four years after the Wasp setback and one year after the DIA agent had been exposed would be devastating. Even worse, Victoria was a repository of knowledge concerning Cuban Intelligence; she could give away agents in Europe and Latin America, too.

For him it would be the end. He would be sent into retirement, no doubt. Thirty-dollar-monthly pension, no more complimentary rations of food, clothing, and toiletries for the whole family, no more Lanceros, either. Never again would his grandchildren vacation at a nice beach all expenses paid. He would be kept under constant surveillance for the rest of his life, in case he considered following her steps. Lastra found himself wishing Victoria were dead.

Had she defected, he deserved the punishment for being so stupid, if for nothing else. Were that supposition correct, he had been tricked into believing what had in fact been a masterful performance. No, it was more than that. She had set a perfect trap into which he had ambled sight unseen. Well, come to think of it, he'd fallen for both things: the masterful performance and the perfect trap. The minister had, too, but the poor man's brain only functioned in combat. In his mind's eye he could see her standing at the rigid position of attention, ranting, "I serve the Socialist Revolution!" It was perhaps the single moment when she had overacted. An intelligent individual behaving like a soulless automaton. No, not even then; that line of verse had been intended for the minister, not for him. So good, she was sooo good.

Suddenly the most probable reason for the desertion exploded in his mind like fireworks. His surprise was so overwhelming that he kicked the brakes, and escaped getting rear-ended by a few inches. Seeing a guy in mufti and the civilian plates, the driver behind him tooted the horn in anger for several seconds before calling Lastra a shit-eater. Dude was right on the money, the general thought, he *was* a shit-eater. Lastra swerved to the right lane, pulling over to the curb at Twenty-sixth Avenue between Twenty-fifth and Twenty-seventh Streets. He killed the engine, turned the headlights off, and, puffing on the Lancero, took a moment to consider what had dawned on him so unexpectedly.

She had told them the truth: Pardo was the XEMIC thief. But they had acted in collusion! Both had been considering desertion for years! Not before they had the money to live comfortably the rest of their lives, though. Victoria had defected for $2.6 million! The enemy had not recruited her; she had not been pissed off. She and her cocksucker husband had achieved a master coup and now wanted to enjoy the fruits of their labors! However, for certain reasons he could not immediately come up with, they decided to set the trap and stage the comedy. Maybe to gain time until they were ready to leave, or to have an alternate solution available. He would find out eventually.

Okay, what should he do next? First, calm down, take it easy. Maybe his perfectly understandable occupational disease—suspecting everybody—had evolved into a disorder requiring medical treatment. Maybe Pardo had just killed her. He chuckled at the *just*. Assuming that nerdy, coolheaded sons of bitches murdered people. What he ought to do was show concern for his most brilliant subordinate, keep his suspicion to himself, and wait to see how things worked out. He turned the key in the ignition.

Three blocks from his office, at Calzada and Second Street, he remembered the server's report. That was probably the detonator that had caused this explosion. Had to be. Pardo had bungled badly when he accessed his offshore bank account, the Jersey bank, from home. Victoria knew that the network administrator had to make frequent reports and would mention it. The scheming cunt had covered their asses immediately and brilliantly with the most audacious diversion! He had been preempted with a stunning red herring! Chances were Victoria Valiente was alive and kicking, on board a plane or a boat, already in another country maybe.

The guard at the entrance to the garage gave him a martial salute that he distractedly returned, cigar loosely held between forefinger and middle finger. He steered the car to his marked parking bay and rode the elevator to the ninth floor, where the officer on duty was standing watch. Lastra turned the handle and pushed the door open; the man jumped to his feet.

"Good morning, Comrade General."

"Good morning, Major. What's new?"

The man lowered his eyes to the logbook. "The UN mission's chief of station sent an urgent message at 0254 hours; it's already been decoded. At 0322 hours, the counterintelligence officer on duty informed us that nothing suspicious was found at the apartment you asked to be searched. We've been getting hourly reports on a Tico parked in Matanzas, as well; nobody has approached it. And at 0531 the Revolutionary Navy reported a patrol boat missing."

Poker-faced, Lastra kept his eyes glued to the officer, processing the information, wondering whether . . . "You mean missing as sunk by an enemy craft or missing as . . . disappeared?"

"No specifics on that, Comrade General."

"Anything else, Major?"

"No, Comrade General."

"Okay. Take care."

Lastra ambled to his office, pressed his right thumb on the Chinese-made fingerprint lock, pushed through the door, went to his desk, and logged on to CNN International. He double-clicked on the headline "Four Cuban coast guard members defect." He read on. "Four camouflage-clad, Cuban coast guard members arrived Monday morning in Key West, where they told police they had raced across the Straits of Florida in a Cuban patrol boat they took while on duty, police said."

Lastra learned that the four men had grounded the thirty-five-foot escape boat on a beach, walked into town, surrendered to a police cruiser, and applied for political asylum. One had a Chinese handgun that the police confiscated. Two AK-47s and eight loaded magazines were found on the boat. The radio was monitoring the U.S. Coast Guard frequency.

The general mulled things over. Too strange a coincidence. He did not take comfort from the fact that the four deserters were men. Lastra suspected two things: that Victoria and her husband had fled Cuba on that boat, and that Pardo was not among those who had surrendered to the police. Somehow the couple had managed to escape Key West authorities undetected. Or maybe not. Maybe she called the FBI office and said: "Hey, guys? Want to learn a couple of things about Cuban espionage?" Had she, her defection would not be made public until she had been squeezed dry, weeks from now. You win some, you lose some.

He knew the first thing he should do to confirm his suspicions. Ask Military Counterintelligence where the patrol boat had been based—Matanzas possibly, unless the "heroine" had abandoned the

Tico there as another misleading clue—then ask Edmundo to find out if Pardo had recently visited relatives or friends who lived close to the naval base or worked there. He would not move a finger, though. He would play dumb for a while, let someone else figure it out. He wondered what the Chief would say when told that the woman he had vaunted so much, maybe even had slated to be the next chief of intelligence, had deserted and joined the ranks of his enemies. And guess who he would take it out on. Lastra felt he was finished.

An idea came to his mind like a snake slithering slowly out of its cave. Had Victoria fled in that boat, maybe she was on her way to Miami. If so, she may try to contact the network to obtain false documents and IDs. Now, if he warned the resident director that a traitor might try to establish contact . . .

Seven

The bus taking Manuel Pardo and Victoria Valiente to Miami was twenty or thirty minutes away, depending on traffic, from the city's international airport, where the ride ended. Even though spring was no big deal this far south, the sun shone in the clear sky, and the leaves of trees and shrubs, the fronds of palms, and the lawns reflected shades of newly arisen greens.

Four and half hours earlier, relieved from anxiety and utterly exhausted, Victoria had fallen sound asleep. Now she was dreaming that someone had seized her right wrist and was forcing her to take hold of a thick broom handle. With eyes rolling beneath their lids, Victoria wondered why she had to clean up the apartment right away. The mass meeting would begin in a few minutes. Which was it? May 1? Twenty-sixth of July? Or was it one of the numerous rallies staged in front of the United States Interests Section? She could not recall. Her hand kept being pressed down on the broom handle. Muscles refused to respond; she was unable to break away. Frowning in disgust, she half turned away from the window, started to wake up, and opened her eyes. The broom handle turned out to be Pardo's erect penis, pulsating beneath the cashmere of his slacks.

Coming to her senses, Victoria smiled broadly. He grinned, too, and let go of her wrist. She had a good stretch, yawned, and looked around. She was free, rich, and in good health. Her husband, an intelligent, brave *macho*, lusted after her like no man ever had. Starting to feel sexually aroused, she gazed around again. No, impossible. The elderly couple across the aisle, now staring out the window, seemed straitlaced. They could look this way any moment, frown upon a woman giving a headjob to her man in broad daylight on board a bus. Not the best behavior for tourists arriving to the Land of the Free. Then again, they might enjoy watching. Better not risk it. She fixed her gaze on her husband and her fingernails journeyed from the base of his dick to the glans several times. Breathing hard, Pardo watched her with the inflamed look she knew so well. Insomnia acted as a potent aphrodisiac on her husband. He always got a boner whenever he missed a few hours of sleep or stayed up all night.

"We are in Miami," he announced.

"Are we?" and she shot a glance at her naked left wrist, clicked her tongue. "What time is it?"

"Nine thirty-eight. Within a few minutes we'll get to the airport."

"Then we better calm down," she whispered and, changing position, fumbled with the lever in order to sit upright. Pardo imitated her, crossed his ankles, and tried to distract himself from libidinous thoughts by looking out through the windows. She returned Pardo's jacket, drew a comb and cosmetics from her purse, and spent time getting herself presentable.

The bus turned off U.S. 1 and followed Le Jeune. Victoria finished sprucing up, cleaned off her glasses with the hem of her dress, put them on, and stole a look at her husband. Men and their beards. Having shaved less than eighteen hours ago, already his chin was sprouting stubble. Obviously impressed, Pardo's gaze moved over facades, cars, and pedestrians. Mentally prepared for the visual shock—the clean streets, well-dressed people, thousands of cars, and tall buildings as seen in movies and documentaries—Victoria found herself marveling not at what passed before her eyes but at the dissimilarity with Cuban cities and towns.

Two years earlier, tourists in Havana that had strayed from the trodden track would wonder whether a war they knew nothing about had recently taken place in San Isidro, the neighborhood in which she had been born. Its decay had become so embarrassing, especially when compared with the renovated section of Old Havana a mile away, that the city government began filling potholes there, removing rubble, and selling paint to those homes whose frontage would improve somewhat with a lick of water-based color. Interiors, however, remained ruinous. The true purpose had been to deceive wandering foreigners, not to furbish up. In stark contrast, the Palace of the Revolution had already been undergoing alterations and improvements for thirty years. Some well-traveled journalists considered it the most resplendent presidential palace in Latin America.

Victoria tried to spot one structure in this section of Miami that needed a coat of paint. She gave up after twelve blocks.

At the airport they boarded a taxi and asked the driver to take them downtown.

"Downtown?" the hack, turning in the seat with raised eyebrows, hoping for a more specific address. Black, in his fifties, his radio was tuned to a station that, to Victoria's ears, sounded like it was broadcasting in French, or Creole.

"Yes, downtown," Pardo repeated.

"What part downtown?" with a strong accent.

Pardo turned to Victoria with puffed cheeks.

"Courthouse," she said to the cabbie.

The man nodded, shifted the stick to drive, and pulled away. Pardo gazed into his wife's eyes. She silenced him by rolling them heavenward.

Back to Le Jeune, left on Flagler. Past Twenty-seventh Avenue everything started looking less affluent; after Fifteenth Avenue Victoria spotted some houses that could use a coat of paint, a few in bad repair. *Do not prejudge,* she said to herself again, this time smiling. Nothing remotely comparable to Cuba, though. Were they heading downtown? Had the hack misunderstood her? Her eyes went to the meter: $23.75? The taxi crossed a bridge over Miami River, turned left on Miami Avenue, pulled over past First Avenue.

"Courthouse," the cabbie announced.

$25.65. Victoria estimated that the fare over the same distance in Havana would not exceed $4.50, maybe $5.00, tip included. Pardo gave the man a twenty and a ten. They got off. The cab pulled away.

"You keep throwing our money away like that, soon we'll be paupers," she commented while looking around. The courthouse was a gray four-story building. Across the street stood another government-looking building, newer and higher. Policemen were all over the place, shooting the breeze and smoking, as if not on duty. She eyed them curiously. Waiting to serve as witnesses at trials? All but a few looked under thirty-five, cocky compared to Cuban cops, healthier and better fed, hip holsters positioned so the butt of the gun angled outward away from the body, gunslinger like, as with many young Cuban cops. Boys will be boys everywhere, she thought. They would grow up, hopefully. Cafeterias and shops thrived in the vicinity. Was that a train going overhead? It looked like one.

"How about breakfast?"

"Not a bad idea. Will you tip the waiter ten bucks?"

Pardo shook his head sadly, took hold of her elbow, steered her to the corner, and waited for the light before they crossed First Avenue.

"How did you know where the courthouse was?" he asked.

"Internet. Wires and articles on the Wasp network trial."

"Oh."

As head of the Miami desk of Cuban Intelligence, Victoria could close her eyes and see in her mind a map of Dade County with all its public buildings and certain specific addresses. She refused to brag about it, though.

They used the restrooms first. After washing, Pardo stripped away four hundred-dollar notes from his money clip and put them in his wallet. They had a hearty breakfast, then returned to First Avenue to look up domestic banks in the Yellow Pages hanging from a pay phone. At the Bank of America branch on Third Avenue, Pardo asked a teller to break the four hundred-dollar bills for him, in tens and twenties, please. Next the couple set off for clothing stores in the vicinity. Cursing under their breath the airline that had lost their baggage, they stocked up on inexpensive casual wear at a nondescript haberdashery in which they also acquired a decent roll-on to pack all they had purchased. At the First Street Payless they bought cheap trainers for him and a pair of black pumps for her. Her high heels went into the roll-on, and she left the shoe shop shod in the pumps.

At a bookshop they picked out a good city map before checking the Yellow Pages for hotels. Pardo argued in favor of a two-star without pool, gym, and restaurant. It was probably the kind of inexpensive place where lower-middle-class Latin American tourists stayed, he said. Besides, the Lexington was very close, on First Street. Victoria had no reason to oppose her husband's choice.

But before heading there, to avoid going insane with curiosity, they wanted to find out how things were going in Key West. Suspecting that the story had broken much too late to make the morning editions, Victoria searched for a public library in the green pages that listed government buildings and found that the Miami Public Library was at 101 West Flagler Street, a short walk from where they were standing at 12.44 P.M.

Shortly afterward, they ascended the ramp access to a modern, somewhat Moorish-looking building across the street from the courthouse. Three smokers were standing outside, near plastic ashtrays. Making the most of a partly clouded sky, several people on their lunch hour were munching their snacks or chatted at a small plaza dotted with white plastic tables and chairs. An automatic door slid open, they went in and asked the receptionist what they had to do to check their e-mail.

"Just go to one of the computers upstairs," the woman explained, "but you can't take that roll-on in," she added.

Realizing that he would grasp the main points of unfamiliar software faster than she would, Victoria decided she would stay in the lobby. By 1:17, Pardo had signed for a desktop and logged in to the *Miami Herald* website, where he learned that four Cuban coastguardsmen had grounded their cigarette boat on Higgs Beach, surrendered to the authorities, and applied for political asylum. "Their spur-of-the-moment sprint for freedom apparently caught officials in both countries by surprise," the piece said. Victoria chuckled with delight when Pardo told her this. They wondered where the four deserters had hidden their money.

The hotel was not a fleabag, but the room was austere. It had a seventeen-inch color TV set on a metal frame screwed to a wall, an old air conditioner, a phone extension, a double bed, two bedside tables, a lamp, a window from which the magnificent view of a bare cream-colored wall could be contemplated, and a small bathroom. While frantically undressing, Victoria quipped that, although it was a radical change from a two-story penthouse in Vedado, they could get over it, and the thirty-dollar rate was very reasonable. Pardo concurred and the buck-naked couple hurried to the tiny shower stall. Victoria realized she still had her glasses on, stripped them off, backtracked to the room, placed them atop a bedside table, and rushed into the bathroom.

Their huge sense of accomplishment elevated their sexual desire to new heights. The notion that they had been accomplices in criminal acts and were looking forward to committing a few more didn't cross their minds.

Under the shower, while soaping themselves, they engaged in hurried foreplay. After hastily drying each other, they flopped onto the bed. Uncontrollable passion made them dispense with fellatio and cunnilingus. On top, facing Pardo, she filled herself with him and came for the first time. Victoria's second orgasm likewise happened with her on top, but facing his feet. Her third took place when they were side by side. They reserved the rear entry position, Victoria's "prehistoric fuck," for her fourth, most intense orgasm and his enormously pleasurable ejaculation. The whole act lasted only half an hour, but its intensity was supreme.

This time, though, their lovemaking had something different that neither lover would have found easy to define. Both were wondering about it as overpowering drowsiness began turning off sections of their consciences. A subtle physical poetry in each movement, a delightful rendition of a song in which sighs and moans of ecstasy and mumbled terms of endearment substituted for musical notes and lyrics. Such tenderness, affection, mutual understanding, or whatever it was had been absent in the past, or they hadn't perceived it. Was it brought about by the risks and fears shared? By the promising future? Whatever the reason, in the last few days something important had burgeoned.

They slept soundly for nearly five hours. Hunger and a stiff awoke Pardo. Dusk was in its final stage, the room in shadows. He began kissing his wife's arms, shoulders, back of the neck. She stirred, turned. A second, more reposed and sophisticated round of sexual activity began. It was completely dark by the time it ended.

"I am so hungry," Pardo grumbled after a while, breaking the spell.

"So am I."

"Should I go out and bring something in or you want to come, too?"

"Let's go find a McDonald's. Those quarter-pounders look so tempting."

"Ughh. Junk food."

"Tell that to the Cuban woman in the street. Besides, I have to make the first phone call."

"Right. It slipped my mind completely."

"Nothing can slip our minds, *macho*. Nothing at all."

Following the cheeseburgers and sodas, Victoria went to a pay phone, dropped in thirty-five cents, and dialed a number.

"Bonis Landscaping," a machine said. "Leave your message."

"Hi, Mr. Bonis. This is your new client, Olga Villalobos," in Spanish, enunciating clearly. "I hope you are well. Would it be possible for you to do my garden next Monday, May 6? Would 9:00 A.M. be okay? Thank you. Bye-bye."

"Olga" indicated that a passport for a white woman in her forties was needed. "Villalobos" signified that other identity papers under the same name on the passport, such as a social security card or credit cards, although not indispensable, would be most welcome. "I hope you are well" meant that photos of the woman would be delivered. "Would it be possible" said that two days were to be deducted from the delivery date mentioned. "My garden" specified that the live drop where the photos were to be handed over would take place at the Burdines store at 22 East Flagler, fourth floor, luggage department. "9:00 A.M." in reality meant six hours later: 3:00 P.M.

"That's it?" Pardo asked in amazement once Victoria replaced the handset.

"That's it."

"But how can this . . . guy?"

"Shush. Don't ask," taking his hand and walking away from the pay phone. "It's very simple, really, but too complicated to explain. I just memorized what I had to say. Olga indicates that a white woman in her forties will use the passport. If the name is . . . any other, it means a woman in her thirties, or in her fifties, or in her twenties; dark-skinned black, or light-skinned black, or Asian, or half-Asian. Maybe Gladys means a black woman in her forties, I don't remember. Every possible situation is included, or so we think. The illegal has these words and phrases in a diskette, the real meaning next to each, so he decodes what I said, word by word. 'My garden' means a place for a live drop, 'my backyard' means another, 'trimming the garden hedge' a third. It's no big deal."

"Well!" Pardo was smiling and shaking his head. "I thought you'd use colored chalks, secret writing paper, coded pads, or microdots. This is so . . . passé."

"Communication is severely restricted at present," Victoria explained. "Even radio messages. What you just heard is the backup emergency code."

"What happens if he doesn't have a passport that belonged to a white woman in her forties?" asked Pardo, his eyes on the sidewalk.

"We wait, keep in touch, call him every Tuesday and Friday at 11:00 P.M. sharp, and listen to the recorded message."

Pardo's facial expression—lips curved downward, raised eyebrows—showed his doubts that this could work. "Poor bastard; what a life," he sympathized.

"I'm not so sure of that. Maybe he derives intense satisfaction from his secret mission, believes he was born for it."

"You think so?"

"Politically motivated illegals are in a class of their own. Their psychological profile is extremely interesting."

"Well, they are all crazy, if you ask me."

"I wouldn't expect your purely logical, mathematical mind to reach a different conclusion. Politically motivated illegals come from the worst kind of idealists: poets, writers, artists, especially frustrated actors. The cream of the crop is indifferent to money and willing to postpone social recognition for posterity."

They went over it some more on the way to the hotel, Pardo mostly listening attentively. In the end, both admitted they lacked the stuff good spies possess in abundance.

"I'm so tired," Victoria moaned inside the elevator cage.

"Me, too."

They made it to the room at 11:22, undressed, and were fast asleep in a short while.

. . .

At 11:17 A.M. on Tuesday morning, Victoria pressed the buzzer of a metal box to the left of a gate closing the entryway to a huge one-story, L-shaped residence painted gleaming white. It had a gabled green-tile roof, tinted-glass louvered windows, and privet hedges alongside a well-tended lawn. Two slender date palms and beds of flowers flanked the ninety-foot-long concrete footway to the front door. Three paved parking spaces by the sidewalk substituted for a garage. Tall treetops toward the rear of the lot suggested a sizable backyard.

Neither the psychologist nor her husband had any notion what that kind of mansion, on a lot this size, in such an exclusive neighborhood, could possibly be worth. A fortune probably. 101 was a perfectly paved, one-block street in the strictly zoned, 103-acre west islet of Bay Harbor Islands.

"Yes?" came from a speaker.

"Good morning, madam," Victoria said.

"Good morning" a woman's voice, heavy with Spanish accent.

"Are you the lady of the house?" deliberately worsening her accent.

"No. Who is this?"

"My name is Angela. Can I speak to the lady of the house, please?"

"Lady expecting you?"

"No."

"What you want lady of the house for?"

"We, my husband and I, are looking for part-time work. We clean houses, pools, mow lawns . . ."

"Mire señora, óigame bien, la dueña de la casa está ocupada y, además, aquí no hace falta nadie. ¿Me entiende? Mi esposo y yo nos bastamos y sobramos para hacerlo todo. Así que pueden marcharse, ¿me entiende?"

Strike one, Pardo thought. Victoria shrugged and smiled at him. The Spanish-speaking servant at the intercom, having identified from Victoria's accent that she came from a Latin American country, had refused to let them speak to the lady of the house. The servant didn't want competition. They had not pondered that possibility. They moved on to the next residence, same sidewalk, where their second deflecting maneuver of the day was to take place.

They had got up at seven, rested and euphoric, and donned items of the tawdry casual wear bought the day before, the kind most recent poor immigrants can afford. Forced to carry the gun, the cash, and the other things he could not leave at the hotel room, Pardo had to wear his jacket, too. After breakfast at a Cuban cafeteria, the couple had rushed to the downtown bus terminal. It had not been easy to figure out the proper bus route to take by looking at schematic maps, but they correctly deduced that a Route H bus would take them to Bay Harbor.

"Bay Harbor, Bal Harbour, what's the difference?" Victoria had asked, not expecting her husband to provide an explanation. She had been standing on the sidewalk by the bus stop, looking at the map, gazing around. The air of affluence was impressive. The beautifully landscaped Bal Harbour Shops, nestled between sea grape trees and silver buttonwood and patrolled by security guards in red-and-black British-looking uniforms, indicated that it was a fashion mecca for the very rich. The natural aromas of seabreeze, earth, flowers, and evaporating dew blended with the artificial fragrances of the priciest French perfumes, genuine leathers, single malt whiskeys, and wet enamel paints. This world was not 180 miles away from Cuba; it was 180 light years away.

"Beats me," Pardo had mumbled after a moment, moving his eyes away from the Sheraton Beach Resort to his wife. "Maybe to live in Bay you must prove a net worth in excess of five hundred million, whereas a mere two hundred million will gain you admittance to Bal."

"You take that down to fifty and twenty, respectively, I'll buy it."

"Sold."

Making fun of themselves for having overestimated their riches so much, acknowledging that in all probability $2 million was the deposit a butler had to make to get a job at either place, they had taken Kane Concourse on foot, crossed the eastern islet, and reached its sister at a quarter to eleven, nearly an hour past their schedule. Tropical vegetation thrived everywhere, and the royal palms made them feel somewhat nostalgic. The difference with the other islet appeared to be the absence of condominiums, apartment buildings, or other kinds of multifamily dwellings. Just stately homes to north, south, east, and west. The impression was of an architectural competition in which the most money didn't always bring about the finest result. The two-story house whose intercom button Victoria pressed next, not as pleasing to her eyes as the first, served as an example.

Sitting twenty or so yards from the ornamental white picket fence by the sidewalk—ineffectual for protecting the manicured lawn, flower beds, and shrubs from being trampled— it also had a gabled roof, but in red tiles. Its cream-colored exterior matched the sash windows painted white. High treetops at the back and swimming pools hidden from view seemed to be standard features in Bay Harbor.

"Who is it?" the cultured voice of a woman.

"My name is Angela, madam. May I speak to the lady of the house, please?"

"Speaking."

"Madam, my husband and I are from Costa Rica. We are looking for part-time jobs. We clean houses, pools, mow lawns, scrape and paint walls, all this at very reasonable rates. If there's something you need done, we would do it gladly."

Several moments slipped by.

"I do not need your services, Angela, thank you. I already have people who take care of that." No foreigner this one, Victoria thought. Maybe a slight upper-class Boston accent?

"Well, thanks anyway, madam. Do you happen to know if a neighbor or friend of yours living nearby could be interested in our services?"

The second pause was longer, as though the woman was carefully pondering what to say.

"No, Angela, I don't. Nevertheless, assuming you and your husband are decent people trying to make a living, let me give you a piece of advice. In Bay Harbor, your approach is wrong. Nobody here will admit perfect strangers into their homes. In point of fact, some may call the police and report you. I suggest you either ring doors somewhere else or place a classified ad in a newspaper. Have a good day, Angela."

The couple stared at each other. They had not considered this obvious danger. Their rounded eyes proclaimed: *"Have we turned stupid overnight?"*

"Thank you, madam."

"You are very welcome."

The speaker clicked, signaling that the intercom had been turned off. Somewhat stunned, Victoria and Pardo started walking toward the adjacent house.

"After all the trouble, I think we ought to go for it, anyhow," Victoria opined.

"Right. And if she turns us down, get the hell out. Fast."

"Immediately."

The next residence was Maria Scheindlin's. Pardo pressed the buzzer. Their eyes roved about the front garden, the colonnaded entry, the overhanging balcony, the slate path leading to the front door.

"Who is it?"

Victoria repeated her pitch. A tiny wireless microphone, disguised as a dry twig and secured with superglue atop the concrete column in which the intercom was embedded, picked up her words.

"No thanks, honey. I don't need anybody. Take care."

The intercom clicked.

"Let's call it a day," urged Pardo.

"Not a minute too soon," Victoria commented.

From a mansion across the street, a video camera followed them.

Half an hour had gone by and they were sitting in a bench on Collins Avenue, waiting for the bus, when Victoria drew a conclusion.

"Remember in Key West you said I never made mistakes? Well, this trip here today was a crass error of judgment. This is a new world and we're outsiders, we don't get to first base here. We don't know habits, patterns of behavior, security measures, nothing. So, I'm telling you, we must be very, very careful, *macho*. Take nothing for granted."

. . .

Thirty-three hours later, at the FBI's safe house, Elliot Steil was watching a large-screen TV in fascination. Yes, no doubt about it. But how had these two made it to Miami? That the FBI was keeping Maria Scheindlin's home under surveillance was almost as surprising as seeing the spurious XEMIC executives walking the streets of Bay Harbor. Hart, McLellan, and a third man introduced as Mr. Smith peered closely at Steil, who shook his head in wonder, turned away from the screen, and addressed Hart.

"Those two," he said pointing at the screen, looking and sounding astonished, "are Carlos Capdevila and Berta Arosamena."

The special agent turned to Smith, a smile dancing on his lips. McLellan reached for the remote and pressed a button. The frozen frame showed the backs of Pardo and Victoria.

They were sitting in the living area, Smith and McLellan in armchairs, Steil and Hart on a sofa, all facing the TV. Each held a can of soda; Hart had handed them around minutes earlier. No sooner had Steil made Victoria and Pardo's positive identification than Smith placed his Coke on the coffee table, pulled a cell phone out, and pressed keys. Three pairs of eyes went to him.

"Positive ID, begin search," he ordered after a moment. He punched a button to end the transmission and slipped the phone into the pocket of his suit coat.

"You don't know where they are?" asked Steil in full amazement.

"No," said Smith.

There were several moments of silence. Steil wondered whether he should ask the next question that came to mind and stole a look at Smith. Nearly sixty, five-foot-nine or so, and 150 to 160 pounds, his sandy, half-inch-long stuck-up hair was rather thin at the top. Dark, short, thick eyebrows hovered over gray, or green, eyes, depending on the light. The rubicund full face had few wrinkles, something Steil judged remarkable considering the guy's line of business. He clipped his fingernails short. Dark suit, white dress shirt, light blue tie, highly polished black lace-up shoes. A classic, including the Coke and the crew cut. Probably liked books by Mickey Spillane and songs by Frank Sinatra. Army background? Steil wondered. Probably. Judging from the respectful looks Hart and McLellan were giving him, the dude obviously was at least a notch or two above them in the federal government's hierarchy.

"How come?" Steil said, breaking the pause.

"They approached two other houses first, rang but weren't admitted. That made our people curious. But when they heard her pitch, they assumed they were recent immigrants trying to make an honest buck. No reason to tail such people."

Steil nodded. The schemers. Now they were needles in a haystack. Over two million resided in Greater Miami.

"And how did you come to suspect they might be the same people that approached me in Havana?"

Smith tilted his head in Hart's direction. "Brent figured it out. You don't easily come across strangers in Bay Harbor. Sometimes a week goes by without any outsider driving by or pacing out that particular block," he said, nodding toward the TV screen. "So, our watchers feel like hooraying and waving the flag when someone does appear, have something to show for their efforts, know what I mean? Even if it's nothing more than a couple of drifters who will work for food."

Steil liked Smith's style: easygoing, restrained, no tough-guy scowl or big-shot attitude. Hart and McLellan believed the number of times a day they pissed was top secret.

"Yesterday evening they gave Brent the descriptions of these two birds," Smith went on. "He compared them with the descriptions you gave of the Havana couple, found a close match. This morning he asked for the tape to be taken to the office."

Steil nodded. He wondered if the bureau had checked INS records for Cubans who had arrived in Miami in the last few days, had asked the U.S. Interests Section in Havana whether Berta and Capdevila had applied for and obtained visas. Maybe they were here legally. Cuban officials had recently been admitted to sign trade deals. But he was loath to be too inquisitive lest it get him more involved.

"Now, Steil, this roundabout way of reconnoitering the territory gives these two away," Smith said. "There's no doubt: They are full fledged enemy agents who pose a serious security risk to this country."

"You think so?"

"Don't you?"

Steil scratched the back of his head and appeared puzzled. "I suspected they were State Security agents when they approached me in Cuba. I suppose that video confirms it. What I can't figure is this spoof they did. What were they after?"

"Check the place out," Smith said. "Entrances, exits, traffic, surveillance cameras, that sort of thing."

"But suppose Maria had said 'Sure, come on in, I want you to clean my pool?'"

Smith smiled condescendingly. "Would've tickled the hell out of them. Seeing the layout of the house, meeting her in person, would make planning ahead much easier. They would've cleaned the pool, collected their money, and got out not believing their luck."

"I see." Then Steil considered a possible aftereffect. "But that would've given Maria a good reason to get pretty mad if the same people came to collect the money."

"Someone else may do the collecting."

Again Steil nodded. This was getting too complicated for him. McLellan finished his soda and crushed the can. Hart sipped from his. Elliot became aware that neither man had uttered a word after Smith made his phone call.

"But I don't think they pose a serious security risk to the United States," the Cuban opined. "They didn't strike me as being the kind of people who plant bombs or crash planes against buildings."

"Leave the assessment of what kind of security risk they pose to us, Steil," deadpanned Smith, a steely nuance in his voice now. "We'll handle that. But you'd make it a lot easier for us if you help us some more."

"What do you think I'm doing here?" raising his hands palms upward.

"I know. And we value highly all you've done. Listen, Steil, let's cut the bullshit. I understand your position. We are a pain in your ass; you've put in long hours and haven't made a buck from this. You feel like telling us to go break somebody else's balls but refrain from saying it 'cause you are a resident here and don't want to risk getting your residence revoked. We understand all that. We are not stupid, you know?"

"I know."

"Okay. Now try to see it from where we sit. You were and are working for the widow of the man who started this, or that the Cubans claim started this, we don't know yet. You were going to Cuba; you are fluent in English. With that candidate at hand, would it be sensible to approach anyone else?"

"No, I guess not."

"Exactly. So it's not like we singled you out from a hundred prospective candidates, right?"

"Right."

"Then, what about helping us out some more?"

"What do you want me to do?"

"We want you to call the widow and ask her to see you. We think she'll say sure, drop over. She may think it's some business matter you want to discuss. Then you tell her you feel guilty for having left her holding the bag in this XEMIC situation, are sorry for that, and are willing to help her out if she needs any assistance to deal with it."

Steil grunted, looked at the floor, smiled, and shook his head. "She'll think I'm in cahoots with those two," pointing to the screen.

"Don't anticipate what's going to happen. She may say 'Yes, help me out,' or 'Thanks, no, I'll take care of it.' Leave it to her."

"Okay. I'll call her tomorrow."

"We'd appreciate it if you'd call her tonight. From here. We'd like to hear what her reaction is."

"Isn't it a little late?" stealing a look at his watch.

"I don't think so."

"Okay. Where's the phone?" He straightened up.

...

"Curiosity killed the cat," Victoria scoffed, then did a stretch.

"C'mon, you are free now. And you know I can keep a secret."

It was May 2, Thursday, 9:55 P.M. They were sitting on the loveseat of a single efficiency room at the Comfort Inn on 3860 Tollgate Boulevard in Naples, Florida. One hundred and eight miles away, FBI agents were patiently, but by now somewhat worriedly, trying to learn where the couple had holed up. Twenty-six hours had gone by since the desk clerk at the Lexington had quite forthcomingly identified Pardo and Victoria the moment he was shown the photos printed from the surveillance video. Those two had checked out early in the morning of May 1 without leaving a forwarding address, the clerk had gabbed.

Not knowing that the FBI had launched a manhunt after them, the couple had kept to their original plan of spending the least possible time in Miami and traveled to Naples, their designated base of operations. Making conversation after a nice meal, Pardo wanted to learn more about Cuban espionage in Miami and about Pola Negri in particular.

Why do I still feel like I should keep this to myself? Victoria wondered. *Because lifelong habits are hard to shed,* she told herself. Her husband, on the other hand, meant more to her than any other person ever had. Anyway, by now a lot of her former colleagues were suspecting that she was babbling to the enemy. She would not, though. All she wanted was to quit and be free to roam the world. Thanks to Pardo, she would achieve that and live comfortably the rest of her life. Victoria supported her head on the back of the loveseat and, looking at the ceiling, began telling the story.

"Well, following the collapse of communism in Poland, one of their purged Intelligence case officers approached our guy in Berlin and asked whether we'd be interested in a six-page report he had prepared on the life story, legend, and cover of a good Polish agent based in Miami. He asked for five thousand dollars, although he felt sure the FBI would gladly fork out twenty thousand. He'd sell it to us for a fourth of its value because he had moral scruples about turning the agent over to the enemy. A friendly service would take care of her. And there were so few friends left, the sonofabitch moaned.

"Our man reported to Papa, who said he was interested, but wouldn't go above twenty-five hundred. You know Poles drive hard bargains, so this dude said that, considering he was doing business with comrades, he'd accept four thousand, but not one dollar less. Back to Papa, who raised his bid to three thousand. The Pole swore thirty-five hundred was his final word or he'd contact the FBI. Papa ordered our guy to pay the fucking bandit.

"That's how we came to know Maria Berkowicz. She was born in 1947, of Jewish descent. She joined the Communist Youth in '62, was recruited by Polish Counterintelligence in '65 or '66, I don't remember exactly. Graduated from the Institute of English Philology, University of Wroclaw, in '69. Rated a very promising cadre, she was transferred to Polish Intelligence in 1970 and trained to become an illegal in the West for two years. In October 1972 she was assigned to the Polish mission at the United Nations in New York as a junior office clerk. Following orders, she deserted in 1973. Her center hoped U.S. Intelligence would recruit her and she'd become a double, but once they debriefed her, the CIA lost interest."

"Lost interest? The Cold War raging on and they lost interest?" asked Pardo.

Victoria turned her head and gazed into his eyes.

"I'm quoting from the report we bought. According to it, after the debriefing took place, neither the CIA nor the FBI expressed any interest in her. Imagine. Such a careful plant, all she could do was visit Polish émigré circles in New York, reporting on what the geezers said."

"Let me guess: Then she met Scheindlin."

Victoria returned to her previous position, eyes on the ceiling.

"In '74, by chance, according to the report. Life is amazing. Two people bump into each other in a certain place at a certain time on a certain day, and an unimaginable chain of events is unleashed."

"Like us."

"Happens all the time."

"And Scheindlin fell for her."

"Big time. She asked for instructions. After checking him out, the center told her to cling to the guy as though he were president of the United States. According to the Poles, Scheindlin was Mossad's resident director in Florida."

"No!"

"An exaggeration, no doubt. I don't think the Poles ran the kind of operation capable of infiltrating Mossad at the level required to determine who was their top man in Florida. Perhaps Scheindlin collaborated with Mossad on a regular basis. With all those contacts in South America, he would've made a good cutout, courier, or bagman. It's possible. But I think he wasn't a handler, let alone a resident supervising case officers and networks statewide."

"You sure?"

"*Macho,* in this business, nobody, ever, is sure of anything."

"Right. So when did she marry Scheindlin?"

"In '76, a week after his divorce was final. They shacked up together in '75. He bought the house we saw the other day in '77, a few months before their daughter was born. I hope she felt something for the man. Must've been hard to be married to someone you are not attracted to and spend thirty years pretending."

"A lot of money provides a lot of comfort," he retorted.

"Yeah, I suppose so." Victoria lifted her head, straightened up, crossed her legs. "Anyway, by 1992 the lady hadn't heard from her center since '89, so she figured she was off the hook. Then our recruiter knocked on her door. Figure of speech."

"Wait a second. When did we buy the report?"

"Must've been 1990. I don't remember exactly."

"And we waited two years before putting the squeeze on her?"

"Don't forget the ministry imploded in '89. Reorganization picked up steam in 1990. Then the USSR and the whole socialist bloc went up in smoke. Our once-friendly colleagues, Vadim Bakatin, Markus Wolf, Pruszynski, and birds of a feather started getting very chummy with the NSA. We and the Chinese were the only serious players on the field. Everybody thought we'd go down the drain any minute."

"Right."

"Besides, we had to check her out, and get a line on Scheindlin and IMLATINEX as well. The possibility that we'd been sold a playback was weighed, too. Why didn't the Pole put the squeeze on her? He could've blackmailed her. The answer to that was he'd been expelled from the service, was known as a case officer to the FBI, and couldn't gain entrance to the United States. On top of that, he was sixty-two years old and had a serious heart condition. He just wanted to take things easy.

"Maria didn't look promising, either. She had never contacted the foundation or any other Cuban exile group, and with her cover and legend, it would have been odd if she had suddenly taken an interest in things Cuban. As it turned out, Cross-Reference reported that her husband had been doing business with XEMIC through Trans-Caribbean Trading since the early seventies. Right off the bat, the manager and the coaches wanted her sitting on our bench."

"You were a rookie utility infielder then."

"Yeah, still pretty green. She was one of the first profilings I was asked to do."

"How did she take it? The recruitment I mean."

Victoria rearranged herself on the seat. "She took it well. She's a pro, you know. I recommended saying to her that she'd been trans-ferred to us, not sold; that her Polish case officer wanted to protect her and help us out. I suggested appealing to her internationalism, her communist ideals as well. Lastra approved my plan. And of course, it worked. It gave her the opportunity to save face, nothing more. She knew what could possibly happen if she refused to collaborate. Therefore, she pretended to go along with the recruiter's arguments. Bullshit, of course. By the nineties she had probably come to share Orwell's—and our own—perception of communism. Besides, by then she had lived the good life too many years to still be sorry for the oppressed proletariat."

"She been useful?"

"We wouldn't be here if she hadn't."

"No, I mean to the Directorate."

"So-so. Most important thing she said was the Jewish business community in Miami is planning to invest heavily in Cuba the minute the embargo ends, regardless of who is at the helm. It seems the Israelis exporting the Jagüey citrus are impressed; they send glowing reports to Tel Aviv and the word gets around. Maria affirms she frequently carried out our request to subtly predispose her husband toward Cuba. And Scheindlin became more agreeable to XEMIC's requests for bet-ter terms and conditions since she began working for us. She said her center had overrated his link with Mossad. He had never given her any reason to suspect he may be an agent or a handler. Informer? Of course, she said. His age, his life story, he had to be."

They fell silent for a while. Pardo gazed pensively at the blank screen of the twenty-five-inch TV set they faced.

"Why Pola Negri?" he wanted to know next.

Victoria chuckled, folded her legs under her, and rested her right arm on the back of the loveseat. "When the recruiter went to Havana, she said the woman was suntanned to the point she seemed black, kept referring to her as *La Polaca Negra*. Then a guy remembered that Pola Negri was Polish. Negri is one vowel away from Negra in Spanish. So, we gave her that code name."

"Makes sense now," Pardo said and got to his feet. He ambled to the refrigerator, got a can of Heineken, and showed it to his wife, a questioning expression on his face.

"No thanks," Victoria whispered.

Pardo returned to the loveseat, popped the tab, sat down, took a pull.

"I suppose she was placed under Bonis," he guessed.

"She changed gardeners, yes."

For a few moments Pardo squinted at the floor, considering something. He drank more beer.

"Is it possible that in '73 she was turned?" he conjectured.

"Never say never" was her reply. "Although the consensus reached at the Directorate is that she's not a double. Had she been one, when the Wasp network was broken, Bonis's cell would have been broken, too. He has handled her for nine years now, more than enough for the FBI to know how many hairs stick out of his nostrils. The Bonis cell is part of Pitirre, our best Miami network. Pitirre provides almost all the top-quality intelligence we gather there. An all-star team, I tell you. There's a guy been doing it for thirty-nine years, can you believe it? It's composed of five three-agent cells, four couriers, three cutouts, a cobbler . . ."

"Hey, hold it. What's a cobbler?"

"Expert forger. Nothing happened to any member of the Pitirre network. But . . ."

Victoria paused.

"But? But what?"

"But Maria could have been turned as soon as she defected in '73, in which case she fed crap to her center until the very last. Then, having become redundant once Solidarity took over, she was transplanted to us. Such a wide range of possibilities is what makes espionage the perfect fertile ground to breed paranoids and schizophrenics. And Fisherman might be feeding us crap through her."

"Who's Fisherman?"

"Nathan Smith, the bureau's chief of counterintelligence at the South Florida field office. He knows that the Israelis and the Cubans are his only serious concerns. Considering Mossad is a friendly service, I'm sure we are his number one priority. And he may have turned one or two of our agents."

"You think so?"

"No, I don't, but it's in the cards."

"Do you trust anyone, Vicky?"

"I trust you. Nobody else, not even my mother, my father, and my two brothers. I know it sounds extremely callous, but it's a feeling all professionals share. What do you think CIA or FBI people experience when they find out one of their own has been selling secrets to the Russians? Guys like Ames, Hanssen, Howard? They start wondering if their superior is a mole. You only dealt with the technical side, Pardo. Computers, cryptography, and software. The first time you voiced your dissent to me, I suspected you. I suspected you for months."

"You suspected me?" pointing his thumb to his chest, eyes wide open.

She nodded emphatically.

"Oh, really? Least you could do is tell me what cleared me."

"The most absurd and irrational of feelings: love. Feeling that you love me and that I love you."

Unprepared for such an astonishing admission, Pardo could not think of something appropriate to say and opted for finishing his beer. The unromantic consequence was that he belched loudly just as something came to mind.

"Excuse me."

"You are excused."

"Is it because of this fear of being double-crossed that you changed your mind about the pickup?"

"Yes and no. Yes because this concern is so embedded in intelligence and counterintelligence officers that it influences our patterns of behavior. No because if it hadn't been for Pola's neighbor the day before yesterday, it would have taken me much more time to realize how ill equipped we are to adjust to a different country. Any foreign country, in fact, but less so in South America, Spain, the Caribbean. Here? Here we are babies learning to walk. Suppose Maria has installed tiny surveillance cameras and mikes at her place."

"Victoria, please!"

"Many people do, you know? She's filthy rich, can afford cutting-edge technology. Just to keep an eye on the help. Or to tape conversations with her lawyers or accountants, or with her manager, this Steil. To have proof of what was said or agreed upon at a certain date."

"You are taking things . . ."

"Isn't it logical to assume"—cutting him short—"that a trained, veteran spy would want to have on tape the dude who comes to pick up the money? Have this little insurance policy stored away in a safe just in case one day she needs it?"

"If you put it that way . . ."

"Always err on the side of caution."

"So, you'll ask Bonis to collect the cash."

"He personally requested and collected our first loan. He paid her back with the Guelph lot. She'll be more comfortable dealing with her handler than with a couple of strangers. In fact, she probably expects Bonis to act as a go-between. Steil is our stand-in in case something happens to Bonis. Maria's neighbor made me realize it would've been a mistake to meet her in person. You'll give Bonis my photos and a note asking him to do her garden on May 8 at 11:00 A.M. He'll bring the cash to us."

"Is that the right date and time?"

"Time, yes. But the right date is one day earlier, May 7."

"Has it occurred to you that the network's field officer may already have been warned that something is amiss?"

"Of course they have contacted him. Chances are they've sent him an urgent message. 'Unexpected situation. Bolster countermeasures.' I sent him a similar message when Fisherman iced Wasp. But Lastra won't freeze our best men, and Bonis is one of them, before making sure what really happened to me. Maybe I drowned in the Florida Straits, maybe you murdered me, maybe I'm alive and kicking but won't squeal on my former comrades. Time is on our side, *macho*. When there's an alert and communications are restricted to a minimum, like right now, because of my disappearance, I supersede Bonis's superior. For Bonis, I'm still Papa. And in this note you'll pass to him the day after tomorrow, I'll say something to justify the alert. The pianist at the Cuban Interests Section in Washington defected, for example. 'But don't worry, we are just playing it safe. The traitor doesn't know about you,' I'll add."

Pardo kept shaking his head. "Victoria, tell me, how come you don't get lost in this netherworld of facts and fictions, truths and half-truths and outright lies? Don't you risk getting dates and codes and . . . stuff mixed up? Confusing places for live drops and dead drops?"

"When you are at headquarters, desk job, nothing happens if you forget something. Sure, you try to memorize, open files in your mind. Like you said: fact, fiction; true, false; name, cryptonym; live drops, dead drops. But if you have a memory lapse, you reach for the hard copy. In the field it's another story. Not easy, *macho*, not easy at all. It requires many years of considerable effort. I spent the last three years training for these days."

"And you've performed admirably."

"Thank you. How about in bed?" with a sly wink.

"Best fuck in the world."

"Atta boy. What do you say we pay for one of those adult movies? We could find some inspiring example to follow."

"Good idea."

"Get me my glasses, will you?" as she reached for the remote.

...

Maria sat back on the sofa and gazed at Elliot thoughtfully. After an instant, he looked away. The man wasn't easy to stare down. At their first meeting he seemed self-assured, remarkably composed. During her visits to the warehouse he had proven to be a knowledgeable, quite capable executive. However, since his trip to Cuba he had changed. And tonight he looked so different: discomfited, evasive, and . . . ashamed? As if he was doing something he regretted? *Be careful,* she said to herself.

"Well, that's quite decent of you, Elliot," smiling, feeling her way. "But I've also done some reconsidering. On the evening you told me about the Cuban request, I acted rudely, failed to see things from your perspective."

"It was I who failed to see things from your perspective."

Make him feel guilty, Maria decided. "No, no. It was my fault and I apologize. I was thinking only of myself. I didn't see that your involvement in this mess could get you in trouble should it somehow become public that Ruben had been buying medicine for Cuba. Then the other day? When I asked you to call Havana? It wasn't nice to say I would've made the call myself had I been fluent in Spanish."

"Don't worry about it."

"Later I realized I hadn't been fair to you. You could be accused of acting on behalf of the Cuban government, be expelled, or deported. I'd never forgive myself if that happened and I was to blame. Never. You've been so cooperative after Ruben's death. I depend on you so much. The firm depends on you."

"You are flattering me, Maria."

"Not in the least. We've already discussed Sam. He's a wonderful human being, but he's too old. You are capable, intelligent, and much younger. You are an invaluable, intangible asset we—Jenny and I—can't afford to lose."

The term "intangible asset" made Steil blink. Having claimed to lack all knowledge about business matters, for the second time Maria had properly used a specialized business term. Part of the guilt he felt for concealing his collaboration with the FBI from her evaporated. There was something about Maria, inconsistencies, or concealed abilities, or simulated weaknesses, he wasn't sure, that nagged at the back of his mind.

"Thanks, Maria. I don't deserve your praise. It's you who deserve more cooperation from me on this issue. It was inconsiderate of me to come here, drop the problem in your lap, and walk away after washing my hands of responsibility."

Maria smiled, took a sip from a glass of grapefruit juice, then dabbed at her lips. They were sitting in the same pieces of furniture they had chosen on two previous occasions: she on the sofa, he in a club chair in her living room. This time she was barefoot, sporting blue culottes and a light blue T-shirt. Steil wore Dockers, a dark green polo shirt, and brown loafers.

"Okay, let's make a deal," she said, returning the glass to the side table. "If I need you, I'll let you know."

"Fine. But don't hesitate to call me. I can drop around at 10:00 or 10:30 on the eighth if you want me to. It'd be best if someone's with you when the man comes."

Does he want to be present? she wondered. "I'll let you know," Maria reiterated.

"Good. I feel less guilty now."

"Conscience doth make cowards of us all."

Again, Steil blinked. It sounded familiar. Was it a barb? Did she suspect him?

"Just a minute. Let me think. Bacon?"

"Warm."

"Mmm. Shakespeare?"

"*Hamlet,* 3.1."

Steil nodded a couple of times and a few seconds slipped by as he meditated. "Well, I guess I'd have a problem translating that into Spanish. In English, conscience is frequently associated with feelings of guilt. In Spanish, conscience is used in a broader context; it's considered a philosophical category. Every individual has a conscience, according to some schools of thought. Having a conscience wouldn't make a person a coward, per se."

"I see your point. You feel less guilt but are not a coward."

With eyes roving about the room, Steil tilted his head to one side, then to the other.

"I'm not saying I'm a fearless man. I have experienced fear. All I'm saying is the Bard may have hit the nail on the head for English audiences and readers, but missed the nail completely in the case of Spanish-speaking people."

"Only if his translator into Spanish is not up to the author."

"So true. I stand corrected."

"In this particular case, Elliot, you are guilty of nothing. Nor do I think you a coward. So, don't fret."

"If I had to deliver a hundred thousand dollars to a stranger, I'd feel better if I had friends around."

He does want to be present, Maria concluded. "Well, it depends on where you stand," she said. "If I were picking up a hundred thousand dollars from a stranger, I'd like to have some backup. 'Has this woman reported the situation to the police?' the person may wonder. 'Will they collar me? Charge me with being a Cuban agent?' The courier should be much more worried than me."

"That figures."

"I'll let you know, okay?"

"Okay," forced to stand up by the finality in her tone.

Once the sliding gate clicked shut, Maria Scheindlin closed her front door and slouched back to the sofa, squinting at the floor, lost in thought. She sat and, taking small sips from her glass of juice, reviewed the whole situation.

She had learned about Elliot Steil in 1995 following the murder of Ruben's secretary. One evening her husband had told her the strange story of the Cuban teacher working for him. Save for the rich American father, he was just one more fleeing Cuban; there had been no reason to mention him to her gardener. By 1997 she had heard Ruben praise Elliot's aptitudes more than once, so when she learned about the successful conclusion of the probate process that made the Cuban rich, she had pointed him out to her gardener. Bonis had listened intently, made her spell out Steil's surname. In 1999, Ruben had termed Elliot an intangible asset whose value would increase considerably the day the embargo ended and IMLATINEX could open a Havana office. She had reported that to Bonis, too.

Over the course of time, as Ruben got accustomed to the Cuban's effectiveness, Steil ceased to be a topic of after-supper conversation and she forgot the man existed. Bonis had brought him up a few weeks before Ruben's death. Her gardener had said Steil had applied for permission to visit relatives in Cuba. Bonis had wanted to know whether she could learn when he was planning to go and where he would be staying in advance. This had taken her by surprise. How could she? she had asked the gardener. She had not met the man. Her husband had not mentioned him for over a year, maybe two years. Should Ruben comment on the trip, she could ask when and for how long. But if he didn't, she could not ask without making her husband wonder why she wanted to know. Bonis had seemed to accept her reasoning.

Then Ruben had died on her. Four days after the funeral, once he had expressed his condolences, Bonis intimated that perhaps now, as heir to the family fortune and majority shareholder, she would be interested in sounding Steil out, see for herself if the man was as good as the late Mr. Scheindlin had said. The tactful Bonis had not reminded her what he wanted to find out more immediately. He knew it wasn't necessary. But at his next visit, once he finished the yard and while sipping the lemonade that she always prepared for him, he had explained that the center required, once again, her invaluable collaboration.

A hundred-thousand-dollar loan was requested. It would be reimbursed within six months—after only three months was possible, too—with real estate in Canada worth at least 10 percent above the borrowed amount. As in the previous loan, that signified a 20 percent annual interest rate, 40 percent if repaid in ninety days. Would she be willing to help the center again?

A lengthy discussion had followed. She had warned Bonis that money always leaves a trail. He had countered by affirming that he would personally make sure it could not be traced to her. She'd spend years in jail, she had insisted, should it be found she had loaned cash to Cuba, not to mention what would happen if her past and present collaboration with communist intelligence agencies were to be detected. The gardener had said not to worry. Only four persons in the world, three of whom lived in Cuba, knew about her solidarity with the Cuban Revolution; he was the fourth. In the end she had agreed to make the loan, provided Bonis made clear to his superior that she hoped no further requests of this sort would be presented to her.

Bonis had then mentioned that communications with Havana were severely restricted. After the Wasp ring was broken, the FBI had stepped up electronic surveillance of radio signals, phone calls, and letters. Therefore, Bonis had gone on, during Steil's visit to Cuba, the center would approach him with a story concerning business dealings with Mr. Scheindlin and ask him to please refer it to her upon his return to Miami. The story would include the exact date on which the cash was to be delivered. One day earlier than the latest date mentioned, at the same time.

It had sounded weird to her. Communications had to be restricted after the Wasp scandal, of course. It was an elementary precautionary measure. But to the point that a single coded message with a date couldn't be transmitted? Why involve Steil in this? Were they trying to recruit a man who had fled Cuba and was well off? Not a good candidate, she judged. That could not be the reason. Maybe Bonis needed the money for something unrelated to espionage. But if such was the case, why involve Steil? She had not been able to figure it out. The first loan had been repaid with the lot in Guelph, which yielded a nice profit by the time she sold it two years later. Anyway, refusing the second loan was not an option.

At the time, she had begun considering moving to another country. Ruben's death provided the perfect opportunity to sell IMLATINEX and emigrate to Spain, France, or Australia. That would sever her ties with Cuban Intelligence. She was of value to them as long as she lived in Miami and Scheindlin was alive. As a widow and in a different country, she could not tell them anything. Maybe they would blackmail her, though.

Consequently, meeting Steil and pumping him for information was necessary. She had enjoyed playing the game she had not competed in for so many years. Having studied the guy, she concluded he was the kind of man most people would like to consider a friend. But after his return from Cuba, he had acted strange. Some change was to be expected, naturally. But on the evening he had told her the Havana story, he surprised her when he said he wanted his participation to end then and there. She had expected the opposite: The perfect gentleman would offer his services. Later that same evening, mulling over his refusal to be involved any further, she admitted to herself that she had been unfair. Why should he want to help her out? She was not a beautiful young woman, he wasn't making a buck on this either, so why should he?

Then, the afternoon she had asked him to make the call, at the warehouse, he had appeared upset for being left out. He had wordlessly reproached her with his eyes. *"Are you leaving me out of this?"* And tonight he had come to beg her to be present. However, something in his expression smacked of pretense, of acting against his will. Something she had not seen before. Was somebody pressuring Steil to witness the loan? Bonis? Of course not. He would probably be the one picking up the cash. Then who?

You better be careful, Maria Berkowicz, she admonished herself. Get some plausible story ready. You are too old and too rich to go to jail.

...

Victoria and her husband slept late on Friday, May 3. They had a light breakfast before going to a photo studio on Peeblebrook Drive, where Victoria paid for six passport-sized photos. In a short while they walked out of the studio with the photos. The rest of the morning was spent pacing around Old Naples, window-shopping in the apparel shops and gift boutiques on Third Street, Victoria marveling at the prices and snorting at the offbeat odds and ends. At an office supply store they bought a pack of letter envelopes.

After lunch, in their room, they flipped over the pages of the

Miami Herald until finding and reading a piece on the four Cuban coastguardsmen. The men insisted that they had made their decision on the spur of the moment, motivated by the lack of opportunities and intense repression in Cuba. All four wanted to apply for asylum under the Cuban Adjustment Act. The Cuban government had demanded the immediate repatriation of the deserters and the return of the speedboat. What puzzled everyone was how easily the cigarette boat had sneaked in. The embarrassment of the Coast Guard spokesperson could be sensed. A suspicious reader might hypothesize that some editing out had taken place. No self-respecting journalist would have missed the opportunity to speculate about whether Osama himself was lurking somewhere in the continental United States, two portable nuclear-bomb suitcases by his side. But the article had nothing of the sort.

"It's over," Victoria said, folding the newspaper and dropping it on the floor. "Let's take the rest of the day off. Before going to bed tonight, we'll check the plan for tomorrow. Now let's forget everything, okay?"

"Okay," giving her high fives.

After purchasing basic beachwear and sunscreen, around three in the afternoon they went to the pool and reclined on loungers under a beach umbrella until ten past four. Then they swam a little, took in the sun again for a while, and sipped iced tea until dusk. Conversation focused on things American: from the fact that, at street level, downtown Miami came across as a Latin American city colonized by Anglos, to the amazing contrast between Bal Harbour and the dingy old city center. After supper they spent an hour and a half going over what had to be done on Saturday and turned in early.

The next morning the suntanned couple took a taxi to the bus station on Davis Boulevard and at 9:35 departed for Miami. Around 11:30 they entered the Miami Public Library and stayed there the next two hours surfing the Net. They checked Google, AskJeeves, and other search engines for Cuban news. None gave them cause to worry. Lunch consisted of glasses of orange juice and *medianoches*. When Victoria came out of the ladies' restroom, Pardo went into the men's.

She then left the cafeteria unaccompanied and covered the two blocks to Burdines, taking in her surroundings and window-shopping. She pushed in the heavy glass door on the First Street entrance at 2:43 P.M. and, looking around curiously, approached the nearest perfume counter.

Seven minutes later Pardo came in through the same door. He spotted his wife immediately. She smiled fleetingly and looked away. Pardo rode the escalator to the fourth floor. Victoria let two minutes go by to make sure no one had followed her husband, then took the escalator. She entered the luggage department at 2:55 and glanced distractedly right and left before ambling to the men's fashion department. She positioned herself by a circular rack of shirts from which she could keep an eye on what went on while affecting to glance over the garments.

After a minute or two, a balding man in his fifties came onto the fourth floor. For a moment Victoria thought herself mistaken. This could not be Bonis. She shot a glance at her watch: 3:00:10. Had to be. Could not be. Many times she had tried to form a mental image of this and other officers and agents whose files lacked photos. She had pictured Bonis as a short, dark-haired, mustachioed, and sort of fat Cuban who possessed a green thumb, cracked jokes at himself, and played dominoes on Sunday afternoons—a guy nobody took seriously, except Papa. What she had before her eyes, however, was a human powerhouse who brought to mind a jaunty, rough-grained, battle-scarred general; or one of those old-style business tycoons who made fortunes out of sheer willpower and balls. A splendid specimen from the rare genus she called "the upstagers," people whose great charisma draws attention everywhere they go. What a waste, she commiserated.

He wore an ivory-colored sports coat over a deep blue cotton pullover, black jeans, and heavy-duty shoes. Very much in shape, not an ounce of fat around his torso, a couple of inches shorter than her husband. His green eyes bristled with . . . hostility? distrust? alertness? on a weather-beaten, deeply lined face. The dark blond thinning hair was the only indication of something in decline. For an instant, as he scanned the floor, their eyes met. He seemingly dismissed her, kept checking out other customers. When he found Pardo, his gaze returned to Victoria for an instant, as if intuition had told him she was Olga Villalobos. She fought off the man's mesmerizing effect, returning to the shirts. Then Bonis strode past counters, edging up to Pardo while pretending to examine pieces of luggage. It took him a minute to reach the cutout.

"Excuse me, I can't make up my mind," he said in Spanish. "What brand do you prefer, Halliburton or Philco?"

"Neither. Hartmann is best," Pardo said, leaving a folded white envelope atop a twenty-six-inch Upright Suiter.

Bonis reached for the envelope, slipped it into a pocket of his sports jacket, and moved along, his eyes on the merchandise. He spent another minute doing this, then chose a cheap, medium-sized tote bag, paid with cash, and rode the escalator down. Victoria selected a shirt, paid, then descended to the third floor to check the lingerie. Pardo told the Honduran saleswoman at the register that he wanted to look around some more and walked away six minutes after Victoria, ten minutes after Bonis.

The couple reunited at the corner of Biscayne Boulevard and Third Street at 3:30.

"Well?" asked Victoria.

Pardo stared at her. "You want to know what I'm thinking?"

"Of course."

"In certain people, courage and the power of reason are inversely proportional."

"Interesting thought. Would you care to elaborate?"

"That man is a brave man, no doubt about it. But he's risking life imprisonment to serve communism, a cause that has proven to be the twentieth century's most shocking political and economic debacle. A cause that has repressed more people than any other in recorded history. He's not motivated, as are those at the top, by holding on to power, by privileges or perks. Living here, with full access to all sorts of newspapers, magazines, and books, if he fails to perceive that he is serving a lost and unjust cause means he must be intellectually deficient, even if immensely courageous. Fanatics must unavoidably be slow-witted."

Victoria took his hand and they started walking toward the bus station. She considered what Pardo had just said for nearly the minute they spent covering one block.

"Your hypothesis implies that cowards abound among the highly intelligent."

Pardo had not studied the corollary of his theory. "Probably. Yes. But exceptions prove the rule."

"And that man, couldn't he be an exception?" tentatively.

"What do you mean?"

"Brave and intelligent."

"Could be," he conceded.

"So, even if your hypothesis is proven true, it seems difficult to determine at a glance who is brave and foolish, or brave and bright, or cowardly and bright, or cowardly and foolish."

"I guess so."

"Let's return to Naples, *macho*."

Eight

T he gray 1995 Chevrolet Astro van that entered Maria Scheindlin's driveway on May 7 was towing an open, black trailer carrying lawn care equipment, and had BONIS LANDSCAPING and a phone number in vinyl on its sides. Across the street, through binoculars, a spotter watched as the driver got out, the gate slid shut, and the widow opened the front door. The second spotter zoomed in the video camera on the van's plates first, then on the man and Maria as they shook hands and chatted. Eugenio Bonis had on dark blue trousers with a large pocket on each side and kneepads, work boots, a long-sleeved denim shirt, and a Florida Marlins baseball cap. Maria was in a bathrobe and slippers. Within a couple of minutes she went inside and closed the door. The gardener unhurriedly approached the trailer and set about unloading the tools of his trade.

The FBI spotter with the binoculars reached for a two-way radio and pressed the send button.

"Base, Team Four," he said.

"Go ahead, Four."

"A gardener just came in. 0905 hours. Drives a Chevy van that says Bonis Landscaping. B-o-n-i-s."

"Same guy was there two weeks ago?"

"We weren't here then."

A short period of silence followed.

"Okay. Provide subject's description and vehicle's plate."

The first thing Bonis did was set the frame of his rotary riding mower at the highest height. A first application of complete fertilizer two weeks earlier had given a very healthy blue-green color to the four-to five-inch-high St. Augustine grass. The gasoline-powered engine coughed into life, and the gardener proceeded to mow the lawn down to three inches, at the front of the house first, the courtyard later. It was 10:25 when he rode the lawn mower back into the trailer. Bonis left the cut grass on the ground, but blew back to the lawn those clippings that had fallen on the slate path at the front, and by the granite path, cemented area, and tiled poolside floor in the courtyard.

Having restored the blower to the trailer, Bonis asked Maria to turn the irrigation on in the front yard. He pulled on a pair of gloves and began moving young plants grown in four-inch pots from the van to the courtyard. He also took a drain spade, a warren hoe, and a half-full bag of fertilizer, then called for the front yard's irrigation to be turned off. Flower beds of butterfly bush, coreopsis, lion's ear, hibiscus, plumbago, and ruelia graced Maria's garden with shades of blue, lilac, yellow, orange, red, pink, and violet. On his knees, Bonis started replanting the flower beds with young plants. Soon he was drenched in sweat. His nimble hands occasionally plucked weeds out of the ground and dead leaves off shrubs. He slogged it out until half past twelve, when he hollered for the widow to turn the courtyard irrigation on.

The sprinklers had been scattering water for a few moments when Maria came into the courtyard, a pitcher of cold lemonade and a tall glass on a tray. She had changed into Bermuda shorts, a print blouse, and sandals. Smiling, Bonis pulled his gloves off, stuffed them into the back pocket of his trousers, and reached for the glass. She poured for him. He avidly drank the whole content and returned the glass to Maria, who asked whether he would like more. He said he was fine now and thanked her. She went inside for a moment to leave the tray atop a side table and came back to the courtyard immediately.

"It's getting pretty hot for this time of the year," he said.
"It sure is."

"Excellent weather for those perennials. I incorporated compost in the soil last time I was here, so those young plants will prosper soon."

"I'm sure they will. You are an excellent gardener, Mr. Bonis."

"Thank you. How's your daughter?"

"She's fine, thank you. Off to a photo shoot in West Palm Beach or some other place. Will be back tonight."

"Please tell her I've checked on the impatiens. They are not suitable for your garden. Their tolerance to salt is poor and you are too close to the sea."

"Oh, I see. I'll tell her."

"Thanks. Do you have the loan ready?"

"I do."

"As I said? Hundreds and fifties in a plastic bag?"

"Exactly."

"Could you bring it now? I'll put it into this fertilizer bag."

"Of course. I'll write you a check for today's work. How much is it?"

"I paid seventy-five for the young plants, so it's a hundred seventy-five."

"Be back in a moment."

Maria went indoors. Bonis recovered his tools and the bag of fertilizer, retraced his steps to the back door to wait for her, and dusted his clothes while doing so. After a few minutes the widow reappeared with a plastic shopping bag in her right hand, a check in her left. Bonis seized the plastic bag, opened it, peered into it, nodded, and put it into the fertilizer bag. Then he took out his wallet and placed the check in it.

"Someday your commitment to the cause will honor you, Mrs. Scheindlin," he said while pocketing the wallet.

"I hope so. However, I'd like to remind you of how wary I am about making these loans. As I said . . ."

"Don't worry, ma'am. I've been given assurances that we'll never bother you again with this sort of favor."

"I most certainly hope so."

"You can be sure of that. Now you should turn the sprinklers off. May I use your bathroom for a minute?"

"But of course, please come in."

Ignoring Maria's protestations that it was not necessary, Bonis removed his work boots. Of course it was necessary, the gardener insisted. Otherwise he would soil the beautiful hardwood floor. When he entered the house, Maria indicated where the ground-floor visitors' bathroom was. As he strode past the furniture to it, she noticed that Bonis was wearing white cotton socks; like athletes, she thought. She turned the irrigation off and remained waiting for him by the back door. A little over a minute had gone by when the gardener came out and drew near Maria with just a hint of a smile. She wondered what the strange tool he held in his right hand was. It was a 9mm Beretta 92 Compact automatic, its numbers acid-burned, a silencer attached.

The gardener was less than three feet from the petrified Maria when he extended his arm and pulled the trigger once. The bullet went in through the victim's right eye, departed through the back of her neck, and embedded itself into a wall. She crumbled to the floor soundlessly, the final moments of her life a whirling kaleidoscope of memories. Bonis contemplated her with a self-possession that, under the circumstances, most people would have considered scary.

"That'll teach you and your buddies not to screw us," he said in Spanish as he thumbed on the safety lever. His tone lacked rancor; it sounded like a passing comment.

Bonis spent approximately two minutes searching for the casing and, having found it, dropped it into the empty glass on the side table, then slipped the glass into a side pocket of his pants. Next, he hurried to the front door, spied for a moment the gate's control panel by the burglar alarm, and pressed the "open" button. Through the peephole he made sure that the gate was opening, then slid the gun into the empty side pocket, stripped off the pair of latex gloves he had pulled on in the bathroom, dropped them into a pocket, and gained the courtyard. He put on and laced up his boots, then seized his tools and the bag of fertilizer before walking to the front of the house.

After putting everything inside the van, he closed the rear door, climbed behind the wheel, and turned on the ignition. The vehicle took a left on West Broadview Drive, then a right onto Broad Causeway to return to the mainland.

"What's she waiting for to close the gate?" asked Spotter One to no one in particular.

"Maybe she's going out in a while," guessed Spotter Two.

"Yeah, maybe," reaching for the two-way radio. "Base, Team Four."

"Go ahead, Four."

"Gardener left at 12:56."

"Okay. Out."

...

Victoria argued that Pardo should make that evening's phone call and that they should record it. Bonis had met him at Burdines; he would identify his accent and voice. The possibility that her husband could misinterpret a place, time, or password should not be ruled out, Victoria reasoned. We are only human, she asserted. Correcting a misunderstanding would delay them. To preclude this, they ought to record the call, she insisted.

Pardo demurred, arguing that she was underrating him.

Victoria maintained she would record the call if she were making it. She reminded her husband that, to make sure he did not mix things up, Bonis always recorded incoming calls. Now *they* would learn from *him* where the second live drop would take place; they could not afford a mistake. Finally, Pardo yielded.

At a Collier Avenue electronics store, they paid $184.55, sales tax included, for a clip-on telephone recorder. According to the salesman, the device simply had to be clipped around the telephone cable or the handset cable. It recorded the conversation without the need to cut or bare any wires.

At a quarter to four, having read the manuals, certain that the gadget worked once Pardo called their room from a cafeteria five blocks away and she recorded his voice, Victoria gave her considered opinion on the politics of the whole thing.

"I still can't get used to the idea of stores selling to the public telephone listening devices, tap detectors, wired and wireless hidden cameras. Things that record the number of strokes you type on your keyboard, voice changers, a thousand things. Gives me the creeps. In some states you don't need a permit to buy a shotgun or a rifle. Not even blank pistols or hunting knives are for sale in Cuba. A Cuban dissident tapes a phone conversation with a State Security officer in which he is threatened, he takes the officer to court, plays the tape, the dissident goes to jail."

"Why are you telling me this, Vicky? I know all that."

Victoria was taken aback. "I'm not telling you. I'm reflecting on the differences between both systems."

"But we've reflected on the excesses of democracy and the short-comings of communism a hundred times. Are we going to do something about it? No, right? So leave it to the naive dissidents who risk their freedom, maybe even their lives. They haven't figured out that when communism falls, Cuban-Americans will give them a medal and a pension before rigging the elections and taking charge. Politics sucks, Victoria. Forget it. Let's focus on the job at hand."

Feeling mildly berated made Victoria a little angry. She believed him right, but it was frustrating to have her observations dismissed as well worn. Sighing, she reminded herself that it was Pardo who had sharpened her meditations on the shortcomings of contemporary societies.

"I'll scout a little for an enclosed phone booth," Pardo announced. "Are you coming or do you feel like a nap?"

"I'm going with you, but hold it a minute, okay? If we play it by the book, we shouldn't call from Naples. Give me the map."

They discussed Estero, to the north, and Copeland, to the southwest. Both appeared to be small towns in which a closed phone booth may not be easy to find. Fort Lauderdale on the East Coast seemed perfect, a bigger city opposite to where they were, but it involved a three-hour round-trip by bus.

"Aren't we overdoing it, Vicky?" Pardo wondered. "This man has been an illegal for . . . how long?"

"Twenty-two years."

"Is there any reason to suspect his phone line has been bugged since you called him?"

"Not to my knowledge."

"I don't want to sound like I think I'm an expert on this. You are. But what's the problem with calling from here? Not this hotel, of course. I mean calling from Naples."

"No problem. It just isn't the sensible thing to do. Fugitives— it's what we are, whether we like it or not—are not supposed to call from a place they can be easily traced to. Naples is not New York or Chicago, you know? Oh, hell, maybe I'm being too theoretical and negative. Let's go find a booth at a big hotel."

...

To say that Eugenio Bonis had endured an adventurous although pathetic life would be quite an understatement. His grandfather, a foundry worker victimized during the first years of corrupt Cuban capitalism, joined the Communist Party in 1925, at age thirty-five. His father, a dropout and shoeshine boy indoctrinated by his ancestor in proletariat ideology, signed up with the Communist Youth in 1935, at age fifteen. Eugenio Bonis, whose real name was Alfredo Aparicio, had been merely nine years old when he started hawking a communist magazine in 1960, sixteen months after the Batista dictatorship had been toppled, one full year before the Chief proclaimed the communist nature of the Revolution. Alfredo joined Cuban Counterintelligence as an informer in 1966, three weeks after his fifteenth birthday.

In postcapitalist Cuba, the overwhelming majority of card-carrying communists under thirty belonged to the Union of Communist Youth, the party's junior organization. Gaining admittance into the party at a younger age was an honor reserved for those who excelled at something, from science to sports. Precious few were granted full party membership at eighteen—in most instances for having distinguished themselves on the battlefield or in matters related to the security of the Revolution. Alfredo was one of those.

He had been admitted to the party at this tender age for spending 1968 and 1969 in a prison camp, purportedly doing hard labor under the Vagrancy Act. In fact, he informed on Catholics, gay men, and hippies who had been convicted for their religious, sexual, or cultural beliefs and practices. Alfredo ate lousy food improperly cooked, slept on lice-infested bunkers, spent nine hours daily from Monday through Saturday—plus four on Sundays—tilling the land, and lacked proper medical care. Despite all this, he enormously enjoyed snitching on the papists, degenerates, and joint-smoking longhaired drunks he pretended to befriend.

Such self-sacrifice won him the respect of State Security's top brass. From June 1970 to December 1971, at an SS farm fifty-five kilometers from Havana, he passed a course on the theory and practice of Intelligence and Counterintelligence with flying colors. His total commitment to the cause and to espionage, and an everyday conduct premised on total obedience, made him the consummate agent, the sort of hand every skipper wanted on board. Thereby, throughout the seventies, Alfredo lived a peripatetic life. He smuggled weapons, explosives, and money into Nicaragua and El Salvador; trained agents in Argentina, Chile, Peru, and Venezuela; liaised between field spies and their case officers in four African nations; smuggled gold worth several million dollars out of Lebanon, executed two traitors, and learned passable English and Portuguese.

Even though most females considered the heterosexual Alfredo an extremely attractive man, he didn't see much difference between ejaculation and defecation. Both were physiological functions, unavoidable discharges. For many years he masturbated ten times for every occasion he took a woman to bed. In his thirties he came to the conclusion that ignoring overtures from members of the opposite sex seemed to make him even more fascinating to the ladies, so he practiced a limited, easy flirtation that worked with most. The notion of starting a family had never crossed his mind. Alfredo had two loves—the homeland and the Revolution.

In 1978 the Chief decided to revitalize and improve upon what up to then had been a rather amateurish—albeit fruitful—intelligence-gathering effort in the United States by planting experienced cadres in Miami, Key West, Tampa, New Jersey, and New York. American and Cuban embassies in all but name had already been opened in Havana and Washington. He had authorized Cubans residing abroad to visit relatives living on the island. The bleeding heart liberal in the White House would most probably win a second term in office, he told his brother. The timing was perfect. Alfredo Aparicio's name had been the third on the list, following the resident director and his deputy, which the Commander personally approved.

Sent back to the farm, Alfredo learned gardening in the mornings and contemporary espionage technology in the afternoons. In the evenings, he perfected his English. The course was nearing completion when, in April 1980, the Chief set in motion the Mariel boatlift. The minister of the interior judged the occasion made-to-order, a comment that elicited an enigmatic smile from Number One as he gave the go-ahead. Under the name Eugenio Bonis, Alfredo Aparicio was locked away at Combinado del Este, the oversized Havana penitentiary, and twenty-six days later he became one of several thousand convicts that Castro shipped to the United States.

Unsuspecting American institutions took Bonis at face value and issued him the proper documentation to find employment and housing, to be allowed to travel, open bank accounts, obtain credit, get free health care and tax exemptions. During his first weeks in the United States, caring Cuban-Americans provided what he needed, from clothing to money. Bonis applied for and was granted citizenship in 1986. He opened his business with an SBA loan. Five years later he married an Anglo woman to bolster his legend. "Taking advantage of the contradictions of imperialism"—communist terminology to describe the opportunities existing in democratic, First World societies—was not a situation fraught with difficulties.

By 2002, Bonis had successfully pursued landscape gardening and espionage for twenty-two consecutive years. As baseball-mad Cubans like to say: If not a record, a good batting average.

Now, driving along the causeway into Miami, the gardener found inner peace. He felt at ease, especially after completing a mission. This, however, was a strange and surprising emotional state. He sensed that the most important years of his life were nearing to a close, that he had accomplished the mission for which, in the distant future, when exploitation no longer existed and imperialism had been resoundingly defeated, his deeds if not his name would merit a few lines in history books.

Returning to the fold—the secret yearning he had refused to cherish to avoid frustrating postponements—seemed closer than ever. In a few days he would be leisurely strolling along the Malecón, getting drunk, smoking a real cigar. This coming July 26 he would celebrate in style. He would do the things that had been forbidden to him for so long. Entering a cane field, machete in hand, to cut a ton of cane stalks; riding a crowded bus; visiting the few old comrades still alive; reading newspapers that denounce imperialism. And he would at long last get to visit his father's grave and say to him: *Viejo, I did my duty. I followed your example.*

He would get his ass off this neon-lit sewer. Never see again its revolting class structure: the dirty rich riding Rolls-Royces at the top, the despicable traitors who betrayed their homeland only to end up begging for coins in the streets at the bottom. He would not have to endure anymore of those cowards who, from the air-conditioned studios of American radio stations, urge Cubans living on the island to take up arms against the Revolution. Those who pay mercenaries to plant bombs in Havana and want the U.S. Army to do the job for them, the same bastards who hope to exploit the Cuban people like their forefathers did in the past. The shysters, pushers, addicts, gamblers, shylocks, corrupt officials, and alcoholics. The hypocrite papists who molest boys, the faggots, and the prostitutes who sell their bodies to rich old men, or rich old women. At last he would leave behind that human flotsam.

Of course, there would be parties, celebrations, and a decoration. After a week or two, though, he'd rejoin Counterintelligence to operate against the so-called dissenters, independent journalists, and human rights activists who within Cuba denigrated the Revolution on a daily basis. Was the Chief going soft on them? Why did he let them meet with foreign politicians, grant interviews to journalists, talk on the phone with Miami radio stations? It had to be part of a strategy and, as a soldier, he had no right to outfox the Commander in Chief. A revolutionary never questions the party, and he prided himself on his discipline. He felt sure that, sooner or later, the order would come to squash them without mercy. Then he would volunteer to arrest and/ or execute as many as possible.

Once in North Miami, the gardener realized he had to concentrate on his immediate plans. First he called his wife (an intensive care nurse at Cedars Medical Center on the 3:00 to 11:00 P.M. shift) from a pay phone and told her not to wait for him for lunch, he'd be late. Then he drove along 125th and parked three blocks away from a rent-a-car outlet. Twenty minutes later he parked a Chevy Impala behind the van, moved the bag of fertilizer with the money and the tote bag he had bought at Burdines, now holding a fresh change of clothes and a shoulder holster for his Beretta, to the rental's trunk, then locked the van. He dropped Maria's glass and the casing in a sewer before driving to a motel on Flagler and Thirty-seventh, where he rented a room. Before showering, he tore up Maria Scheindlin's check and flushed it down the toilet, then ordered a pizza and a beer. After lunch, satisfied and unconcerned, he asked the desk clerk to awake him at four. He took a long nap and dreamed he was hawking *Mella* magazine at Havana's Central Park.

At a quarter to five, neat in the fresh set of clothes, he steered the rental to the home of Ms. Gene Hagstedt, a widowed retired realtor who owned a modest house at Ninety-sixth Avenue and SW Thirty-second Street, West Wood Lakes. To supplement her pension, she ran an answering service with ten steady and several temporary clients to whom she charged thirty dollars a month. The gardener had chosen her because people learned of her business by word of mouth. She was not registered as self-employed, nor did she pay income tax on what she earned as a service provider.

At no time had Ms. Hagstedt asked Eugenio his marital status, yet she firmly believed that the calls she fielded for him were of the sort a married man couldn't take at home. Although seventy-seven years old, the lady still had an eye for attractive men. She considered that if there were two middle-aged hunks in Miami, the Cuban gardener was one. He got just three or four messages a month and nearly all came from Ana, a husky-voiced woman who merely said "Please tell Eugenio Bonis to call Ana." Ms. Hagstedt thought that if Eugenio was half as good in bed as he appeared to be, both his wife and Ana were extremely lucky women.

Once or twice a month Eugenio dropped over unannounced around half past five in the afternoon. He said something sweet about her blue eyes, her smooth skin, or how absolutely lovely she looked in that forty-year-old photograph atop the mantelpiece before sitting to read a magazine or watch TV until, when the clock struck the hour, her phone rang. He'd answer it, listen for a while, jot down something or say or read from a piece of paper a phrase or two in unintelligible rapid-fire Spanish, then hang up. On these occasions he tipped her a fiver.

"You look ravishing," Eugenio said when Ms. Hagstedt opened her screen door on the afternoon of May 7, 2002. "I feel like getting down on my knees and begging you to marry me."

. . .

Pardo and Victoria took a taxi to the Hyatt Regency Coconut Point, found their way to the golf course's clubhouse, and from its lobby called Bonis's number at 6:00 P.M. sharp.

"Call my other number, please," the machine said.

When Pardo told this to his wife, she knitted her brow and squinted suspiciously.

"Okay. Hang up and dial 305-555-1965."

Pardo did as told. Ms. Hagstedt's phone rang.

"Hello?" the gardener said.

"Uh, Mr. Bonis?" Pardo probed.

"Yes."

"This is Mr. Villalobos."

"Right. Tell your wife I found your geraniums," he read from a handwritten note he had taken from his wallet. "I have to leave for West Palm Beach early tomorrow, so I'll leave the seedlings in your front lawn at 7:00 P.M. today. Good-bye."

Pardo hung up and echoed the message to Victoria. Blocking from view his maneuvering to unclip the recorder, she tilted her head and frowned, slightly intrigued. They made it back to the Comfort Inn and Victoria asked her husband to rewind and play the tape. She listened to it standing by the chest of drawers.

"Didn't I say it word by word? Almost?" Pardo wanted to know, hoping for a compliment.

"Shush. Play it again."

"Why?"

"Play it again, Pardo, please."

Pardo heaved a sigh and pressed buttons.

"Okay. Let's decipher," Victoria said. Sitting on the bed, she emptied her purse on the mattress. Pardo rewound. She took off a hairpin, bent it backward, and with one end repeatedly picked at the stitches in the purse's internal protective lining, alongside the metal frame, until a piece of thread came off. From between the lining and the fake leather, she extracted an A6-sized page of paper with both sides printed in the smallest typeface.

"Give me a blank page. Play it again."

"Again?"

"And make a pause every five or six words."

"You got it."

She wrote down each word. When the recording ended, Pardo turned off the gadget.

"Unless I'm much mistaken, 7:00 P.M. today means 1:00 A.M. tomorrow, right?" he said.

Victoria nodded while shifting her gaze from the note she had just made to the code page.

"What does the rest of the gobbledygook stand for?" asked her husband.

Victoria finished making notes, then said: "West Palm Beach means Miami International Airport, Flamingo garage, second level. He said 'leave' twice to indicate he's got both things, my passport and the cash, ready for delivery. Geraniums, plural, indicate we both have to be there. And that he'll leave the seedlings in my front lawn means he has lost contact with Havana."

"Okay. Let's go take a bus to Miami."

Victoria remained sitting, reflectively gazing at the wall ahead.

"Why does he tell me he's lost contact with Havana? He knows I know that. Why does he ask for the two of us to be there? That's a mistake."

"Beats me."

A short silence followed.

"Is there any way to find a map of the airport's garage?" Victoria wondered.

Pardo pressed his right hand under his left armpit and cupped his chin in the palm of his left. "I'm sure we can print a map from the airport's Internet site," he said a moment later. "Concourses and gates and shops, that sort of map. But I don't think they'll have a map of the parking garages."

"Let's find out."

"It's early, Victoria. A quarter to seven."

"Let's head to Miami. We'll go to an Internet café. And we should get to this airport garage as early as possible. Try to be there three hours ahead of time. There's a snag in that message that I can't figure out."

...

Nobody heard the shrill scream that Jenny Scheindlin let out at 9:06 P.M. Then she started spinning around several times, dreading an assassin in hiding, and scurried from one place to the next turning on all the lights in the living area. When the notion that nobody was lurking in the shadows sunk in, Jenny stared at her mother's body for almost a minute while biting her closed fist. She was unable to muster the necessary courage to get nearer, much less search for vital signs. The inertness of the body made her feel sure Maria was dead. A hot sphere climbed up her esophagus and she vomited gastric juices on the polished hardwood floor. Breathing deeply, Jenny recovered enough to wonder what she should do next. She rinsed her mouth with water in the bathroom where Maria's murderer had put on his gloves and drawn his gun. At 9:14 P.M., shaking uncontrollably, Jenny gathered her wits and dialed 911.

Two minutes had gone by when a Bay Harbor Police Department cruiser, its flashers spinning wildly, arrived at the scene. The officer steered the car through the open gate, screeched to a stop, killed the engine and the lights, and got out. Jenny stood silhouetted in the wide-open front door.

"Base, Team Four," the intrigued-looking spotter on the graveyard shift said into the two-way radio.

"Go ahead, Four."

"A police cruiser just went into the subject's driveway."

"Come again, Four."

The spotter used exactly the same words.

"Why?" Base wanted to know.

"I have no idea, sir."

The Bay Harbor police officer, who was new on the job and had never seen Jenny Scheindlin, followed the hand signs made by the obviously terrified and seemingly mute young woman. Without touching the body, he doubled back to Jenny, gently steered her to a club chair, told her not to move, and talked into the mike on his left shoulder. Bay Harbor police will not touch a murder with a ten-foot pole, so the dispatcher called the North Miami Beach Police Department. At 9:29 a Crime Scenes Unit team arrived at the Scheindlins'. A Miami Medical Examiner Department vehicle came in at 9:45. Practically all the lights of the house were turned on. The FBI spotter reported these developments to Base as they unfolded.

For its part, Base frantically tried to ascertain what had taken place. A dozen phone calls and some computer-assisted personnel search revealed that the photographer on duty at the North Miami Beach Crime Unit had applied for a job with the bureau seven months earlier and would probably be willing to explain what the hell was going on at the Scheindlins'.

The man's cell phone rang at 10:19. An FBI photographer identified himself and asked his colleague whether he could possibly spare a minute and get to a private place where they could talk. He sure could, the North Miami Beach photographer said. Walking around the edge of the pool, staring at the underwater lights that someone had inadvertently turned on, he reported that a deeply suntanned woman in her fifties had died as the result of a gunshot wound in her face. The weapon was nowhere to be seen, no casing had been recovered, and gunpowder marks on the victim's face suggested she had been shot at close range. Her daughter had discovered the body. He had heard the ME estimate that the stiff had died between eight and ten hours earlier. The photographer believed she had been murdered.

Brent Hart called Nathan Smith at 10:44.

"Sorry to wake you up, sir, but things have taken a turn for the worst."

"What is it?"

"Maria Scheindlin is dead. Probably murdered."

Smith swung his legs out and sat up in bed. "When?"

"Between eight and ten hours ago."

"Hold it."

Smith placed the handset on the mattress, rubbed his face, pressed his eyelids, recovered the handset. "Lay it on me."

Hart rattled off what the North Miami PD photographer had said.

"This happened after the gardener left?"

"Apparently."

"You checked him out?"

"I did."

"Tell me."

"Eugenio Bonis. Cuban by birth. Boatlifted in 1980. Served time in Havana for privately cultivating and selling flowers, or so he said.

Owns a landscaping business. Naturalized in 1986. No criminal record, married a WASP nurse in 1991. No children. Contributes twenty dollars a month to the Cuban American Foundation but is otherwise indifferent to politics. Lives at Fifty-seventh Street between Third and Fourth Avenues, Hialeah."

Smith processed the information in silence for a few moments. "When did he leave the house?"

"12:56."

"You got him covered now?"

"Two cars, one on each corner of his block. They got there fifteen minutes ago. Except for the porch, lights are out; air conditioners too."

"Phone?"

"We're working on it."

"Okay. Any chance the killer got in and out unseen?"

Thirty years married to the man had not inured Smith's wife to such exchanges. She turned on her right side and covered her left ear with her hand.

"Theoretically, yes," Hart said. "He could have jumped the backyard fence. Also, had our guys been reading girlie mags or playing cards . . ." He left it there.

"I'll be at the office in thirty minutes."

"Okay," Hart said and hung up.

...

At a Cyber Net Café in the NW section of the city, seven minutes away from the airport by car, Victoria and Pardo examined the terminal's map onscreen. There were two multilevel, long-term parking garages, rather flippantly named Flamingo and Dolphin, connected to the terminal by a moving walkway on the third level. The map, however, lacked specifics concerning their perimeter, the number of cars each level could hold, or any other significant information, so they decided not to print it. They walked out of the café at five minutes to nine.

Their taxi arrived at the terminal at 9:15 and they got out at the entrance to Concourse E. After some pepperoni pizza and sodas, they used the restrooms. An elevator took them to the third floor and they entered the Flamingo garage through the moving walkway at 9:55. The sheer size of the square-shaped area surprised them. It seemed capable of storing over one thousand automobiles although only a few dozen were there at the moment. It had the usual ramps for vehicles and elevators for pedestrians. Despite the lighting, the place was gloomy.

"The floor below is probably exactly like this," Victoria whispered, her eyes roving all over the place, searching for surveillance equipment and dark corners. "We'll hide behind one of those columns."

"No, this part's too bright," Pardo said, looking around. "We should go all the way to the back, crouch behind a car, and hope the owner is in Shanghai."

"I think halfway might be better. Let's go down."

"Just a minute, Vicky. Are you telling me we're going to stand around here for over three hours?"

"Yes, *macho*. I want to see Bonis come in, have a minute to see how he acts, walks, and moves around. In Burdines he was too alert, distrustful. Something's amiss here. We are using him for our own ends and I don't know whether he has grown suspicious, wants to ask what's the money for, feels entitled to decide whether he should trust us. In my book he's a fanatic, but maybe I'm wrong. Maybe he has changed over time and wants to keep the money for himself. Or maybe the Feds got to him and turned him. Either way, I want to preempt him."

They were just strolling now, taking in the place.

"Is that possible?" Pardo asked.

"Everything is possible. And without that money and a passport for me, I'd be stuck here."

"Only for a few days, darling. I'd fly to Europe, open an account here, transfer some money from the Jersey Islands bank into it, then fly back. Three days tops."

"I hope we can stick to Plan A. The sooner I leave the United States the better. The INS catches me, I get fingerprinted and photographed; leave a sample of my handwriting, too, in the forms I'll have to fill out."

"I know, I know. But Vicky, he arrived at Burdines on the dot. Why should he be early tonight?"

"That's the point; he shouldn't be. If he gets here five minutes ahead of time, everything's fine. But the earlier he comes, the more reason we'll have to worry. It means he wants to stake *us* out, or to check if *we* arrive early to stake him out. Either way, it's a sign he is up to something. He walks in one or two hours early, you get ready, and I mean ready, for the unexpected."

Pardo scratched his temple and looked off thoughtfully. "How should we deal with him in that case?"

Victoria's gaze kept scanning the place. "I don't know. Let's consider it. What do you think we should do?"

...

Elliot and Fidelia were experiencing the early, non-REM stage of sleep, in which the brain does whatever it is that unplugs people completely, when the phone rang. Elliot started dreaming he was sitting behind the wheel of his car at a railroad crossing, watching two blinking red lights and hearing a bell clang stridently. He would be late for the meeting now. The train was nowhere to be seen. There had been ample time to cross the tracks safely. Trains here were endless, had dozens and dozens of freight cars. A hand shook him by the shoulder and he woke up.

"It's for you," Fidelia said, extending him the handset.

He reached for it. "Hello."

"Mr. Steil?" a female's quivering voice.

"Speaking."

"It's Jenny."

"Who?"

"Jenny, the daughter of Ruben and Maria Scheindlin."

"Of course. Excuse me, Jenny. I was sound asleep. What can I do for you?"

"Oh, Mr. Steil . . ." her voice choked.

Elliot could virtually see the remaining cobwebs in his mind fall away. A sobbing Jenny Scheindlin calling him at home in the middle of the night?

"What's the matter, Jenny?"

He heard her blow her nose, sniff. "My mother is dead."

After a moment of total immobility, Elliot slid his feet to the floor and sat up in the bed. "I beg your pardon?"

"My mother was murdered, Mr. Steil. She was taken to the morgue half an hour ago."

Elliot rubbed his forehead and ran his fingers through his hair. Confusion made his mind go blank. He wanted to say something, but nothing came.

"Mr. Steil?"

"Yes, Jenny."

"Did you hear what I said?"

"Yes, yes I did. I'm . . . stunned. I don't know what to say. How did she . . . ? I mean—"

"She was shot in the face."

"And . . . and . . . who did it?"

"I don't know."

"Are the police there?" He had not finished saying it when he realized he had asked the most stupid of possible questions. The body was in the morgue.

"They were. House was full of cops. The last two left a while ago."

"Jenny, listen. Are you alone?"

"No, I called two friends of mine. They are here now."

"Good. I'll be right over."

"There's no need, Mr. Steil. Really. I called Sam first; I didn't know he was in New York, his wife told me. Then I thought you, as company manager, should be among the first to learn the news. I found your home number in Mom's phone book."

"You did right. I'll be there in a while. Wait for me. Okay?"

"Okay."

"Bye now."

"Bye, Mr. Steil."

Elliot broke the connection.

"What happened?" Fidelia asked as he stood.

"Maria Scheindlin has been murdered," hurriedly putting on slacks.

"What?"

"That's all she said."

"Said who?"

"Her daughter. Get me a clean shirt, will you? This seems like a bad dream to me."

...

Eugenio Bonis parked the Chevy on the Dolphin garage's first floor at 10:07 and entered the terminal six minutes later holding the tote bag that now stored a hundred thousand dollars. To his complete surprise, he found there were no red-eyes to Ottawa from Miami International. After one that had departed at 4:00 P.M., the next would be a Delta flight at 6:45 A.M. to Atlanta, where it would connect to another flight to Ottawa. Well, he thought, that forced a change of plans. He would drive north, then fly from Orlando in the morning.

At 10:35 he doubled back to the Dolphin parking building, took the elevator to the second floor, and through a connecting passageway crossed to the Flamingo garage. He devoted a minute or two to glancing over the parked vehicles, ramps, and emergency stairs, choosing the place in which he would ambush the traitors. Not knowing which of the six elevators they would take, any dark corner would do; trying to find him, they would pace the garage over. No surveillance cameras or parking attendants were to be seen. While at this, an elevator discharged a woman who hurried to a red Toyota 4Runner, heels clicking on the cement floor. She boarded it, started the engine, turned on the lights, and drove down the ramp.

Bonis had been warned that Miami was one of the places the two deserters might be heading to. If they got there, they could try to contact him and, through him, other agents or informers. Nobody in Cuban Intelligence knew that he had unwittingly liaised for Victoria for years, nor that Pola Negri had loaned her cash and that a new loan was in the making. On May 2 an unsuspecting Cuban-American visiting her frail parents had taken to Havana an encrypted message in a diskette. The order sentencing to death the two traitors came in a similar diskette, brought to Miami by another innocent Cuban who had spent a week with his relatives in Santa Clara. That message ordered the gardener back home, his mission accomplished, once he had tracked down and executed the two traitors.

Bonis chose one of the farthest support columns to hide and wait behind. He ambled to it leisurely, the tote bag on his left, resigned to the long, precautionary wait. Although Havana had not given away what the deserters had been, he believed them to be Intelligence or Counterintelligence officers who were well versed in the tricks of the trade. He couldn't afford to give them an edge. He was forty yards away from the chosen column when the short, unattractive female in the unbecoming glasses he had first caught a glimpse of at Burdines emerged from behind a Mercedes.

"You are way too early, comrade," Victoria said, smiling insincerely.

Bonis used to carefully plot every step of the way well in advance, leave to chance only the unforeseeable. He had shunned unpleasant surprises for so long that he felt astounded. The cunt was perceptibly uneasy, though. Her hands were empty. Good. Where was the guy? Close by, for sure.

"Where's your comrade?" he demanded to know, his eyes not quite meeting hers.

"Somewhere else. No reason for him to be here tonight. Why did you come so early, comrade?"

"My instructions are to give this" he lifted the tote bag, "to both of you. He's not here, I take it back to Pola Negri."

The gardener turned around and started to leave. Without breaking stride, his free hand slipped under the sport jacket. Prodded into action by Bonis's refusal to hand over the money, Pardo stepped out

from behind a light gray Buick Park Avenue, pistol aimed at the fleeing man. Neither he nor Victoria noticed that the spy had been reaching for a gun.

"Here I am, Bonis," he said. "Now put the tote bag on the floor."

Bonis turned his head and laid eyes on the cutout's face first,
the gun next. The pistol—a Tokarev?—and the wristlock grip to re-
duce recoil confirmed that he was confronting a professional. Bonis's
Beretta had the safety on—he had meant to turn it off once he hid
behind a car or a column—and he would lose half a second switch-
ing it off, enough for the traitor to put two rounds into his chest,
maybe three. It peeved him to discover that he had underrated them.
His hand came out empty.

"You point a gun at me?" off the top of his head, letting the palm
of his hand rest on his chest to show how offended he felt. "I run
risks for you and you point a gun at me? I can't believe you call yourself my comrade."

"Put the tote bag on the floor, Bonis. Then leave," coming loose
on him.

"What's eating you? What's going on? After all the work and
effort I went through to get this?" lifting the holdall.

"Bonis, don't give me a hard time and put the tote bag on the
floor. Maybe someday you'll learn why I'm doing this. Just put the
tote bag on the floor."

Victoria watched, mesmerized.

"What are you getting excited about? You know how many years
of my life I have devoted to the cause? I don't deserve to be treated
like this."

"Put. The. Tote. Bag. On. The. Floor."

"This is as good as it gets, right? Okay. But I'll report your attitude to Havana," Bonis said before dropping the tote bag.

"I have no beef with you, Bonis. Go take a walk now," Pardo
ordered him.

"Screw yourself."

Pretending to be deeply angered, the gardener stomped off—
five, six, seven heavy strides toward the closest elevator door. Pardo

kept glaring at his opponent, but, relieved that things had been solved peacefully, he lowered the gun. Victoria moved toward the tote bag. Pardo threw a sidelong glance at his wife at the precise moment that Bonis turned and dropped to the floor.

"PARDO!" Victoria screamed the instant she clutched the bag.

Her husband swirled and fired two shots, aiming too high. Bonis, supported on his elbows, squeezed the trigger three times. Victoria watched the flashing muzzle in gruesome fascination, frozen. Two bullets hit Pardo: the first just below the left clavicle, the other one inch above and two inches to the left of his right nipple. Knitting his brow in surprise, Pardo felt his knees buckle and then slumped over.

Bonis turned his attention to the unattractive woman. In a crouch, she was scurrying to the column, still three or four feet away from it. The tote bag lay where he had dropped it. He fired once and missed her back by an inch. Having lost count of the cartridges remaining in the clip, but remembering he would need two for the coups de grâce, Bonis stood erect and dusted his knees before starting to retrace his steps. Had she been carrying a weapon, she would be firing at him right now. He would get to her, there was no hurry. He had taken five or six paces when a 7.62mm slug drilled his left cheek in an upward angle, trepanned the temporal bone, perforated the brain, and, repelled by a too thick occipital, bounced back. It gradually lost momentum while worming its way through both cerebral hemispheres, shattering into millions of tiny fragments the zealot's determination and his swirling reminiscences of a faraway land. Bonis stumbled, dropped the gun, and felt his legs beginning to give way beneath him. He was brain-dead before his face thudded to the floor.

It had been a lucky shot. With his vision blurred and in burning pain, Pardo had aimed for the midsection. When he saw his opponent drop, Pardo tried to take a deep breath, failed, and rested his forehead on the coarse cement floor. Was this what his wife suffered when she had an asthma attack? Feeling utterly winded, extremely weak, and having a strange foreboding, he wondered whether Bonis could still shoot Victoria. He wanted to lift his head and take a look, but all he managed was to scrape his left cheek against the concrete.

Behind the support column, the realization that her husband was hit made Victoria snap out of her immobility. She had recognized the loud gun report of the Tokarev. Had Pardo shot Bonis? She took a peek and, seeing the gardener lying inert, hurried to where Pardo was. She hunkered down by his side. The hairs on the back of her neck prickled when she noticed the blood trickling out of his nostrils and mouth.

"Pardo? Are you okay, my love?"

"I don't . . . think so. Are you . . . hurt?"

"No, I'm fine."

"Did I take . . . the sonofabitch out?"

Victoria lifted her eyes to Bonis's corpse and stared at it for a few moments.

"He's not moving," she reported.

"Fine. Bring the . . . tote bag here."

"What for?"

"Bring it here. Now."

She went for it, returned to her husband's side, and crouched again.

"Open it."

She unzipped it.

"What's in it?"

"Cash. A lot of it."

"Did he bring . . . your passport?"

It took her nearly a minute to check the pockets and make sure there was neither a passport nor other identification.

"No, Pardo. He didn't. He came to kill us and keep the money for himself."

"Okay. Take the . . . cash with you . . . and hide. Take the . . . CD, too. It's in my . . . breast pocket. Wait for me. I've got a passport. They'll take me . . . to a hospital . . . and cure me. Later I'll . . . search for you . . . in Naples?"

"I'm not leaving you, Pardo," as she took his pulse.

"Don't argue . . . with me. I need to . . . save strength. I'll say . . . this man . . . tried to . . . hold me up. Get going. Call an ambulance . . . and go away."

"I won't leave you and that's final."

"You don't . . . have a passport, you don't . . ."

Eighty or so yards away, a Ford Escort ascending the ramp reached the second level. The beam of its headlights momentarily swept over the crouching woman and the fallen men. Startled, Victoria looked up, but they were too far away for the driver to see them and he kept steering his car to the garage's top floor. She lowered her gaze to Pardo in time to watch him cough, gasp twice, writhe spasmodically, and die.

She had never seen someone die before her very eyes. After a minute of disbelief staring at the half-open eyelids of the human being she had loved above all others, as she lost his pulse and registered that he was no longer breathing, a new side of Victoria's personality emerged. "Don't do this to me, *macho*," she implored. Tears were not welling in her eyes, her grief was not incapacitating. *Am I in shock?* she wondered, baffled by her equanimity. *Partly, yes, of course.*

She released his wrist, stood, and surveyed her surroundings. Not a soul. Had anybody heard the shots? She lowered her gaze to Pardo, thinking. The only thing she could do was flee. Having made up her mind, she squatted one final time, turned the body on its back, and retrieved the CD. On its upward trajectory, the bullet that pierced Pardo's left lung had also perforated the disk, rendering it useless. Victoria smiled sadly before picking up her Tokarev. She put both objects into the tote bag, zipped it shut, and straightened up. From behind the column she recovered her purse. She took a last look at her husband and moved away. Passing near Bonis, she saw the Beretta on the floor and noted that it had a silencer attached. So, the only shots that could possibly have been heard by others were Pardo's. Victoria bared her teeth in a snarl, lifted the gun, and fired the remaining rounds into the gardener's head. Then she dropped the Beretta and hurried to the nearest elevator, wondering what to do first.

. . .

The two young men came across as patently gay in their trendy clothing, dyed hair, plucked eyebrows, and effeminate gesticulations, but they were showering Jenny with almost maternal solicitude. The dark-skinned Valerio, a Peruvian with considerable Inca blood in him who spoke impeccable Spanish, held a saucer with a steaming cup of chamomile tea from which Jenny had taken a few sips. The older Chris, New Yorker by birth, fashion photographer by profession, and South Beach resident since 1998, contemplated Jenny adoringly, his hand on her shoulder. All three were sitting on the huge sofa upholstered in striped satin; Elliot was in the club chair he always chose when in the Scheindlins' living space.

"It was the first thing the police asked me," Jenny, answering Steil's last question. "I hadn't looked, so I took them all over the house. The safe is closed, the paintings are in place, no jewels or money are missing from my room. There were four hundred and fifteen dollars in Mother's purse. Her car is in the garage. No, Mr. Steil, robbery wasn't the motive. The only strange thing I found when I came in was the open gate."

Steil rubbed his forehead and closed his eyes. Certainly the police had to know that a closed safe could well be empty. Maybe the killer had forced Maria to open it, taken everything, and closed it. He wanted to ask more questions. Did Jenny know if her mother had a lover? Or any known enemy? Had the widow shown signs of sadness, depression, or acted worried recently? Surely the guys from Homicide had already posed those questions. Besides, he had no right to intrude neither into the young woman's grief nor into family secrets. He lifted his head, turned his gaze to the bloodstains on the floor, then searched Jenny's eyes. She was dejectedly staring at the rug under the coffee table.

"Well, Jenny, I don't know what to say." She locked gazes with him. "Death is always surprising. Your father's, for instance. But he was an old man, and he died from natural causes. This is so . . . un-expected and brutal. I only hope the police get whoever did this as soon as possible."

"I hope so, too."

"Is there anything I can do for you tonight?"

"I don't think so. Thanks. Chris and Valerio will stay with me."

"For as long as she wants us to," Chris added, unasked. "We're also trying to talk her into spending a few weeks at our place. We'd be delighted."

"That's very nice of you, gentlemen." Then, turning to the emaciated young woman, "Okay, Jenny. You have my home number and you know the company numbers, too. If you need anything, give me a call."

"Thank you."

Steil placed both hands on his knees, ready to stand up, then hesitated, clearing his throat. "On the way here I considered whether I should tell you what I'm about to tell you now. I know it's not the right moment to bring this up, but I feel it's my duty to tell you now. When you feel better, you need to learn some basic facts about IMLATINEX. You'll have to consult with your lawyers, maybe ap-point people to represent you."

First Jenny frowned in incomprehension. Then her shoulders fell slightly, as if a physical object had landed on her back. "Yes, I suppose I have to, right?"

"Yes, you have to, Jenny. There's no escaping the fact, and the sooner you do it the better. I don't mean tomorrow or the day after. Sam and I will try to act in your best interests for as long as you need: a week, two, three, whichever. But my advice, unsolicited advice I should say, is that you discuss the situation with your lawyer," he concluded, getting to his feet.

Jenny stood, too. Valerio put the saucer and cup on a side table and imitated her. Chris also rose. Steil shook hands all around and Jenny escorted him to the door.

"I'm really sorry, Jenny. Your mother was quite a woman."

"Yes, she was. Thanks, Mr. Steil."

Driving to Miami, Elliot reflected on what he ought to do next. He had to call Hart, of course. In the middle of the night? What could Hart do? Nothing. Police dealt with murders. Besides, the FBI had filmed Capdevila and Berta when they went to Bay Harbor, so they had the place under surveillance. No hurry then, he would call Hart in the morning. Sam Plotzher was in New York. Mrs. Plotzher had probably called him right after Jenny gave her the news; no point in calling, him, either.

He remembered that in a few hours someone would be coming to the Scheindlins' to pick up a hundred thousand in cash. Carlos Capdevila and Berta Arosamena? What a surprise awaited those two. *Wait a minute!* flashed in his mind. Had they come a day earlier to claim the cash, argued with Maria, and murdered her? He shook his head. He was of a mind that they were not assassins. Could he be sure they were not? Could he be sure the murderer had nothing to do with them? From that perspective, reporting the murder to Hart ASAP seemed much more urgent. Right now, he decided. He spotted a gas station at the corner of Sixty-sixth Street and Biscayne, across from the American Legion Park. He pulled into it, went past the pumps, killed the lights and the engine, and got out, searching for a pay phone. He looked up the number Hart had given him, dropped in the coins, and punched it.

"Federal Bureau of Investigation."

"This is an emergency. I need to talk to Special Agent Brent Hart."

"Your name, sir?"

"Elliot Steil."

"Hold the line."

Elliot figured the call had to be rerouted to Hart's home. His watch read 12:16. He extracted another quarter from his pocket and dropped it into the slot, just in case. He started to have second thoughts. Making Capdevila and Berta suspects in a murder case was not nice. Although they were no angels, he had no proof. But you never know. About two minutes had gone by and he felt disinclined to finger the Cuban couple as suspects when Hart's deep bass resounded in Steil's ear.

"Steil?"

"Yeah."

"What's on your mind?"

"Listen, I know it's pretty late, but do you know that Maria Scheindlin was murdered tonight? I mean, yesterday. At her home. I just left the place."

"No, that's news to me. Calm down. Begin at the beginning," Hart said.

Steil talked uninterrupted for roughly three minutes. Hart patiently heard him out. He was in his office, working the case. The spotter had radioed Steil's plates in when he got to the Scheindlins' and within ten minutes Hart had learned who the driver was. The special agent also knew about Chris and Valerio. The time when the Cuban departed had already been reported as well. However, other people's versions were always welcome; they provided confirmation or, less frequently, reported something others had not seen. The call, as all others, was being traced and recorded.

"Driving home it occurred to me maybe Capdevila and Berta are somehow connected to this. I don't think they killed her, mind you. Those two don't look like assassins to me. But I wanted to know if you had told the police about them and how they fit in. I'm calling from this gas station because my . . ." he hesitated, "friend is at home and you said she should be kept out of this."

"You did right. I'll get in touch with the police department immediately, find out the details. Thanks, Steil."

"It's okay. I suppose neither of us will sleep tonight. Bye."

"Bye."

Elliot hung up, took a deep breath, and got into his car. He drove home feeling he had done the right thing.

The building where he rented, on Coconut Grove's Virginia Street, was nothing to be proud of. Although thirty-seven years old and architecturally insipid, the landlord had increased his apartment rent 25 percent in seven years. He had grown accustomed to the place, the building, and the block.

He parked at his designated space in the lot and headed for the building's main entrance. The security guard in the foyer buzzed Elliot in the minute he saw him on the other side of the glass door, then turned to say something to a woman sitting on a bench. Steil pushed the swinging door and stepped in. The woman turned to face the newly arrived. Elliot froze. He felt the door's closing mechanism operating behind his back. Its hiss seemed to come from the snake in the grass coiling up into a straight position.

"This lady is waiting for you, Mr. Steil," said the guard, who seemed bemused.

...

Elliot watched her come near. The poised, self-assured executive he had confronted in Havana had vanished into thin air. There was little color in her face, and she gave the impression of being uptight and feeling lost. Her relieved expression the minute she caught a glimpse of him indicated she had high hopes. Had this woman gone mad? What was she doing here? He was reluctant to see her. A black purse *and* a holdall? Planning to spend the night here? In a black halter-neck evening gown, of all things.

To compound his annoyance, Victoria had the nerve to give him a peck on the cheek.

"What are you doing here?" he asked gruffly, leery of her.

"I need to talk to you."

"You need to talk to me?" curled fingers, thumb pointing at his chest. "Are you out of your mind? When did you get here? How did you find out where I live?"

She looked over her shoulder, checking on the security guard. "I can explain everything, Elliot. Can we go to your apartment?" trying to keep her voice low, patently struggling to be in control of her emotions.

"No, I'm not taking you to my apartment. That guy doesn't understand a word of Spanish. You can talk."

"Please help me," beseechingly. "Pardo was murdered. I don't have . . ."

"Pardo? Who's Pardo?"

Victoria realized she had slipped badly. "I'm sorry. Pardo was my husband, Carlos Capdevila. I called him Pardo in private, because . . . his complexion was a tad dark."

Having met the man, Elliot could have argued that Capdevila's complexion had not been in the least dark, but shaken by the news of another murder, he missed the inconsistency. "Just a minute," raising both hands to ward her off and lifting his gaze to the ceiling in search of understanding.

"Let me see if I've got this straight. Are you telling me that you were married to Capdevila and that he has been murdered?"

"Yes."

"Was he shot?"

"Yes."

"When?"

"Two hours ago, more or less."

"Why? What happened?"

"We were held up. He resisted. I don't know the man who did it. Everybody here is a stranger to me."

"Where were you?"

"At the airport."

Elliot blew his breath out, looking off toward the bank of elevators. Was she telling the truth or was she playing damsel-in-distress? Curiosity stirred inside him.

"Did you call the police?"

"No. I ran away. I'm an illegal here. Listen, Elliot. You are the only person I know in Miami. I need your advice; I need your help. Cut me a little slack. If you won't let me into your apartment, then, please, hear me out in your car."

Elliot vividly remembered that he had extricated himself from quite a serious situation eight years earlier thanks to Scheindlin. Ever since, he had been receptive to other people's predicaments and willing to help. Berta seemed to be in a very tight spot, with good reason if her boss, friend, lover, husband, or whatever Capdevila was had been murdered. He would not put his hide on the line to help her out, but he ought to hear what she had to say, advise her to turn herself in, call Hart. Apart from that, he was eagerly interested in knowing what was going on. The anger he had felt a minute earlier petered out.

"My wife is upstairs. She may want to know who you are, why you are visiting at this hour, what the problem is."

"It's her place. I wouldn't mind."

"I'm not going anywhere near this, Berta."

"I know. You said so in Havana."

Elliot gazed into her eyes and saw despair. "Let's go."

He took her elbow and steered her around. "The lady is coming up with me, Lee."

"Fine, Mr. Steil."

Inside the elevator cage, Elliot wanted to know how Victoria had learned his home address.

"The form with your visa application."

"Ah."

Once in his living room, Victoria arranged herself on a loveseat and surveyed the place. A woman's hand showed. No markedly masculine man decorates his living quarters with lace window curtains, fine porcelain dishes upon a wall, figurines on the side tables, a wood pedestal with a sheepherder carved in olive green serpentine, beautiful candles on the coffee table. The black, genuine-leather suite seemed opulent to her, the big-screen TV princely, the wooden desk elegant, the glass-fronted china cabinet delicate. A subtle and pleasant perfume filled the room. It helped obliterate the stench of blood, gunpowder, and exhaust fumes lingering in her nostrils. Victoria loosened up somewhat.

After signaling Victoria to take a seat, Elliot entered the bedroom and woke Fidelia. He gave her a quick overview of Maria Scheindlin's murder, then explained that a Cuban businesswoman he had met in Havana two weeks earlier had arrived unannounced and was now in the living area. She seemed to be in serious trouble, wanted to confide in him, and would probably ask for help. She would tell her story much more freely if Fidelia was not present. Would she mind? No, she would not, Fidelia said as she got up and slipped into a robe. Nonetheless, out of politeness she should meet her and ask her if she felt like an espresso. Then she would go back to bed.

But for the gravity of the situation, Elliot would have found Fidelia's reaction amusing. Beneath the civility with which she greeted the stranger, her scrutiny of a possible rival was noticeable. A spark of curiosity shone in Victoria's eyes as well, who comprehended the reason that had smoked the wife out. That Steil was married was news to her; the visa form he had filled out said his marital status was divorced. During the exchange of courtesies, she learned that Fidelia was a lawyer and assumed that to practice law in the United States she had to be an American citizen. A possibility she had not considered budded in her mind. Yes, if things went from bad to worse, it might be an alternative.

Fidelia perceived that this woman wasn't Elliot's type and relaxed. For the next fifteen minutes all three acted as if it were perfectly natural for a stranger to arrive unexpected to a couple's home in the small hours, accept a demitasse of espresso brewed by the lady of the house, and remain conversing with the husband after the wife went back to bed.

"Well, let's have it, Berta," Elliot said when Fidelia closed the door to the bedroom behind her.

Victoria concocted a mixture of fact and the version prepared in case the authorities in Key West intercepted them. She and her husband had become disenchanted with the Revolution in the eighties, she began, and dreamed of coming to the United States, but as party members and executives of XEMIC, they could not file applications. They would have been considered traitors, expelled from their jobs, and prevented from emigrating for the rest of their lives.

"I know how it is," Elliot interrupted. "Cut to the chase. How did you manage to come here? To the States, I mean."

"We paid a smuggler."

"You what?"

The first time they made an inquiry, human traffickers charged two thousand per person, Victoria cooked up, drawing from what she had learned as an Intelligence officer. The only way they could possibly raise that kind of money was by peddling their influence when making XEMIC's purchasing decisions. She was ashamed to admit it, but believing that the end justifies the means, they had started demanding kickbacks and commissions from suppliers. Over the course of time, prices rose sharply. By 1996 they had three thousand saved, but the price had gone up to four thousand per head. When they had nearly six thousand, a single ticket was worth five thousand. Therefore, they had kept taking under-the-counter money. Last March they finally raised the sixteen thousand two tickets cost in 2002.

All they had told Elliot about Scheindlin was true. He had a hundred thousand of Cuban money that they planned to keep and use to start a new life. But even if Maria Scheindlin had refused to give back the money, they would have come anyhow. Communism sucked and the Chief had gone over the deep end.

"I know that, Berta," Steil said impatiently. "Have you been to the Scheindlins'?"

"No. Of course not. We weren't supposed to go there until today."

"Yeah, right."

It was the first thing she had said that Elliot knew was a blatant falsehood, and the hardness of his stare bespoke his irritation. Victoria realized something had gone wrong, but had not the slightest notion what it was. He tried to make his gaze neutral and failed. Victoria raised her guard and her eyes crinkled a little.

"Well, downstairs you said you needed my advice. You still do?"

"Of course."

"I think you should call the police right now. Report what happened at the airport. Make a full statement and apply for political asylum under the Cuban Adjustment Act."

With her gaze fixed on him, eyes rounded, Victoria blinked twice. She had expected that suggestion and, knowing that it would be a mistake to brush it aside, had prepared for it. She thought it wise, however, to pretend that the notion had not crossed her mind and she was considering it.

"You think so?"

"Absolutely."

"Umm. Yes, you are right. But don't you think first I should collect the money the widow has?"

If she doesn't know Maria is dead, neither she nor Capdevila killed her, Elliot reasoned with some relief. Should he tell her? No, not for the time being.

"I mean," Victoria went on, crossing her ankles, "Pardo was murdered three hours ago, his killer must be in hiding or in full flight. Reporting his death right now won't bring my husband back. And that money means a lot to me, Elliot."

Steil considered Victoria an extremely hardened woman. She had not shed a tear in his presence, her corneas were white. She was asking for help, not consolation. Greed overcoming grief? Or maybe she and Capdevila had not had a relationship of any kind. Either way, it taxed him to mask his dislike for a person who had been cleaning the floor with him since the day they had met. On the other hand, she could not imagine that the FBI would be waiting for her at the Scheindlins' with open arms. She would never touch the money.

"Let me think about it," Elliot said, aware that he had remained silent for too long. The notion of letting her walk unsuspecting into the trap, however, was repugnant to him.

Neither rival surmised that each was ignorant of something the other knew and that they were locked in a duel of lies and half-truths.

"No, Berta, the situation you are in, you should forget about the money. Report Capdevila's murder to the police and then apply for political asylum. I have a friend who's a police officer. I can call him now and ask him to come over."

Victoria unzipped the tote bag and extracted the Tokarev. "I'm sorry, Elliot. But you leave me no choice," she said ruefully.

Nine

E lliot had always considered that cornered individuals are liable to become desperate. If armed and dangerous, they shouldn't be contradicted. Berta was armed, and the impression that in a tight spot she could become quite dangerous began to loom large in his mind. After dropping all pretenses, she had grown pale again, had a haunted look about her, and seemed nearing desperation. He held up his hands, palms outward, then shook his head and clicked his tongue.

"No, no, maybe I didn't make myself clear," Elliot said. "I won't force you to do what you don't want to do. I made what I thought was a helpful suggestion. You think I'm wrong; do what you think is best. You want to leave, I won't stand in your way."

Victoria nodded in slow mo, thinking ahead. "That's very understanding of you, Elliot," she sneered. "Thank you. I appreciate that, even if it's at gunpoint. But no, I'm not leaving. And if you try to pull a fast one on me, I won't hesitate. I will shoot you. We clear, Elliot?"

"Very clear, Berta."

"Good. Now I will ask you to stand up and open the bedroom door. Let's join Fidelia."

"Listen, Berta. I'll do whatever you say. But leave her out of this."

"I think I know why she was given that name. Like many others born in the sixties to destitute parents, they named her after the Commander in Chief, right?"

"Right."

"And ten or twenty years later they regretted it. Am I mistaken?"

"Leave her out of this, Berta."

"Right now the sweet, kind, espresso-making Fidelia is standing right behind that door, eavesdropping on every word being uttered in this living room."

"I don't think so."

"You can bet your life she is, Elliot. I don't know how American wives react to this situation, but a Cuban wife won't go to bed and leave her husband talking to a strange woman in her living room in the middle of the night. So, stand up, Elliot," Victoria said as she got to her feet, "let's go join Fidelia."

When Elliot opened the door to the bedroom, he found a fiercely glaring Fidelia standing by the bed, arms crossed, still in her robe. Her face was taut.

"Okay, Fidelia, just in case you missed something, let me run it by you," Victoria said from behind Elliot. "You two do what I say, I won't harm a hair on your heads. But I'm telling you: Don't try anything. I'm desperate and you won't have time to regret it. Okay?"

The balking lawyer remained silent. The corners of her mouth, curved downward, showed the intense aversion to the intruder she had developed in a minute or two.

"Did you understand what I said, Fidelia?"

No response.

Victoria pressed the muzzle of the Tokarev to the back of Elliot's neck. "My husband was killed less than three hours ago. Would you like to experience what I'm experiencing right now?"

"No."

"So drop the attitude. Will you cooperate?"

"Yes."

"Good," Victoria said and drew back the gun. "Where's your passport?"

Elliot immediately read her mind. Fidelia took a moment to think. "In the second drawer of that chest."

"Get it for me."

Victoria inspected the lawyer's American passport using her left hand only, shifting her eyes from the document to the hostages several times. Flipping through the pages, she found Spanish entrance and exit stamps, nothing else. She bore no resemblance to her, though. Not that Fidelia had a beautiful face; they just were different in physiognomies. It had to do, though. If asked, she could always say she had sued her plastic surgeon. Victoria slipped the passport beneath the right cup of her bra.

"Okay. Now get a pair of scissors and start cutting that bedsheet lengthwise in four-inch-wide strips."

As Fidelia returned to the chest of drawers for the scissors, Steil saw it coming again. She would instruct Fidelia to tie him up, then order her to lie down and immobilize her, too.

"Before going any further, Berta, maybe you should know where I went tonight," he said, staring at the headboard of his bed.

Victoria squinted suspiciously. "Should I?"

"I think you should."

"Out with it."

"I got a phone call tonight. But just so you don't think I'm making this up, ask Fidelia who called."

Victoria and Fidelia glanced at one another, the lawyer having stopped midway from the chest of drawers to the bed, scissors in hand.

"Well, Fidelia?" asked Victoria.

"Jenny Scheindlin called," the lawyer said.

A three-second pause crept by. The caller's last name made Victoria remember who Jenny was.

"And who is Jenny Scheindlin?" Elliot prompted Fidelia, just in case.

"Jenny Scheindlin is the daughter of Ruben and Maria Scheindlin."

"Now tell her what Jenny told me."

"She told you that her mother had been murdered."

The news jarred Victoria and she was momentarily lost. Elliot could not see her reaction but, sensing that he had gained an edge, he pressed on with his idea.

"It's true," he corroborated, turning his head left to watch Victoria out of the corner of his eye. "Think. How could I possibly know you'd be waiting for me when I got back? How could I know you'd pull a gun on me? Did I have time to cook this up with Fidelia the couple of minutes I was alone with her when we came up? Believe me, Berta. Maria Scheindlin was murdered yesterday at her Bay Harbor home. Her daughter called me and I went there to see if there was anything I could do for her. Right now the police are trying to find the murderer. If you go there tomorrow, I mean, today, you'll be questioned. What are you going to say? You should report your husband's murder right now. Maybe the same person who killed him killed Maria, too. Listen, Berta, this is madness. You are not thinking clearly, you should . . ."

"Shut up!"

A minute of silence ensued as Victoria processed the implications. She *knew* it to be true. She *knew* who had killed Maria. He had been following orders to execute the traitors and return to Cuba immediately. It was why he had picked the airport for the live drop, because after killing her and Pardo, he would take the first flight to Mexico City, Bahamas, Kingston, or any other capital in which he could amble nonchalantly into a Cuban embassy or consulate. Lastra and Morera had decreed that both she and Pardo were to be executed. From a professional standpoint, Victoria discerned that ordering her put to death was technically correct. Nevertheless, how had her superiors inferred that they would be heading to Miami? Had they connected the cigarette boat to her and Pardo? Maybe all resident directors on the American continent were on the alert. She would never know. Her bronchi began contracting and her breathing became labored. *Not now, please.*

Fidelia, seeing how the intruder's face slowly drained of color as she looked off thoughtfully, realized the news had hit her hard. Good; she hoped things would go from bad to worse for the miserable bitch. This was a consequence of Elliot's trip to Cuba. Why were men so hardheaded? She had begged Elliot not to go. But no, he knew best. He always knew best. There was nothing to fear, he had said. She threw him a sidelong glance of reproach.

Elliot perceived despair in Victoria's tone when she ordered him to be quiet. Besides, the duration of her silence, and the soft wheezing that reached his ears, indicated the news had caused a greater impact than he had hoped. She had been counting on the money to get away, he deduced. Now she realized it was out of her reach. That had to be it. He felt sympathy for the woman. She had to understand there was no way she would pull out of this mess by herself. If her boss—or husband or whatever Carlos Capdevila was for her—had been murdered, why was she so reluctant to report it? In all probability she was a State Security officer, granted, but she had nothing to fear. The Cuban American Foundation claimed Miami was crawling with former officers of the Cuban Ministry of the Interior who had grown disaffected.

"From now on, I'll do all the talking," Victoria said at last, absolutely adamant. "Start cutting the bedsheet, Fidelia."

"You're taking it out on us, Berta," Elliot said, reprovingly.

"This gun says I can. Get to it, Fidelia."

When the lawyer had cut two eight-foot-long strips, Victoria instructed her to cut them in half. Next, she ordered Elliot to lay prone in bed.

"Tie him up, Fidelia."

Under Victoria's watchful gaze, the lawyer bound Elliot's hands behind his back with one strip, his feet with another. The psychologist had to order the knots tied tighter, as Fidelia tried to make it possible for Elliot to free himself. When she finished, he found himself tied loose enough not to hinder circulation yet tight enough to be unable to move.

"Great. Now lie down by his side, Fidelia."

Abhorring all sorts of violence, the lawyer did not try anything when Victoria let go of the gun twice, for maybe fifteen seconds each, to immobilize her feet first, then to tie her hands up. Next Victoria plucked the phone cord out.

"Okay, guys, listen up," she said after glancing at her watch. "It's 1:45 A.M. At this hour nothing can be done, and I need to rest a while. I don't want to gag you, but if you holler for help, I will. Try to relax and fall asleep; time will fly."

Victoria used the bathroom before turning off the bedroom lights. Leaving the door ajar, she returned to the living room, approached the loveseat, and eased herself onto it. She let go of the gun, retrieved her purse from the tote bag, fumbled for her inhaler. After shaking the canister she held it upright less than one inch from her open mouth, pumped, and held her breath for a few seconds. She recapped the canister and dropped it into her purse. Fidelia's passport went there next.

Closing her eyes, she took the deepest breath she could. The emotional collapse she had been able to ward off for almost four hours came about and tears started streaming down her cheeks. For over five minutes, not wanting to be heard, she muted her sobs as much as she could and wept and wept. To her surprise, giving vent to her grief and the medication combined to clear her airways perceptibly. Having regained her self-control, she strode to the kitchen sink and blew her nose, then washed her face. Back in the living room, she set the alarm of her watch for 8:00 A.M.

At 2:04 A.M., still angst-ridden, Victoria curled up in the loveseat to find obliviousness in sleep. She felt her emotional foundations shifting, slowly and tentatively attempting to bypass the void created by the death of someone she had taken for granted. She had never imagined he was so indispensable to her. Having been so sure of herself and her actions for so long, it was amazing to realize that much of her strength, decisiveness, and confidence had derived from him. She felt like an earthquake survivor who had lost all her loved ones. There was nobody to comfort her in her tribulation. Her future had faded away in that damned garage. What could she do without him? Following almost an hour of this, at last Victoria Valiente lost consciousness.

...

At 4:32 A.M., a parking attendant taking inventory of the vehicles found the two bodies. Sixteen minutes later two squad cars from the Miami Police Department secured the area; a few minutes before five the Crime Scene Unit began its work.

At 5:54 A.M. a police cruiser pulled over in front of the Bonises.' A uniformed officer got out and pressed the buzzer alongside the front door. The FBI specialists staking out the gardener notified Hart. When the cop departed at 6:16, an unmarked car driven by a man in civilian clothes intercepted him two blocks away. Flipping his badge holder open, the man explained that his superiors needed to know why a police officer had paid a visit to Mrs. Bonis so early in the morning. It was how the FBI learned that the bodies of two Caucasian males had been found at Miami International Airport's garage. The ID on one of them had been issued to Eugenio Bonis. "I didn't tell the missus," the officer volunteered, "but whoever shot her hubby did a thorough job. Guy's got more lead in his noggin than a radiologist in his apron."

Hart's official car went up the garage ramp and screeched to a stop ten yards from the crime scene, now bathed in the klieg lights from three TV crews, twenty-one minutes later. The special agent and Smith approached the man in charge. Having learned the details, Smith used his cell phone to call Dade County's chief of police and the Medical Examiner Department. He requested urgent collaboration in the forensic examinations of the two bodies, the gun, bullets, and casings, and of Maria Scheindlin's corpse, too.

Heading on back to the bureau's Miami division, at Second Avenue, North Miami Beach, Hart took Le Jeune. The sunrise, luminous and cloudless, promised a hot day to the yawning and stretching city. Exhaust fumes spoiled the scents coming from the lawns, shrubs, and fruit trees flanking the wide avenue. The muffled rumble of engines and the hum of tires on the asphalt were the predominant sounds.

"Do you remember how many rounds are in a Beretta clip?" asked Smith as Hart tapped the brakes for the red light at Fifty-fourth. From the median divider, an Aztec-looking man in his forties was hawking bouquets of roses to drivers.

"Eight in a Compact. From thirteen to fifteen in other models."

"Bonis was shot four times. This other guy . . . what's his name . . ."

"He told Steil his name was Carlos Capdevila. The Costa Rican passport was issued to one Evaristo Consuegra."

"Right. Capdevila was shot twice. That's six. There should be two rounds in the clip. There're none."

"Unless there were only six rounds in the clip."

"Yeah, that's possible. But the gun was by Bonis. As if he had shot Capdevila twice, then Capdevila had wrested the gun from him, shot him in the head, dropped the gun by the body, tried to walk away, and fell. It doesn't figure. You ask me, there's a missing shooter."

"Berta Arosamena?" conjectured Hart as he stepped on the gas pedal.

"Possibly. But consider this: Bonis did Maria Scheindlin's garden; when he left, the gate remained open; no one was seen entering the place later in the day. That makes him the prime suspect. Now he's found dead alongside the body of a Cuban agent. What do you make of that?"

Hart moved from the center to the left lane. "That he was a CuIS courier?" CuIS was the FBI's acronym for Cuban Intelligence Services.

Smith nodded, pulled out a cigarette from a pack, and lit up. He took a deep drag, opened the ashtray, snuffed the butt. "Let's recap. We've been on Maria's trail since August 2001, following the tip of an anonymous letter that accused her of spying for Cuba. She was a Polish defector, had been living in the United States for thirty years, had married a lifelong informer for a friendly service who was doing business with Cuba and whose assistant was Cuban. Not a bad candidate for recruitment by our neighbors. Washington didn't think much of it, though. Housewife, never dabbled in politics, no known Cuban acquaintances, quiet life, they pointed out."

"You have to admit the logic of the argument," Hart said, stealing a look at the rearview mirror. "Then we found she went out at odd hours, bought phone cards, and made calls from pay phones."

"And that lent a fresh perspective to the case," Smith went on. "Always a different pay phone, always a new phone card. So far, Steil's phone tap and surveillance have drawn blanks; his anger when we recruited him furnish additional proof he may well be clean. After Scheindlin died, Maria got chummy with Steil, who would be traveling to Cuba soon. She made one of her suspicious phone calls two days before Steil flew to Havana, where Carlos Capdevila and Berta Arosamena approached him and fed him this weird story about Scheindlin having bought medicine for Cuba. Then, a few days later, these two surface in Miami.

"So, we have all this circumstantial evidence linking Maria with four Cubans: Berta and Capdevila, from CuIS for sure; Steil, who is playing for us; and Bonis, the wild card we knew nothing about. This morning Berta and Capdevila were hoping to recover the Cuban money they claim Scheindlin had when he kicked the bucket. The date they told Steil probably wasn't the real date; it's standard practice to move the real date and time forward or backward. We know Berta and Capdevila went to Maria's place and weren't admitted. We know that Bonis did Maria's garden at least once since we began staking out her place in earnest five weeks ago; maybe she had been his client for months, or years. In addition, Bonis emigrated from Cuba.

"So, one working hypothesis might be that Maria was not a Cuban informer; she found the money and agreed to give it back. Bonis, willingly or unwillingly, was courier, cutout, or auxiliary agent handler for CuIS. He picked up the hundred Gs and then got greedy, demanded a share, or for some other reason argued with Capdevila and they shot it out. But why would he kill Maria if she gave him the money? Couriers, cutouts, and auxiliaries are not hit men. A lovers' quarrel?"

"Oh c'mon, Chief; that's stretching it a little, don't you think?" Hart complained. "Surveillance found no indication of her playing the field. Besides, that kind of woman doesn't screw the help."

"Then, a second hypothesis might be that Maria Scheindlin was spying for Cuba," Smith went on, "and for some reason CuIS thought she had betrayed, or was a playback, and ordered her terminated. She may have refused to fork over the dough."

"I know CuIS is strapped, but not so much to kill for a hundred thousand," Hart objected.

"Yeah, you're right. If Bonis killed Maria for reasons related to espionage, he was a full-fledged handler, maybe a ringleader. He knew he'd be the prime suspect and was getting ready to flee."

His eyes on the road, Hart shook his head. "We don't have anything on this guy and he's been here for twenty-two years," he said. "But we should consider whether Maria Scheindlin was somehow involved with CuIS. It would give a rational explanation to all that malarkey about Scheindlin buying pharmaceuticals for Cuba and demanding money. How soon are they performing the autopsies?"

"Right away," Smith said. "The bullets will go to Imaging immediately, to compare with the one dug out from Maria Scheindlin's wall. The gun and the casings recovered back there, too. By ten we should know if Maria was shot with the Beretta."

"So practical having an indoor range at the ME's. Speeds things up."

"And pretty sophisticated photographic equipment at Imaging, too."

"One goes with the other."

Nothing was said during the couple of minutes both men spent reflecting on the most recent developments.

"I think we should send a team to the Bonises'," suggested Smith as they were cruising Ali Baba Avenue. "Tell the missus we'll look for evidence of who killed her husband and comb the place. He may have a computer, records . . ."

"You think so? A gardener?"

"Everybody has a desktop these days."

"Won't she wonder why the FBI is investigating her husband's murder?"

"Well, if she does, tell her the other stiff is a foreigner and that brought us to the case."

"Okay."

...

A voice clamoring for Berta awoke Victoria at 7:13 A.M. Reality overtook her in a millisecond. She got to her feet, seized the gun, rushed barefoot to the bedroom door, and pushed it open.

"About time," Elliot growled. "We pee and shit, you know?"

"Elliot! Don't be vulgar," Fidelia scolded him.

"Okay, calm down. Give me a minute," their captor said upon learning what the problem was.

Hours earlier, nearly forty minutes after Victoria walked out of the bedroom and when all was quiet, Elliot had asked Fidelia to try to untie him using her teeth on the strip of cloth around his hands. Almost half an hour of efforts proved fruitless and the lawyer threw in the towel. Then he had tried to free her using the same method. Twenty-five minutes of futile attempts persuaded him that, besides wasting his time, he risked losing his front teeth. As he was catching his breath, Fidelia had asked whether Mr. Steil considered that, as a victim, she could claim the right to know what he had kept from her concerning his trip to Cuba. "In other words, Elliot, would you kindly tell me what the fuck's going on?" Abiding by his promise to Hart, he omitted his role as FBI informer. When he finished, she could not resist the temptation: "I warned you," she had said in a derisive sing-song. Next, they had searched in vain for a way out. Following a ten- or fifteen-minute silence, Elliot registered that the exhausted Fidelia had drifted off. Acknowledging that the only positive thing he could do was to rest a while, he had soon fallen asleep.

At seven the alarm of their clock went off.

"I'm bursting," Fidelia had said.

Then he had started calling Berta. After wasting several minutes gradually raising his voice, he was forced to holler.

Victoria relieved herself and washed her face before untying Fidelia. The lawyer scurried to the bathroom and six minutes later came back into the bedroom looking fresh and clean. Then Victoria authorized her to untie Elliot. They waited as he used the bathroom. When he got out, the psychologist said they should move to the living area and have breakfast.

While Fidelia heated the milk and brewed the espresso for three *cafés con leche*, Victoria put her shoes on and sat in the loveseat to consider her options. Elliot stared through the window and sulkily stroked the growth on his chin. The shoreline exhibited the aquamarine color that people in the tropics take for granted until they spend a winter watching the Baltic from Rostock, the Cantabric from Gijón, or the Atlantic from Tierra del Fuego. The billowing sails of two boats reminded him that most people live placidly. A gecko climbed up the windowpane. Five stories up. Unbelievable. It reminded him of Santa Cruz del Norte. He wished he were there.

"Move to the kitchen, Elliot," Victoria said, rising to her feet. She had decided to take one step in the right direction. "I have to make a phone call and I need privacy."

"By all means," his tone dripping with sarcasm. "Feel at home. Here in Miami we are used to getting kidnapped by the Mafia every coupla weeks."

When Elliot dropped two slices of white bread into the toaster, the psychologist moved to the wooden desk positioned between the window and the living room's farthest wall. It had three drawers on its right side and a laptop, a printer, and a telephone on its top, plus a pad and two ballpoints. She pulled back an armless swivel chair from the kneehole, turned it left to better keep an eye on her prisoners through the kitchen counter, sat down, and rested the gun by the printer. Then she lifted the handset and dialed a number. For around ten seconds the absence of sound made the line seem dead. Victoria recovered the gun and turned her gaze to the kitchen counter. Steil, his back to her, was saying something to Fidelia. Then the connection was made and someone unhooked a phone after two rings.

"*Ordene,*" said a man curtly.

"Put me through to Lastra, Mao," she ordered.

Nobody had ever dared to call Pernas "Mao" to his face since appointed Lastra's adjunct, in 1991. He found it an honor, but he realized it was meant as an insult. It made him mad to see that certain comrades swallowed capitalist propaganda aimed at defaming one of the greatest historical figures of all times.

"Who is this?" he asked.

"Micaela."

"Micaela! Where are you, Colonel? We've been so worried!"

"Give me Lastra. Right now. I know he's there."

A rather long pause followed as arrangements were made to record the call. This line was for the exclusive use of trusted people whose exchanges with the chief of intelligence were not to be registered, Victoria recalled.

"Micaela! Where are you?" Lastra, sounding cheery, said into his mouthpiece.

Victoria snorted. "Don't pretend with me. You know damn well where I am. I got news for you. You may cut three new notches in your gun's butt. Pardo is dead, Pola Negri is dead, but your assassin is dead, too."

"I don't know what you are talking about."

"All we wanted was to get the hell out, Lastra. We were sick and tired of the repression, the hypocrisy, the lies, the personality cult, and the ever-deepening economic crisis. And yes, Pardo had the brains and the balls to screw you. But let me tell you: Turning in the fools we have here risking their freedom so His Majesty and his courtiers can live the good life never crossed my mind. Behave and I won't. They are just a pack of manipulated puppets, like you and those under you are, like I was until a few days ago. But be warned, Lastra, I'll make a full report, naming all the names and giving all the addresses. You can bet your life that if something happens to me, it'll reach the Gypsy. And you know, Lastra, you know perfectly well that the scandal will make headlines from here to Nepal. So, it's your call, General."

Lastra considered his reply for a few seconds. "You are obviously suffering an altered state of mind. Tell me where you are and I'll send someone to pick you up."

"Good-bye, you pathetic eunuch," she said before hanging up.

Victoria took a very deep breath. So deep, in fact, that she had no memory of ever having filled her lungs so much. This made her smile broadly. Steil seemed to be slathering butter or jelly on toast. The smell of freshly brewed coffee reached her.

"When are we going to have something for breakfast?" she yelled joyously. Then, from the sacred corner that stored her most precious memories, Pardo smiled at her. After an instant of bewilderment, she started sobbing and crying inconsolably. Elliot and Fidelia exchanged surprised looks. Should they wait and see, cuddle her, or run away? They were still undecided when Victoria sniffled back mucus, wiped her nose with the back of her hand, and got to her feet.

"I need something to eat, please," she said. "And a handkerchief."

. . .

Victoria broke the connection at 7:49. At 7:58, Hart's extension rang and he lifted it.

"Hart."

The special agent was in his cubicle, at his cluttered desk, on the second floor of the bureau's Miami division, holding a mug in his left hand. Across from the desk, in a metal and vinyl armchair, Nathan Smith, being fond of making subtle statements, was sipping coffee from a *Washington Times* mug. The metallic drapes to a bigger office in which staff labored were drawn.

"Alford here, sir."

"What is it?"

"Sir, uh, twelve minutes ago a woman made a phone call to Havana from Elliot Steil's number. It wasn't Fidelia Orozco. It was someone else. And . . . I think you should try to make sense of what was said. ASAP."

Something in the specialist's voice made Hart suggest to Smith they should hurry to the recording studio. The instant Victoria identified herself as Micaela, the two men exchanged astonished looks. When the click of the phones signaled the end of the call, they looked at each other.

"Micaela?" Hart, squinching up his face in doubt. "Colonel?"

"The head of the Miami desk?" Smith, also unbelieving.

They had learned her cryptonym from communications with the ringleader of the Wasp network. That a woman was head of the Miami desk had always been in doubt. To misinform the opposition, males have been known to choose female cryptonyms.

"General Lastra?" asked the puzzled Hart.

"The general director?" Smith, wondering if they were being set up.

Both men stared at one another.

"Berta Arosamena is Micaela?" Smith, incredulously.

"Steil is . . . a Cuban agent?" Hart, wholly mystified now.

"It would seem so," Smith said.

"But . . . But . . ."

Alford, the SIGINT specialist, kept turning his head to right and left.

"Order a SWAT team to Steil's place. On the double," Smith said.

"Right away," Hart, turning and rushing for the door.

"I'll be damned," Smith muttered before bolting after his subordinate.

The openmouthed Alford felt sure he had stumbled onto something big.

...

In a conciliatory tone, the muzzle of her gun pointing to the floor, Victoria asked Fidelia to please bring her a cup of *café con leche* and a piece of toast to the desk. The couple was to have their breakfast in the kitchen. She apologized for the inconvenience, hesitated, chuckled while shaking her head, and added that inconvenience did not begin to describe what she had done to Fidelia and her husband, but perhaps one day the lawyer would realize that she had no choice. She pressed a button to turn off the alarm of her beeping watch. Then she dropped the Kleenex she had wiped her nose with into the wastebasket by the desk.

Following breakfast, Victoria told Fidelia that she needed Elliot to drive her somewhere. If he followed her instructions to the letter, she promised that nothing would happen to her husband and he would be back in a few hours. Fidelia countered by saying that it might be best if she drove Ms. Berta to wherever she wanted to be taken. Two women in a car were less conspicuous, she argued.

Steil cut in, "Do you realize that you are talking like I'm a robot that you, Fidelia, own, and that you, Berta, want to rent?"

"I was trying to make your wife understand why I'll ask you to tie her up," Victoria said.

"Tie me up? Again?"

The psychologist, sensing that she was dealing with a woman several removes away from her world of cheating and double-dealing, attempted to make acceptable the unacceptable. "Please understand, Fidelia. You may report what has happened here to the police and that would . . ."

"I promise you I won't report it."

Victoria clicked her tongue and shook her head. Was this lady for real? "Don't you see I can't take your word for it? Listen, I'm trying to work this out with you, make you see things from where I stand, but I have no alternative. Before leaving this apartment I have to make sure you can't lift the phone, or drive to the nearest precinct, and report that your husband has been abducted and is driving a car with plates number so-and-so."

"Okay," Fidelia fumed. "Then just point that gun at us and force us to do what you want. But don't try to make us believe you are the victim here."

"If that's the way you want it . . ."

"Wait!" Elliot barked. "Don't you believe me? You can't go to Maria's home to pick up the money. Maria is dead. You'll be arrested."

"Take it easy, Steil. We are not going to Maria's. I have the money. C'mon, get in bed, Fidelia."

Therefore, it was back to the bedroom at gunpoint. Elliot was twice asked to tighten the strips of cloth binding Fidelia's wrists and ankles. He wondered whether it was true that Berta had the money. What was true and what was false here? Once Victoria felt sure that the lawyer would not be able to free herself, she addressed Steil.

"You have your wallet and car keys on you?"

Steil felt his pockets. "I do."

"Okay. We are leaving now. Let's go," she said, walking backward toward the door to the living room, at no time taking her eyes off him. She picked up the tote bag.

"Okay. Now I will do this."

Victoria cradled the tote bag on her left forearm and put the gun into it, but her right hand remained inside the bag, closed around the pistol's butt, forefinger on the trigger.

"We have to ride the elevator together, cross the lobby, go into the parking lot. You may try to overpower me along the way. Don't do it. I'm warning you: Don't do it. I'm pretty tense, there's a round in the chamber, the safety is off, and I can move fast if I have to. So, don't try anything. I don't want to shoot you. But I will if you try anything. Are we clear on this, Elliot?"

He nodded emphatically. Overhearing the exchange in the bedroom, Fidelia squeezed her eyes shut and muttered to herself: "Elliot, do whatever she says, please."

"Now, I want you to open the front door and tell me if there's anyone in the hallway."

Elliot complied. The hallway appeared to be deserted.

"There's no one," he said, turning to look Victoria in the eye.

"Okay, let's go."

They crossed the threshold into the hallway, Elliot fifteen feet or so ahead of the psychologist. Victoria leaned sideways, fumbled with her left-hand fingers until she found the handle, and pulled the front door closed. She had taken two steps after Elliot when a voice boomed:

"FREEZE!"

Which was exactly what, for an instant of total astonishment, both did. Elliot slumped to the floor immediately. Victoria drew the Tokarev.

"DROP IT!"

She thought things through for what seemed like an eternity. Life without him, penniless, informing on others, cleaning floors or washing dishes until the end? Elliot turned his neck to watch her.

Victoria lifted her eyebrows in resignation and forced a smile before turning the gun on herself and pulling the trigger.

...

Pandemonium followed. Gun-toting men in black fatigues materialized out of nowhere. One knelt before Elliot, placed an ugly-looking 9mm H&K MP5SD with a sound suppressor before his face, and ordered him not to bat an eye. Another kicked the Tokarev away from Victoria. Numbers three and four used a battering ram to break down Steil's front door and barged into the apartment. Two others knelt by Victoria; one placed two fingers on her carotid artery, his partner pried open Victoria's eyelids and stared into her pupils. Fidelia let out a piercing shriek that reached Elliot at the same time that he felt hands palpating him for weapons.

"Hey, what's the matter?" he asked.

"He's clean," he heard over him. "Stand up," he was ordered.

Elliot straightened up looking at a pair of cordovan loafers and suspected he would be facing a civilian, or an officer of the law in civvies. Sure as hell, Smith was glaring at him. To find himself winded, as if he had jogged a mile, baffled Elliot. At the other extreme of the hallway, a neighbor had very cautiously opened his front door just a crack.

"Is she dead?" Steil asked, starting to feel sorry for his captor.

"It doesn't seem so," Smith answered. "Who is she?"

"Don't you recognize her? She's Berta Arosamena."

"What was she doing here?"

Steil turned on his heels. "You are not going to believe it. Give me a minute. Let me first . . ."

Smith grabbed Elliot's arm. "Hold it, Steil. What was she doing here?"

"Wait a moment, Smith," breaking away in anger. "I have to untie Fidelia."

"Hey, Steil, get in here," Hart said in a loud voice at that precise moment as he exited the apartment, looking relieved. The special agent dashed around the SWAT officer lifting Victoria in his arms, stole a look at her face, and strode purposefully to where his boss and Elliot were standing. "Your friend is worried sick," he added.

"Did you untie her?"

"Sure. Go in," reholstering his gun.

As Elliot stormed into the apartment, Hart told Smith they had found Fidelia bound hand and foot, the phone cord plucked out. She had gabbled that a Cuban woman had abducted Elliot at gunpoint. The officer carrying Victoria rushed to the elevator, the door being held open by another cop.

"It looks like she had taken Steil hostage," Hart was telling Smith. "Did you see how fast she drew her gun? Makes me think she had been aiming it at him before leaving his place."

"Take them to headquarters and make sure of that. I'll go to the hospital with the suspect. I want no expense spared to save her life. HOLD IT GUYS," Smith bellowed, and sprinted to the still open cage.

...

As part of the aftershock, Elliot and Fidelia were kept apart and interrogated individually, making both quite mad. Four hours later, incontrovertible proof—the reddish abrasions around Steil's wrists and ankles at the top of the list—had dissipated Smith's last doubts, and Hart tried to make up with the fuming Elliot.

"Listen, Steil. I didn't sleep last night and probably won't sleep tonight, either. I've got a zillion things to do, check, verify, and countercheck. But I'll give you ten because your collaboration in this case is crucial . . ."

"WAS crucial. I'm quitting."

"Okay, fine. You're upset. I can understand that. I don't want you to be pissed off at us, though. So, I'll give you ten minutes, tops. It's 1:12. Listen to me. These are the bare bones.

"This woman called Cuba from your home. She called . . . someone who . . . is a high government official. She is a Ministry of the Interior officer, that's a fact. She had entered this country illegally, a woman she had been trying to extort money from had been murdered, and that woman's gardener had been found dead . . ."

"Who?"

"Eugenio Bonis, Maria Scheindlin's landscaper. Ever heard of him?"

Frowning, Steil looked at the floor and reflected for a few moments. "I don't think so."

"Well, this guy was found dead at the airport. Capdevila, too, same place. Berta was on the run and . . . what comes to her mind when seeking a place to hide? Your place. This led us to briefly consider the possibility . . . that when you went to Cuba . . . perhaps you were blackmailed or coerced into collaborating with CuIS."

"What's CuIS?"

"Cuban Intelligence Services."

Elliot slapped his thighs and rolled his eyes. "That I was . . . ? I can't believe this. You suspected Cuban State Security of doing to me what the FBI had done to me?"

Hart turned his head and let his gaze roam over the interior of his office. The muscles at the base of his jaw swelled. "Steil, you know nothing about the methods and procedures intelligence and counterintelligence agencies employ. Many are patriotic and straightforward. But sometimes they are forced to do things that apparently are unorthodox or ethically questionable . . ."

"Like tapping my phone line," Steil barged in.

"Thanks to which you are now sitting in this office," jabbing a finger at him. "You could be dead, or wounded, or driving a criminal somewhere at gunpoint."

Steil's mental gears begrudgingly turned on that. "True. But why did you tap my phone line in the first place? Did you suspect me of being a spy or what?"

Hart pushed back his swivel chair and crossed his legs. "This case is still open. Years may go by before it's closed, and I can't divulge classified information. I'll say what I can, though.

"Someone intimately associated to a person of your acquaintance was accused of spying for Cuba. When the investigation began, your name came up. You are Cuban; you work for a firm that does business with Latin American countries. At the outset you were only marginally involved. We didn't tap your phone then.

"But two things happened that moved you to center stage: the death of Ruben Scheindlin and your planning a trip to Cuba. That's when we sought authorization to tap your phone. And the tap strongly hinted you were just a victim of circumstance. Which was why we tried to recruit you. But you have a very short fuse, Steil. You were incensed at the airport. However, we were prepared to twist your arm if we had to. So we did."

Hart paused. Steil breathed deeply. "But you kept the tap after I had agreed to collaborate with you."

"On the chance the suspect called you," Hart argued. He glanced at his watch. "And it paid off. Maybe the tap saved your life."

Steil's facial expression was doubtful. "If I had tried to wrest the gun from her, she would've shot me for sure. But had I done what she said, I don't think she would've killed me."

Hart smiled crookedly. "For what it's worth, let me tell you this: Berta may have fired three nine-millimeter rounds into a guy's head."

"Really?"

"We are not sure yet, but it looks probable."

"I wouldn't have thought her capable of that. How is she?"

"It's touch and go. She's in ICU. Prognosis is not good."

"Can I go see her?"

Hart's chest and shoulders shook several times as he chuckled. Irritated by the agent's reaction, Steil nevertheless noticed that laughter made the man's face more human.

"No, Steil, you can't. She's under custody. Jesus Christ! You don't get it, do you? That dame is a dangerous criminal."

"Okay. I guess my ten are up. Can I go?" He got to his feet.

"Sure. But let me ask you one final favor," Hart said as he stood, too. "If possible, try to keep your collaboration with the bureau from Fidelia. I told her that the airport cabbie who drove Berta to your apartment building mentioned her to the police when he learned that two bodies were found at the airport's garage. He suspected her involvement in the double murder because she came from the garage looking very upset. That can provide an explanation as to how we found out where Berta was."

Steil considered it. "Okay. Will you remove the phone tap today?"

"I can't promise today. Tomorrow for sure."

"I got your word?"

"You have my word," extending his hand. Steil shook it. "Bye."

"Fidelia is waiting for you in the visitor's area."

"Thanks."

. . .

The twenty-by-twenty-foot room dubbed the Cauldron in Havana's Palace of the Revolution owed its name to the fact that all the problems of crucial import were cooked in it. The soundproof, most strictly protected meeting room in Cuba was scanned for bugs on a weekly basis and, besides Number One, only nineteen people had security clearance to go into it, two of whom were poor souls that cleaned up, fixed things, and applied coats of paint when necessary. The trash collected there, from crumpled papers to dust, was incinerated.

The Chief opened the door to the Cauldron from his office and crossed the threshold. He had changed from the double-breasted blue suit he had sported in the evening at the University of Havana's assembly hall to his customary olive green military uniform. Number One was extremely pissed off by what he considered President Carter's discourtesy. In the lecture on Cuban-American relations that Carter had just delivered at U of H, the former head of state had mentioned the Varela Project—a petition for a referendum signed by eleven thousand Cubans and filed before the National Assembly. Broadcast live nationwide, Carter's speech had been watched by several million amazed viewers.

People abroad were aware of the Varela Project; the foreign media had reported it. However, for the Chief—and by extension for the Cuban press, government, and party—it did not exist; inevitably, the overwhelming majority had not heard about the dissident movement's initiative. To make matters worse, three of his henchmen, possibly to curry his favor, had expressed their disagreement with Mr. Carter. Viewers' reaction to that would be negative, the Chief felt sure.

Number One had grasped the enormous importance of publicity and propaganda as a young man. In '53 and '54, while serving a fifteen-year sentence for launching a surprise attack against the most important army barracks in the eastern part of the island, he penned anti-Batista articles published by the best-selling Cuban magazine. When the tyrant pardoned him and all the other surviving assailants after only twenty-one months, several newspapers and radio stations let him argue his case before he went into exile. The *New York Times* introduced him to the world in 1957 with a front-page interview. A pirate radio station broadcast his message while waging guerrilla warfare. For several weeks after Che Guevara and Camilo Cienfuegos won the war for him, from Hudson Bay to Tierra del Fuego only Jesus Christ got better press. Having learned the lesson well, soon after deciding he would hold on to power as long as possible, he confiscated the Cuban media and made sure no adversary could present his views to the public. President Carter, however, had accepted his invitation on the condition that he would be allowed to address the Cuban people live. Canceling the visit on a pretext would have been worse.

Beside the Commander's kid brother, the minister of the interior and the chief of intelligence sat on the other side of the Cauldron's rectangular conference table for sixteen. Anger was stirring within Number One's chest. Whenever Interior had to deliver devastating news, invariably the minister told his brother first and then begged him to arrange and be present at the meeting. The Chief believed that losing the perks that went with their jobs terrified many old men who had been fearless idealists in their youth. Which was the reason they supported him all the way. The minister of the interior was one of those.

Most Cubans believed the Commander's kid brother to be the epitome of mediocrity. It seems that he screwed up many times for every single occasion he did things right. Despite Communist Cuba's dependence on the USSR, from the beginning the Chief had realized that in most respects—history, culture, demographics, traditions—both countries were diametrically opposed. His brother, by contrast, had tried to turn Cubans into Russians. In the seventies, entrusted with reforming the economy, he had copied Soviet institutions and procedures in detail, down to naming the new ministries "state committees," as in Moscow. Also in the seventies, and well into the eighties, he had imposed on the Cuban army, navy, and air force all the formal aspects of the Soviet military, from the insignia of its officers and enlisted men to its ribbons, medals, and full-dress uniforms. The Chief felt forced to draw the line to such shameful behavior after a military parade broadcast live. Following orders, Cuban soldiers had shouted "Hooray" three times—as the Red Army in Red Square did every November 7—rather than "Viva."

Had he not been his brother, he would have bumbled along through life obscurely enough, the Chief felt sure. But since babyhood the poor guy had shown him unstinting devotion, shared his moments of glory behind the scenes, comforted him in his darkest hours, and provided unquestioning obedience always. As the lone man he felt sure would never betray him, he had appointed him second secretary of the Communist Party, first vice president of the Council of State, first vice president of the Council of Ministers, and minister of the Revolutionary Armed Forces. Moreover, he had indicated many times, in public and in private, that nobody was better qualified to succeed him than his younger brother, a statement that ranked alongside his most glaring lies.

"What the fuck is the matter?" Number One barked as he closed the door behind his back.

Over the course of time, courtiers and sycophants had learned that when the Chief cussed and swore, he was in a foul mood. His intimates had noticed he was cussing and swearing a lot lately. Refusing to sit was another sign of discontent, so the three men watched expectantly as Number One reached a chair, took hold of its back with both hands, but failed to pull it out from beneath the conference table. His brother cleared his throat. The minister of the interior opened a notebook and uncapped a pen. *C in C asks what has happened,* he wrote.

The worried Lastra instinctively took a cigar from the top pocket of his uniform. This won him a fierce glare. The general realized his mistake and pocketed the Lancero. Ever since the Commander in Chief, had to give up smoking for health reasons, only foreigners could light up in his presence. American businessmen in particular, hoping to ingratiate themselves with their new client, arrived puffing on the choicest *habanos.* They had not a clue that they were subjecting their host to the ordeal of Tantalus. The wonderful smell of a burning *habano* made the Chief remember his years of glory, when taking a deep drag on a Cohiba was among his most cherished pleasures. Sometimes a sassy young visitor asked him why Mr. President was not smoking. His reply, invariably delivered with the resigned look of a Christian martyr, was in keeping with his role of Great Leader. He had quit to set a good example to his people.

"Look, Fidel," his brother began, "there's been a defection. We have a new traitor."

"Who is he?"

"It's a she: Micaela."

"WHO?"

"It's hard to believe, I know, but we are sure. She has betrayed."

The Chief remembered her well: One of his few geniuses. Contrary to rumor, defections failed to make him seethe with rage. He was inured to it. All through forty-five years, in addition to the million Cubans who had chosen emigration to living under communism, and the two-odd million hoping to move anywhere except North Korea, hundreds of trusted members of his inner circle had turned their backs on him. A few had served time with him, fought in the mountains against Batista's army, repelled anticommunist guerrillas years later, renounced promising futures elsewhere. Men and women who had risked their lives, sacrificed family and friends to serve the cause. Micaela was not one of them, but she had gathered, collated, and correctly evaluated the information needed to thwart three attempts on his life. The night he decorated her, she had seemed entranced, her eyes said she idolized him. He made her one of his favorite cadres, gave her a nice place to settle in Vedado, presented her with a car and computers. What were the hard-and-fast reasons for her betrayal?

Number 2 gives C in C the gist, scribbled the minister. An ominous silence reigned among the group.

The Chief squinted, turning his gaze to Lastra. The general was the only one in the room, probably in all of Cuba, capable of providing well-informed answers and plausible conclusions. For an instant, Number One wondered if he should ask. He was aware he would be fed a concoction of a few truths, numerous half truths and exaggerations, plus several outright lies. He had refined and tropicalized Machiavelli's teachings only to become the victim of his success, for his brightest pupils had taken his precepts one step further; Lastra was one of them. The Chief's rosy cheeks became rosier. The gray hairs under his sagging chin quivered.

"What happened, dear Comrade Chief of Intelligence?" he asked in the soft tone people dreaded even more than his explosions of anger.

Lastra stood up. "She placed herself on the auction block, Commander in Chief, and they bought her. She and her husband were spirited away three weeks ago. Both are currently in Miami."

Number One assented thoughtfully. "How do you know this, Lastra?" he inquired next.

The general began giving the carefully crafted, succinct explanation that he had suggested, and the other two participants had approved, three days earlier. The CIA had approached Victoria Valiente's husband during one of his many trips abroad in the nineties. In all probability, American Intelligence just hoped to recruit one more low-level informer. They had no way of knowing who the man's wife was. But then this individual, Manuel Pardo was his name, had revealed to his recruiter that he was married to a senior Cuban Intelligence officer. Lastra admitted to not knowing when or how Pardo had managed to turn Victoria, but it wouldn't be far-fetched to assume that she gave away the Wasp ring to furnish evidence of the sort of revelations she could make if given safe passage to the United States and paid $2.5 million.

Gabriel makes full report.

"Is that what I asked you?" trembling now, knuckles turning white on the back of the chair. What really pissed him off about successful defections was the inability to detect the traitors beforehand and send them to jail. Chief of intelligence, this naive moron! He had lost good agents right, left, and center because of his inability to find and yank out moles. A repository of incompetence is what he was.

"No, Comrade Commander in Chief. Excuse me. I know this because she called me from Miami and let on all."

A short, reflective pause ensued. As usual, Number One's gaze shifted over the room before veering sharply to Lastra.

"You think she denounced Eagle?" he asked. Eagle was the cryptonym of a senior DIA intelligence analyst recruited by the Directorate. Seven months earlier, the FBI had arrested her.

"No, Chief. Micaela didn't know about Eagle."

The man nodded. "Why the fuck did she call you? To repent?"

"She said someone had shot and killed her husband. She suspected I had ordered them killed. She threatened me with making a scandal, saying we order people murdered and so on."

The Chief rested his eyes on his kid brother. He had the sheepish, resigned look he always had in his presence. The minister of the interior, pen poised over the notebook, wished he could have a quick one.

"What proof do you have, Lastra?"

"I recorded her call, Commander in Chief."

"I want to listen to what she said."

Bending laterally to his right, Lastra picked up a briefcase from the floor, opened it, and produced a mini tape recorder. He pressed a button, then closed the briefcase, returning it to the floor.

For six minutes the Chief listened to a composite of the record-ing made at Victoria's apartment the night Pardo "confessed," and fragments of her last phone call. The very professional job had re-quired twenty-nine hours of fine-tuned adulteration and corre-sponded exactly with Lastra's version.

Audiotape played.

The Commander knew that recordings could be doctored; he suspected this call may have been altered, but he could not prove it. The best experts were under Lastra; under no circumstance would they admit having conspired to deceive him. And should they admit it, he would have to sentence them to death by firing squad. That Micaela had betrayed had to be true; these three would not be here otherwise, he reasoned. In a few days or weeks, the American media's field day would confirm it. It was a given that she had fled elsewhere. He would never learn why she had betrayed, though. Another mystery. The list of things he failed to comprehend kept growing. Maybe he had cre-ated too many Lastras. He had taught them to manipulate people and information; now he, his brother, and other geezers who still thought they were in charge, like the minister of the interior, were being un-scrupulously manipulated. They were told only what was impossible to conceal or what their subordinates thought they should know.

"Furry."

The minister of the interior dropped the pen, tried to jump to his feet, failed, seized the edge of the conference table, then pulled himself up. "At your service, Commander in Chief."

"As of this minute, General Lastra is sent into retirement. Six hours from now, I want to read a report on what has been done and what remains to be done to bring back our comrades in Miami be-fore the FBI has them arrested. Spare no expense. In two days I want to read a study on how to rebuild our networks there. Are we clear?"

"Yes, Commander in Chief."

"Lastra."

"At your service, Commander in Chief." The general had ex-pected it. The man had to take it out on somebody and he was the best possible culprit.

"Will you manage with four boxes of Lanceros a month?"

Lastra could not repress a sad smile. The Maximum Leader's parting gesture. He felt sure this was the last time he would see the man. In a few moments he would cease to exist for him. "Yes, Commander in Chief."

"Raúl."

"Yes, Fidel," said the Chief's kid brother as he got to his feet.

"Make sure Lastra gets four boxes of Lanceros delivered to his home every month."

"Thank you, Commander in Chief," Lastra muttered. He knew that later today, probably during the early morning meeting, the minister would be instructed to keep him under 24/7 surveillance for the rest of his life.

The Chief shuffled back to the door to his office thinking his favorite comforting thought. One out of twelve followers had betrayed Jesus Christ. He had millions of devotees, so he should not let a few thousand Judases depress him. Traitors were part of politics and politics was his life. Before operating the lock, he turned to face the three men standing static.

"I don't want to hear the name Micaela ever again," he deadpanned. Then he went into his office and closed the door behind him, wondering which team had won that evening's baseball game.

Gabriel sent into retirement. Report on rescuing Miami agents at 06:15 A.M. Report on rebuilding networks: 48 hours. Meeting ends 00:16 A.M. May 15, 2002.

. . .

On the very same day that Victoria Valiente was admitted to the Jackson Memorial Hospital, a fine medical institution and the nearest to Steil's apartment building, Smith had been warned that the prognosis was dismal. The bullet had fractured her first rib, pierced the intercostal artery, injured her bronchi, and collapsed the left lung. As she was being operated on, it was reported that an asthma inhaler had been found in the patient's purse. Such respiratory insufficiency was another discouraging factor, the physician on duty had warned. Therefore, when four days later the hospital called to report that the patient had passed away, Smith wasn't surprised. He drove there and an intensive-care nurse spent five minutes reading to him from the patient's medical record, a long, incomprehensible list of acronyms and abbreviations.

"But when a patient refuses to get well, medical science is powerless," was how she concluded, then closed the file's metal covers.

"What do you mean?" asked Smith.

"This patient," tapping her fingers on the file, "refused to live, sir. I've seen too many cases. Her eyes said she wanted out."

David Szady, the bureau's chief of counterintelligence, had asked to be kept informed of new developments, which was why, back at the bureau's Miami division, Smith recapitulated before calling him.

Forensic examinations had proved that the bullet that killed Maria Scheindlin was fired by the Beretta. The same gun had ended Carlos Capdevila's life. Eugenio Bonis, already dead or dying from a slug fired by the Tokarev, had been shot in the head at very close range with the Beretta. The Russian gun had Berta and Capdevila's fingerprints. The Beretta had Berta and Bonis's. Swabs of Berta's hands taken at the hospital detected primers, nitrites, and nitrates from the two different kinds of ammunition the guns had. Conclusion: She had fired the Tokarev *and* the Beretta. He and Hart shared the theory that the couple had met Bonis at the airport garage, the gardener and Capdevila shot each other, then Berta, out of anger or in cold blood, gave Bonis the coup de grâce with his gun. What had caused the dispute? The impounded cash was one possibility.

Based on the circumstantial evidence available, Smith and Hart had made a few embarrassing assumptions. Although nothing having to do with handguns or espionage was found at Bonis's home, they had felt reasonably certain of two things: The gardener had murdered Maria Scheindlin, and he was a spy. His records proved he was the landscaper of choice of many rich Cubans, including several directors of the Cuban American Foundation. He had been doing the Scheindlins' garden for over ten years. The videotape established he was the only visitor Maria had received on the morning of May 7. The residence's gate had remained open after he took off. Two airline attendants remembered he had been at their counters, asking for a ticket to Ottawa. He had run a disk wiper to delete the master hard disk of his computer. If it looks like a duck, walks like a duck, and quacks like a duck, then it just may be a duck. However, with him, Maria, and Micaela dead, finding out much more seemed quite a long shot. The reason for recruiting a housewife who lacked connections with the Cuban community was not clear. Maybe, Smith speculated, CuIS hoped to learn her husband's plans with regard to Cuba. Hart had doubtfully tilted his head sideways at this.

For the bureau, however, Bonis and Maria were small fry when compared with Berta-Micaela. The cryptonym she had given during her phone call to Havana made them believe she had been the fabled head of the CuIS Miami desk. Hart defended the theory that she and Capdevila, whose real name had apparently been Pardo, were genuine defectors and Lastra, CuIS general director, had ordered Bonis to execute both, plus Maria Scheindlin, whose cryptonym had been Pola Negri. Apart from that, the special agent had argued, CuIS seldom sent desk chiefs abroad, and when it did they were given diplomatic cover.

Playing devil's advocate, Smith had disagreed. He argued that loyal officers choose death before dishonor, which was what she had done. Berta-Micaela had come to Miami to carry out an important mission for which she needed the hundred Gs, maybe reconstructing the Wasp network, he hypothesized. The code page and the key to a safe-deposit box found in her purse furnished proof of her intentions. The perforated CD, diagnosed unreadable by the bureau's technicians, probably stored information related to her mission. Having failed, seeing her comrade and possible lover dead, she had committed suicide. Berta-Micaela's case broke the mold, he argued.

Hart, considering this possibility far-fetched but not wanting to say so, had opened a desk drawer, extracted a mini cassette that he fed to his tape recorder, then turned the gizmo on.

"All we wanted was to get the hell out, Lastra. We were sick and tired of the repression, the hypocrisy, the lies, the personality cult, and the ever-deepening economic crisis. And yes, Pardo had the brains and the balls to screw you. But let me tell you: Turning in the fools we have here risking their freedom so His Majesty and his courtiers can live the good life never crossed my mind. Behave and I won't. They are just a pack of manipulated puppets, like you and those under you are, like I was until a few days ago. But be warned, Lastra, I'll make a full report, naming all the names and giving all the addresses. You can bet your life that if something happens to me, it'll reach the Gypsy. And you know, Lastra, you know perfectly well that the scandal will make headlines from here to Nepal. So, it's your call, General."

"The scorn and hatred in that voice, Chief, sound pretty real to me," Hart said as he pressed the stop button. "The scorn of someone who had to pretend for too long and at last can speak her mind; the hatred of the lover who addresses the man responsible for the death of her loved one."

Smith enjoyed playing devil's advocate but disliked being considered a dork, so he disabused himself of the "important mission" hypothesis and accepted the defection theory as being the most probable. "I wonder who the Gypsy is," he had mused before concluding the give-and-take.

Having completed the mental summation, he lifted the phone and dialed the Gypsy's number an hour after Victoria was pronounced dead. He gave his superior the news.

"Why did she kill herself, Nathan?" asked Szady. Smith knew it was not a rhetorical question.

"I guess we'll never know, sir," Smith said. "In her phone call to Havana, which she couldn't possibly imagine we were taping, she made very clear she had defected. But would anyone defect and then commit suicide? It doesn't figure."

"No, it doesn't."

"Maybe the clincher was our presence. She may have feared being tortured to death."

"Oh, c'mon, Nathan. She was Cuban, remember? Not an al-Qaeda fanatic."

"Well, sir, you know communists. Children are indoctrinated from kindergarten. We capitalist pigs are bad, we torture and give shots of truth serum and apply electrodes to genitals. That sort of ideological garbage surfaces in critical moments. Losing her man, if this Capdevila or Pardo was her man, may have been a contributing factor to her pulling the trigger. They were sexually involved, for sure. We found sperm on the bedsheets of their room. She termed Pardo her husband, but Hart says in Cuba the word *marido* applies to a lawful wedded husband and to a lover, too. Maybe she doted on him. I don't think we'll ever find out if they were married."

"You think she may have been planning to contact us?"

"Only as a recourse of last resort. In her phone call to Lastra, she said she wasn't planning to turn in her *compañeros* here. But I wish that CD were intact, or that my request for consultation with DGSE is approved. Any news on that?"

"Not yet, no."

"I would appreciate it if you discuss it with the director. Our guys are sure the key belongs to a French safe-deposit box, but we can't determine which bank or branch. There may be fresh evidence there."

"Okay. I'll see what I can do. Shit, I was hoping she'd recover. We've lost a great source. Can you imagine that woman spilling the beans?"

"A watershed. The consummate defector. We would've cleaned South Florida. You know what Hart said when I told him she had died?"

"No."

"Heaven-sent has gone back to heaven."

Szady chuckled. "Nice one-liner," he said. "I don't think I'd heard it."

"The staff at Jackson Memorial did all they could," Smith said. "They pulled her out of cardiac arrest twice."

"I'm sure they did. Well, it's over. I'll let you know what the director says about consulting DGSE. Take care, Nathan."

"You too, sir."

Ten

Fidelia got a call from Hart around noon on May 29, a Wednesday. They had finished with her passport; she could pick it up that same afternoon, if she wished. He would be in his office until seven, the special agent added.

While in Cuba, Fidelia developed a strong dislike for people in positions of authority. This disposition had worsened in the United States. Her dealings with all sorts of government officials, police officers, court clerks, and bureaucrats in general were of an adversarial nature. For this reason, she asked Hart to have her passport delivered to her home, which was where they had taken it from, she argued. The special agent had practice in dealing with uncooperative people. Her home? he asked. To the best of his recollection, Ms. Orozco's passport had been found in the purse of a kidnapper. Apart from that, had Ms. Orozco changed her place of residence to Mr. Steil's apartment? Her registered home address was other than Mr. Steil's. All choked up, Fidelia next learned that a receipt had to be signed, too. Knowing when she had lost fair and square, Fidelia left the law firm earlier than usual, drove to the bureau's building, and picked up her passport. She reached the apartment feeling belligerent.

Elliot's day had not been nice, either. People from the U.S. Treasury's Office of Foreign Assets Control had begun an investigation to determine whether IMLATINEX was the parent company of Trans-Caribbean, the Panamanian firm set up by Scheindlin to front for him in his trade with Cuba. Should it be found in violation of existing rules and regulations, IMLATINEX might be fined to the tune of millions, their executives sentenced to prison. Their lawyers had assured Elliot and Plotzher that Ruben Scheindlin had covered his tracks masterfully, that both Panamanian front men were ready to testify in court should the need arise, and that IMLATINEX would receive a clean bill of health, but Elliot was wary of lawyers' assurances.

That evening the dishwasher was humming quietly in the kitchen and Elliot was at the desk, reading the *New York Times* on his laptop, when Fidelia, sitting in a loveseat, concluded revising one last time a brief she would file the next morning.

"I got my passport back this afternoon," she announced.

Elliot turned in his seat. "Oh, did you?"

"Yes."

"You went to the FBI?"

"I did."

"Did you see Hart?"

"Yes."

"Did he say something new about . . . what happened?"

"To me? Are you kidding? Why should he give me any news if he sees you keeping me in the dark?"

Elliot saw it coming but failed in his attempt to pour oil on troubled waters. "That's not fair, Fidelia. I told you the whole story."

"Oh, c'mon, Elliot. Stop bullshitting me. I'm not mentally retarded, you know?"

"I am bullshitting you? Are you saying that I didn't meet Berta and Capdevila in Havana? That I invented the story of Scheindlin buying medicine for Cuba?"

"What I'm saying is that what you've told me is the tip of the iceberg. I hate overused analogies, but that describes it pretty well. You are keeping from me the chicken of the rice-with-chicken. (Oh, shit, there I go again.) I wouldn't mind, you know, I wouldn't mind at all, really, because our relationship doesn't give me the right to stick my nose into everything you do. I hate seeing you get into deep water because I care for you, but you are a big boy and your life is yours to conduct. However, when I'm threatened, kidnapped, and rescued by a SWAT team, I reckon I have the right to know what the hell is going on. Then you get slippery and mysterious with me, and I just have to stand by and read in the eyes of certain people, like Mr. Great Super Special Agent Hart, 'The dame's a nitwit, Steil sidelines her.'"

Steil logged off and turned in his seat to face Fidelia. "We've been over this before. I've told you all there is to tell. This whole situation began as one thing and ended as another. It seems Berta and her husband were Cuban spies and the FBI was after them. I don't know how they entered the country. She said she had to pick up the money, you heard her, and all the time she had it in her holdall. Did the man who murdered Maria Scheindlin give it to her? I don't know. The dots connect, that's for sure, but how? I don't fucking know. How can I tell you? It would be stupid of me to go see Hart and say, 'Hey, Fidelia and I want to know what went on. Tell me.' The guy would laugh in my face. So, I'm not asking. But one thing I can make pretty clear to you."

He raised and shook his right forefinger.

"I've never gotten involved in something knowing that it would put you at risk. However, I've put your life in danger twice. I know. I apologize."

"Apology accepted. But don't wag your finger at me."

"Oh, I'm sooo sorry," sardonically now. "Thanks for being so understanding. Now, I don't know . . ."

"Do I detect a note of sarcasm in your voice?"

"For God's sake!" rolling his eyes in exasperation. "Let's get serious. I was about to tell you that I don't know what the future has in store for me. OFAC is investigating the company."

She frowned, then asked, "What's OFAC?"

"OFAC is Treasury's office in charge of enforcing the embargo on Cuba. They suspect IMLATINEX of violating the embargo."

"Have you? That's a stupid question. Why did I ask it? You don't have to answer it."

"Not on my watch. What happened before I joined the company is not my concern."

"Right. You are not legally responsible for what happened before 1995."

"I know that. But if they find any questionable transaction between then and now, the company will be fined and Plotzher and I could be sentenced to prison. You may find yourself dragged into deep water. The press would report it. Even worse: Some lifelong anticommunists could accuse me of being a Castro agent and beat the shit out of me, or arrange a hit on me. That would be even deeper water. Suppose you are by my side when I get beaten or shot at."

"You are grossly exaggerating things."

"Right. I'm drawing a worst-case scenario because I want you to take a long, hard look at our future together."

"Hold it, hold it. What does that mean?"

"It means that sharing your life with me may be risky, and if you want out, I'll understand. It's not what I want, but I'll understand."

"Is that so?"

"Don't make up your mind right now. Think it over. Take a week, a month, as long as you want. And factor in my reluctance to make daily reports on every single thing I do or risk I take, because I won't. Okay?"

Fidelia sprang to her feet. "You are insufferable tonight. I'm turning in."

"Sweet dreams, Fidelia."

"Elliot, you are not good at sarcasm. Shut your yap."

...

In her Bay Harbor residence courtyard, beneath the green-and-white striped canvas, sitting in the cushioned armchairs and nursing drinks, Jenny Scheindlin and Samuel Plotzher were concluding a long and interesting conversation. As a pause unfolded, the old Jew contemplated his surroundings through gold-framed bifocals. The garden looked regal, as if in tribute to the deceased caretaker. Framed by the spectacular purple bougainvillea that bordered the property, the flower beds in full bloom created a splendid palette of blues, greens, reds, pinks, and yellows. Perfectionists would argue that the lawn could use a mowing, Plotzher thought. A gentle breeze wafted the scent of flowers, trees, seawater, and wet earth through the community's yards. The ripples it caused on the swimming pool reflected the setting sun and conjured a succession of blinding flashes that forced humans, and the sparrows and hummingbirds nesting in the Roman-tile roof, to blink more than usual.

In her chartreuse, three-sizes-too-big top, Jenny brought to mind a skeletal adolescent playing grown-up in her obese mommy's clothes, but oversize was the trend. She also had on slim, citron-colored pants, mule boat shoes, and designer sunglasses. Jenny took a sip from her gimlet—classic drinks were back in vogue and Chris mixed great cocktails. In the lambent light, with her hair gathered in a satin ribbon, she looked so beautiful that Plotzher stared. He was wearing frayed jeans, steel-toe work boots, and a long-sleeved blue cotton shirt, cuffs folded up to his elbows. His tumbler held Scotch on the rocks. They made quite a contrast: glamour and practicality, art and industry, naiveté and politics, future and history. In reality, though, the business partnership between Sam and Jenny's father, shared cultural values, and secret undertakings in the last three years had forged a close bond between the fashion model and the old man.

"I miss him so much," Jenny sighed, her gaze lost in the light blue sky.

For an instant, Plotzher considered what to say next. "I never thought I would love a man. And I loved him," was what he came up with.

"Mom was like . . ." Jenny hesitated. "Well, you know. She had great business sense and yet . . . basically she acted as if her world of sun, fun, and housekeeping would . . . like . . . crumble if she had initiative. Know what I mean? Then, when she started to come out of her cocoon after Dad passed away, that sonofabitch killed her. Why did he, Sam?"

"I don't know," he said. He suspected why, but did not know.

Jenny glanced at the flower beds and heaved a sigh. "I miss her a lot, of course, but I miss Dad even more. He taught me guiding principles, like, you know, 'study men, save your money, be strong, go after what you want.' From the age of three or four, he talked to me about Israel and the Jewish people with such devotion that I kind of, you know, fell in love with my ancestry. My pride in being a Jew is the result of his teachings and my time spent in Israel."

Plotzher nodded approvingly. "It would've made him happy, and proud, too, to hear you say that. What would've pleased him most, though, is to see how well you follow in his footsteps."

"He was always saying to me: 'Consider carefully what you should do, then act on it. Talk is cheap. To have practical value, talk has to be backed up with deeds.'"

"And you are doing great," looking her in the eye, elbows on the arms of the armchair, holding the glass with both hands. "Your report on the Saudi Arabian sheikh was much praised by Tel Aviv. But let me remind you of something, just to make my final point today. You are in a business in which people retire young, right?"

"Right."

"So, while you pursue your modeling career, bear in mind that five, ten, or fifteen years from now, fashion designers and photographers will no longer pamper you. Don't hold your breath, though. I will be long gone when you reach that stage in your life, so I—"

"Oh, Sam, don't say that," she said, with genuine grief in her expression.

"Don't 'Oh Sam' me. Ruben died, you got over it; your mom died, you'll get over it; I'll die, you'll get over it even faster because one learns to accept death. If I haven't died by the time you quit modeling, I'll be sitting in a wheelchair, drooling and shitting in my pants, God forbid. So, the point I want to make is this. Other models, when they reach that crossroads, marry a rich geezer or become high-paid whores. Not you. You won't have to take shit from anybody. You'll be even richer than you are now. Know what I mean?"

"Sure," remembering that, despite being intrigued, she shouldn't knit her brow. Where was Sam taking her now?

"When your modeling career is over, you will have options; for instance: 'Why should I trouble myself with the firm? I'll sell it and be free to do as I please, go wherever I want to whenever I want to.' Well, it's your life and, of course, you can do what you deem best. But I want you to consider that if you sell the firm, you'd be selling something vital to the security of Israel. We don't ask you for money, we don't ask you to quit your chosen profession; you don't have to ask our permission if you want to marry, have children, divorce, stay single. We'll never ask you to change your lifestyle or expose you to danger. What we ask of you, for the security of Israel and for the good of the Jewish people, is to hold on to your firm and get ready to manage it. Now, would you do this for Israel and its people?"

"Of course I'll do it, Sam."

"Do you believe this in your heart of hearts or are you just giving me peace of mind?"

"I mean it, Sam."

"Then you have to start moving in that direction. The things you have to master can't be learned in a year or two. So, I suggest that as soon as possible you get close to Elliot Steil, learn from him as much and as long as you can. Whenever you can spare a day or two, please call Elliot, go to the firm, ask questions . . ."

"Why should I depend on Elliot? I've got you."

"You should depend on him for two reasons, for three reasons, in fact. The first is, he's the manager. I know little about paperwork and he knows shit about the logistics of the business. We complement each other. But in a few years Elliot will know everything there is to know about IMLATINEX,' cause I'll teach him the logistics. The second reason is that he's a born teacher. He's got the ability to make people understand rather complex issues in a short time. And the third reason is that he's clever and honest; honest to the point of being naive, know what I mean? Now, cleverness and honesty are two great qualities, as long as they are in the right proportion. Excessive honesty is harmful for business. Watch out for Elliot's honesty, but absorb all you can from him."

"I will."

"When you take the reins of the firm, you'll begin a new life: the businesswoman's life. Ruben's blood will make you love it. Only then you'll realize why the most valuable Israeli secret agents are those who operate in the world of business. You are doing fine. But this Saudi Arabian, and others who approach you now, see in you little more than a gorgeous woman they want to take to bed. They make comments in passing, if at all, because they are not thinking politics or business in your presence; they are thinking romance or sex. They underrate you and that is wonderful. Eventually, they'll see in you a very attractive, middle-aged, and rich businesswoman who can negotiate deals, quote prices from memory, meet with government officials, and, after hours and over drinks, discuss current world events. Then, Jenny, you will be in a position to extend the legend of your father, who was one of Mossad's most valuable agents of all time."

Jenny breathed deeply and let her eyes roam over the garden. The thoughts her handler had just planted in her mind, like Jack's beanstalk, sprung up out of proportion. She saw herself walking the corridors of financial and political power, entering the most famous artistic salons, attracting the admiring glances of elegant, cultivated, and rich men who would vie for her company and affection. She would be the status symbol other models now were. The class of women billionaires exhibit at the most exclusive places. This would serve to gather information for the Hebrew people, to protect their hard-won homeland. She would most certainly extend the Scheindlin legend.

"I saw you grow up, I love you, I want the best for you," Plotzher said after a few moments, having considered beforehand that the conversation should end on a very intimate and personal note. "You've lost your father and your mother and I want to know this: Who is your closest living relative, Jenny?"

Her smile was the most beautiful he'd ever seen.

"You are, you old goat. Who else?"

"It's what I thought, so hear this piece of advice. I see only two things that could frustrate your brilliant future: drugs and alcohol.

There's no harm in sniffing a line or downing one of these," lifting his glass. "The problem begins when you have to snort the coke or drink the drink because your brain demands it, know what I mean? When that happens you are in trouble. So, always keep a close watch on yourself. The day you feel you need a drink or a line or a pill or a smoke or whatever is trendy in the market, you are in trouble. Seek help then, from whomever you figure can help you best. Know what I mean?"

"I know, Sam. Don't worry."

"Good." Sam Plotzher placed his glass atop the cocktail table, grabbed the arms of the armchair, and pulled himself up. "Well, dear, let's call it a day," he said.

Jenny quickly got to her feet. "Stay for dinner, please."

"You want the old lady to close me out tonight?"

"Oh, Sam. Don't say that. Esther is the sweetest woman I know."

"Your friends will keep you company. Fags, aren't they?"

"Sam . . . C'mon, don't be homophobic. A guy like you? They are fine people."

"Every generation has their value system. For mine, fags are perverts. I'm too old to change, Jenny. Walk me to the door."

She slid her arm in his and they took the gray granite path that led to the sliding door.

"I think I'll sell this house, Sam. Too many bad memories," Jenny said, her gaze roving about the courtyard.

"I understand."

Crossing the living area, the old man smiled and nodded to Valerio when he stepped out of the kitchen to ask if they wanted something. Jenny thanked him and said no. By the front door, the model went misty-eyed when she kissed Plotzher's cheeks before turning the lock.

The handler of Ruben Scheindlin for over twenty-five years, of Jenny Scheindlin since 1999, the man who wrote the anonymous letter that put the FBI on Maria's trail, got in his car and drove off as the sun set.

. . .

Col. Enrique Morera (cryptonym Bernardo), deputy chief of the General Directorate of Intelligence and head of its USA Department, had lived a largely unpredictable life ever since adolescence. As often as not, when almost everybody was at work, he was sound asleep at home, and vice versa. At midnight on December 31, 1999, as 99.9 percent of healthy Cuban adults, his relatives and friends included, were lifting their glasses to toast the New Millennium, he had been drafting an urgent message to an illegal. Such dedication had exacted a heavy toll on his family life. His first wife had divorced him after five years and their only son, now thirty-eight, was an alcoholic and exhibitionist kept out of prison by his father's friends in police circles.

In 1974, a few weeks after his second wife gave birth, Morera began to make efforts to prevent the same hardships from recurring. When in 1998 their daughter, a microbiologist, married and moved to Sancti Spiritus, he promised his wife that every time he could take a break, they would go see a movie, have a drink, or just sit on the Malecón wall to gaze at the sea and talk a while. Morera had already reached the conclusion that he had lived a dog's life, and for a lost cause at that.

His wife, a retired judge, was now a full-time housewife. Once or twice a month, when she least expected it, the phone would ring and her husband would ask if she felt like letting her hair down. Invariably she jumped at it, hung up, changed, applied lipstick, and boarded the colonel's Lada when he gave a toot on his horn in front of their nice Casino Deportivo residence.

At 5:19 on the afternoon of May 23, a Thursday, Morera and his wife entered a movie house at Twenty-third Street between G and H, Vedado, to watch an Italian film. They sat in the lower level, fifth row of seats counting from back to front, and waited for the matinee to start. Fifteen minutes into the picture a middle-aged woman changed seats to one in the fourth row, behind and to the right of the colonel. The third reel was playing when Morera slowly extracted an 8cm CD in a plastic case from a pocket of his slacks. Holding it with his thumb and forefinger, at no time taking his eyes from the screen, he crossed his legs and rested his arm on the back of the seat to his right, in what seemed a natural change of position. The middle-aged woman reached for the case and dropped it into her purse.

The instant the picture ended, as credits rolled on, the woman hurried out of the still dark theater. She hastened down G Street with long steps, turned right onto Twenty-first, and pulled open the passenger door of a 1953 Studebaker parked between G and H. Having scooted over the front seat, she opened her purse and surrendered the case to the young man with coal black hair and plastic-framed glasses sitting behind the wheel. The driver turned the ignition and pulled away. The woman abandoned the jalopy at the corner of Artola and Vista Hermosa, Jacomino. That evening the young man surrendered the CD to the cleaning lady of the Havana branch office of a Brazilian company. The next morning she gave the disk to the firm's manager.

Five days later, on May 28, Efraim Halevy, head of Mossad, read two messages from his priceless Cuban agent. One dealt with the Micaela case; the other listed the names of nineteen CuIS officers working under diplomatic cover at the Cuban UN mission in New York and in Washington's Office of Interests. Halevy signed an order transferring twenty thousand dollars to the Liechtenstein numbered bank account where the Cuban colonel's greenbacks went.

Recruited in 2000, Morera was the man responsible for the extended honeymoon that Mossad and the FBI were taking. Well aware that Mossad served simply as intermediary, to whet the end user's appetite and in exchange for fifty thousand dollars, in March 2001 Morera had fingered the DIA analyst recruited in 1985. When Mossad's official representative in Washington passed on the information to the bureau's liaison officer, the man chuckled in his face. "Check it out," the Israeli had said. The honeymoon really took off when the FBI corroborated the unimaginable: Castro had ears and eyes at the Defense Intelligence Agency.

To make the intermediary happy, Morera denounced Pola Negri in May 2001. It had been embarrassing for Mossad to discover that Maria's security clearance in 1975 had failed miserably. Those involved had retired or died, so they couldn't be called to account. Ruben Scheindlin, one of their best agents, spent twenty-six years married to a communist spy who had given birth and raised a promising young woman that behaved as a real Sabarit. It was comforting to remember that Scheindlin had been extremely cautious and discreet. He probably never revealed anything of significance to his spouse. Based on Morera's reports, Mossad had instructed Samuel Plotzher, Ruben Scheindlin's handler, to send an anonymous letter to the bureau giving away the agent's wife.

Now Morera was demanding half a million, safe passage, relocation, and to be included in the bureau's witness protection program, in exchange for the Pitirre network. Halevy felt sure the Americans would gladly fork over five hundred thousand for dismantling what Morera described as the oldest, most efficient Cuban spy network, which included agents "nobody could dream had been working for Cuban Intelligence ever since the 1960s."

The logistics to smuggle out a guy like Morera and three relatives had to be particularly complicated, Halevy pondered. As the Directorate's second-in-command, the Cuban had to report his whereabouts at all times. Maybe while Morera and family were on vacation. Were he given the job, Halevy mulled over, he would slip a submarine in the dead of night into a deep, wide Cuban harbor lacking port facilities on the southern coast—Bay of Pigs, for instance. But that was not his problem; he just had to serve as go-between. Halevy pressed a button to call his adjunct.

"Take this down, Yossi," he said after a man carrying a notebook entered the office. "Memo to Washington. Please forward to friends list of Cuban diplomats in the United States who . . ."

...

At a quarter past 6:00 P.M. on June 7, inside IMLATINEX's glassed-in cubicle, Samuel Plotzher was checking off items on a list atop his clipboard and Elliot Steil was revising specifications in a contract when the Jew did a big stretch, stole a look at his watch, and addressed Steil.

"Hey, Elliot, would you give me a lift? My car's in the garage, tune-up."

"Sure thing," Elliot said, who immediately began closing folders and plastic binders to mask his astonishment. First time in eight years that Plotzher had asked him for a favor.

They got into Elliot's recently acquired charcoal gray '98 Saab 9000 two minutes later. Less than twenty seconds after leaving the warehouse things got even weirder.

"Pretty hot, isn't it? What do you say we go to South Beach, have a drink, and watch pretty asses and tits?" Plotzher asked.

Steil wondered whether he had heard well. Sam Plotzher wanted to ogle naked young women? "It's not a bad idea," the Cuban said, rather noncommittally, "let's do it." He then took a left onto North Miami Beach Boulevard.

Considering Sam a member of the strong, silent type, Steil concentrated on driving and nothing more was said during the thirty-five-minute ride. The Saab was cruising by the Delano Hotel, at Collins Avenue, when Sam spoke again.

"Park anywhere you like, Elliot. Let's take a stroll along the beach."

Elliot found an empty spot at Collins and Twelfth, at Lummus Park. Both men got out and, burning with curiosity, Steil locked the car. Plotzher ambled over to the seashore, leaving deep imprints on the hot, ivory-colored sand. His Cuban associate tagged along. The fading cloudless afternoon promised a splendid sunset to onlookers. Surprisingly, none of the few people in the vicinity were buck naked. However, a six-foot-tall topless brunette in a skimpy bikini bottom caught Elliot's eye. With muscles rippling under the skin of her thighs with each step, she ambled due south over docile wavelets that broke and died at her bare feet. The soft breeze lovingly swayed her ponytail, pulled out the back of a khaki cap. Her left hand rested over the cap's visor, the better to squint at several sail-boats that seemed to be taking part in a race. A body that deserved to be worshipped, Elliot thought. Hairball, a Cuban he knew, always said the same thing when confronted with a woman like this: He'd start licking the bed's legs.

"The real reason I asked you to bring me here, Elliot," began Plotzher, his gaze scanning the eastern horizon while still ten or so yards from the shore and seemingly oblivious to his surroundings, "is that electronics advances by leaps and bounds. You can never be sure nobody is overhearing you, and I want to lessen the odds on someone getting on tape what I have to say to you."

Elliot took his eyes off the brunette and caught up with Plotzher. He was the dirty old man, not Sam. He braced himself for something truly important.

"Maybe these guys from OFAC planted a bug in the office. See if we let on something about Trans-Caribbean. Let's deal with that first. Chances are they might suspect we've been sidestepping this stupid embargo law, but they won't be able to prove it and won't take us to court. The way things are changing with all these authorized sales of poultry, cereals, and stuff to Cuba, we'll probably be given a warning and that'll be it. Don't worry about it, okay?"

"Okay."

Plotzher came to a halt by the shoreline. With eyes fixed in the distance, he checked what he would say next. Elliot stole a look at the retreating brunette. Only one word could define her figure: perfect.

"Before changing the subject, I want to tell you that I appreciate your telling me about what happened to you in Cuba and later here in Miami. You did it after everything was over, though. Your private life is your concern, but if it affects the company, it is my concern, too. You were dragged into the whole thing because you manage IMLATINEX and because Trans-Caribbean sells to XEMIC. You should have told me the day you flew back. That's water under the bridge now, but next time I need to know. The sooner the better. To plan ahead, maybe help you out. We clear on this?"

Elliot nodded his agreement. "I didn't want to trouble you, Sam."

"Well, I appreciate that. But in the future, you let me know, okay?"

"Okay."

Sam took a deep breath and looked around. "This coming December I'll be sixty-nine. Started making a living when I was eight, shining shoes, selling papers, running errands. I've been dreaming about retiring at seventy since my sixtieth birthday. After Ruben died, Maria said to me the same thing she said to you: that she didn't want to sell IMLATINEX. I thought in a year or two, you could get the hang of a few tricks you haven't mastered yet, and we could have instructed Maria on the fundamentals of the company. She didn't know shit about trading, but as a responsible adult she would watch over the company just to make sure she, her daughter, and a conceivable grandson or granddaughter would live comfortably all their lives."

Plotzher turned to face Steil. "But now I don't think I will retire anytime soon. Maria is dead and it's a twenty-five-year-old fashion model who owns 79 percent of IMLATINEX. This kid thinks types of fabric, colors, the length of the skirt, the shoes, the camera, and the lights. She doesn't know the difference between a ball bearing and a bolt, between a chain saw and a lawn mower, between an invoice and a bill of lading . . . You think it's funny?"

Steil shook his head and stopped chuckling. "It's the way you put it, Sam."

"It's not funny."

"Okay. Sorry."

"It's not funny because her father built this company from scratch, because I've devoted almost twenty-seven years of my life to it, because I don't want to see it sold to a drug dealer that will use it as a front for money laundering and/or to smuggle coke and heroin. You understand what I'm saying?"

"I think I do."

"I had a talk with Jenny a few days ago. She swore she won't sell the firm and will try to learn trading. But that's just words, and you know what words are."

"Cheap."

"Exactly. So, I want to trap her into something and I want you to help me do it."

Steil knitted his brow. "Trap her into what, Sam?"

"Trap her into loving the firm, trading, and doing business."

Steil clicked his tongue and shook his head. "And how do you think you can pull that off?"

"She's got Ruben's genes, or part of them, so maybe she inherited his business acumen as well. She'll turn into a businesswoman if we make trading attractive to her. What are you shaking your head at?"

From the sand, Steil raised his eyes heavenward. "Oh. C'mon, Sam. Genes have nothing to do with vocation. Henry Ford's parents were farmers; Tchaikovsky was the son of a mine inspector; Stephen Hawking's father was a doctor and wanted his son to study medicine; millions of cases prove that. You just said it: All she thinks about are photo shoots, keeping her nice tan, and sipping the drink in vogue at the 'in' bar with guys from the fashion crowd. If she drops that for contracts and invoices, I'll cut off my balls and throw them to the dogs."

Plotzher smiled briefly, then grew serious again. "She won't drop fashion, fashion will drop her."

Elliot cast Sam an intrigued look. "What do you mean?" he asked.

"In modeling, people are old at thirty, geriatric at thirty-five. She knows that. She's twenty-five. It's just a matter of time. Eventually she'll realize that her well-being depends on IMLATINEX, not on modeling."

Elliot gazed reflectively at the horizon. Maybe. "And how can we make trading attractive to a woman like her?" he asked.

"You tell me. You are the teacher."

Elliot pretended to guffaw with delight. "Me? Are you serious? C'mon, Sam, get real."

"Listen. I saw her grow up. I'm like an uncle to her. She loves me, but seldom do people learn from those they love. When I try to explain something to her, she only pretends to pay attention. She interrupts, makes jokes, laughs, hugs me, kisses my cheek. She won't do that to you. She'll respect you. You are a trained teacher, better educated, you handle the company's managerial side. Younger than me, too, so the generation gap is narrower between you two. If anyone can make trading attractive to her, it is you. I'm asking this as a favor. Will you do it for me?"

Elliot raised his eyebrows and pursed his lips in concentration. Two favors in eight years, both on the same day. Mission impossible, he thought. Such a radical change was doomed. It would be akin to teaching mechanics to a poet, or sexual mores to the pope. But he couldn't refuse.

"Tell me, Elliot, eight years ago, could you have foreseen that you'd learn so much and be so effective that you'd end up as the firm's manager?"

Plotzher had a point, Elliot conceded, looking at the toecap of his shoes. But it was different. For him, everything was at stake. For Jenny, nothing was at stake.

"No, Sam, I couldn't. But in Jenny's case I think you are wrong. Nothing in her past indicates that she'll take an interest in trading, much less master the business. *Now* I love the business, but eight years ago I had no alternative. Jenny has alternatives. She can sell the firm and with the proceeds live the rest of her life comfortably. But I'll give it my best shot. As a favor to you. What happens if she decides to sell the company?"

Sam Plotzher gave Elliot a wide smile. "You buy her out."

"WHAT?"

"You buy her out. I know it seems impossible. How can you pay for the firm? Perhaps a bank loan. But discussing that possibility is premature. Here comes the brunette again. Quite a woman, ain't she?"

Without breaking stride, Ms. Perfect noticed the old man who was eyeing her knowingly and the slack-jawed, middle-aged goof who was staring at her with intense concentration. She looked daggers at the jackass. What was the matter with him? Never seen a woman before? She took her eyes off him in disgust and kept puttering along.

There was no way she could divine that the expression on the schmuck's face had nothing to do with her body. When she crossed his line of vision, Elliot Steil had been wondering whether Sam Plotzher had gone gaga or if, once again, fate was conspiring to make him a victim of circumstance.

"Now take me home, Elliot," Plotzher said, then turned around. "I don't feel like getting a glow while you guzzle Seven-Ups one after the other. Let's go."